LUCIFER
WITH A BOOK

a novel by
JOHN HORNE BURNS

 A BARD BOOK/PUBLISHED BY AVON BOOKS

AVON BOOKS
A division of
The Hearst Corporation
959 Eighth Avenue
New York, New York 10019

Copyright © 1949 (renewed) by John Horne Burns
Published by arrangement with the author.
Library of Congress Catalog Card Number: 77-72940
ISBN: 0-380-01666-4

First Bard Printing, June, 1977

BARD TRADEMARK REG. U.S. PAT. OFF. AND IN
OTHER COUNTRIES, MARCA REGISTRADA, HECHO EN
U.S.A.

Printed in the U.S.A.

In somma sappi che tutti fur cherci
E litterati grandi e di gran fama,
D'un peccato medesmo al mondo lerci.
—*Inferno*, xv

I

The Book
of
Genesis

1

When Miss Sophia went walking, she created two separate clouds of dust. One was nebulous and tentative from the toe of her cane in the road. The other was a small enveloping cyclone scuffed up by her swollen old feet. She walked every morning at nine o'clock. If it rained, she carried an ancestral umbrella which had been baptized in a cloudburst on the day of the Battle of Chancellorsville. But her walking costume was the same, rain or shine. She wore a frog-green bonnet with a straw visor that always threatened to close down over her peering old face. A high lace choker loomed over her green silk waist. And her crinoline billowed as she limped over the road; it too was rusty green and stained at the hem with silt. The brown bird's-hand that clutched her Malacca cane glittered with a single emerald. In a reticule of net Miss Sophia carried a bag of Turkish paste to give to the village children. Few came near her. From a long perspective on herself she knew that, as she rocked along, she looked like a benign and leisurely old pagoda.

It was July. The humid air was militant with invaders of ragweed sperm. Miss Sophia couldn't see them, but she awakened this morning strangling with asthma. She'd cursed in a ladylike fashion; and lifting her constricted bosom from under the counterpane, she'd read a passage from the Song of Songs. But even though she was to die of suffocation she'd determined to take her morning walk.

She was in the habit of walking just to get away from The Manse. It had been in her family for more than two hundred years, built by the hands of her great-great-grandfather Obadiah in 1657. All the children of her family had been born into this solid old white house. And the money that built The Manse and maintained it had seeped even into the water in the well—a faintly metallic taste, redolent of the

3

sweat of whores and the blood of black slaves. For that was how Miss Sophia's ancestors had amassed their riches. And now as a kind of penance the life force of her family had run its race and spent its strength in that house. She sensed that the duration of an American dynasty could be no longer than two hundred years: the stream of vitality, passing from the predatory stage into the vegetative and artistic, finally chokes out like an old river forever turning on itself in a weir. Yes, Miss Sophia, meditating acidly at midnight by the hearth of The Manse, decided that her own interesting theory of decadence was the only way to account for herself and for her brother Hooker, who for twenty years now had been bringing to perfection a single watercolor—of twigs leaning over a stream.

Into The Manse she had been born, her first wail an attempt to shatter the corset of tradition that had bound her family for six generations. Miss Sophia knew from her reading in dangerous French books of political theory that tradition is inimical to American life. And she'd regarded nineteenth-century America from the parlor window of The Manse and had diagnosed it as dynamic and terrible. Her static family was irrelevant to it all! But because she was born to their myths, being of their blood, she bowed her head to a transgression of natural law that had been set up before she was born. She was following out logically the original hypotheses of The Manse when she found herself a spinster at sixty-five, living with her brother Hooker. Though when she was twenty she'd known she would end this way.

Yet for forty years in her own stylized way Miss Sophia had been subtly flouting the traditions of her family. They would never quite bring *her* under their yoke. This revolt was more symbolic than actual, as a dying person refuses to lie down in bed. But she put on her green bonnet and walked determinedly forth. Sometimes she thought it would be better if some day on her promenade she dropped dead on the road. The Italian gardener or the coachman would find her and bring her home, a spent lizard half melted from the sun. And the papers of America would murmur gloatingly of the demise of a spinster of wealth, patriarchal descent, and great sensibility.

Miss Sophia's asthma got a little less asphyxiating as she

4

put some distance between herself and The Manse. A clump of trees now shut out the view of the dreadful house that she loved and hated. Tottering on her cane, she stood still in the road and fought for a deep breath that would either kill her or fill her lungs with life and air. Then her chest opened up and the warm rich air filled her bosom. For an instant she was giddy, and felt like a young girl again. And she spoke aloud her gratitude to her favorite Old Testament prophet:

—O thank you, thank you!

Or perhaps she said it to Saint Paul, whom she preferred as he'd been before his conversion. She believed she descried his lineaments in her great-great-grandfather Obadiah, the founder of that line which was ebbing out in her and her brother Hooker.

After that grateful breath of air Miss Sophia smiled to herself, a smile she'd never have permitted anyone else to see. She shoved her cane into the dust and hobbled on.

—Perhaps, she thought, I shall die today. It must be an omen: That sudden breath of air. . . .

And The Manse, that exquisite while charnelhouse which had bleached her into a tired old woman, receded behind her in space and in her consciousness. The clicking of her cane reminded her of a skeleton castanet, and she thought upon her own death.

Death is a frequent guest with old American Protestant families like Miss Sophia's. She'd been born into death rather than into life. And she knew that to belong insistently to an old family is to insist on the dignity and validity of death. She'd been doing it all her life. She had lived with portraits and hopechests and spinning wheels of her progenitors. Willy-nilly, therefore, she recapitulated their thoughts. She'd lacked the courage to set up her own pattern of life by cutting loose from them. And so this July morning she was haunted by a sound reminiscent of her asthma. It was herself gasping on her deathbed.

Now there was nothing terrible in the thought of death to Miss Sophia. It meant simply unrolling a long sheet of memories and regrets she'd been weaving all her life. It meant leaving her canopied sighing bed in The Manse and moving to a more permanent manse by the whitesteepled church. She would tenant a bed of grass at a discreet distance from her relatives, virtuous and stiff in the soil that had been theirs for living and dying for generations. And who knew but what they would murmur chastely upon her arrival in the graveyard those decorous emptinesses remembered from her childhood?

—Sophia's come to join us, Em. A little late, but she's come. . . .

Miss Sophia smiled and shook her head. Knowing herself alone on the road, she lifted her cane and made a graceful and coquettish arc through the air, as though she was disputing a fine point in croquet with an imaginary partner. And some of the old girlish revolt awoke in her. She'd last evinced it forty-five years ago at Mount Holyoke. She spoke aloud to her ancestors:

—O, no, my dears. I shall not come to you with my hands full, as all the rest of you did. . . .

She paused and considered the implications of this revolutionary comment.

—But what *will* you do, Sophia?

Then she knew what her last derision of the world would be. The people of the town expected her to leave them her fortune. A stately public library? A baroque urn on the village green? Not Miss Sophia. She was casting about for a scheme to make her money live after her. This life-in-death of money was to her one of the most miraculous things in American dynamics. Children and loves she had none, but there was a residuum of untapped power stored in her fortune that lay snug in banks and stocks all over America. This realization gave her a passionate sense, like the carnal pleasure she never had known. She wasn't a staid old virgin after all; she was a rich and influential woman!

Gasping with delight, Miss Sophia tried to plant her heavy black cane in the road. But she lost her balance and fell onto the shoulder of the path, into green grass ready for haying. Even as she fell, she laughed. She refused to be panicky as old people are, in a tumble, fearful lest they break a hip. Yet as she lay there, face down, still laughing a little, she knew that she'd done herself a dreadful harm by her fall. There was a cold knife of pain in her pelvis; she couldn't lift herself to her feet. Her cane lay beside her on the grass.

All her life had been a vague polite shadow of pain. But she'd never really suffered like this before. Her brown old lips winced together to keep from screaming. Yet even in

6

this agony she was sufficiently objective and amused to recognize that some such pain as this might, forty years ago, have driven her out into the real world, cutting the bonds of The Manse. She had lacked the motive of true anguish.

—Well, she said, well. So this is the way I'm to end? . . .

She thought of her brother Hooker up there in The Manse, putting in another eight hours on that watercolor he was unable to finish. She thought of his peevish old face when they told him they'd found his sister lying in a ditch, just like any drunken operative from a factory. She heard his fretful voice:

—Sophia, didn't I *warn* you? . . .

Then her pain increased, and reality was with her again as she heard a wagon rumble up on the road. It was a bosomy tuft of new hay on wheels. High on the front of the rick sat a young farmer and a little freckled boy. The farmer's great-great-grandfather had come over from Devon with Miss Sophia's great-great-grandfather Obadiah. When the farmer saw her outstretched on the shoulder of the road, he clucked to his horse. The wagon stopped, and he and his little son hopped down. The farmer bent over her:

—Mam, if I didn't know you for a respectable lady, I'd think you'd been. . . .

—I wish I *had* been, she answered, stifling a groan.

—Paw, what kin I do? the little boy said.

—Go away, both of you, said Miss Sophia grandly as she lay, face down. You love this spectacle. You'll tell it all over the village tonight. . . .

The farmer gave directions to his son:

—William, fetch me them there sticks off the toppa the rick. This lady's hurt bad. . . .

—I am, Miss Sophia said. And rather enjoying it.

While the ruthless pains seemed to gather and increase in her body, the farmer and his son improvised a litter of sticks and a jacket.

—I learned these tricks at Bull Run, mam, the farmer said. You'll be light alongside some I've toted.

—At Bull Run? she whispered. I wish *I* had been there. I wish that I had been born a man. . . .

Her groaned pleasantries were the last thing she remembered. Then the world all turned to night and rushed in upon her. She thought: Ah, so? This must be death. This is

7

the black velvet waistcoat of my grandfather, which he used to throw over my head when I was a little girl. I hated it, and him with his booming laughter. . . .

Presently she found herself lying in her own wide bed in an upper room of The Manse. Her corset had been slit, and all her clothing stripped away. And by the hands of men! She felt a splint thimbling up the lower part of her dry old body. She couldn't move. Standing by her bed and smiling fatuously was Doctor Ellsworth, with his silly valanced face, though he was a cousin of General Grant. And there was her brother Hooker in his gray beard and fingers stained with paint. And there were the young farmer and the boy William. Also her lawyer, Judge Hopkins, rubbing his hands, all ready for a fat fee. Miss Sophia knew quite well what was happening. It was the first and last time in her life that her maidenly bed was to be the center of attention.

—We're sorry, mam, the young farmer said.

—Not at all, Miss Sophia said weakly. I had this coming to me. All of you please go away. . . . Boy, stay here. I want to talk to you.

Unmanned by her feeble imperiousness, her brother Hooker and Judge Hopkins and Doctor Ellsworth vacated her bedroom, backing out anxiously, as though taking leave of royalty. Only the boy William now stood by Miss Sophia's bed. He didn't fidget, and he looked through her with dry blue eyes. The frayed shoddy of his overalls just touched the elegant white of her counterpane. Now Miss Sophia had always conserved within some closet of her heart a tenderness for children. She was anything but a sentimentalist, but she saw in them, even in their noisiness and destructiveness, a dignity and a wonder that human beings slough off all too soon. Children filled her wizened heart with an excitement and an optimism she knew could never be fulfilled. Yet this elation was born anew with each generation she saw, as if the human race never could give up *trying*. Young boys, before they got beards and ragged voices, seared Miss Sophia especially. She liked the way they stood, careless yet intense. She liked their eyes, dreaming things they could never explain, and herself only foggily surmise from her reading in suspect French literature. Miss Sophia turned her face to the boy William. He'd been looking at her all the while—not in

8

alarm or teary concern—just a long cool stare.

—How old are you, boy?

She was in great pain, and talking was like knifing.

—Ten, mam.

—Are you good, boy?

—Not very often, mam.

—You are honest too, she said musingly.

She wished she could sit up and look at him. For this young William had filled her whole room with light and air and motion as though, even in pre-puberty, he'd ravished all the old customs that lay about her chamber in unseen but unsweepable cobwebs.

Miss Sophia was also well aware that, like all young persons and Negroes, this farmer's boy was consciously eluding her every effort to know him. He kept a secret and true part of himself tucked away, to be shown only to the open sky and other friends his own age. And the more she probed, the more wilily would he conceal whatever she wished to know—as misers hide, in obvious places, jewels, where they are sure to be overlooked. But the boy William had for her a relish like a piquant fresh sauce. She desired to taste him in small mouthfuls. She was incapable of deceiving herself, old Miss Sophia. She knew he didn't particularly care to be wasting his time in her room. So she determined not to condescend, nor yet to address him on his own plane.

The agony at the base of her spine and in her hip continued. She shifted a little in her bed to see if she could tease her pain into biting back at her. It did. Yet she'd always experimented in thresholds.

—Boy, what is your mother like?

—She's always nervous about me, mam.

—That's the way it is, Miss Sophia said irrelevantly. We *are* nervous. And you have made us that way. . . .

—Mam?

—Do you want to leave me, boy?

She wished again that she might lean up on her arm and look at him. It would make her feel more mistress of a situation that she feared was running away from her. For the first time the boy William didn't look at her:

—My paw will be needin me to git back hayin. . . .

—Suppose I need you too, boy?

Not since her childhood had she coquetted so with a man.

Her old age permitted her the queenly lasciviousness of saying to this child overt things impossible to younger women.
She saw that he squirmed under her remark. But even
though he was a farm boy, he wouldn't yet be susceptible to
certain nuances and intensities....

—Will you pour me a glass of sherry, boy? she said suddenly, fearful of losing his attention.

In the room soft with the glint of drawn blinds Miss
Sophia watched his overalled figure, relieved to translate his
anxiety into action, walk toward a decanter on her night
table. In handling the slender precious glassware he was discreet and cautious, as he must have been told to be with rich
folks' things. He poured out a glass of wine slowly and with
infinite elegance—not as though he'd been born to serve, but
as though he enjoyed his own motor sensations.

—My maw says ladies oughtn't drink.

—Your mother leads a life of drudgery, Miss Sophia answered tartly.

It astonished her to find that she was irked and jealous
of his implied analogy. He snapped right back at her:

—My maw's a farm woman. She *has* to work hard....

The boy William approached her bed. Miss Sophia looked
with gusto at the velvety liquid in the glass and at the boy's
sunburnt face above it.

—You must feed it to me, boy, she whispered. I cannot
lift my head.

He bent down and put the rim of the glass against her
lips, tilting it as she needed it. He was dryly gentle with her;
he seemed to be meditating on the propriety of putting his
hand under her neck, to buoy up her white head.

Then she noticed that his hands were covered with welts.
And the warm spicy trickle of the sherry choked her; she
pushed away the glass and dabbed at her lips:

—Who has beaten you, boy?

—Teacher. I go to Dame School in the village . . . sixth
grade....

—She beats you? With a ferrule?

—We always git thrashed when we don't know our sums.
Paw says it is meet an just....

—I thought that teaching was a labor of love, Miss Sophia
said slowly.

And a new spasm in her hip carried her back to her own

girlhood—to her Swiss governess, to the patient slow lessons. It had never occurred to her before now that most American children are not schooled in this fashion. She looked again at his young hands, mottled from the beating he'd received —and from a woman who was supposed to enlarge his mind.

—Do you read books, boy?

—What use are books to a farmer? he said sullenly.

And the boy put his bruised hands behind his back and edged away from the bed. But the swallow of sherry and the desire to override the shooting mortification of her body made Miss Sophia as eloquent as her ancestors—those who had been clergymen. In her zeal she almost sat up in bed:

—Education, boy, is not something to prepare you for life. That is a vulgar American error. . . . It's something to take you *out* of life. Don't you want to have some small kingdom of your own that no one can take away from you? You have one now, but when you are older it will slip away from you, and you will never know why you are poor. . . . That is what you can get from books. That is why everyone has the right to education, true education. . . . Boy, the things on the printed page are at least as real as life. They last longer than life. And that proves that they have an independent existence that is deeper and longer than life. . . . And every American (and you too, boy) owes it to himself to know much or a little of what has been thought and said before him. Then he loses some of his sense of loneliness, which is our lot. Thus by education he merges with the whole, and will not be just a sore thumb. . . . Boy, go away. I don't want it said in the village that you saw an old woman weeping. . . .

The boy William went out slowly, his head turned so that he could see her as she lay in her bed. He didn't skulk. But a flash of understanding and pain—his in prospect, hers in retrospect—had been established between them. It was the closest and warmest contact Miss Sophia ever had with a human being. It was worth every moment of the other niggardly sixty-five years. And as she wept for pain and delight, she thought there must be some conserving process whereby much of their impromptu sweetness and justice would always be kept in children. Not through the ministrations of Dame Schools, which beat their scholars.

Because she was old and low in stamina, Miss Sophia

wandered into dissociation and pneumonia from lying with a broken hip. In a few days she died, a slow insensible extinguishing of her longings and her rough edges. She went at high noon, amid the peony smells and haying of July. Her spirit left The Manse forever while downstairs her brother Hooker worked at his one watercolor, which was to be perfection of all American art.

But before she sank into the murmuring oblivion of great American families, Miss Sophia called in her lawyer, Judge Hopkins, and whispered a new will. She made him and his heirs her executors. The Judge rubbed his hands. Then his hairy ear prickled at what he heard next—that sighing petulant voice saying:

—Listen carefully. Being of sound mind. . . .

2

She was buried in green ground by that white church which her great-great-grandfather Obadiah had helped build when he came over from Devon. At her own request she was laid away in the farthest available spot of the family's acre—not too near her Aunt Emily, who had had a heart attack from reading Mrs. Stowe's novel in its first edition. No, Miss Sophia's grave was close to a lazy river, a stream so still that, if she could listen, she would hear the meandering of that water on which she'd gone boating as a girl.

Over her mound, which from erosion soon lapsed into a sunken plat, grew ferns, hollyhocks, and daisies—flowers suitable for a maiden sepulchre. By moonlight water rats and beavers made shortcuts and expeditions through the cemetery; by daylight children ventured to picnic there. But always in this place of pastoral death there was a muffled sound of scurrying and activity, a hint of life itself. Miss

Sophia wouldn't have been offended, because she'd regretted that tradition had cut her off from rhythm and movement in America.

And over her grave, a symbol of her own frigid hope, lifted the white cheroot of the meeting house tower.

Her will was heard at the next town meeting because it concerned the whole village. Judge Hopkins read aloud its revolutionary proposals in a banal and political voice. Inside he was shaking. And when they heard it, the townspeople decided what they'd always suspected about Miss Sophia —that she was not only queer, but heretical. But there was no known way in nineteenth century America to set aside the wishes of the dead, particularly of a rich old woman like Miss Sophia. Her testament to the future was in one paragraph. This is the way the muttering villagers heard it from the unctuous throat of Judge Hopkins:

Let my monies be laid away in the wisest and most prudent investment for fifty years after my decease. To this end I appoint Judge Hopkins and his heirs and their heirs as my executors and trustees. Let there be an old woman's curse upon these monies unless they are husbanded and employed wisely, as in the parable of the talents in Scripture. And after fifty years, or at such time as these monies shall have accrued the sum of four million dollars, let there be erected, built, and maintained a school to my memory; this is my last and dying desire and command. This school shall be an endowed Academy for the education of the boys and girls of America. This Academy shall have its premises on the estate of my family, known as The Manse. One-third of the student body shall be drawn from boys and girls of the town in which I lived and died, and which I loved, though it did not return the compliment. But I have no objection to deserving and qualified boys and girls from anywhere in America enrolling in my Academy. I desire further that its standards of admission and of curricular scholarship be as high as is consistent with the best young intelligences in America. No deserving scholar, however indigent or mean, shall be excluded from enrolling in my Academy. Nor am I so presumptous as to stipulate what subjects may or may not be taught in this hereinafter-existent Academy. There may be included any subject or course, ancient or modern, or discovered in the future, which shall tend to contribute to the dignity, usefulness, and scope of human life. Christianity shall be the official religion of this school, but I would not bar from my Academy any color, sect, or creed. And let this school function in my memory as the vessel and contributor and maintainer of American life, as it has been and always will be lived, in decency and cheerfulness, so long as this country shall endure. . . .

The townspeople sat and listened to the reading of this single paragraph. There was a long silence at the end; an August fly heckled Judge Hopkins's bald head. At last they arose and left the Town Hall in silence, husbands taking their wives' arms and looking grim. On the steps outside there broke forth a chatter of whispered rage and thwarted cupidity. Miss Sophia had her first laugh:

—Abner, I declare! An ole fool of an ole maid! Shoulda had children of her own. That's the best way to shut up silly wimmin. . . .

—Why, we already got a Dame School and a Latin School here! Durn good ones too. . . . She and her furren idears. . . .

In the first fifty years of her long slumber under the burdocks and mallows, Miss Sophia's America changed more than she could ever have conceived—she who guessed at what a flux it really was.

Little towns, such as where she had lived and died, ceased to be self-sufficient agrarian cells. No, the machines invaded the towns. And little proud businesses, such as her ancestors had put their faith in, were swallowed up by bigger and more ruthless corporations, impersonal in their wolfery. The thin worried men and women of Miss Sophia's day, who had done the nation's toil for slave wages and slave treatment, organized themselves out of the pit of their wretchedness. Yet her money flowed on down the years—a trickle here and a trickle there—but always attracting fresh capital to itself, as is the way of money on paper.

Her capital had its share in the plummeting of 1873. Miss Sophia's phantom hovered behind William Jennings Bryan

14

as he hallooed about a cross of gold. Or dressed in muslin, her specter was a spirit-lobby of one, stalking the White House and bristling the mustaches of Teddy Roosevelt. She helped finance young Henry Ford in his machine shop. Yes, within fifty years after her death Miss Sophia percolated to nearly everywhere in the world—cents of her here, dollars of her there. Quite a few of her dollars ended up at the Hague Conference of 1912. To all these places Miss Sophia went without once quitting her grave by the white prim church.

And her brother Hooker died after her, at ninety-seven. He left unfinished his one masterpiece of painting, the twigs kissing the stream. But he added his fortune to hers, to swell and accumulate in the endowment of her Academy. In his last days he was as petulant as an old prune, for he'd sent young painters to study in Paris, and somehow they disappeared there with their scholarship money. He was determined to make America the place to study what he called The Fine Arts.

In good time there died also the learned Judge Hopkins, whom Miss Sophia had designated her executor. In the burial ground he was planted twenty yards away from her, so that she could audit his stewardship even in death. Yet still her trust fund went on, accruing, accruing, drawing interest multiple and compound. This momentum of Miss Sophia's money took the shirts off the steel hunkies in Pittsburgh and the smocks off the yellow backs of newly arrived coolies in San Francisco.

In the fifty years after her death the bankers and lawyers who handled her money changed, just like everything else in America. She'd known polite plump gentlemen, refined leeches swollen from sucking the blood of the economic system. But now they were less and less like that portly and insular aristocracy Miss Sophia had known. By the twentieth century they'd become notorious and inaccessible barons who hid themselves away in granite castles in New York, Philadelphia, Chicago, and San Francisco. These new bankers and lawyers hired young Sicilian gunmen to protect themselves and their castles and the accruing monies of rich dead old ladies, like Miss Sophia. For hold onto this money they did. Their honor toward their dead clients was as scrupulously medieval as the soul of a usurer. And if ever these bankers or lawyers betrayed their patrons—why, they jumped out of their office windows in skyscrapers. They symbolized the only honor and ancestral worship that had survived in America: the adoration of a Dead Hand which had adjured them to husband wisely mountains of greenbacks left in trust.

Eventually, in the early years of the twentieth century, the trust fund of Miss Sophia and her perfectionist brother Hooker rolled up four million dollars. Though this sum was actually on paper, broadcast all over the world, the shrewd gentlemen in New York knew of its fruition the moment it passed from $3,999,999.99 to $4,000,000.00. They were notified by telegram, by ticker, and by adding machine. It was a day like any other in America: millions of agonies, 287 suicides, and 13,587 births. But it was the day for which Miss Sophia had been waiting for fifty years. Doubtless she knew of it even in her cool green grave. Perhaps after half a century of listening and waiting, she resigned herself to the law of Adam, and crumbled finally and irretrievably into a packet of dust in her green silk burial gown. Perhaps a sigh of consummation went up all over the cemetery, a suspiration of ancestral and matriarchal relief:
—Four million at last, she says, Em! Fifty years the poor soul's been awaitin and amummifyin! . . .

That very afternoon the four million matured, a meeting was held in a marble and plush room in New York. The air was thick with cigar smoke; the Louis Quinze chairs creaked under lawyers and bankers stuffed with lobster Newburgh. The present trustees of Miss Sophia's estate sat around a long Directors' Table, a stately checkerboard for high finance and chicanery. Now this meeting was no labor of love for the twelve trustees, who were just as self-perpetuating as the four million dollars. They'd been ordered to convene by the Governors of half a dozen states. It was a hot summer day, like that one on which Miss Sophia had died fifty years ago. These trustees had been haled into New York, sleepy stewards from their vineyards all over the United States: one from Nahant, one from Newport, one from Sea Island, Georgia. Several of the younger trustees had had to be torn from the talcky embraces of rising actresses, whom they'd

16

promised dinners at Delmonico's. There was even an old cattle baron from Wyoming, who'd brought his spittoon to this portentous and austere rendezvous of Big Money with Idealism.

And presiding over the conclave was the grandson of the first president of the Board of Trustees. Miss Sophia would never have recognized Judge Hopkins III, for this sultry afternoon his breath was fruity with bourbon and panatelas.

After several parlor car stories (such as Miss Sophia had never heard) and some swigs from a flask which was making the rounds of the Board of Trustees, Judge Hopkins III bethought himself of his ulcers and of his duty. He arose, cleared his throat, and said:

—Well, boys, let's look into this goddam business of The Academy....

They decided to settle it, what with the heat and pressing social engagements, as everything else is settled in august circles—by the Appointing of a Committee. Judge Hopkins III was unanimously voted Chairman. The committee drew themselves up a liberal Expense Account and voted themselves into a junketing tour of inspection of all the Great Schools of the United States. Their mission was cut out for them: to discover the first principal for Miss Sophia's Academy. They wanted a man not young, not old—with vision, scholarship, and a Good Head for Business on His Shoulders. Each member of the committee knew perfectly well what sort of Principal they were searching for. They didn't even need to articulate their ideal. As they got their hats and the blank checks for their expense accounts, they muttered rosily. They bumped into each other in the Florentine marble doorway of the secret room where they had met. They knew that somewhere along their route a bell would ring in their collective heads when they saw their man. They were fired with their responsibility to the youth of America. What they wanted was an aggregate and composite image of themselves—a soldier, a saint, a statesman, and a poet. Only in America could such a type of man be bred. But they would find him out.

Yet their exploratory journey lasted four months, into the fall, with chill success. They looked into every school worthy of the name in the United States. Perhaps secretly they hankered to offer the job to Teddy Roosevelt or to the presi-

17

dent of Standard Oil. But Miss Sophia had stipulated that the salary of her Principal was to be ten thousand dollars —no more, no less.

And since they were men of business, the committee searched with considerable acumen and plan. Every morning of their trip they had hangovers, and they smelled of waitresses from little overnight hotels. Judge Hopkins III carried a roadmap which he covered with colored pins as they canvassed school after school.

The committee sounded out old and established Principals of successful schools. None of these would accept a new job, since they'd developed or founded their own personal academies—why leave the known for the unknown? The committee discovered to their chagrin the odd proprietary nepotism of school Principals, who gather their schools around them like a blanket. When they are ready to die, they lie down in them. The committee discovered with a pleased awe that there is no position in the United States so powerful, autocratic, and absolute as to be Principal of a school. And these old successful Principals informed the committee with courtly innuendo that they were quite happy where they were, thank you.

One afternoon a bright young committeeman observed to Judge Hopkins III:

—Is it possible, Judge, that America does something funny to her teachers?

The jovial Judge, surprised by his very own thought, answered his junior partner with hearty nonchalance:

—O, horsewash, T. J. A good man wouldn't *stay* in teaching. . . .

—Does seem sort of a pity, though, what we've seen, said the young committeeman, scratching an ear.

—Heat's got you, T. J. Let's get on with our knitting. . . .

(Judge Hopkins III's favorite and only poem was Tennyson's one, about The Charge.)

Finding no consolation or abetment for Miss Sophia's money from Principals of long standing, the committee were about to give church schools the once-over. Then one of the lawyers recollected Miss Sophia's stipulation that her Academy must be nonsectarian. Thus they couldn't offer the post of Principal to a young Anglican priest, or to a Mormon, or to any Protestant minister. A committeeman who was a

Cowley Father sighed audibly at this reminder. He had visions of Gothic chapels, of chaplains in cassock and surplice coaching saintly football teams.

—Well, Judge, T. J. said. What about the *public* schools?

(T. J. was known in Wall Street as a hustler. And after three and a half months of this nonsensical fandango through the United States, he wanted to hustle back to his business and to his new house in Scarsdale.)

—*Public* schools? said Judge Hopkins III, mopping his forehead and lighting a cigar. No *class*, T. J. . . . And my grandfather distinctly told me when I was a tyke that Miss Sophia hated the public schools and the way they beat the children. . . .

—But, Judge, T. J. said, do you think she meant to found a factory for *snobs*?

Judge Hopkins III purpled a shade:

—O I don't know what the hell the old girl wanted. All that concerns you and me, T. J., is that she left four million smackers to found a school. . . .

—Old ladies are sorta nuts, now that you mention it, T. J. said, eager not to offend the potent Judge.

And on an afternoon when it looked as though their quest was hopeless, the committee arrived at a mining town in Pennsylvania. It was disfigured by slag heaps or by striking miners rolling drunk in the streets. Those members of the committee with coal interests looked virtuously the other way.

—Black bastards, Judge Hopkins III said. Ought to be home taking care of their wives and kids. They're the anarchists who make trouble in this great country.

Cold and tired and thinking of the delights of New York, the committee groped their way to the nearest tavern. Thinking of Miss Sophia's seemingly unexpendable four million, and of their four months wasted out of Christian Duty, they drank several brandies in peeved silence. Only one member of the committee abstained from these fortifiers. And this clergyman spoke up for almost the first time on the junket:

—You gentlemen, he said softly and wheezily, are forgetting your sacred duty to the Little Ones of America. . . .

—O my God, Reverend! cried Judge Hopkins III. Do you know what I wish Miss Sophia had done with her four mil-

lion? So far as I'm concerned, she can take the whole ka-
boodle and shove. ...

In order not to have to cover his ears with his soft white
hand, the clergyman interrupted:

—Suffer the Little Ones. ...

As the waiter, he too impregnated with coal dust, brought
the fifth round of brandies, Judge Hopkins III clapped him
fraternally on the back:

—Goddam it, lad. Do *you* want to start a school?

The boy wiped his coal-back hands on his apron:

—No, sir, but I know someone who does. ...

—Who? the committee cried in unison, gagging on their
brandy.

—They's a Friends' School up the road a piece, the boy
said. An they's a teacher there named Pilkey. A balla fire.
He's burnin up the Quakers even. They got smoke in their
eyes. ...

Judge Hopkins III hooted deliriously, arose, and smashed
his pony of brandy on the floor of the tavern.

—Take my hand! he shouted. Lead me! ...

3

But he hesitated more than was his wont before he lifted the
knocker and shivered it down on the escutcheon underneath.
Indeed from this solid neat door emanated the fiercest radiance of power, as though the eye of God was peering at him
from behind it. Himself a strong man, Judge Hopkins III felt
as if his spacious stomach had come smack up against an
unyielding buttress. But summoning up his manhood and
remembering what Jay Gould had once said to him, he
rattled the ornate and sneering knocker. Almost at once a
Negress answered, as though she'd been hulking there, waiting for him to make up his mind. Through the passageway

behind her tremendous back came the smell of heliotrope, tapestry, and bourgeois upholstery.

—I wish to see Mr. Pilkey, the Judge said shyly. It's very important.

—Well, he jest ain't to home raht now, the Negress said. Dere's jest me and da two Missus Pilkeys.

—Then I will call on *them*, said Judge Hopkins III.

He wondered if he'd bumbled into a Mormon ménage.

With her scent of coffee and pork the Negress led him through a sinister hallway into a large drawing room. It had the air of being a set-piece in a period museum. The Judge could have sworn that the chairs and divans had been nailed to the floor. The flowers on the coffee table seemed to have been frozen immediately after picking. The room was lined with books in sumptuous matching sets, but these books seemed to be really tiles to wall up whatever corpses had been stowed in the wainscoting. There wasn't a speck of dust on the waxed floor—no sign of children's play, in fact no indication that human beings had ever lived, laughed, or loved in this room. Judge Hopkins III felt a hand about his windpipe.

And seated on a sofa at the far end of the room two ladies were regarding him. One was old and mummified, her white hair coiled up on her pin-head and skewered with a comb. This lady knit on unconcernedly after she'd shot the Judge one look of profound malignity and vengeance. As she purled, she kept sucking in her denture. The old lady wore furlined slippers which she kept up on an ottoman. The Judge saw that bandages rumpled the contours of her stockings.

The younger of the ladies hopped up from the couch. She was dressed in a bedspread which she must have wrapped about her that morning. Her hands palpitated in front of her narrow bosom like bony leaves. Her black hair was braided over her brow. The eyes in her brown bony face were piercing, but they shot around the drawing room as though its very perfection still didn't satisfy her. Judge Hopkins III decided that she was either mortally afraid of him or was going to convert him to some new missionary work.

He held his Homburg against his generous belly and made both ladies the bow that in court disarmed all his witnesses:

—The two Mrs. Pilkeys, I presume?

21

—Presume on nothing, the old lady said. And if you're selling anything, we don't want it.

The younger lady went through motions suggestive of an Indian squaw about to give the flame signal. She ran straight at Judge Hopkins III and spread out her fluttering hands. Whether it was a gesture of welcome or dismissal he couldn't for his life have told.

—I don't know that it concerns you, she said. But I am Mr. Pilkey's wife, and that is his mother.

—Word of your husband's fame as a teacher has reached us, Judge Hopkins III said.

—I only know he's made me a wonderful son, the old woman said from the couch. But that's because I trained him in the way he should go. Many a cuff I gave that boy. . . .

—He *is* wonderful, Mr. Pilkey's wife said. That's why I married him. It took a *man* to lure me away from my art. *He* did it, though. . . .

—Your art, mam? Judge Hopkins III said weakly, looking about the room.

—She's a very great artist, Old Mrs. Pilkey said. As a matter of fact we make a specialty of greatness in this house. . . .

Wishing he might be offered a chair, Judge Hopkins III looked about the morgue of a room. But now for the first time he noticed something distinctive. Besides the books and a few pretty-pretty landscapes he observed quantities of china and pottery standing about in kittenish attitudes on top of the mantel and the bookcases. These were bas-reliefed or colored in mezzotints.

—Those are *her* work, Old Mrs. Pilkey said, dropping a stitch from pride. Ceramics. . . .

Judge Hopkins III turned courteously to the younger woman, who was still trembling and dancing about him:

—You mean, you make *pots*, mam?

—She is an artist, said Mr. Pilkey's mother with hoarse finality. Probably the only one left in America. That is why my boy married her . . . her sense of perfection. . . .

Suddenly Judge Hopkins III concluded that he was carrying on a conversation with two crows which had somewhere learned human speech. Since he hadn't yet been asked to sit, he strolled appreciatively about the room, murmuring over Mrs. Pilkey's china and urns. He mooed mad nothings, like

22

a bull caught in a Fine Arts class. And always behind him he could hear young Mrs. Pilkey on tiptoe, ready to sue him if he smashed anything.

—Lovely, lovely, the Judge said, trying to summon up the deliberate ecstasy of the connoisseur. My wife would give her eyeteeth for some of these. . . . Real antiques . . . aren't they?

—My art is above price, said Young Mrs. Pilkey. No, I take it all back. If I were paid what my art is worth, I would have several million dollars.

—As it is, she does pretty well, croaked Old Mrs. Pilkey from the couch. The orders pour in from all over the country.

The Judge went into a spasm of ingratiation:

—Perhaps, mam, my wife would send you an order. . . .

—Impossible. I create only for My Custom. That is true art. . . . I . . . I don't know your wife. All I know is that I am in complete revolt against mass production. My only interest in life (besides Mr. Pilkey) is restoring dignity to art and handicraft. Workers today are unhappy because they have no share in the product they turn out. . . . Whereas my own happiness is consummate, because *all* of me goes into my work. It is a labor of love. . . .

The old lady's commentary from the divan went right on:

—Yes, she's unique. In fact all of us in this house are. . . . They talk about rugged individualism in America. Well, that's a lie. One hundred million people have been brought to heel by the system. Only three are in revolt against it: my son Mr. Pilkey, Mrs. Pilkey there, and myself. . . .

—Why, I think that's wonderful, the Judge whispered.

It was almost the first time in his life he'd been put in his place. He had the sensation of being kept after school, of being rattaned and lectured at. He believed that he could gratify these two ladies only by bursting into tears. Feeling a little faint, Judge Hopkins III groped about him and sat down heavily in the nearest chair. The younger Mrs. Pilkey whirled on him:

—Please get up at once! That chair is not for sitting. It's function is the Chair to Stand by the Fireplace. I designed it myself. Good furniture is to be appreciated for its lines.

23

Mr. Pilkey and I have tried to make this room a projection of our spirits. . . .

—It's a perfect marriage, cried the old lady. They see eye to eye on everything. Not like young folks nowadays. More like wedlock when I was a girl. . . .

—If you must sit down before ladies, said Mr. Pilkey's wife, sit between Mr. Pilkey's mother and myself on the couch. . . . Though we don't know what you are doing here.

Judge Hopkins III took out his huge linen handkerchief and mopped his forehead. Then he staggered to the divan and lowered himself between the two ladies, taking pains not to contaminate the thigh of either with his thick masculine one. Once he was ensconced between them, his hostess stared straight ahead. Old Mrs. Pilkey knit madly, sucking philosophically on her denture. But here there was no consoling perfume, such as normally soothed the good Judge in the proximity of women. He smelled only soap, carbolic acid, and functional talcum powder. Not after a long and distinguished career at the bar had Judge Hopkins III ever been closer to snapping than now.

He addressed the younger of the women, who was staring in front of her at her gaunt folded little hands:

—Children, mam?

The younger Mrs. Pilkey made a frenzied wave about her icy drawing room, including all the gossamer crockery on the shelves.

—O your *pots*, the Judge said under his breath.

—Any woman can have children, said Old Mrs. Pilkey. I did myself. And often I wonder the worth of it . . . except for Mr. Pilkey, of course. Sometimes I think that women should refuse to bear any children for a generation or so. It might improve the caliber of the human race.

—It might at that, you know, said Judge Hopkins III.

He wanted insanely to cross his knees or do something relaxed with his red furry hands.

—You ladies mind if I have a smoke? he asked.

—If you mean cigarettes; no, Old Mrs. Pilkey said. We believe that sucking cigarettes is another symptom of these degenerate times. Mr. Pilkey himself smokes only a pipe. But we agree that that is justifiable as a manly habit of the heroes of English novels. . . . Mr. Pilkey occasionally takes

a glass of rum, too, though neither his wife nor I approve. . . .
But I suppose we must allow males their minor vices. . . .

(Judge Hopkins III pricked up his ears at the mention of rum. It might be just the bait he needed.)

—Just what, mam, said the Judge, do you do for amusement besides your Art?

The old lady made her first spontaneous gesture of the afternoon. She spread her arms over her bosom, which was deeper than that of Mr. Pilkey's wife:

—Innocent merrymaking. They read aloud to each other every evening. They take hampers of lunch to the woods. They play charades. They go to church. And they play backgammon and Chinese checkers. . . .

—A much fuller life than most of us Americans know, Judge Hopkins III sighed.

—You may say that, said young Mrs. Pilkey, beginning to fidget.

Just then the Judge heard a tremendous roaring in the street outside, a bumptious baritone over the bleating of childish voices—a shepherd dog herding a flock of sheep. He heard a sound of many feet in a stampede, but of one heavy pair of heels that seemed to be chasing the lighter ones. The Judge stood up from the divan:

—Are they having labor trouble in this town?

Old Mrs. Pilkey giggled and threw down her knitting:

—Bless you, no! That is only Mr. Pilkey frolicking with his pupils on the way home from school. . . .

Strangely stirred by the uninhibited and genial boorishness of the sound, Judge Hopkins III walked to the window. He peered out into the mean and rubbishy street of this Pennsylvania mining town. And he saw a procession that seemed to prance out of the Crusades. A cloud of boys and girls was billowing about a man of thirty-five, thickset and tall. The laggards in the race he caught and cuffed with a certain grim affection. He shouted continuously at them, as though he resented having grown up at all. Catching hold of a ripening little girl, he spanked her in an important place. She screamed with pleasure and grabbed his wrist:

—Oooh, Mr. Pilkey, you're awful! I'm gonna tell your wife!

The Judge watched, delighted and almost certain. This

25

man had the face of a lion, benign from feasting well. He waved his great arms and shouted afresh when the tumult gave any sign of dying down. To Judge Hopkins it seemed that Mr. Pilkey scuttled instead of running. A mass of graying hair plopped into his eyes, and Mr. Pilkey shook it out again, pummeling his charges. The teacher was dressed in a football uniform, its shoulderpads accentuating his prophetic torso. And Judge Hopkins III at the window found himself nodding his head vigorously. There would never be vacuum, repose, or inanity in any place that Mr. Pilkey found himself. And what a way with children!—bullying, fond, and somehow deliciously condescending, as though they were his playthings. And Judge Hopkins sensed that the man didn't so much love the young as seeing in them a fruitful soil to plant his own personality. Yes, Mr. Pilkey was the personification of Flying Will. The Judge now knew that the cosmic energy of Mr. Pilkey had flattened out his wife and his mother.

Musing and enthusiastic, the Judge turned from the window. He was, after a quest of four months, pleased with, and reconciled to, the world. There was a little tic in his eyesocket that might have been the remote control of Miss Sophia nodding from her grave. Accustomed to judge his man by criteria financial, energetic, and predatory, the Judge had already formed an opinion of Mr. Pilkey. He was in fact a little terrified of this man he'd watched chase fifty yelling children through the streets. In his world the Judge was cognizant only of vitality and drive. He was indifferent to delicate issues. Was this what he'd been searching for? What would a school do with an ascetic, a pale poet, a yearning introvert? Mr. Pilkey was as juicy with red blood as a thick steak. No, what the Judge was seeking was push, a sense of dedication and organization. *What* was dedicated and *how* it was organized was, he said, none of his business. . . .

The elder Mrs. Pilkey was clutching her breast maternally:

—You've seen him? That's my son. And I tell you, he is a masterpiece.

—He is indeed, mam, said Judge Hopkins III softly.

—That's my hubby, said the younger Mrs. Pilkey.

It was the first time she'd lapsed into the vernacular of the day.

The Judge was still smiling almost tenderly at the two ladies when Mr. Pilkey slammed into the drawing room, tearing off his shoulderpads and football helmet. Some of his meaty white chest under the jersey was exposed to the delicate ladies, but Mr. Pilkey didn't seem to care. He threw down on the elegant bare table a huge brown paper bag streaked with grease.

—Hullo, hullo, hullo! I bought porkchops for supper!

Then Mr. Pilkey threw himself down in Mrs. Pilkey's Forbidden Chair and began to strip off his cleated shoes. As yet he hadn't noticed the Judge, who had retired to the window. A fierce aliveness exuded from Mr. Pilkey that would have blotted out anyone else in the room anyway. The Judge wasn't displeased from his point of vantage and momentary anonymity. He listened.

Mr. Pilkey, practically undressing before the ladies, had a rich zealous voice that just went on and on. He didn't care whether anyone was interested in what he had to say. His words kept coming out in a wall of sound—anecdote, aphorism, and jest. His humor was accompanied by rich snorts. He simmered with heartiness. Judge Hopkins wondered if perhaps Mr. Pilkey mightn't even talk to himself in an empty room, just for the persuasive opulence of his own voice. Yet there was always the hint of a magisterial threat behind that voice. Judge Hopkins felt that he was being bullied by it, that it had him up against a wall and was going to murder him slowly and genially—all for his own good. Yes, there was somehing massive about Mr. Pilkey; he hurled himself at life, and God help life for standing in his way.

Mr. Pilkey kicked off his football shoes. He stood up and unabashedly opened his football pants, unlacing them to ventilate his crotch. Then he tossed the luxurious bang of graying hair out of his eyes and attacked his wife and his mother. He gave smacking unsexual busses, though Judge Hopkins was positive that so masculine and lordly a man was capable of other caresses, far less genteelly connubial than these. He could be stud for a score of mistresses. And perhaps he was, for all the Judge knew.

—Dearie! said Mr. Pilkey to his wife.

—Dearie! said Mr. Pilkey to his mother.

Then he charged into an exuberant recitation of his day—every detail from the moment he'd left the house that morning. The two women listened with glistening proud eyes. It was evident that Mr. Pilkey was interested in every facet of his life, that he accepted his world like the God who had created it, finding it good and zestful. And the Judge marked him down as one of those men who need the company of women to expand in, needing them perhaps as much for their approbation and applause as he needed them for the solace of their bodies.

Because there was something magnetic about the fullness of Mr. Pilkey's embrace of human beings lesser than himself, Judge Hopkins III found himself drawn and wandering timorously toward the threesome. And then the wife tugged at the ranting husband's arm.

—Dearie, she said, almost graciously. I forgot. We have a guest. He wants to see you. . . .

His football trousers still unlaced, his hip pads jutting, Mr. Pilkey clapped Judge Hopkins on the shoulder and crushed his hand. The Judge looked into two gray eyes that were hard and strong and somehow without mercy, except as the man-god interpreted it:

—Why, welcome to my poor house, sir! Stay and take pot luck with us for supper . . . porkchops and a tossed salad, for which I am famous. . . .

—Just *one* of his accomplishments! his mother cried.

Judge Hopkins III spent a long, thrilling, and enervating evening with the Pilkeys. After that overwhelming greeting he noticed that Mr. Pilkey really didn't have any manners. He wasn't a barbarian; he just didn't go by any earthly code of etiquette. Nor was he aware of Judge Hopkins, except as a listening mosquito in the monsoon of his eloquence. Mr. Pilkey crammed down great mouthfuls of crisp pork and his own tossed salad, snorting with gourmand happiness. And talking, always talking, his mouth full and his eyes gleaming with tears of laughter at his own stories. Mr. Pilkey was also a moralist; he paraded for the Judge's edification judgments of everything that was happening in the world that year. (And it was mostly all to the bad. We should return, said

Mr. Pilkey, to the stern decencies of our forefathers. He lamented the invention of the electric light and the automobile, for Softness had slithered into the world. Only *he* hadn't been made flabby.)

So Mr. Pilkey talked. For dessert he sucked the sweets out of half a dozen eclairs with sensual gusto. And he wiped his mouth with a great sigh and belched several times. His tongue went to work cleaning the shredded food out from the crevices of his white teeth.

The Negress did the dishes, and Mr. Pilkey and Judge Hopkins III withdrew to the formal living room. They were replete with food. But the Judge wasn't allowed to nod in his chair. Mr. Pilkey bullied him into a game of backgammon. Thrice the Judge caught him cheating like the craftiest child, and Mr. Pilkey roared with laughter and dug him in the ribs.

And when the ladies joined them, they sat with brandy in Napoleon glasses and Mr. Pilkey observed that brandy and rum were the only things he ever touched. With unusual delicacy Judge Hopkins III strove to change the tone of the conversation, which was getting like a locker room, with stories of Mr. Pilkey's prowess and impressions on everything.

—And what do you read, sir? asked the Judge, mincing bookishly and nodding to the two ladies, who were also sucking food out of their teeth.

—Dickens, English history, and the Bible, sir. Everything else is frivolous nonsense. . . .

Judicially the Judge closed his eyes and tilted his brandy in the womblike glass. Then he spoke very slowly, trying to suppress the excitement he'd been feeling in this house:

—And what would you do, Mr. Pilkey, if I gave you a school to play with?

Mr. Pilkey leapt to his feet and brought his fist crashing down on the table. The heavy oak seemed to shiver. O my God, thought Judge Hopkins III, I am in the presence of Moses. . . .

—*Play* with it, sir? Are you joking? That's no game! I'd give my life to a school I believed in!

The ladies smiled and sighed. Judge Hopkins III laughed, sipped his cordial, and urged on his new Principal.

29

4

Physically The Academy was a place of beauty and poise. From her dust Miss Sophia would have rejoiced in its easy elegance. Yes, her corseting and her opulence and her hope had been projected into the buildings and landscape of her school. It was separated from the village by that narrow rushy river. But this medieval moating-off of The Castle incurred the resentment of the villagers, who began to mutter about Town and Gown. Forgetting their history, they said that Miss Sophia had been One of Them, but that her school was not—and all on account of the snobbishness of That Old Bastard. Mr. Pilkey was never mentioned by name in the village.

And on his side he maintained that Education is a separating and conserving process, by its nature womblike and maternal. Students should be segregated from American life, which he called decadent and dangerous. Almost tearfully on his jubilees he read a statement to the newspapers that security and isolation are necessary to the growing mind. Thus he deliberately removed his students from life. He said that if stability and offishness (*not* snobbishness) were inculcated for the first twenty years, the gyroscope would obtain for the rest of the individual's life. He disregarded genially all protests in the name of John Dewey and the progressive schools.

Early in the twentieth century Mr. Pilkey had been considered a great liberal in American education. He did away with fraternities at his Academy, said Negroes were welcome at his school, even though none ever came. His school was, he said, classless and Utopian. But by the middle of the twentieth century, secure at the sheltered helm of his Academy, Mr. Pilkey had forgotten in the flush of his triumphs

30

that the radical of one generation is the fogy of the next. He would never know. For he had taken his school out of the real world.

For his new and enlarged catalog he had an aerial view taken of The Academy's grounds. Seen from the sky, it had a tranquil and noble appearance. This geometry of red and white and green seemed to frame a nursery for gentle thought. There were acres of greenery where once Miss Sophia's Manse had stood mumbling by the river. Outlying the plant were the rectangles of athletic fields and the ashy streaks of running tracks. The glass of the gymnasium roof looked like a little dihedral mirror.

In spring and summer and early fall the grounds were feverish with flowers and the woolly outlines of shrubs and bushes, held to the tolerance of one-thousandth of an inch, for Mr. Pilkey's wife preyed on the grounds crew when she was dissatisfied with the pruning. Dominant also were a chapel and a dining hall. The whole campus had an air of mellow discipline, seeming to say: This Is The Way It Should Be.

Nothing new architecturally had been invented for The Academy. A few said they hated the plant, for it merely repeated the prim scholastic architecture of dead generations. But such criticisms never reached the ear of Mr. Pilkey. Most people were breathless over the beauty of The Grounds, for most people think that a school should look like a greenhouse out of doors. And the people who most loved the looks of The Academy were the parents of these children being schooled there. These parents felt an almost crawling humility toward the school, as though it was an altar on which they had laid the bodies of their sons and daughters for sacrifice.

Mr. Pilkey's interest in things pertaining to his Academy is benign and bland if he is not aroused to the wrath of Isaiah. He is now sitting at his desk (called The Den) in a huge brick building he archly calls The Schoolhouse. Over his alcove is a portrait in oils of Miss Sophia in bonnet and kerchief, looking down as though she might smile, if she wasn't fearful of cracking the canvas. In front of Mr. Pilkey's desk every member of the Boys' School must pass all morning as one class lets out and another begins. The Principal may seem to be dictating to his secretary, but he has an eye

31

peeled for the expressions of the faces of students and faculty as they pass in review. Often he has told Mrs. Pilkey that he can read their minds from the expression on their faces. Perhaps he can after twenty-five years. At any rate he is Keeping In Touch.

Mr. Pilkey is now threescore and five years of age. The days of his reign in Israel are a score and five. And though he is now and old man he does not dream of retirement, though his alumni murmur of it and his trustees perhaps wish it. As he sits at his desk, genial and in control of his empire, he thinks often of that verse in Ecclesiasticus:

—Let us now praise famous men, and our Fathers that begat us....

II

The Book
of
Fall

1

In September of this year the tired sunlight singles out Miss Sophia's grave with a lingering brightness. She has been dead eighty-one years now; perhaps there is nothing beneath her headstone but ashes of cloth and that prayerbook she was buried with. There is a smell of late asters on the air; the horizon crackles with fires from sheds where they are curing tobacco in the leaf. The graveyard is not less frequented than on the day she was laid there, for a state highway passes one hundred feet from her headstone. In the afternoons there crawls a humming clicking stream of those chromium alligators which are called automobiles. Miss Sophia had never seen one, but in a day or so they will come in herds, observing prim lanes in the road, carrying boys and girls ticketed for a year at The Academy.

America has come through two World Wars now. Parents of these boys and girls in recent years have scrounged their meat or bought it at black market prices—while their sons and daughters were getting Culture, Religion, and Democracy. These parents bless themselves that their boys and girls are a little young to have taken part in the recent carnage. Yet they have observed how their children are different from the kids before 1941—how they stay out at night, how they talk knowingly and furtively among themselves. It must be the fault of Those Veterans! These returning soldiers from the Second World War have injected something new and anarchic into America! For now the country is jaded and weary and sinister and nervous all at once. And the children are different too. Miss Sophia would never have recognized this America. In the very state where she lies buried there is now a cynical laughter and an un-Calvinistic experimentation, even among the very young, who in her day were thought to be rosycheeked. During their vacations now schoolchildren don't stay at home. They hitchhike over the country, where they learn a thing or two. Probably from Those Veterans! The age of snuffling is over. And during the Second World War the doctrine of individual responsibility, a favorite tenet with Miss Sophia, has died, along with most vestiges of Christianity. There is less hypocrisy—and yet more of it—in America. Could Miss Sophia return, she'd phrase it in a euphemism, observing that America has passed from the Age of Cicero into the poisonous ripeness of Caligula.

Mr. Pilkey, the aging Principal of her Academy, knows more of this than Miss Sophia. For he has firsthand, if groping, experience of it among his boys and girls. He inhaled his education in the nineties, when William James and Royce and Muensterberg were the last word. But his sly and quick old mind detects aura and nuances among his students which are different than they were in, say, the Class of 1941, most of which sallied gallantly forth into the Armed Forces. Last year he was at a loss to cope with certain sinister and giggling goings-on in his school. Something inside him said that what his Academy needed was a resident psychiatrist. But under the proddings of parents and the insistence of Judge Hopkins V, now President of the Board of Trustees, Mr. Pilkey turned his face backward and engaged a resident chaplain, an octogenarian who admires Phillips Brooks. Mr. Pilkey counts on the Reverend Doctor Smedley to cope with the moral morass of postwar America. This pious old gentleman dotes on long prayers, and will bludgeon the old prewar God into young American hearts.

It is September at the close of the first half of the twentieth century. The Academy is reopening. This is a jubilee year for Mr. Pilkey, his twenty-fifth as Principal. He has no thought of retirement; isn't he at the peak of his mature virility? In his morning prayers he promises himself and his school all sorts of treats to signalize this *annus mirabilis:* small raises for deserving members of his faculty, a drive for new building funds (possibly a dormitory to be named after himself), a program of publication of textbooks by the faculty which will cause a renascence in the book industry.

Each September (and this September too) The Academy reopens on a Saturday evening. Last week Mr. Pilkey sent out the glad tidings by mimeographed letter to faculty, secretaries, and janitors, inviting them to the Annual Reunion Frolic. He believes that his staff has been in Limbo or exile all summer, waiting and holding their breaths for the re-opening of school. He knows that teachers are not happy during their vacations, for he himself gets to feeling nervous and superannuated at his house in Maine, with nothing to do but eat lobster, read Dickens and English history, and scheme for the triumphs of the coming year. But this Saturday evening he's Getting Into Harness Again, and he knows that everyone else is as expectant as he.

This Reunion Frolic is held on the lawn of Mr. Pilkey's Cape Cod house, which is set a little off from the quadrangle of the Academy. For twenty-five years he has tried to evolve a gracious custom of Going To the Principal's House—but few of his faculty or students ever come, except on business. Tonight they must come.

Mr. and Mrs. Pilkey are forming a reception line of two, by temporary tables laden with chicken salad, rolls, and iced tea. Mr. Pilkey is wearing a white suit and a yellow ascot. Under his flowing white mane he looks the gay old dog he is. He seems a successful senator about to give himself a testimonial dinner. He is proud of his tan, got on a Maine beach while Mrs. Pilkey painted her plates.

This afternoon Mrs. Pilkey is wearing pongee slacks, a green blouse and a picture hat. She has always refused to keep up with styles, wearing what she *feels*. Her hair is white too, though still in coronet braids. With the Second World War she decided that dyeing it was frivolous and un-American. And she hasn't been well since the birth of Herman, twenty-five years ago. In old age she still reserves herself for her art—those fragile dinner dishes which she paints and ships out all over the country. Her fame as an artist in ceramics has spread all over the world. Every newly married member of the faculty is expected to purchase a set of Wedgwood beautified by her brush.

And Mr. and Mrs. Pilkey stand together by the tables for the buffet supper. She is keeping a birdy eye cocked to the Polish steward and his wife, the school dietitian, who are setting up the tables of goodies. Mrs. Pilkey is as conscious as ever of symmetry. At last she cries out to Mrs. Miekewicz:

—That pitcher of iced coffee is two inches off center!

The steward's wife, sweating in muslin, lumbers over to right the pitcher. She sputters in Polish. Mrs. Pilkey suspects that she is swearing, but says nothing, for the steward and his wife have been twenty years with The Academy.

Old Mrs. Pilkey, the Principal's mother, is not to be at this Reunion Frolic, the first she has missed in twenty-five years. The old lady is ninety-two, and as armored as a turtle. Last night she ate lobster salad, and now she is upstairs in the Cape Cod house with ptomaine poisoning, under the care of the Negress, who fans her.

—Mother was in tears to miss our party, says Mr. Pilkey cosily to his wife. Well, anyhow I've got *you*, dearie. . . .

She gives his arm a little squeeze and giggles girlishly:

—Hand in hand together, up and down this vale of tears. . . .

—So it's been *that* bad? Mr. Pilkey whispers in her ear.

And, as on such occasions, he remembers how as a young teacher he wooed her thirty-five years ago, because she was an artist and a perfectionist.

Mrs. Pilkey shifts restively. Standing at attention on her slender old legs sets throbbing her varicose vein. Now she stands only when she daubs at her pottery. But she has played the Great Lady of the Manor for twenty-five years, even though it costs her time away from her ceramics. Yet she gives vent to the spleen of a tired old woman:

—Where *are* they all? If we had cocktails, they'd have been here an hour ago. . . .

Mr. Pilkey puts his fingers together and reflects delicately:

—My faculty are more spoiled children than my students. . . . But dearie, we will *never* serve cocktails at Reunion Frolics. Goddam it . . . forgive me, dearie . . . I want the fun to be spontaneous, like what you and I have together. People in this day and age have lost the joy I knew as a boy. Thank God, *we* still retain it. . . .

These two old people, prince and princess of a great school, look at each other, a little dubious and a little lost. These moods have been stealing over him as he ages into a kind of marble poignancy. But her preoccupation with her art prevented her noticing till recently how old he is. But now she knows, with a shiver that is an echo of her girlish tremulousness, that he is an old man and she an old woman. And that they are still living in a different world from the

38

swift sad one of the late nineteen forties. Then she speaks out in a chilly whisper:

—Dearie, don't be angry . . . but do you think they really *like* to come to these Reunion Frolics? Isn't it after all . . . a little like being presented at court?

—Why, nonsense, dearie!

And Mr. Pilkey looks at her from under his marble brow as though he wonders why he ever married her. Mrs. Pilkey sighs a little. She knows it is never his habit to apologize. He looks away from her massively and snorts. She feels hurt, but like an artist, she can't express her feelings. People are coming. . . .

First to arrive is a group of janitors and their wives, starched, Sundayish, and uneasy, and wedged together for their own social protection. Mr. Pilkey doesn't suspect the anguish he causes by forcing faculty, secretaries, and janitors to meet socially over chicken salad on that first Saturday. He is merely insisting on the democracy that permeates his school. By God, they *will* get together and have fun! This faculty are snobs. Only yesterday he told some reporters that The Academy was a microcosm of the United States of America. . . .

But the janitors and their wives aren't coming up to be received. They just stand there twisting their hats, and their wives are panting from respect and fear. He will show them! He sweeps down upon them in all his majesty, carrying along Mrs. Pilkey because he's pinioned her arm. He shakes hands with the janitors; their wives curtsy, pleasing Mr. Pilkey·and embarrassing Mrs. Pilkey. He booms forth:

—Twarkins, old boy, how are you? Have a good summer? . . . And Mrs. Twarkins, as I live and breathe! Still the village belle you were twenty-five years ago. The boys still on the farm? . . . Hello, Mr. Higby! And Mrs. Higby too! . . . And the Jasons and the Tomkinses and the Reynoldses . . . God love you all! So good of you to come to our Reunion Frolic! I often ask Mrs. Pilkey, where would a school be without its janitors? . . . There's more than enough chicken salad to go around. . . .

The dietitian, running around with iced tea, murmers something in Polish. Mrs. Pilkey gives her a look. The janitor's wives peer damply at Mrs. Pilkey, waiting a smile from her, as bedraggled flowers await the sun. No smile is forthcoming. So the head janitor, older than Mr. Pilkey and crippled with arthritis, sidles forward to show The Boys he knows how to bluster a bit:

—Well, sir, what do you think of the Republican Party?

—Well, sir, Mr. Pilkey roars, what do *you* think of it, Twarkins?

After this sally there is some indecision among the gray little knot of janitors as to whether it is permissible to nudge one another and Mr. Pilkey. For they are restless and a little naked without their brooms and mops. Finally they all start laughing, the way old men do when they have mislaid their false teeth. None of them is under fifty, and nearly all have been mopping The Academy buildings since those ivied walls first lifted their heads. Mr. Pilkey knows that their pride in the school and in himself is blind, puzzled, and unchanging. They go to every game The Academy plays. And now their wives, taking the cue from their husbands, give out a panicky giggle.

—O relax! cries Mr. Pilkey with a festive wave. Enjoy yourselves!

Mrs. Twarkins, gathering about herself the shreds of etiquette, says to Mrs. Pilkey:

—That chicking salad sure looks fine, mam. That would win a prize at *any* church supper!

Mrs. Pilkey is caught offguard. She wishes to be gracious, but she's been thinking of a set of plates she means to fresco tomorrow:

—O yes? Well don't touch *any* of that food till everybody gets here....

Because of her gaffe she retreats into icy jitters. Mr. Pilkey, his duties done, shepherds the janitors and their wives into a remoter plot of the lawn:

—In the meantime, friends, just chat and mingle among yourselves....

Some of the janitors' wives are blushing and hemming and hawing. They put their heads together and whisper. But Mr. Twarkins, as head janitor, takes them in hand, just as he drives their husbands through the corridors on their cleaning forays:

—You heard what the Big Boss says, boys and girls.... Or are you deef?

—Wonderful people, wonderful, Mr. Pilkey says. I sometimes wonder if my faculty, for all their educational advantages. . . .

The electricity of his own autogenerated hospitality is charging him. He bears Mrs. Pilkey back to their stance by the tables.

—You know, she says softly, next year why don't we *try* cocktails? . . .

—Dearie, says Mr. Pilkey, mopping his brow, which is moist from the frenzy of his joviality, let's not have any more of that cocktail nonsense, please. . . .

—But, the old woman pleads, this is all so . . . stiff. . . .

—All in your own mind, dearie, Mr. Pilkey says huffily. *I* am relaxed. . . .

—Then where is the faculty?

—*That* I can tell you, dearie. In their homes. Drinking coffee. Sucking cigarettes. . . .

Further tension is obviated by the arrival of The Academy's seven secretaries in party frocks. Mrs. Pilkey feels more at her ease because the stenographers, who know all the dirt of the school, enter chattering in their birdlike fashion, as staccato as their typewriters. They have also an esprit de corps which the janitors' wives lack. Mrs. Pilkey beams at them. They range from fiftyish Miss Pringle (who takes down Mr. Pilkey's ideas in shorthand, wears high velvet buttoned boots, and has an occasional epileptic fit, which insures her lifelong virginity) to nineteen-year-old Miss Budlong, who is a graduate of the Girls' School, and whose spectacular face and figure cause most of the Boys' School to wander into her office on the pretext of buying postage stamps. And the middle one of these lady clerks is Miss Robenia Hoskins, a special favorite of Mrs. Pilkey's because she is a warm steady talker, whereas Mrs. Pilkey rarely has anything to say at all. Miss Hoskins is the only woman with whom the Principal's wife has ever felt easy; so the two ladies kiss genteelly:

—Dear Miss Hoskins! says Mrs. Pilkey.

—You darling! shrieks Miss Robenia Hoskins. You old darling! I call you that even though all the girls in the office know you're just as chipper as the youngest sprat in the Girls' School I'm always saying that am I not girls? Mrs. Pilkey so help me Hannah I'm singing your praises night and day and of course everyone else in the office agrees with me only the

41

other day Mrs. Budge was saying that you had the face and manners of a queen don't blush now Mrs. Budge you said those very words with your own tongue and teeth my stars she's blushing like a bride isn't that the prettiest sight, don't you think so Mr. and Mrs. Pilkey? Well I never guess what I heard as I was dressing for this party. . . .

Mr. Pilkey bows low to the seven secretaries; his wife notices that he gives an extra glance of approval at young Miss Budlong:

—Dear ladies, what a pleasure to welcome you back! And I tell my faculty that it would be well for them if they could make their self-indulgent wives look half as chipper as our office force does. Don't I say that, dearie?

—He does say, answers Mrs. Pilkey, that more women should work for a living, as you ladies do. And it is a fact that some of the faculty wives are hopelessly spoiled, what with only one or two children to take care of, and those sumptuous apartment we give them to live in. . . .

The seven secretaries bow their heads and flush a girlish scarlet, depending on their ages. There is nothing they can say to Mr. Pilkey. Some of them hate the ladies of the faculty; some are bosomclose, and swap gossip with them, in that intense partisan life of offices. Miss Pringle, the First Lady among the secretaries because she takes Mr. Pilkey's dictation, puts her buttoned boots firmly together, rolls her green spectacled eyes, and wonders if a fit is coming on. But Miss Robenia Hoskins charges right in:

—There isn't another school I'd dream of working at except The Academy I think it has A Tone about it which makes it quite different from what you might call normal office work only the other day I told Miss Pringle that a girl here gets so cultured that in no time she's typing letters in Latin and Greek ha-ha didn't I say those very words Miss Pringle? . . .

Mr. and Mrs. Pilkey extricate themselves from the cluster of the seven secretaries. He points out to them the bereft little group of the janitors and their wives:

—Now you girls just go over there and be sociable. I think you know all those ladies and gentlemen? . . .

Miss Pringle winces at the idea of fraternizing with the janitors. Her caste at The Academy is unique. As The Principal's Secretary she knows everything. She wishes she were home working on her translation of Sappho. For before her epileptic fits Miss Pringle was Dean of Women at a Western university. Nevertheless she purses her lips and trots over in her high boots with the six other stenographers.

Mr. Pilkey is balling and unballing his great white fist. He is sweating under his white suit like a polar bear. Mrs. Pilkey knows that he is growing irked:

—Where *is* my faculty? Sometimes I believe that they deliberately and slyly insult me. . . .

She looks at the tables behind her:

—The ice is melting in the iced tea. . . .

—Let it melt, damn it. I'm melting too. . . .

Mrs. Pilkey sighs. She feels her varicose veins clamoring from her long standing. But now to ease Mr. Pilkey's wrath the entire faculty of the Girls' School is approaching, chaperoned by their Directress, Mrs. Mears. Mrs. Mears derives her authority from mandate of Mr. Pilkey. She is wearing a vast picture hat and waves a paper fan. She is an ex-librarian of the village, to whom Mr. Pilkey gave her position as a sop to the townspeople. His gesture had no effect whatever on the village's hostility to his school. Indeed Mrs. Mears talked her way into her job on the death of her husband, a cousin of Judge Hopkins V. She is a huge woman of fifty, noted for her bulldozer charity. She understands almost nothing, but gives the impression of authority by never allowing anyone on her faculty or student body to get a word in edgewise. She is a born executive, for she hounds her school with the voracious righteousness of anyone who has passed the menopause unscathed. She is like an abbess who has swallowed a phonograph.

Mrs. Mears is shaking hands with Mr. Pilkey; she pecks his wife on the check:

—The lord and lady of our manor!

Then Mrs. Mears steps back and fans herself, squinting at the Pilkeys as though they were disciplinary cases in the Girls' School, which she handles with steamroller justice.

—Minerva Mears, says Mr. Pilkey with intense cordiality.

Then Mrs. Mears sweeps in her faculty of twelve ladies, clutching her picture hat:

—Girls! Step up and speak your pieces! Don't be nerrrvous!

She addresses her faculty in the same tone of voice she uses on her girls.

One by one the teachers of the Girls' School mince by the Pilkeys, shaking hands, and muttering something tense and appropriate. Two or three are ladylike married women with English accents who are eking out their husbands' stipends by pumping history, Latin, and manners into American girls. And there are a couple of raging young spinsters just beginning to get tizzicky about their prospects for marriage: some took their jobs in order that they might meet eligible young men on the faculty of the Boys' School. These younger women teachers drink and smoke on the sly; they wear dungarees and saddle shoes and do their hair in a feverish upsweep. Mr. Pilkey isn't much interested in the Girls' School of his academy, and he distrusts female teachers. But Miss Sophia established a school for girls too, much as he begrudges their expenditures for chalk and paper and electricity. So he beams on them all.

Then he notices at the end of the line a handsome little thing holding back, with something of animal panic in her eyes. She wasn't on the Girls' School faculty last year. And he burbles gaily:

—Why, Mrs. Mears! Is this a new adjunct to our halls?

—Betty, cries Mrs. Mears, didn't I warn you not to be nerrrvous? . . . This is Miss Betty Blanchard, our new Spanish teacher. . . .

And Mrs. Pilkey, shaking hands with Miss Blanchard, is aware that finally a beautiful woman has come to teach at the Girls' School. The aging woman feels a soft fragrance of pity for this new teacher. She wonders what will happen to Betty Blanchard after a year at the Girls' School. Mrs. Pilkey's sense as an artist is in strife with her position as the Principal's wife. Miss Betty Blanchard puts out her hand to the Pilkeys and says fuzzily:

—I. . . .

—O she's gone and got nerrrvous! Mrs. Mears shrieks.

And with a shove of her muscular arm, that has haled weeping girls into her office, Mrs. Mears propels Miss Blanchard in such a way that the girl must end either in Mr. Pilkey's arms or at his feet. In a pass of spicy masculinity he catches his newest and loveliest teacher and holds

44

her for a moment against his chest. Mrs. Pilkey sighs again and glances at the iced tea.

—There, my dear, Mr. Pilkey says paternally. You're going to be very happy with us. . . .

—I hope so, thank you, Betty Blanchard says.

And with something like pettishness she disengages herself and joins the other lady teachers, who are regarding her as a new saboteur to their ranks.

—Betty's nerrrvous! Mrs. Mears shrieks. Just like one of my girls!

After making obeisance the faculty of the Girls' School withdraw from Mr. Pilkey's presence, just as people, after a nervous peep at the Holy of Holies, drop the veil and step out of the sanctuary into prosaic everyday air. Another reason that the ladies move on is that they observe their archrivals, the faculty of the Boys' School, coming up to do homage to the Pilkeys. There is supposed to be a social amboid welding together all the elements of The Academy in the eyes of the world, but actually this unity exists only in the mind of Mr. Pilkey and in the printed catalog of his school. Here, as in the world, there are the fiercest cliques and rivalries.

—Well, finally! Mrs. Pilkey murmurs, feeling a throb in her varicose vein.

—My faculty! says Mr. Pilkey in magisterial irony.

He folds his hands over the breast of his white jacket and waits in grim humor, as though he is adjusting a black cap on his head. The faculty of the Boys' School and their wives enter in a primly joyous group, though they've just been briefing one another on what to say to the Pilkeys in this first official reunion of the school year. It is the same every fall; most of them have been through it ten times or more. Although they dislike and envy one another with a cordial litotes, they have been exchanging congratulations, murmurs, and gossip. Mr. Pilkey knows this, and he must divide and conquer them. They have probably been comparing notes on their salaries and have been sighing that the old ratrace is beginning all over again. He regrets that this muted hostility over the commencement of another academic year is the one unanimous consensus among all his employees, with the exception of the janitors and secretaries, who love their work and bite into it, because mere

45

minions love the feeling of *belonging* to a great institution. . . .

There is a long-fixed protocol of precedence, of who goes first to the Pilkey's reception line. Married teachers come first with their wives, depending on the calendar year (according to the catalog) in which they were hired. And as he waits to have his hand shaken, Mr. Pilkey is not unaware that some of these older teachers, because of the security he has given them, have the settled and ruminant air of ancient cows. These older men think only in terms of the school's curriculum and points for graduation. They are in that frozen rigidity which besets old teachers, who resent any deflection from the norm they knew before the system turned them into ice. Mr. Pilkey tells his trustees that They Haven't Grown in their Profession. These older men are prolongations of various facets in the Principal's personality —as an armed force needs an infantry, an air arm, and a navy. . . .

And the older wives chew on their narrow reddened lips; their girdles pinch them, but they're going to be Gracious Ladies, damn it! Some are already grandmothers. By a life of glittering penury and by planning their children's clothes three seasons ahead, they have managed to work their way into a semblance of elderly gentry: they own farms in Vermont, and Miss Sophia's retirement annuities guarantee that they shall live out their lives as titled arthritic wives of elderly schoolteachers, used up and turned out to pasture like fire horses which have done their duty.

—Beware that solid phalanx! cries Mr. Pilkey to his faculty.

He says it to be jovial and to split up their incorporate mass. He doesn't care for mobs, except when they're organized the way he likes them—as, say, when he is haranguing the school in assembly He is irked the way his faculty comes to greet him, like small children afraid to let go one another's hands and groping their way in the dark.

First to be received are the Comptroller and his wife, Mr. and Mrs. Whitney. The Whitneys have been with the Academy since its first year, for, though every Principal would prefer to be his own treasurer, the Trustees have decreed that there must be an official Cerberus to snarl over the purse strings. Mr. Pilkey spends Miss Sophia's money pretty much as he pleases. The trustees back him up on most of his outlays, but nominally it is little Mr. Whitney who signs the school's checks. In the Middle Ages Mr. Whitney would have been a Jew, with a chamois purse suspended round his neck. But the Better Business code of the mid-twentieth century requires that now he wear a pencil-striped double-breasted suit. For twenty-five years now Mr. Whitney has been a most scrupulous steward to Miss Sophia's Endowment. Each year The Academy's books end in the black. But the little dapper Comptroller has a squeezed look about him as though he were being pressed between sheets of bullion and is fearful of oozing out one red cent of sweat. Mr. Pilkey is aware that not one soul on The Academy's faculty likes Mr. Whitney, for all his good heart and accuracy in accounting. The ladies of the faculty can't have their apartments done over with costly wallpaper, and the young unmarried Marxian Socialists whisper that Mr. Whitney is enriching himself out of the withholding taxes on their salaries. Of course none of these opinions ever rises above a sibilant murmur because of Mr. Pilkey's diplomacy in playing both sides of his faculty against the middle. But there is a haze of tension and mutual suspicion every time the faculty gets together en masse. And little Mr. Whitney often weeps in his office, which says BURSAR on the door. And in his cups at private poker parties Mr. Whitney calls himself a croupier to Diamond Jim Brady. This is one tidbit that Mr. Pilkey has never heard from any source. . . .

And now Mrs. Whitney, the Second Lady of the Faculty, is kissing Mrs. Pilkey on both cheeks. Neither lady can endure to be in the same room with the other, for Mrs. Whitney tells her bridge club that the First Lady exploits her art as an exemption from the normal duties of a Principal's wife. But Mrs. Whitney is a comfortable middle-aged person, her gray hair done up in a Regency style she has read is modish for a matron. She has a face like a tart bursting with meringue. In the privacy of her boudoir (she does no essential work at The Academy except to keep the younger women in line by insisting loudly on her prerogatives as Second Lady) Mrs. Whitney devours boxes of peppermint patties and bestselling novels. She spends whole months lying on an ocher chaise-longue having headaches and telling Mr. Whitney that, now she is old and fat, he no longer loves her. He married her thirty years ago, when she was a gumchewing stenographer in his office, and he couldn't penetrate her rubbery vitality without dropping a ring on her finger. Now she makes up for the education she never had (and that a Second Lady needs) by guzzling the *Reader's Digest*, ladies' magazines showing stylish American homes in color and plastic, and historical novels. Mrs. Whitney is at her best as a bosomy heroine in Sumatra in 1745. All her children have gone out into the world, cringing from her demands that she wasn't loved. She never got off her chaise-longue, except to open a can of beans for the little Whitneys. But, by God, Mrs. Whitney is still Second Lady of the Faculty, and that will not be taken away from her till she collapses of an exploded pancreas from munching chocolates. When she isn't reading or suffering, she flirts a little with the young unmarried men of the faculty—those whom she doesn't suspect of being Marxian Socialists. Or when her darkened room gets too dull, she sallies forth for a bridge marathon with the Third, Fourth, and Fifth Ladies of the Faculty. She is a raging tigress in manipulating little pasteboards and tallies. In contract bridge, in the name of divertissement and good fellowship, Mrs. Whitney manages to claw all the junior ladies of the faculty and their husbands. Then, clutching her winnings, she buys herself several pair of nylons and retires to her historical novels, pouncing every evening on little Mr. Whitney when he comes in tired from the Bursar's Office. . . .

Mr. Pilkey is still shaking hands with Mr. Whitney, and Mrs. Whitney is giving Mrs. Pilkey half a hundred smacking kisses to show the rest of the faculty just how affectionately the First and Second Lady regard each other. Mrs. Whitney's permanent is bobbing so fast from her kisses that she all but bites Mrs. Pilkey on the ear.

—Our artist! cries Mrs. Whitney to Mrs. Pilkey.

—Our hostess! cries Mrs. Pilkey, all but suffocated with the fat woman's cologne.

And Mr. Pilkey, shaking his Comptroller's hand, drops into his honeyed Man-to-Man tone, which he uses at Trustees' meetings:

—Herb, this year I swear to you that I'm going on the strictest economy. You might call it an Austerity Program. You know I never was a Rooseveltian spender. . . .

Mr. Whitney smiles and sighs and winces. He knows. With

just some such declaration Mr. Pilkey will be quite capable tomorrow of pillaging one thundred thousand dollars from the Endowment to build a new biology lab, all made of glass bricks.

—Well, we'll see, Mr. Whitney says, waggling a tremulous finger at his boss.

Twenty-five years ago he formulated a policy of passive resistance, of never committing himself to the Principal. For he has been reduced to a dummy who sits in an office and signs checks for educational expenditures that would make a Jesuit blush. . . .

Having done their duty, the Comptroller and his wife retire to inspect the chicken salad and the iced tea and to compute the cost of the Reunion Frolic. Now Mr. and Mrs. Pilkey wade into an orgy of handshaking. To a few of her favorite faculty ladies Mrs. Pilkey vouchsafes her famous dry kisses. Mr. Pilkey expands hugely at this love feast of sentiment and homecoming. He is instinctively a distributor of largesse, the Maecenas, the benevolent patron. He loves to have people warm themselves at the fire of his cordiality. Perhaps at his birth the Fates decreed he should be Principal of a school. . . .

But Mrs. Pilkey is in a mild nagging agony from her varicose veins. Her heart is beginning to skip too. She knows that really she should be upstairs in the Cape Cod house, just like Mr. Pilkey's mother, cared for by the Negress Florinda. Yet she forces herself through her act of graciousness, a tired, dubious, resentful old queen of the revels. Since she is also an artist who paints butterflies and portraits on plates and urns, she has often a frenzied desire that all these chattering falsely gay people will go away and leave her in peace.

The Principal and his wife continue to greet almost a hundred faculty and ladies. The air twitters with sweet nothings and mangled epigrams. Some try to get Mr. Pilkey's ear for schemes of their own or for gossip; some of the ladies are fulsome in their praise of Mrs. Pilkey's hat and slacks. But most of the ladies and gentlemen, unless they are favorites of the Pilkeys, are hustled in and out of the reception line.

The men teachers at Miss Sophia's Academy are old and young, vain and retiring, virile and swishy, geniuses and louts, mannered and boorish. Some of the unmarried ones dress exquisitely; some of the married wear those casual tweeds which indicate they are concerned about their children's next pair of shoes. But all have that fixity of expression, a certain air of being rapt into essential or nonessentials which is characteristic of teachers. There is an odd light in the eyes of nearly all—in the young men it is sweetly fanatical; in the older it is rheumy and prismed. Those glances seemed to say in arrogance, humility, and confused wonder: We are American teachers; we are the Platonic policemen; we are the Conditioners; the Benders of the Twig, the Prop, the Crutch, the Spoonfeeders. And nobody really cares. . . .

The ladies of the faculty are of a different plumage than the men. Since teachers' wives, except those with children, do nothing all year long, they wear a fatuous and excited expression of frustrated birds. Faculty ladies are aware that they belong to some sort of indigent American aristocracy, that they must act with Manner and Culture. For they are teachers' wives. They feel instinctively and resentfully that they cannot act like normal American women. How shall they comport themselves? Nearly every one of them has her attitude, her individuality, her intellectual passion, which she strikes as repeatedly and monotonously as a triangle in an orchestra. Since their husbands are supposed in The Academy's catalog to be complete and dignified human beings—not union artisans at machines—the ladies play the grande dame to the hilt. Nearly all are somewhat decayed gentlewomen who are neither wholly gentle nor wholly women. The only happy ones among them are those who have children—and even now they are thinking of these children, at home, and tended by a baby sitter at fifty cents an hour. For Mr. Pilkey insists on all ladies putting in an appearance at these jamborees. Only those few well-born ladies with private incomes can afford to be a little minxish and satirical of Mr. Pilkey's lordly paternalism toward his faculty. These dress themselves dramatically; their children wear clothes from Brooks Brothers. But they are a minority. They deem themselves the true oligarchs of the faculty, the unacknowledged First Ladies. They have no time for Mrs. Pilkey nor Mrs. Mears nor for Mrs. Whitney. Those few rich ladies who happened to marry teachers out of lust or love have their own salons and serve sherry and coffee to their favorite unmarried teachers. All other ladies of the faculty (dependent on Miss Sophia's stipend) loathe, fear, and envy their elegance and independence.

Miss Sophia, of another age and breeding, would have smiled at the poorer faculty ladies eyeing the chicken salad on the tables behind the Pilkeys. She would have found them affected, distorted, desperate, and more than a little pitiful. Their conversation might have struck her as a macaw-screaming to drown out their own bitterness and bemusement. Most strident of all is the voice of Mrs. Doctor Smedley, wife of the new school chaplain, who is trying to manage things as a minister's wife should, at a Church Supper. She is telling a group of younger ladies (thinking of other things and waiting to get their own conversational oars in) how she packed a hamper of goodies and took it to a family in the village who keep a Mongolian idiot upstairs in their attic.

The arms of Mr. and Mrs. Pilkey are now nearly wrung off. The reception line is down to its Lowest Third; nearly all the respectable married couple have gone through. The Dubious Fringe is coming up for a greeting. These are the unmarried teachers. They are the shifting sands of Mr. Pilkey's geopolitics at his Academy because he can't build securely on them. Yet nearly a third of his teachers are bachelor, and flagrantly so. A school is the last stand of the bachelor in America, for there he can flaunt his crotchets as nowhere else. Among his younger teachers Mr. Pilkey counts precious scholars and elegant athletes from the last five classes of Ivy League colleges. He is suspicious of the masculinity and loyalties of some of his more gifted young teachers and coaches. They have their own clubby, snorting, and tweedy world, to which he can never quite penetrate, no matter how many extra jobs he thinks up to keep them busy. He distrusts young unmarried teachers, for he himself wed Mrs. Pilkey when he was barely out of Dartmouth. These racy or arty young men lack the respectability and the smugness which soon snows under married instructors. Yet Mr. Pilkey likes to have them around, because much of their libido goes into their teaching and coaching. What bothers him is the devotion of the boys to some of these bachelors. He finds something covert and cloying here. . . .

Mrs. Pilkey reels back in the reception line, clutches her husband's arm, and hisses:

—Look at Herman. . . . I think he's intoxicated. . . .

The Pilkeys' son and heir is weaving before them. He is a

burly counterfeit of his father, something like Mr. Pilkey when he began to teach at the Friends' School in Pennsylvania. Herman almost broke Mr. Pilkey's heart by drunken pranks at Dartmouth. And Mr. Pilkey knows too well (and rationalizes) the faculty's aversion to Herman's presence on the staff of his father's school. Yet the Old Adam in the Principal is proud of his only son, who has inherited his rudeness and vitality. Herman Pilkey is a gorgeous boor. But last year he regained his father's good graces by marrying a southern belle and has already begotten a little Pilkey on her. Mr. Pilkey often chuckles at Herman's procreating. Herman appears in his father's consciousness as a thick and reassuring obelisk, a battering ram of Pilkeyism to coming generations. When Mr. Pilkey passes away (though at sixty-five he has many more years) what fonder dream than that Herman and the little Pilkeys should continue Miss Sophia's dynasty at The Academy? Mr. Pilkey is busy even now insinuating Herman's praises as an executive into the inclining ear of Judge Hopkins V, President of the Board of Trustees. Certainly a whole line of Pilkeys as Principals—that is what Miss Sophia would have desired. And Mr. Pilkey is a great interpreter and codifier of other people's wishes, according to his own lights. But here is his own son, drunk at a Faculty Reunion Frolic!...

—Herman, says Mrs. Pilkey with a catch in her voice, you've been drinking....

Herman kisses his mother with alcoholic lips:

—Aw, Mum. You know how damn dull these parties are. Everybody thinks so. But they don't dare open their yaps....

A flash of brilliant cobalt passes in front of the Principal's eyes, something like his old rages in the early days of his Academy. Family solidity is a fetish passed on to him from his mother, who lies upstairs ill. And now his son, before his faculty, is knocking his fondest beliefs into a cocked hat. With his own hands the husky old Principal thrusts his son from the reception line:

—Goddam it, Herman, go away some place....

Mrs, Pilkey's heart strums. An artist, and she brought forth this drunken gamin! But now Herman's wife sashays in and kisses her in-laws:

—Honeys, ah think these sho are the sweetest pahties. Ah'm *happy* heah....

—Thank you, Nydia dear, the Pilkeys rejoin with dignity.

Nydia has made Herman a fertile wife, but she hasn't tamed his gaucheries. At first the Pilkeys believed that Herman was marrying beneath himself when he wed an Atlanta heiress. But now that Nydia has produced an heir she is forgiven. The young Pilkeys couple in a hot mist of Georgian accent and honeys. . . .

The rest of the faculty haven't missed This Incident in the reception line. They turn away their faces and gossip over it. Mr. Pilkey is embarrassed, for he sees them nudging one another with that clinical gloating of persons who live in tight communities and do not enjoy even that delicious liberty of picking their intimates.

Mrs. Pilkey's eyes mist up at the defection of her son, and she holds on to her husband's arm for support. But then the Principal's mighty chest breathes a sigh of gratitude, for he sees approaching his favorite teacher, his confidant and henchman, Mr. Philbrick Grimes, hastening to him on shoes filled with eagerness. Mr. Grimes bows over Mrs. Pilkey's brown veined hand:

—Madame! E monsieur aussi . . . quelle réunion joyeuse . . . je suis ravi. . . . O, I'll just say hi. . . .

—At last, says Mr. Pilkey, relaxing. At last, Philbrick.

Now Mrs. Pilkey's eyes really fill up after her crucifixion by her son Herman:

—Dear boy. How happy we are to see you again. The summer's been so long without you. . . .

Mr. Philbrick Grimes is the choicest spirit among the unmarried men at Miss Sophia's Academy. He is slender and jittery, his agile head skims with executive ideas. He is only happy when he has a finger in every pie—which to Mr. Pilkey is the sign of Growth in a young teacher. Mr. Grimes simply can't stand or sit still for sheer exuberance. By term end time he will have brought off so many coups as Mr. Pilkey's right-hand man that he will spin like a top from his own adrenaline. Mr. Grimes is really the only soul on the faculty to whom the Pilkeys, lonely autocrats, commit their bosoms. He is now thirty-seven, an age when it is believed that he will never marry. Thus his bride is The Academy, and all his energies are wedded to her furtherment. Teaching is but a fraction of Mr. Grimes's career. He does everything else too. He arranges flowers for Mrs. Pilkey so that she can work in lovely surroundings, and he informs Mr. Pilkey of any subversive fume in the school. Mr. Pilkey often proclaims in faculty meeting that perhaps only Mr. Grimes is really earning his salary. There is little evidence of his ever sleeping. He knows everything that will happen, and when it doesn't he makes it happen. He draws his nourishment from panic, gossip, and disorder. He is the essence of Pilkeyan humility: subtly disparaging himself, he has built himself up into the wheedler, the propagandist, and the Doer of The Academy. In some respects he is almost as powerful as Mr. Pilkey, but the Principal doesn't mind. If there weren't Herman, the Principal would be willing to see his mantle drop on the slight shoulders of Mr. Grimes. Yet he tells the Pilkeys nearly everything, prefacing his intelligence with a curdling whisper:

—Now, sir, I *may* be wrong on this deal; so just tell me what *you* think....

There is no question to Mr. Pilkey of the devotion, generosity, intensity, and worth of Mr. Philbrick Grimes. He is the head of the most informed and literate clique of the faculty. Their claws are long, and their ostracism finally and conclusively damning. Mr. Pilkey doesn't mind—in his old age someone has to watch out for his interests. No, now that Mr. Pilkey is old, Mr. Grimes is the living lobster-pincers of the Academy's ethical and disciplinary system. He is the camouflaged forceps of Mr. Pilkey's Puritanism, of his gumshoeing cynosure, of all his violence shaped in velvet....

Everyone is eating chicken salad and drinking iced tea. The Polish dietitian is swearing to herself about the way these whitecollar workers gobble up free food. The Comptroller is worrying about this feast's putting his books into the red, and at the very beginning of the Fall Term.

But Mr. Grimes and the Pilkeys are tied up together in a little loveknot of brilliant talk, unmindful of everyone else on the faculty. He flutters like a hummingbird between them, plying Mrs. Pilkey with potato chips. He regales them with international gossip, for he has just returned from a summer in France. According to him, postwar Europe's sufferings are vastly overrated. Mr. Grimes knows how to flatter the Pilkeys by seeming to crave their advice, then giving his own opinion. He works with a gossamer touch to assure the Pilkeys that they are more than an old man and an old woman who reign over a famous school—he makes them seem something pompish and purplish out of ancient Egypt. The Pilkeys see themselves in cloth of gold when Mr. Grimes is around; and he often is. To them he has devoted at least half his day and night for fifteen years, dancing courtesies upon them like a dancing master, for he is light on his feet.

—If they were all like you, this spoiled faculty of ours, Mrs. Pilkey says with glittering eyes.

—Please, please, says Mr. Grimes, you'll have me in tears. . . .

And looking over his shoulder to see that no faculty member is near to encroach on his precious time with the Principal and his wife, Mr. Grimes in humble whispers pours his latest scheme into Mr. Pilkey's ear, an idea he hatched in France this summer. It will mean work for everybody on the faculty, but it is Mr. Grimes's brainchild. Mr. Pilkey edges in to hear the secret.

—Why yes! says Mr. Pilkey. Yes, of course! Why didn't I think of that, Philbrick?

—But you did, sir, you did. You mentioned it to me last June. It's your very own idea. . . .

—Bless you, my boy, so it was, so it was.

And he looks ahead into the shrubbery with his gray eyes, thinking that he is getting a bit forgetful in his old age. And suddenly Mr. Grimes leaves off his whispering, for someone is coming toward the Pilkeys:

—Mon Dieu, you will pardon me. Here's a Little Person I haven't had the pleasure of meeting. . . .

Nettled in their clandestine delights of eavesdropping on the ironies and profundities of Mr. Grimes, the Pilkeys whirl toward a young man who now presents himself to them. He has a plate of chicken salad in his hand. Mr. Pilkey feels angry and slighted:

—I didn't see *you* in the reception line.

—No sir, the young man says. I'm tired of all that folderol. In the army we did nothing but queue up. . . .

—*Folderol*, sir? cries Mr. Pilkey.

Then he gets a grip on himself and presents the young man to his wife:

—Dearie, I don't know if you remember Guy Hudson, whom I hired last spring? He's a veteran, and I thought he showed promise. . . .

55

—I don't remember him, Mrs. Pilkey says, And from the way he speaks to his betters, I wonder if I ought to give him a howdy-do. . . .

—How do you do anyway, Mrs. Pilkey? Guy Hudson says, bowing over his chicken salad.

One eyebrow raised at such insolence, Mr. Grimes gives the new faculty member a swift sweeping glance. Then, because he has been interrupted in his tête-à-tête, he shoots off into the garden party to spread and pick up tidbits. He rarely speaks anyway to a new member of the faculty for the first five years.

Mrs. Pilkey is looking hard at Guy Hudson. The artist in her trembles at this young man. Why? He is tall and red-headed, with an air that she can call only arrogant. He has a cleft in his chin, and the left side of his mouth is horribly scarred and turns upward in a permanent sneer. She supposes he was once handsome.

—A veteran? she says weakly to her husband.

—Yes, dearie. And I said in this year's catalog, my school was accepting all the challenges of the postwar world. . . .

Guy Hudson speaks up, still holding his chicken salad. She guesses that humility, the humility of the artist, is dead in him.

—Don't let my mouth get you down, Mrs. Pilkey. A mortar shell exploded near me at Malmódy. In December, 1944. Remember?

—Of course I do! cries Mrs. Pilkey. Many a prayer I sent up for the boys over there. . . .

—They are grateful, Guy Hudson says, bowing again.

—We know you'll be happy here, Hudson, Mr. Pilkey says. This is just the school for you. Just what the doc. . . .

—I shall try to be happy here, Guy Hudson says.

And bowing again, he walks away with swift robotlike strides.

—What does he mean? What does he mean? cries Mrs. Pilkey.

—He needs rehabilitation or some such nonsense, Mr. Pilkey says. Well, he'll get it here. But in my day, dearie, he would have been called a young whippersnapper. . . .

And after they have finished their salad and their iced tea on the Pilkey's lawn, the faculty of Miss Sophia's Academy settles down to an evening of what Mr. Pilkey calls Innocent Merriment, organized by himself. Whether they will or not, old and young, men and women, of learning, poise, and education, are forced to play games—charades and potato races out of Mr. Pilkey's youth, Snap the Whip, and Leapfrog. The climax of the evening is a free-for-all, a Battle of the Sexes, and some of the more delicate or neurotic ladies of the faculty weep for chagrin and physical pain. As the games get more violent, the Principal grows happier, shouting encouragement and insults to those who do not Enter In. The air quivers with the outraged feelings of clever and educated people bullied into making fools and ruffians of themselves. Guy Hudson finds himself on the bottom of a pile of men and women, being gouged by a Ph.D. from the Latin department:

—What the hell is this? Playtime in a nuthouse?

—God, I don't know, the Ph.D. gasps, sobbing for breath. The Old Boy is a fine Freudian example of suppressed ferocity. He loves to humiliate people. . . . But why give you a briefing on what it took me a year to learn? . . . You'll find out soon enough. . . .

2

To insure their humility Mr. Pilkey started off his young teachers in what he called Modest But Sufficient Bachelor Quarters. By this he meant a garret room in a dormitory, with walls not so thick as to shut out the hubbub of students living on the same corridor.

Mr. Guy Hudson, newly of the history department, had an attic on a lower-form corridor of the Boys' School. Since the Reunion Frolic of last night he'd been having misgivings. Did he know too much of the world to be a bright-eyed scoutmaster for shrieking kids of twelve and thirteen? Yet he moved into his room.

Over his fireplace he'd hung two German student sabers and between them a captured Kraut helmet of an Oberst who'd tried to shoot him. He hung a Picasso and a Piranesi. He owned also a pornographic etching he'd looted from Berchtesgaden. Already he'd capitulated to the probable artistic taste of the Pilkeys by consigning the etching to his closet.

But he hadn't slept well in this new room; he'd tossed like a novice on her first night in the convent. And after the Reunion Frolic he'd walked to the town across the river and got stinking drunk. He'd returned to this cell after midnight and thrown himself down on the palletlike cot which was supposed to remind a teacher that his life must be monastic and austere.

Before he fell asleep last night, a drunken rage had besieged Guy Hudson so that he cursed and beat his pillow. Since he lived icily enclosed in himself, his fury took the form of raging images projected on the screen of his brain. He was furious with himself for taking on this teaching job at Miss Sophia's Academy. So far he hated everything he'd seen of this school and everyone he'd met in it.

Wasn't *his* reality after combat in France and Germany a stronger and truer one than these people who chattered as though life was an intellectual garden party and themselves sophisticated marionettes? What after all was the point in going back to teaching? The anguish that he'd seen during the war in Europe had sickened his brain. Nothing here in these so-called academic circles seemed to have any relevancy whatever.

Before he fell asleep, almost weeping with anger, Guy Hudson believed he *saw*. Was it perhaps that all these people who called themselves custodians of education were merely spineless dolls with guts of sawdust, living in pretense because they refused to accept life as it was? Was it that those who called themselves teachers were merely playing politics on an enclosed checkerboard and parroting the thoughts of the Dead Great because it gave them a vicarious importance and authority? Did America perhaps justly laugh at her teachers and humiliate them because they asked for it?

And yet his rage tapered off, and Guy Hudson slept. Be-

fore he dropped into clammy nothingness, he believed that
the solution for him might be to become the antichrist of
this whole scheme, to flaunt its hollowness before the world,
a diabolic Punch and Judy.

And now the morning sun came into his room, striking
his head burrowed under his single sheet. He was sleeping
on his belly; he rolled over, groaned, and awoke. The sunlight refracted the reddish hair about his collarbone into
prisms of steel wool. The sunlight also picked out and made
ruby the slash along his scarred mouth.

Upon awaking Guy Hudson was aware that he was a man,
and still young. With a sleepy gust of sensuality he would
reach over to awaken with a caress whoever was lying beside
him. No one! He sighed in thwarted amorousness; he wanted
someone, anyone, badly, and there was no one in his bed.
In France and Germany, whenever he was off the line, he'd
never slept alone. The relief in wartime of having another
body alongside his each morning had made him a resolute
yet goalless satyr. In college he had been reserved and
scholastic, taking his sex when he could get it, often leaving
it alone. But now it soothed his nervousness like a new
reflex. Like many other American young men his sensuality
was now desperate—he had to have it, and it didn't matter
much with what or with whom. He and other veterans had
to touch and be touched the last thing on going to bed and
the first thing upon waking in the morning. Even when the
panic and the danger of combat had lifted, his indiscriminate
desire went on and on like a rocket.

Guy Hudson's hand came back empty after questing all
over his narrow bed:

—O damn. Not one teeny goddam lover. . . .

He closed his eyes, for he remembered a voice saying to
him:

> —Wenn du Geburtstag hast,
> Bin ich bei dir zu Gast
> Die ganze Nacht. . .

(He must have been in love, that April of 1945.)

There's nothing so delicious as making love, lazy light
lovin, in those moments after awakening. He knew he should
have picked up something last night in the village when he

was drunk. And have brought it back here, to the chaste walls of his room in The Academy. What a laugh! The only copulation permitted here was the chaste coupling on the beds of the married faculty. He didn't know yet what the boy and girl students might be up to. But he laughed as he thought of himself and his hypothetical pick-up of last night, stealing through the dormitory, to be pounced on by the Pilkeys and Mr. Philbrick Grimes, who would then have a really juicy tidbit to regale his gossips with. Well, what do you know? Broth-er. That Mr. Hudson is no chaste young dominie, teaching out of a thwarted libido. . . .

He sat up in his bed, affectionately scratching the hair on his chest through his skivvy shirt. That wrath with which he'd fallen asleep was ebbing. There was only a tart taste of whisky in his mouth. After the Reunion Frolic some of the young bachelors of the faculty had invited him simperingly to A Party. He'd refused. All the bachelors his own age at this school were rather like giggling male nuns. They just didn't know what he knew. The war had made him into a lone wolf, an introverted arrow that shot silent and solitary to his target for the moment. He'd become an opportunist of sensation and esthetic. It was something he swore he'd never be, when he was a bright history major at Amherst.

Why had Mr. Pilkey hired him to teach? For all his act of the country squire, the Principal was no fool. He must have observed something dangerous in Guy Hudson's truculence, in his shattered mouth. Was he sorry for him? No; the Pilkeys of this world are innocent of compassion because they go back to the Hebraic code. Why, Mr. Pilkey must have known that a wounded ex-lieutenant of infantry was no fit subject to instruct the sons of the National Association of Manufacturers—to guide their feet in the paths their fathers wanted, the path of American prosperity, the shibboleths of University Clubs, the credos of normalcy, home grown on Main Street. Had Mr. Pilkey, wily old devil, really taken his measure? Did he really want on his faculty someone who would keep the magnesia perpetually stirred up?

That's what Guy Hudson would do, for the last years in Europe had stripped him down to a lynx, a lecherous and clever lynx. And teach he would, till be got fired, tarred and feathered by the horrified complaints of his students against him, by yowling letters from parents, and by anathema of

Miss Sophia's twelve trustees. He *would* teach these boys and girls. He didn't believe that you can really teach anybody anything about life. What he would do would be to torture his students, to badger them into a little thought, to shatter their complacency.

Thinking these bitter yet somehow consoling thoughts, he noticed that the tumuscence of his morning desire had abated. He could now leap out of his bed into the shaft of sunlight without looking like a Priapus from Pompeii. For, like all honestly sexual men, he was modest. He looked down at his slender body in its white shorts. Since his release from the army he'd never slept in pajamas—and this was part of the reduction to simplicity of his life.

There was a knock at his door. He shuddered, since panlike men dislike being caught undressed in their bedrooms, except by the companions of their pleasure. He wondered if perhaps Mr. Pilkey, through telepathic scanning of his thoughts, had already decided to fire him. He pulled down his skivvy shirt over his drawers and called out:

—Damn it, come in! Unless you're a lady of the faculty. . . .

The door flickered open swiftly and delicately; Mr. Philbrick Grimes entered with a show of concern for the invasion of privacy. It seemed almost as though he'd materialized out of a mist, for the door opened and shut faster than Mr. Grimes could have squeezed through the aperture he'd made for himself. In a crook of his arm he carried a lacquer clipboard. He was already busy in the labors of the vineyard.

—A most unusual greeting, mon vieux, Mr. Grimes said. Who knows? Perhaps you're the breath of fresh air we need Around Here. . . . He bustled into conversation while Guy Hudson gathered his clothes from where he'd thrown them in his passion of last night:

—Don't take this badly, please. But I felt that you weren't happy at our little orgy last night. . . .

He laughed nervously. Guy Hudson wrestled into his shirt:

—O, was that an orgy? I didn't know. It seemed like Merrymount getting raided by a bunch of Puritan divines.

Mr. Grimes answered with a specious thrust of confidence:

61

—You have a fine historical sense. You will be an ornament to our department of Social Studies. That's what you must call it, you know the name of History is old hat. . . . But seriously, we have more fun Around Here than you might suspect. . . .

And Guy Hudson, for years on the defensive, was aware that he was being tickled, sounded out by the feather of Mr. Grimes's secret service. From his training in the war he suspected that anything he might ever say to Mr. Grimes would be used against him. And by the time he'd buttoned his shirt and zipped up his trousers, his barrier was erected.

While he finished his dressing, Mr. Grimes talked purringly, seeming modestly to avert his eyes. Yet Guy Hudson knew that he was being sized up by those Siamese eyes, that every detail of his body and his clothing was being salted away for future reference. They would be served up that afternoon in faculty kitchens all over the campus. Mr. Grimes talked constantly, out of a basic horror of being known and pinned down, just as salesmen filibuster customer resistance. He was demure and violent, witty and platitudinous. And since he kept up a figurative rubbing all the time he talked, like a cat sounding out a hearth, Guy Hudson concluded that he was subconsciously begging to have his fur stroked. And he decided also that Mr. Grimes was a male virgin with a horror of sex and its dishevelments, who sought constantly to spice up his conversation with irrelevancies, as persons sprinkle in garlic when their tastebuds have atrophied.

—We work hard Around Here, Mr. Grimes was saying. Yet I always say that's one of the satisfactions of teaching . . . outsiders like yourself might conclude that we're squirrels on a treadmill. . . . But that's the raw impetus of a teacher's life, don't you think? We couldn't get the results we do Around Here if we weren't all jazzed up. Yes, this constant benzedrine jag is one of the stimuli of the teaching profession. For friction produces fine results through the discipline of corseting. . . . Take the fourteen lines of the sonnet form. . . . By the way I read a very interesting little book lately. . . .

The sterile excitement in Mr. Grimes's conversation led Guy Hudson to believe that there was nothing wrong here which a little lovin wouldn't cure. But perhaps Mr. Grimes was by now beyond the need for human love. . . .

—Don't judge our Principal too quickly. He has parts (in the eighteenth-century sense of the word) that are not at first obvious. And I've got a Trade-Last for you: Mrs. Whitney the Comptroller's wife told me you were a very interesting-looking man. Though she suspects you of being a Marxian-Socialist. And Mrs. Pilkey likes you very much, if you'll only give her a chance. . . . You can't afford to be bitter Around Here. . . .

Guy Hudson was on the point of asking Mr. Grimes why he'd snubbed him last night at the Reunion Frolic, but he bit his tongue. He couldn't be frank with this creature; the whole façade was against it. If one outright thing was ever said to The Academy faculty in the interest of clearing the air, the whole business would probably fly into the air like a mine long unexploded. But he loathed himself for starting off the morning with one of those dissimulations he'd forsworn. He felt as though he'd been wrapped up in cotton batting. Why had Mr. Grimes come to call on him? Perhaps, like an evil old man who pretends to have at heart the interests of young newsboys, he'd come out of ambiguous generosity, to offer *his* special brand of friendship. The secret Guy Hudson had already divined: Mr. Grimes hamstrung people by disarming them. He wished he had a cup of black coffee to clear his head. Then he could fight back on these cobwebby terms. And he offered Mr. Grimes a test case:

—I invite you over to the village for a cup of coffee. . . .

Mr. Grimes held up his slender hands in horror, waving his clipboard:

—Mon vieux! What can you be thinking of? That's not the way we do things Around Here. This isn't the army, my dear Doctor Hudson.

Thus the hand had been forced. Guy Hudson saw that he was in the presence of a Born Organizer, who pretends to infinite leisure.

—But you must come to my apartment soon, said Mr. Grimes, for one of my Little Dinners. I've made a study of bachelor cookery. May do a book on it some day. . . . Right now, my dear Doctor, we're going to make out Study Cards for our students. I'm in charge. It's a bore. . . .

—I am not a Doctor, Guy Hudson said, knotting his tie, only a poor M. A. . . .

—To me all Nice Guys are Doctors, Mr. Grimes said fidgeting.

With such deprecations and murmurs Guy Hudson found himself being hustled downstairs.

—Did you say we have to copy out Study Cards? What about all those stenographers I saw last night?

—Mere front, Mr. Grimes giggled. Around Here the faculty does the clerical work. The Head pretends that doing these dirty little chores gives us an in on the executive side of things. We are not deceived. . . .

Guy Hudson wasn't taken in by such coyness. He was being goaded into his first protest against The System. And whatever he said would eventually reach the ear of Mr. Pilkey. So for the second time this morning he censored his own thoughts. This was awful! At this rate he would be pummeled into a law-abiding faculty member by the end of his first day at The Academy. He looked uncomfortably at his companion, who was skipping down the stairs at his side. The lithe man guessed his thoughts:

—We work very hard Around Here. What do you think you get four months' vacation for every year? And we *are* a little proud of our work, you know. . . .

—But is it all *useful*?

—There are many questions, said Mr. Philbrick Grimes, that a teacher may ask himself. But only in the privacy of his own closet. Things left unsaid here are sometimes more important than things said. And that's a saw, mon vieux docteur. . . .

—I am *not* a Doctor, Guy Hudson said, and then he was silent.

Mr. Grimes was not ungenerous. He was giving gratis a lesson in diplomacy to a new teacher. Guy Hudson was being beaten into shape. Perhaps he was being unjust to resent Mr. Grimes's attempt to put him wise. That fabulous Old Stager had already noticed his own malcontentment and had determined to prevent his spewing out like a keg of ale. But still Guy Hudson squirmed under what seemed to be the officious ministrations of a maiden aunt. Suddenly Mr. Grimes said:

—You're not a very happy young man, are you, Doctor?

He was tempted to reply acidly:

—Neither are you, Mr. Grimes. . . .

But already he knew that Mr. Grimes would go mad or

vanish in a puff of sulphur if a mirror was ever brought up against his true self. That was the reason this poor insect talked so fast and zoomed around making important notes on his clipboard. Finally Guy Hudson felt almost sorry for the little man, as one pities a mouse constantly repairing her burrow of straw.

—Are we friends, Doctor? Philbrick Grimes said quickly, peering at him.

—Of course, of course....

In the early September morning the quadrangle of The Academy was a precise rectangle of emerald, diagonally cut by paths. Along the dormitories Mrs. Pilkey's asters were still in bloom. Members of the faculty of the Boys' School scurried about, looking portentous and worried, as though they'd just left an idea lying somewhere. Guy Hudson wondered if they tore about this way because they were really in a hurry—or whether Mr. Pilkey liked nervous scurrying for its own sake, a counterfeit of important business at hand.

Faculty members greeting one another with a calculated brightness, intended to convey that they were all apostles in a confraternity, that this was the gayest and most portentous little community in the world. Guy Hudson found it rather eerie to watch older men dressed in the negligent garb of American students—battered unclean saddle shoes, sport jackets with chamois patches sewed over the elbows. And some of these older men gave out with jive greetings that could only have come out of a jukebox.

—Teachers never grow old Around Here, Mr. Grimes said, seeming to read his thoughts.

—How? Do they suck the blood of their students; or is it vice-versa?

—You are a wit, Doctor, Mr. Grimes said, giving his twitching smile.

Guy Hudson, looking with the sharpness of novelty, observed also big blond boys, loafing about the campus, relaxed and cynical in contrast to their keyed-up teachers. These students were indolent, handsome, and milkfed. He thought of the students of Europe whom he'd seen during the war—hollow-eyed, frightened, yet determined. These boys had the genial raffishness of unfocused personalities. They called out studiedly sophisticated greetings to one another and to the faculty, whom they treated with respectful condescension.

In spite of their elegance and good looks he found them vulgar; their speech was the argot of refined muckers. How he'd changed? Hadn't things been so at Amherst eight years ago? Now he resented it all. . . .

—Those are Student Councillors, Mr. Grimes said, pattering beside him in his gumsoled shoes. We govern ourselves Around Here.

—Seventeen-year-olds? Impossible. Don't tell me that in this school Mr. Pilkey encourages the fallacious nonsense of a democracy inside of an oligarchy? Don't the students often get the faculty by the balls? Who runs this school? The kids?

—You must read our catalog, Mr. Grimes said. Student government is the backbone of The Academy . . . preparation for world federation . . . democracy hic et ubique . . . what's the difference, Doctor? I never thought you were a reactionary. . . .

—Jesus Christ, you're kidding. . . .

On the path leading to the Study Hall they met a fat little man with bald spots like tundra. He wore a checkered tattersol and a yellow ascot. He spoke with a thick suety accent and addressed himself at once to Guy Hudson, peering damply through his thick lenses:

—O you there, Mister Hudson! Lissssen, I've heard you're a veteran. Well, so am I, my dear, of that pukey little 1918 war. We'll be great buddies won't we? I jussst *know* you'll hold your classes in line. The manners of a drill sergeant are what these little bastards need. But discipline is a thing of the past Around Here. . . . Lisssen, Guy (mind if I call you Guy?) here's some advice from an old hand. . . . Give it to em. . . . *Give* it to em . . . but hard . . . as much as they'll take of your sssstuff. They *love* it. . . . Kids do, subconsciously. . . .

And after passing his hands in greeting over most of Guy Hudson's body, the little man careened off, his fat rear bobbing through his tight sport pants.

—Well, Guy Hudson said with a whistle. That would be Miss . . . ?

Mr. Grimes daintily ignored him, snapping his clipboard:

—That is Doctor Sour. Head of the department of Modern Languages. He's a fixture Around Here. And don't start thinking things. . . .

They entered the Study Hall, where Mr. Grimes took things in hand. Like a tobacco auctioneer he cajoled fifty

66

faculty members into copying out the Study Cards for the Boys' School. The faculty must do it, he explained sweetly, because kids are prone to error. Besides, the Principal claimed that one of the talents of the true teacher is a high clerical aptitude. Mr. Grimes, something like a supervisor in an insurance office, was as light as a butterfly, as perfectionist as a martinet. He made a game of the whole business as the faculty copied down Latin I, English I, French I, Algebra I. This copying and collating went on for six hours.

At a desk opposite Guy Hudson sat a beautiful girl, her brow furrowed at the arid and ghoulish paper work that is synonymous with high organization in American schooling. He remembered her from the Reunion Frolic of last night. Sometimes he stole a look at her, and his scarred mouth tickled. Was her name Betty . . . Blanchard?

At the end of the third hour of copying (for which these men and women had gone to college and become specialists in various subjects) the lovely girl raised her head and took off her Oxford glasses. She spoke to Guy Hudson in her low somewhat studied voice:

—I was a captain in the WAC. But this is sheer dry guillotine.

3

The solitary hermit thrush was wrangling with a worm that had been teasing her by poking out exploringly from the crust of a grave. Finally she got its juicy body into her neb, wound it around like a strand of spaghetti, and flipped the whole ruddy thing out. Then this thrush took to the air from the cemetery churchyard, mounting up steadily in the September afternoon till she came to rest on an eave of the white meeting house. She sat there making appreciative sounds to herself inside her dowdy feathers and swallowing her lunch.

After making her repast, she squatted on the belfry and looked down on a chain of automobiles inching along the macadam road below.

One of these was a rouge Cadillac stuffed with the impedimenta of a schoolboy—golf clubs, tennis racquets, yoyos, and luggage. Inside the Cadillac an airconditioning unit was whirring for the comfort of the three occupants. And the rear turret window clicked with Venetian blinds. Driving was Mr. Marlow Brown, alone on the suede upholstery of the front seat. He was dressed in white whipcord which almost concealed his little pot, for he'd been an athlete at Princeton, class of '15. He was fretful to leave his plastic factory even for a day. But the compensation is that he must drive his only son Buddy to The Academy. His hypertension wasn't so bad today, for Mrs. Brown wasn't nagging him on his driving. She sat lachrymose and upset in the rear seat. She wore a toque with a bib that crossed under her chin which was beginning to sag, though she'd once been a Junior League beauty. For today she had to call a three-month halt to her liaison with her blond Praxitelean son. This tenous incest had been going on since Buddy's birth eighteen years ago. She called it mother love. Consequently at this moment, with The Academy a mile away, Mrs. Cynthia Brown was exacting the last caresses from her son. He sat as far away as he could from her on the back seat under the clattering Venetian blinds. He wanted to drive the Cadillac on this last progress into The Dungeon. But he couldn't get so far away from his mother that she mightn't clutch his hand. The rings on her fingers cut into his tanned skin with the exigency of her mother-passion.

—Aw, Mom, Buddy Brown said fretfully. Lay off. It's hot today....

He was a Nordic of an accepted type. Cynthia Brown all last summer had rejoiced in watching her boy's muscles flex when he was on the beach in his swimming trunks. Now he was dressed in his Going Away to School Clothes—a striped seersucker suit, a bow tie, and polished loafers. Buddy Brown was what this mother and father, who made scads in the recent war, had brought him up to be. He was a walking talking eighteen-year-old tribute to conspicuous consumption. To him life was little else but looking like a Neat Little Monster in his eleven suits of clothes, playing pinball machines, getting drunk, and picking up girls with his buddy on the beach. But that was all over now. He'd been kicked out of New Trier High for various unspecified enormities; and the Browns, taking council together as they rarely did since his conception, decided that, damn it, they were Well Enough Off to afford a private education for their Kiddo. His named dropped wistfully from their lips. Buddy. A private education was more classy anyhow. Their son had picked up bad habits from That High School.

Mrs. Cynthia Brown was in tears as her son attempted to elude her last display of affection. With one taut handsomely manicured hand she struggled to hold on to Buddy's wrist; with the other she smoked a long scented cigarette in a chromium holder inscribed with the initials of her maiden name. (Her analyst had advised her to this, as a reaffirmation of what he called a beautiful poetic ego that had been stifled.) All three lay back in the furry seats of the airconditioned Cadillac as it purred along by the old white church. For they were entering the village where The Academy had its seat.

—Damn it, Cynthia, Mr. Brown called over his shoulder. Let the kid alone. Or did your analyst tell you to maul your own son?

—Thanks, pop, Buddy Brown said.

Mr. Marlow Brown beamed. For eighteen years he'd been groping toward some sort of camaraderie with his only son. But kids were different nowadays. Mr. Brown was a Self-made Man, who'd gambled on plastics and was now raking in the profits of a brilliant guess. The gnawing sorrow of his life was that Buddy always evaded his advances, except when the father gave him hush money in the shape of a new convertible (with white-walled tires) or a check to buy himself those clothes which seemed unnecessarily loud and slavish to advertisements in magazines for young men.

Buddy finally wriggled free of his mother's caresses by something close to a slap. He reached out of his luggage a tiny silver case, which turned out to be a portable radio, giving out with music as soon as he opened its top. As the Cadillac swung around a corner, the handsome hard boy tapped his loafer in time to the voice of a Negress moaning about her Body and her Soul. Mr. Brown couldn't understand why she clipped the ending off all her participles. But

69

there was much that he didn't understand these days, he told his associates in the plastic business.

—Yeah, said Buddy Brown in a gutty whisper, yeah, sister. . . .

Mrs. Cynthia Brown was awed and a little horrified to hear her beautiful boy so intimate with the trappings of the passionate life. To be sure her girlhood had been in the fevered twenties when everybody drank gin and talked sex. But children today were different—less open. Often he'd come home stinking of bourbon. But that was over now. The other night as she'd packed his things with her own jeweled hands she'd burst into tears and told Buddy the only love an eighteen-year-old should have was his mother. And he'd snickered at her out of his chilly blue eyes.

After a few moments of the radio music Mr. Brown, still holding onto the wheel of the Cadillac, reached around and batted the portable radio out of his son's hand with an executive and paternal smash. It fell to the floor of the car; the Negress's voice was strangled off as the lid snapped down. Buddy and his father glared at each other; Mrs. Cynthia Brown took a puff on her cigarette. She'd have much to tell her analyst when she got home.

—Pop, Buddy said. For Chrissake. . . .

—Listen, son, Marlow Brown said. This is our last five minutes with you before we leave you at The Academy, and you insist on listening to ragtime. Son, it's insulting to your mother and I. It's not decent . . . it's not . . . manly. . . .

—Listen to your daddy, Buddy, said Mrs. Brown sniffling. She felt a psychic headache coming on.

—What for, I'd like to know? Buddy Brown said, picking up the portable radio from the floor of the car.

He had an impulse to fling his radio into the shatterproof glass of the Cadillac's window. That churchyard he'd just seen depressed him. But then under his blond curly head there flickered a thought that was almost relieving. In a few minutes he'd be rid of three months of these sniveling old fools who'd brought him into the world, and tried to make him believe he owed them something for the favor. By God, the least they could do was give him cars and Neat Clothes. The mere prospect of getting away from his mother and father for three months made the imprisonment and castration of boarding school almost inviting.

70

—Why wouldn't they let me bring my car to school? he asked his father for the hundredth time.

—You're here to study, son.

(He'd read this in Mr. Pilkey's own prose in the catalog.)

—I'll study shit, said Buddy Brown under his breath.

Marlow Brown, as a successful businessman, has always believed that rationality, straightforwardness, and tenderness would solve everything between himself and his goodlooking son. He did so want this boy to be his pal—to go on fishing trips with him, to strut a little before his friends at the Country Club. Was there something he'd left undone as a father? He didn't believe so. He boasted to his business associates that Cynthia and himself had Given Buddy Everything: a trumpet, a set of drums, a convertible, a speedboat, a princely allowance. . . .

Mrs. Brown snuffed out her cigarette, removed it from the holder, and burst into tears. She didn't even bother to take out her lace handkerchief. She intended to ruin the fine pastels of her makeup.

—Well, what's eating *you*, mom? Buddy said, sulkily looking at her from his corner of the rear seat.

—It's just . . . O my darling hero, it's just that I won't be seeing you for another three months. . . . But I'll fly up every other weekend. I'm sure my analyst will permit that. . . . O my darling, if you just say the word, I'll have Daddy turn the car around, and we'll all three go right back home. . . . You don't have to go to this dreary old Academy if you don't want to. . . . Tell your mom. . . .

While Buddy revolved these possibilities in his cunning mind, his father turned the steering wheel so hard that it cracked, and the Cadillac swerved wildly:

—Shut your mouth, Cynthia. The boy is going to this school whether he likes it or not. . . .

—That's my pop, Buddy murmured in a worried tone.

He took out a cigarette and lighted it with considerable show. He flicked the match with his thumbnail and cupped his palm about the butt, puffing nervously yet coolly, like Robert Mitchum. It was one of the devices that caused beach girls and waitresses to admire his tigerish good looks.

—And put out that damn cigarette, his father roared. You

71

know you can't smoke at The Academy. Start breaking the habit right now. . . .

—If I have to keep that rule, Buddy said calmly, I'll be home at the end of a week. . . .

—You do, my fine young fellow, and I'll put you to work on a plastic dye-stamper. In the factory. . . .

—Christ, Buddy said, stubbing out his cigarette.

The remainder of the mile to The Academy was completed in a suffocating silence, in which many suppressed feelings crackled. Mr. Brown chewed on his cigar and wielded the wheel of his Cadillac. There might be heard the sobbing of Cynthia Brown, for she felt her nerves crackling. Buddy sat rigidly at attention, nursing his portable radio and glaring straight ahead. There was a ruddy mist of rage in his eyes; his good looks were taut with broodings of revenge, which he meant to take out on the whole damn world. He would find ways to make an abattoir of this Academy, for he knew all the meannesses that eighteen-year-olds learn in pool rooms. He would unleash them all, by Christ. He would be a BMOC simply by virtue of his exquisite sadism. He crossed and uncrossed his loafers in an ecstasy of scheming. As they drove through the village his eyes lighted, for he saw a greasy snackery, with a juke box and a slot machine, purple with Coke ads and menus of monster sundaes. Outside loitered young men in dungarees and sweaters with football letters. Local high school. Buddy sniffed. But these gees were heckling one another and passing girls in bandannas and bobbysocks. This was for *him*! He'd find his way over here as soon as possible.

The Browns drove into the campus of The Academy. Marlow Brown's chest throve with a certain pride of display. His boy was going *here*! Meet the right class of people. And to himself Mr. Brown made a mental reservation that if Buddy disgraced himself in this classy layout he would tan the kid's hide. Indeed during the last half mile he'd been throttling a compulsion to stop the car, take Buddy into the bushes, and thrash him. For after all Marlow Brown wasn't any less a man than when he'd stroked the Princeton crew in '15.

Buddy was peering at the sauntering students and at worried little men who were obviously faculty wage slaves:

—Some dump! Looks just like a school!

Mrs. Cynthia Brown dried her eyes and sighed:

—O, it's lovely, sonny! Has atmosphere, just like the catalog says. . . .

—What the hell do you think we're paying $1800 a year for? Mr. Brown said genially, tapping his cigar.

After some inquiries, which were answered with lazy good manners by loafing students, they found Buddy's dormitory. It was in a place called Hooker Hall, camouflaged with ivy and shrubbery to look older and more traditional than it really was. The room was on the second floor of a corridor that smelled of oiled floors. There were only two beds, two dressers, and two Windsor chairs. And a French door opening onto a balcony that overlooked the quadrangle. The chamber smelt of September and the longing of several generations of boys who'd lived here. Their initials covered every inch of the woodwork.

Buddy Brown swaggered in, followed by his parents.

—Wait till I get my hands on roomie, whoever he is.

The veil under her toque swaying in the warm breeze of fall, Mrs. Brown looked with horror at the empty double room. For her vivid imagination, conditioned by gay chambers in women's magazines of smart decoration, had expected pennants, chintzes, ottomans, beer mugs, crossed fencing foils. That was the way a Boy's Room was supposed to look. She took her husband piteously by the arm:

—Honey, he *can't* live here! Why, he has a *sensitive* soul! See somebody at once and get the room assignment changed!

—I shall do nothing of the sort, said Marlow Brown.

And he rushed to his blond son and confiscated a pack of cigarettes protruding from the sharp seersucker jacket.

—You won't need these for another three months, my fine fellow.

Buddy spat in the wastebasket. He flung himself into one of the Windsor chairs and brooded horribly. His father and mother went down to the Cadillac to bring up his bags. Buddy kicked off his loafers and extracted a stick of bubble gum from a secret pocket. He peeled it and put it into his face. He snapped and smacked it with preoccupation while his eyes cased every detail of his prison. His white teeth gnashed; his blue eyes flickered like a cornered rat's.

In ascending the stairs to the second floor of the dormitory, which was called Hooker Hall, the Du Bouchets stepped humbly aside to let pass a florid man and an overdressed woman who were coming down. There were three Du Bouchets, all carrying luggage, which they had just unloaded from their rattling station wagon. They were a little frightened and a little gay to be at last at this Academy.

Father Du Bouchet was an artist with mustaches and the sprightly air of the nonmaterialist in poverty. He never tired of good dialect stories, good wine, and painting marine landscapes. He knew that the visual arts were all washed up by the twentieth century, but he went right on practicing them, because he loved them. He owned a little bungalow near Cape Hatteras, where he eked out what income he didn't get from marine landscapes by renting a motor launch and farming lobsters. This weather-beaten little house of the Du Bouchets was always full of guests, talk, and music. They were almost in need, but without the sordidness that comes from poverty in American life when it is subject to invidious comparisons and the bait of advertising. The Du Bouchets kept aloof from life and lived with a curious, not ingrown, sweetness.

Mother Du Bouchet was a tall, stern woman, who had been faced with cracking or hardening. She had hardened—but not into the negation of Puritanism. She was the gyroscope of the family. Her hardness consisted only in checking the centrifugal and merry force of her husband, in denying him that third bottle of wine. She had a sad grasp of decencies and proprieties. She did needlepoint for rich women. She lived only for her husband and for her son Ralph, who was eighteen yesterday. And watching the passionate silence of her only boy, she thought that he might be a specter from Father Du Bouchet's student days in Paris. She loved Ralph more detachedly than most mothers love their sons. She confessed that she didn't come within a mile of understanding him, though sometimes she thought she did, in their silences.

Ralph Du Bouchet brought up the rear of this little caravan. He was wearing a Tee-shirt and slacks that revealed his slender graceful body. Something in his face bespoke a re-

moval from life, a melancholy, and a focused intensity undreamed of by most American boys of eighteen. His eyes
were curtained by the fringes of long black lashes. Until
puberty he had seemed almost a girl—not effeminate, but
secret and grave. Now dark instincts swirled inside him. In
some respects he was an old man. Under one brown arm he
carried an old suitcase covered with scratched labels of
French provincial hotels, and a belt around it to keep it
from flying open. Under the other arm was his violin.

Ralph was musing on a redheaded man with a scarred
mouth who had just passed him in the quadrangle. He knew
that he'd have no peace until he spoke with this piercing
person. Perhaps the man had answers to some of his questions? Ralph was never at ease with boys his own age. He
preferred to be alone with his music, his black head bowed
over the oxblood wood of his violin. And he felt many
strange things when he rowed out after lobsters.

Father Du Bouchet started first up the stairs, pert as a
gamecock. Under his arm were two of his marine landscapes
that he counted on hanging in his boy's room. Mother Du
Bouchet was panting under a suitcase and some rich dark
curtains she'd stitched up for Ralph's windows. She dropped
back a step in the slow procession, groping in that twilight
that seems to hang in the corridors of dormitories. Outside
from the quadrangle of The Academy there was the noise
and clatter of hundreds of students, banging their trunks,
greeting one another after the warm hibernation of the summer:

—Ja have a good summer, Kirkpatrick?

—Ah, drop dead, willya?

After they'd climbed the stairway, Mother Du Bouchet fell
back and peered at her son, moving in a dream with his suitcase and violin. She nudged his arm gently, for she recognized an insuperable abyss between them, which must be
bridged by loving indirection:

—You haven't said a word in the last hour.

—I'm wondering if I'll be happy here.

He was always truthful.

—O, she said, relieved. Aren't you being a little silly? It
preys on your mind that you're a scholarship boy. No one
will know it, dear. No distinction is made. The catalog distinctly says so. . . .

—We're church mice, Ralph said. Happy ones, though, mother. I don't belong here. I feel something strange and false already....

—It's the chance of your life, she said devoutly but uneasily.

—I wonder if there's really a place here for my music and the things that interest me....

She felt a pang like that moment in which she knew she was with child:

—Why, how silly you are, dear. This is a Great School! Where else could you find a concentration of the Finer Things?

—I don't know, Ralph said.

His father, bustling a little, had been reading aloud the numbers on the closed doors of the rooms on the second corridor. At last he came to Number Sixteen, sighed, quipped, and, because his hands were laden with his painting, kicked open the door. The sunlight of the room shot out into the obscure corridor. The three Du Bouchets stood blinking on the threshold. Ralph saw a handsome blond boy charge to his feet; he'd been in the act of spitting a ribbon of bubblegum with his forefinger:

—Wrong room, my friends.

—Why, I beg your pardon, sir, Father Du Bouchet said pleasantly yet humbly. This *is* the right room. Number Sixteen....

—Well, whaddya know, the blond boy said, sauntering to the French window and whistling.

Ralph Du Bouchet, setting down his valise and violin on one of the cots and relieving his mother of her burden, hated his father for using *sir* to the blond boy. But he hated the blond boy even more. Already their backs arched at each other. Ralph wondered how he would ever be able to live eight months with this boy. He wasn't afraid, only nauseated. And the blond boy sat down and put up his loafers on his cot springs while Mother Du Bouchet was standing up, still unpacking.

—So you and me are gonna be womb-mates, the boy said. I'll keep you in line, I guess, I think, I know....

—You're a fine young fellow, sir, Father Du Bouchet said to the blond boy.

Ralph winced.

—O, I know crap from shineola, the boy answered, laughing loudly.

Ralph watched his mother stiffen, but she went right on putting things away in drawers.

The next half hour poured venom into Ralph's heart. He was by nature delicately antisocial. This intercourse was all the more unnatural since by the laws of lottery he had to live with this boy, who announced his name, under the wheedlings of Father Du Bouchet, as Buddy Brown. Presently the Browns returned, loaded with costly gear. And Ralph had to witness the obscenity of his mother and father condescended to by this vulgar man and woman—he boasting of his plastics business, she with her bleary eyes under a toque and veil, smoking scented cigarettes from a chromium holder. The garishness of Mrs. Cynthia Brown turned the quiet fatigued dignity of Mother Du Bouchet into a faded old post. Ralph wasn't ashamed of his mother and father; he was only sick at heart. At one point Mr. Marlow Brown offered a cigar to Father Du Bouchet:

—So you're an artist, hey? Why, a man in my plastics plant makes more in a day (even with the goddam union) than you do in a week of watercoloring. Correct me if I am wrong. Sure, there's a place for art in America, though I can't guess where. Maybe you artists should join a union too. Only the other day I said in a speech to the NAM. . . .

—We don't seem to agree on how this room should be decorated, my dear, Mrs. Cynthia Brown said to Ralph's mother.

—Why not leave it up to the boys? Ralph's mother said in her soft voice.

—O, boys are pigs and like to live in pigpens, Mrs. Brown said.

—I don't agree with you there.

At last the Browns and the Du Bouchets left. The final surgery came for Ralph when Marlow Brown pressed a twenty-dollar bill into his hand:

—My son Buddy is used to living high, wide, and handsome. This will help you keep up with him for a day or so. . . .

And when their room had only themselves in it Ralph and Buddy sat in their respective desk chairs and regarded each other. It was the way dogs sniff each other out. Buddy popped his bubblegum. He'd spread his stockinged feet all over the desktop, cynically airing his crotch with the relaxed air of a male-man taking his ease.

—I saw that my pop's twenty dollars burntya.

Ralph said nothing. Normally he would have crossed the room politely and laid the greenback on Buddy's desk. But the steel in him whipped up and convexed like a tested blade. He put the money on his fingers and flicked it into his blond roommate's lap. There was a silence, broken only by the popping of gum.

—Gee, thanks, roomie, Buddy said, pocketing the money.

He stood up, strolled to the fireplace, and looked at the seascape by Father Du Bouchet:

—This picture will have to go.

—It's my father's masterpiece, Ralph said.

—Yeah? Well you know what ya can do with masterpieces. Tomorrow I'm goin over to the village and get some pinup girls.

—I'm not going to live with Varga girls, Ralph said softly.

He knew he didn't sound prissy or priggish, for a cold flame was stammering inside him; and no high wind would extinguish it.

—Hell, boy, Buddy said manfully, I'm not askinya. I'm tellinya. . . . O by the way, I notice ya got a violin. I mean a squeakbox. Well, I'll thankya not to saw on it while I'm in this room, see? I brought a hundred good platters of hot jazz, and you're welcome to play em any time, if you don't break em. Thanks a million, he says. . . . But this longhair stuff is just shit and sugar to me, see?

Ralph laid his face in his hand. He couldn't bear to look at Buddy, but his voice was like ice:

—I think we'd better reach an understanding. . . .

—Yeah? Impossible with me, sweetheart. . . .

Ralph stood up at his desk. He found that he was trembling, but not from fear. He went to his closet and got a spool of stiff thread his mother had left him to darn his socks with. He unraveled it and tightened it into a barrier diagonally across the wide airy room.

—You stay on your side, and I'll stay on mine.

—Christ! Buddy Brown said slowly and judicially You *are* a meatball and a character.

78

4

Miss Betty Blanchard lived in a huge gabled attic on the third floor of the house of Mrs. Mears. Her room was lovely and hushed; it looked over the churchyard where Miss Sophia lay buried. When she moved in, Mrs. Mears gave her what she called The Run of the House:

—I don't want you to think of me, my dear, as dragon, concierge, or landlady!

Nevertheless, the fact remained that Mrs. Mears locked her doors at eleven each night, and the lady teachers had better be in at that time or sleep on the village green. Mrs. Mears also said that she had no great objection to Betty's smoking, but would she please do it in the parlor? These old houses were *so* inflammable! They might even go up themselves of spontaneous combustion!

Betty Blanchard already knew better than the Directress what caused the spontaneous combustion. In this white clapboard house, that bore a plate telling interested observers that it was built by Ebenezer Wilcox in 1670, the true tension came from a volatile tinder of nothing but women. On the ground floor lived Mrs. Mears and her daughter Midgie, who was President of the Student Council in the Girls' School. Midgie dressed in sweaters, bandannas, and dungarees, and Betty Blanchard had already privately christened her La Vache. She was blonde and loud and bedizened; most of the Directress's income went to keeping her daughter in clothes. The rest of the time Mrs. Mears kept herself from brooding by her own highpowered executive tactics. She did most of her pondering in a seventeenth century study, surrounded by mementoes of her dear husband, a lawyer and friend of Judge Hopkins V. And now there remained to her only Midgie and the Girls' School. With them she fought off the atrophy of a proper widowhood. The lines around her mouth told Betty Blanchard that the Directress was battling nearly everything.

As Betty stood dressing, the murmur of a houseful of women floated up to her: that panic and sizzling that is heard only in girls' locker rooms and offices of bachelor insurance girls. For in this seventeenth century house ten women dwelt without benefit of men. And the sound of these starved women was something Betty Blanchard knew well, and feared. In young girls the hubbub was pretty and somewhat sparrowlike. But the sound of women's voices mounted in desperation and stridency as they grew older, until finally a houseful of mature women becomes an aviary of hysteria and petty hypocrisies.

As she dressed, Betty could hear Midgie downstairs screaming at her mother that she couldn't find her loafers. Next door she heard a rustling from Miss Demerjian, the mustached teacher of French, who'd been moaning in her sleep all night long. And on the second floor she heard Miss Tucker, the brawny gym teacher, tell her roommate Miss O'Leary that she couldn't couldn't do that acrostic in the *Saturday Review,* and would Miss O'Leary kindly wash her own ring off the bathtub?

Betty shuddered as she buttoned her skirt over her waist. All her life she'd been among women's voices—at Wheaton, in the WAC, and now here as a new teacher at The Academy. These voices were like nettles. Her own was shy, prim, and slow—like these functional oxfords she was wearing this morning. She wondered if perhaps she had some sort of Convent Complex, a reversion to the society of her own sex —most of whom she couldn't stand. Had her three years in the WAC finished her at twenty-five? She'd been in Algiers and Naples as a lady captain in charge of a signal corps switchboard. She'd thought it would be an adventure. But overseas she'd noticed herself flinching back from life. The enlisted women had been shut up every night in the WAC-ery at curfew time. But the WAC officers! Betty's eyes had been opened. The lady lieutenants and captains of her detachment in Africa and Italy had given themselves brazenly to army officers, pretending that each night of pleasure would be their last. It was a fearful thing, to her taste, when women abrogated to themselves all the opportunistic prerogatives of men. The WAC officers of her acquaintance had surrendered their intactness of body and soul. Others, in a febrile intoxication with a military corps of women, had taken up fierce friendships with one another—or with their enlisted personnel. The WAC taught her what she'd suspected at Wheaton: that women together are a suffocating lot, like waves of steam from a drier in a beauty salon.

Why had she shut herself up in the purgatory of a Girls' School? She was afraid. Her paradox was that she wanted both sanctuary and freedom. On those few dates she'd had after returning to America in 1946, she'd been horrified and made sick. The American men with whom she'd gone out for an evening, who had hitherto been shy and gallant according to the Old Code, had become soggy and crass from the war. They expected from her the same violent evenings they'd had from hungry Italian and French girls. Thus she discovered that she'd kept her virginity to no purpose, to have it hustled and insulted in postwar America. And so she'd returned to teaching. This place would be her final burial-alive. Here her juice would dry up under the heat of young girls and withered teachers. Soon she would lose her fresh beauty. And perhaps that would be for the best.

As she brushed her hair and prepared to go down to breakfast, she pondered on what she'd already learned of Miss Sophia's Academy. She remembered Mr. Pilkey's clasping her at the garden party known as the Reunion Frolic. The old lecher! He was just like some army colonels she'd known. And she was already a bit raw from the claws of the other schoolmistresses: they had such nice ways of jabbing with their understating phony English accents! She laughed at what she'd seen of the men teachers, especially the long-married, who'd observed her out of a corner of their puffy eyes till they caught their wives' transversal stare.

But there was one male teacher who haunted her horribly —the redheaded one with the scarred mouth, the ex-lieutenant of infantry. Mr. Guy Hudson. He was the sort of purposeful icy man she most feared. He was as cynical as herself, but he knew a great deal more. Would he track her down? He seemed to have all the instincts of a weasel. Well, she would sit in her room at night and listen to Miss Demerjian talking to herself next door. She would read her *Don*

Quixote and her Calderón and her García Lorca, and watch the moonlight in the cemetery.

After breakfast there was a phone call for her in Mrs. Mears's study. She hesitated.

—Take it, take it, my dear! screamed Mrs. Mears. This house is yours as well as mine!

She knew how to construe such a noisy generality, but she walked into the cosy study of the Directress. On the walls were pictures of the last twenty-five graduating classes from the Girls' School, all flourishingly autographed to Mrs. Mears. There were also evidences of the extravagance of maintaining Miss Midgie Mears—an open checkbook and a pile of clothing bills. The phone lay by its cradle; Betty picked it up:

—Miss Blanchard? said a tinny voice.

—Yes, she said, swallowing dryly. Is this . . . Mister Hudson?

—Miss Blanchard, tee-hee! No, this is Philbrick Grimes. . . . Has Mr. Hudson called you already? A Nice Guy, I might add. . . .

—Go on, please, Mr. Grimes.

Her color had come up, for she'd given herself away.

—Well, Miss Blanchard, I always take the liberty of finding out how our new faculty members are doing. . . . Have a good breakfast? Happy? Don't think I'm a sniveling busybody. I know how institutions are . . . a little impersonal till you get acquainted. . . . I remember when I was new here . . . a little warmth never hurts our profession; does it now? Or am I wrong? . . . Miss Blanchard, are you there?

—Go on, please, she murmured, swallowing again.

—Remember my name: Philbrick Grimes. Remember that if I can ever be of assistance to you, to call me at the Boys' School.

—You're very kind, Mr. Grimes, she said, and hung up.

She felt as though a mouse had run up her arm. Was 'he kind? Was he kidding? She could have bitten off her tongue for mentioning Guy Hudson's name.

—Blanchard, you're a fool, she said, striking the telephone with such rage that her bracelets clattered.

She strode out of Mrs. Mears's house and across a lawn tc the Girls' School, which was a chaste pillared building looking like the Parthenon in wood. She looked over her shoulder at the cemetery, the only prospect from her room. The September morning was as lucid and tinkling as a bell of air. The sun was gentle; she heard the voices of fall cicadas in the bushes around the school building.

On it were converging a hundred girls, more raucous than the crickets in the shrubbery. The boarding girls were trotting from their dormitory—the Fat Little Girls with hairy legs, the Magnificent Queens, the Born Organizers talking and gesticulating, the Pimply Ones creeping drearily along under their calamine lotion. And clambering out of their cars were the Daygirls, calling out taunts to the boarders; some were hunched down under their dashboards for the last cigarette till afternoon.

The girls walked arm in arm and sang snatches of popular songs. Miss Blanchard, putting in the aloof manner of a mistress of Spanish, noticed a standardization in their dress and manner: a hectic cadence of the voice intended to indicate Pep, the bandanna about the hair, the slippers or moccasins in place of shoes, the wad of gum which each chewer genteelly spat out before she flounced into the school building. They had essentially the air of shopgirls reporting to punch a timeclock, yet their faces showed that many were the daughters of the well-to-do: the heads showed delicacy and inbreeding; many affected languid accents or Hollywood diction.

—Gloria, don't forget four thirty! cried a girl with hair like steel wool.

—No indeedy-weedy, Audrey! another called.

Hey bop a-re bop! still another.

The Daygirls exchanged their exploits of the preceding evening for the benefit of the boarders, who were locked in at sundown. There were shrieks of rage, gossip of who stole whose date. . . .

Betty Blanchard entered the whitewashed corridors of the Girls' School, clutching her books to her sweatered breasts, and keeping a little clear of the milling mob. The air shivered with the crash of feet running to classrooms, streaks of bobbing pastel socks, the smell of perfumed young bodies and the plump of new flesh as girls knocked one another down at corners of the corridors. But everywhere there was this madrigal of high voices that went through her like a file. It was an orchestration of shrieks and giggles, as though the girls

83

couldn't say one syllable without jumping an octave.

Miss Blanchard inspected the bulletin board, a strip of framed cork stuck with memoranda for somebody to meet somebody somewhere, with sheets of laundry cardboard reminding the girls of their posture and to contribute to the Red Cross. A tea was being held by the Junior Class for the Sophomores; everyone had better be present. There were trellised sheets of paper for tennis and squash ladders, announcements of elections to the Student Council. And a list of daily demerits. Miss Blanchard read how one Ellie Newcomb had been fined two weekends for dropping a salad bowl in the dining room. From this bulletin board she noticed a sort of organized hysteria, a conflicting of academic and extracurricular interests, as though the girls were trying to do everything at once. Was this a school? No, she decided. It was a nursery, a home for wayward foundlings, a cafeteria, and a bazaar all rolled up into one. There was a mad refinement about the whole business, an insistence on petty detail, in the giddy hope that perhaps enough frenzy and folderol would turn out the Disciplined Young American Woman.

At the whirring of an electric bell (Mrs. Mears threw the switch) Betty Blanchard drew open the door to a classroom she knew was to be her own preserve all that year. She threw back her shoulders and walked in with glacial composure. It was so bright inside the room that she saw nothing; she heard only a gasp. It was a few seconds before she got used to the brilliance of the illumination from the floor-length windows. She walked to the desk, set down her books, and put on her glasses to ascertain just what manner of class Spanish III was going to be. Now these glasses, she knew, were a trifle chi-chi. But they turned her good looks into something clinical and cold. She wore a pair of Oxford eyeglasses which ran on a little chain into a metal burse fastened to her sweater. And as she whipped out the disappearing chain and put the glasses on her slender bony nose, Betty Blanchard heard another gasp from her class, then a titter. She should never have bought those glasses. They were suitable for genteel old ladies who taught dancing schools.

Fifteen girls sat rigid in one row of movable chairs with armrests. Betty noticed that these fifteen were taking in every detail of their new mistress. They looked like dolls surprised

84

in a midnight ballet in a toyshop. She knew she was smartly and severely dressed, but the glasses on a chain were a faux-pas. She stared back at her girls, particularly at those who were wearing harlequin spectacles. Each had her legs crossed at precisely the same angle; each had an open notebook on her armrest. Their cynosure was fifteen times as intense as that stare one woman gives another upon first meeting. The only girl Betty knew was Midgie Mears, who sat on the left of the row. Midgie was wearing her Student Council locket, which rose and fell with the breathing of her fabulous breasts. The intensity of the girls' appraisal continued. When it became a sheet of plate glass moving in on her, Miss Blanchard spoke, her voice brittle and professional in the still class-room:

—Girls, don't let your eyes pop out. You'll be seeing me all year long. . . .

There was a murmur of approval and of disapproval, but the tension was attenuated. Well, wasn't she *nice*? Or, She wasn't going to get around *them* that easily! A few stared even harder than before. She was going through that hideous icebreaking which is the first test of a new teacher. Her success or failure would be decided forever in the next minute or two.

A mouselike little girl in blue leapt to her feet:

—Please may I leave the room?

—Sit down. You've had half an hour since breakfast. . . .

There was a genuine giggle this time. Then Midgie Mears arose without invitation and put her knee on her chair. She leaned chummily toward the class:

—Kids, let me introduce Miss Blanchard, our new teach. Betty Blanchard to us. On dates she answers to Butchie. . . .

A horrible giggle overgrew the entire class. It was the most menacing sound Betty had ever heard, like a ripping of platinum. And she saw thirty little claws preparing to rend her. But she'd seen bombs fall on Naples and she'd wrestled with drunken majors in jeeps; so this foray upon her dignity was no worse than the cawing of vulturettes in their nest. She said quite softly:

—Sit down and shut up, Midgie. I'd hate to make a disciplinary example of the daughter of our Directress. . . .

Midgie plopped down in her chair like a deflated sow. First a scowl overspread her coarse pretty features, then a pout:

—I only wanted to help.

—Even God can't help a teacher. And next date you go on, try answering to the name of Butchie. . . .

The class were on her side now; they laughed.

—I'm gonna tell mom, Midgie whimpered.

—Go right ahead. . . . Now, girls. . . .

Though she'd taught for a year after leaving Wheaton, Miss Blanchard in the next forty-five minutes learned something she'd only guessed before. She knew her Spanish so well that part of her brain was always free to wrestle with that inertia which lies dormant in every class. She never tried to fool her students. Once she admitted to not knowing the answer to a question.

At the end of the first class she was tired, cool and triumphant. She knew the immense delight that comes from creative teaching. After a morning of four classes her head was singing with nervous fatigue. She'd never known quite this exhilaration and quite this peace. She saw why teachers get very old and stay very young. For there is no closer probing of the mind—not even in psychoanalysis.

The entire Girls' School, day and boarding, lunched together in the cellar of Mrs. Mears's house, which had been converted into a refectory, but was still obviously a cellar, dank and cool. They ate Waldorf salad and drank iced tea—that kind of luncheon which is considered calming to young women, and, incidentally, economical. The hundred girls sat at ten long tables, presided over by the Student Council. The mistresses sat at Mrs. Mears's table, who dished out the salad as though it were boeuf à la Vichyssoise and she chatelaine of a manor. When the voices of the girls rose to a shriek (they were conversing with mouths full), Mrs. Mears tinkled a little bell that sat by her knife. This meant that everyone was to stop talking for a minute. Then the babble would begin all over again from a mumbling, till it built up to a shivering scream; and Mrs. Mears would tinkle the irritable little bell once more.

The Directress did her bit in the hubbub, for she reached

across the table, laid a hand on Betty Blanchard's arm, and shrieked:

"Are you happy, my dear? You seem less nerrrvous. ...

—Happier than I ever dreamed.

—Well, you're a nice addition to our roster. I've asked the girls, and they *like* you. ...

—I don't think that matters, Betty Blanchard said, but inaudibly.

—Shhhh! said Miss Demerjian.

After lunch the girls had a Quiet Time so they wouldn't get nerrrvous while they were digesting their salad. Mrs. Mears served coffee to the married and unmarried ladies of the faculty in her seventeenth century drawing room. Betty looked forward to this ritual of leisure until she found out what it really was.

Mrs. Mears sat behind a Chinese Chippendale lowboy and poured thick strong coffee from a solid silver service that had been one of her wedding presents. For a while there was a Quiet Time here too, in which the faculty ladies sipped and looked weary and retrospective, as teachers do in the early afternoon. Then suddenly, as though she feared the silence was getting a bit subversive, Mrs. Mears leaned forward in her tailored suit of tweed, her white head austere over her huge bosom:

—Well, ladies, well? Who speaks first today?

Spatters of a fine unholy hail began to shoot through the calm room. Betty Blanchard was reminded of a parliament of cats honing their claws. Each of the faculty ladies in turn described everything she'd done that morning, and in such studied minutiae that she could be saying only what the Directress wished her to say. And every girl in the school was discussed. The girls were referred to clinically, by last names only. But what froze Betty Blanchard was the morbid manner in which each mistress spoke of the minor malefactions of Taylor and of Biddle and of Rovetti, tagging each case history with the loving intensity of a research technician staining a spirochete on a glass slide. Mrs. Mears listened to these recitations with fierce pouncing scrutiny, taking notes in a little Florentine leather notebook and narrowing her brilliant eyes behind her wrinkles.

—Yes, Yes? Go on, she would say in her husky screechy voice.

Every detail of the morning's teaching, discipline, and study periods was covered by an auditing analysis that made Betty Blanchard feel she was suffocating. It was like a juvenile court fumbling around to dissect the brains of delinquent children. These ladies, especially the spinster ones, were obsessed with their work—and with their pupils. They weren't so much teachers as tamperers with the souls of young girls. Betty was chilled. She had to listen to how Mueller had changed her hairdo—for no good reason, so far as Miss O'Leary could discover. How Epstein had taken to using too much lipstick. How Anderson had been heard to say *damn* under her breath in the corridor. And all were to be summoned to the office of Mrs. Mears for further inquest that afternoon.

—And now let us hear from Miss Blanchard, said the Directress, seeming to lick her chops.

Betty Blanchard paused, clutched her pearls, and said in a level voice:

—I'm afraid I have nothing to report. I consider that I spent a constructive morning. . . .

There was a silence, followed by a gasp. She knew that every woman in the room was looking at her as though she'd dropped a sanitary napkin from under her skirt.

—What did you say, my dear?

—I have nothing to report, Mrs. Mears.

The Directress leaned forward and looked at the strained faces about her drawing room. She made a helpless gesture to Miss Demerjian:

—Did I hear right? Am I getting a little deaf, Habib?

—No, mam, Miss Demerjian said. Miss Blanchard said *rien*. . . .

Mrs. Mears swept the coffee table away from her and stood up, pulling her jacket about her and buttoning it.

—You noticed nothing . . . psychiatric? she said.

—I thought psychiatry was a science for sick souls, Betty Blanchard said.

—You will have to do better than this, my dear.

Then she left the room, followed by the other lady teachers. Betty sat on a windowseat looking out at the grave of Miss Sophia under the light of an early September afternoon. Then she went up to her attic and wept.

5

A bell as fat as a Chinese gong went off every morning at two minutes after seven. But he'd been up since six, watching the gradual magic of an October sunrise from his window. He hadn't slept much since four, what with thinking of the responsibilities, extraneous and essential, that had been dumped on his shoulders. It was the second month of his teaching, but when this stabbing bell began, the mood of the sunrise vanished into irritability, as though some officious warden had stuck a nose into a tranquil green jail he'd built for himself. This bell was for Guy Hudson the only music of Mr. Pilkey's personality, the only tune he understood. It was the Onward, Christian Soldiers of a twentieth century intellectual factory. And whereas in the army he used to scream at his platoon to Rise and Shine, here he was within an inch of yelling Shuddup at the bell. Still it yammered and sprayed, a stream of enuresis turned to iron.

He'd watched the sunrise in shorts and skivvy shirt, but now to the intermittent bell (every two minutes) he washed his face, shaved, and dressed. He heard his corridor of lowerformers wake under the proddings of the bell. In the room next to his he heard two boys tussling; there was the mellow clump of a pillow thrown against a wall. And yet he envied them their sleep, the deep repose of young students worn out with books and athletics. His own was fitful and fraught with crazy dreams and frustrations. He remembered how in Europe he used to watch the sunrise with his companion for the night.

He dressed slowly and vengefully; the hubbub on the corridor waxed. It began every morning shortly after seven and was never still till ten at night. Only in nine hours of darkness was he free of the shouting and wasted energy of young America.

Now he heard the drubbing sound of students washing themselves with a lick and a promise. He smelt the sour chowder of the urinals, which were always backing up from the effluvium of many boyish kidneys and bed-wetters.

Guy Hudson walked down the dormitory stairs, his red head bowed in thought. A sort of apprehension of the day was seeping through him. Students greeted him:

—Good morning, sir!

The *sir* of American secondary education was as offensive to his ears as the *sir* of enlisted men when he was an officer. For it was neither cringing nor respectful. It meant nothing. Nevertheless, he raised his head, smiled with his misshapen mouth, and returned their greeting. He knew it was ridiculous to take out his resentment of the system on children who were trapped in it.

He walked through the crispening October morning and entered the dining hall, which was a vast roofed arena. The faculty sat at one end on a dais, which Mr. Pilkey insisted must be called The High Table. It was Mr. Pilkey's theory (set forth in the Academy catalog) that the faculty's eating in the same room with their students created the cozy atmosphere of those Fine Homes from which the boys had come. Below the dais three hundred boarders of the Boys' School were making their breakfast on packaged cereals and milk. They grabbed food from one another and insulted the waiters, scholarship boys in white coats, who looked piqued or returned the insults.

This dining hall, which rumbled like a cafeteria in a railway station, was painted dead white for the illusion of aristocracy and sanitation. The walls were hung with portraits of distinguished alumni, dead faculty, and assorted worthies calculated to inspire the young to pious emulation as they dined. After nearly a month at The Academy Guy Hudson believed that the real reason why the faculty ate with the students was for supervision—to see that no beef stew got hurled at these somber canvases. Indeed the whole aspect of this roomful of American students breakfasting was of wellborn young convicts dunking from a common trough. They swaggered in, wearing dungarees, their hair uncombed, their voices querulous from sleep. And upperformers filched the milk and cereal of the lowerformers, who looked after their vanishing breakfasts with idolization and fear. For the older boys (by the Pilkeyan doctrine of Student Government) kept the younger in line. These traditions of the piracy of food would be continued when the little boys got bigger. They would Take It Out on succeeding classes.

He sat down with six unmarried faculty at a maple table on the dais. Red-eyed, they were listlessly crumbling cereal and swigging gray coffee. Over the bachelors' table hung that curtain of hopelessness, chagrin, and austerity that descends when unmarried men dine together at seven thirty every morning.

—Good morning, gentlemen, Guy Hudson said, pouring some coffee.

—Listen to him, said a physics teacher. When he's been here twenty years, he won't be so goddam chipper.

—Eat your oatmeal and pipe down, an athletic coach said.

—Ah, youth, the fifty-year-old organist said. I had a toothache and didn't close an eye all night long.

—He's got a bad tummy, a French teacher said. Something screwy in his duodenum. . . .

—Didn't shut an eyelash last night, the organist said again.

—Hell, Amos, have your prostate looked at, another voice said.

Guy Hudson's stomach quivered, but he broke up some dry cereal and drank his coffee, brooding on the gracelessness of the male just out of bed, and of dyspepsia and of senility. He'd been told in a whisper by Doctor Sour that the Pilkeys and the married faculty felt quite unconcerned about these ghoulish breakfasts for the derelicts of the Boys' School, for *they* dined at home on waffles and sausage and thick cups of fragrant coffee. Guy Hudson watched a bright-eyed young hyperthyroid from the English Department take his place at table, tear open a russet banana, and scrunch down the pistil of brown fruit upon the table. Then this young man stalked out, crying audibly to the whole dining room:

—Are we expected to teach all morning on *these* calories?

—*He* won't last very long, a bachelor said hopefully.

—Well, it's not as bad as C-ration, Guy Hudson said to his neighbor, a liverish young mathematician.

—Ah, you veterans. You come back with a bad case of self-pity.

Guy Hudson was silent.

He pushed back his chair and walked angrily from the dining hall. He saw the scurfy heads of the unmarried teachers as they champed on their shredded wheat. He watched a fat upperformer trip a little scholarship boy struggling through the swinging pantry doors with a tray. And last of all he eyed the motto painted on a scroll over the main doors to the Dining Hall:

MEAT FOR THE BODY   FOOD FOR THE SOUL
MAKE THE CITIZEN-SCHOLAR WHOLE

He walked in the quadrangle sparkling with the first frost of October. The dormitories were astir with housekeeping—the banging of iron beds and the whisking of brooms. Windows clacked up and down as mops were shaken out of them. Guy Hudson knew. Mr. Pilkey boasted in the catalog that students took care of their own rooms. No pampering—that was the democracy of The Academy. What Mr. Pilkey didn't mention was how much he saved on janitors' salaries. What cleaning force there was complained constantly that the faculty were dirty; the little old men spent their time mopping around Mr. Pilkey's desk, where results showed. But in such wise little economies were rationalized into educational virtues.

Those bells began ringing again: they were pealing forth in burring dissonance from every building in The Academy. Boys stopped making their beds and issued forth in demented hundreds toward the chapel. Curses and singing filled the October morning. Chapel was compulsory for Gentile, Jew, and Negro (there was one), for this was a Christian school. Mr. Pilkey had said in his catalog that there is no substitute for beginning an educational morning in the Right Way—that is, by prayer.

Guy Hudson followed the crowd into a long low building that looked like a greenhouse. Outside in its paneled hallway students lingered till the last possible moment before entering the Divine Presence. They gossiped in not too hushed a fashion under bronze plaques of Academy boys who had been killed in both World Wars. There was also a marble

92

tablet, fringed with myrtle and laurel, dedicated to a teacher of manual training (called Handicraft in the catalog) who had dropped dead in this corridor after leaving a service of worship. Guy Hudson hesitated in the passageway; then a voice spurred him on with a genial and godly conviction:

—Upstairs, upstairs, young man! Have you forgotten that Young Faculty sit in the Choir Loft?

It was Mr. Pilkey who spoke. He was rosy and freshly shaved: his breath exuded the incense of a rich hearty breakfast he'd just demolished in his Cape Cod House. He carried a prayerbook in his hand.

—O good morning, sir, Guy Hudson said.

The Principal smiled and lumbered off to accost those students who were blocking the doors to the chapel:

—Goddam it, fellows, move on, move on! Are you *afraid* to go to church?

And he snorted at his own little joke. His students did too; the clusters of talking boys melted away as he bore down on them. He atomized them. He was charged with holiness and purpose, for it was the beginning of a new day.

Guy Hudson groped his way up the dark stairs to the Choir Loft. There, overlooking the chapel below them, sat most of the younger men of the faculty like a flight of crows in caucus. They were taking attendance of the pews beneath them. Each absence or tardiness they checked off with little sighs of auditing satisfaction, for teachers love to Make Notes on Things.

He sat down on a hard bench behind the rows of recording angels. He surveyed the chapel from the vantage of God. It was really a big nondenominational auditorium, designed to accommodate the entire Boys' School for state or for disciplinary occasions. But this chapel had whitewashed walls, intended to suggest that peace which surpasseth understanding. Its decorative characteristics were mostly negative, in that anything which should suggest the symbols and outer trappings of worship, or the richness of Popery, had been excluded. It was really only a huge room with uncomfortable pews.

These pews were roosted on by four hundred boys from twelve to twenty years of age. They acted more like a theater audience, for their chatter could be heard over that tentative organ playing which is the prelude to worship. Tiny lowerformers sat near the rostrum, the seniors and Student Councillors in the rear. It was one of the privileges of seniority that they might be the first to tear out of the chapel. Already Guy Hudson had heard apocryphal stories of how Mr. Pilkey was quite capable (in his younger and more fiery days) of rushing off the platform at vespers and bashing together the heads of lowerformers who giggled at vespers.

On that very platform now sat Mr. Pilkey and the school chaplain. Mr. Pilkey's vestments, since he wasn't a minister of the gospel, followed his own rubric—a black satin gown with a revers of deep purple, a token of that time when his own college, Dartmouth, had awarded him an LL. D. for his pioneering in American education. But Doctor Smedley, the official Jesus to the school, wore a dark business suit. For the rest there was an American flag, its folds hanging according to the artistic directions of Mrs. Pilkey, and a heavy mahogany rostrum with a Bible.

To quiet the murmur, Mr. Amos James, the Academy organist and handyman of music, threw on more stops. The faces of boys and faculty became more solemn under the booming diapasons and brilliant reeds, for a worried reverence is the stock response of the American male to loud ecclesiastical organ playing.

A twinge of sacred boredom crossed the faces of Mr. Pilkey and the resident clergyman as the prelude reached a full cadence and went right on. A sigh of expectation unfulfilled passed over the student body. Mr. Pilkey, out of the folds of his robe, seemed to make a sign to Amos James to cease and desist. But the skeletal aging man bowed unheeding over his three manuals and pedals and modulated with eclat into F-sharp major. The brilliance and uproar of the full organ became intolerable; the panes in the chapel windows rattled. Perhaps this morning the poor organist planned to annihilate them all by sound. Mr. Pilkey and the official chaplain settled back against their cushions. Guy Hudson smiled to himself. This was the last protest of a numbed artist against his bondage. And it went on for four more minutes. And when the prelude was really ended the two on the podium couldn't quite be sure that there was no more music, for it echoed in the porches of their ears; they sat under the organ pipes. Finally in a grisly silence of ruptured eardrums Mr. Pilkey arose and addressed the Boys'

School in his easy almost wistful manner. He always sounded to the uninitiated as though he was supplicating the indulgence of his audience. But woe betide that boy whose attention wandered!

—Fellows, last spring I talked with members of the Student Council, who, like all of you, come from devout homes. They spoke of the inadequacy of the religious background here at The Academy. In my heart I agreed with them. We talked together about how this school is a bulwark against the chaos and heartsickness of the outside world. . . . As the old fellows know, in the past I conducted most of the religious services here at school. Perhaps that was a wee bit presumptuous of me. For I am not an ordained minister. I have no orthodoxy. If you don't know what that word means, fellows ask your English teachers in class this morning. But I tell Mrs. Pilkey sometimes (here the Principal chuckled richly and intimately) that we have our own brand of religion: plain commonsense Christianity. . . . But now all that is obviated. In memory of Our Gracious Foundress a chair of theology has been established at this Academy. The sum, fifty thousand dollars, is not important. What matters is that from henceforth the school will have its own chaplain. . . . Fellows, take Doctor Smedley to your hearts. . . . He understands you . . . is in fact one of you, though he's four times your age. . . . The last school he was in, the senior class spent all their time in the Smedleys' house. Couldn't be driven away, so eager were they to talk with a good Christian. . . . You fellows are going to find Doctor Smedley as hospitable as any couple already here in residence on our beloved and gracious faculty. . . . May I introduce Doctor Smedley to your affections? . . .

As the old minister arose, there was a sprinkling of applause from the pews of the lowerformers, swiftly extinguished by a glare from the Principal. Three Student Councillors rushed from the rear of the chapel and patrolled the offending pews. Doctor Smedley shook hands with the Principal and walked rheumatically to the rostrum. For a long time he leaned on it silently, as though he was imploring the assistance of God in this, his latest and possibly final mission in life. Then he stared out at the congregation as though he was taking the measure of its collective soul. Guy Hudson was embarrassed for the nice old man. Coughs from the

95

student body and squirmings told him that the keener adolescents were feeling similar sentiments. But Guy Hudson pitied the old guy while probably these kids didn't. Finally Doctor Smedley cleared his throat and spoke in an aged voice, which he strove to fill full of portentous intimacy:

—Not so long ago I was a boy myself. . . .

Then gathering momentum and velocity, like an old fire horse, he preached on in the stunning empty periods and cadences of the homiletics of 1880, such as would have moved Julia Ward Howe. He told little jokes that were no longer funny because they depended on Puritan slang such as By Gosh, By Jinkers, By Gum, By Jeeper, and Twenty-three Skidoo. And he rose to terrific climaxes where his thought (always in platitudes and truisms) was insufficient ballast for the blustering of his voice. To Guy Hudson the poor kind old man seemed fuddled and slightly ridiculous, well meaning when he inveighed against the vices of a world he knew only from stories heard at the dinner tables of rich bankers, for Doctor Smedley had once had a wealthy parish. He had, however, never really lived life, as a Bunyan or a Calvin had. There was in him a fatuous sweetness, of Jesus Christ emasculated and translated into a novel by Anthony Trollope. And Guy Hudson knew also, since the war had taught him pity, that the undergraduates found Doctor Smedley merely silly. He himself had some idea of what made Dr. Smedley what he was. They saw the minister as a fussy old man who had long forgotten (if he ever knew) the tumult of youth.

And finally the chaplain concluded his squeamish sermon, geared to Arouse Young Minds to a Darn Good Fight:

—Boys, I leave this thought with you. Years from now you may remember an old man's wisdom. . . . Make your algebra a prayer, your French a prayer . . . and yes, even your chemistry with its strange smells from the laboratory. *That* can be a prayer too. . . .

After dismal shuffling silence from the student body, Mr. Pilkey shook the hand of his new chaplain. Guy Hudson wondered whether Doctory Smedley wasn't perhaps a better Christian than the Principal. The strong old executive and the querulous old Christer.

Then they sang a hymn. It was the sort of choral song that

Mr. Pilkey loved, the only music he had any time for; what he called a Darn Good Tune, rhythmic and athletic, written in 1874 by a man named Henry Smart, (a perfect name) exhorting the world to shake itself from sloth and win for Queen Victoria and the House of Rothschild. Then Mr. Pilkey prayed to God on terms of the most august intimacy: to make himself a fit executive and his school a torch of learning and gentlemanly manners. Then to a reprise of the day's hymn the student body filed out pale and rather chastened. Guy Hudson was dizzy with the foul hot air that had seeped up into the Choir Loft.

But the faces of the boys as they reached the corridor were a testimony to their resiliency against Pilkeyan religion. It was as though Phoenicians had been subjected against their will to one half hour of Christian Doctrine. Just outside the chapel their faces metamorphosed from the mask of gloom, that badge of piety, into schoolboys, discovering again that it was an October morning, that Christ was two thousand years dead, that the adjurations of Doctor Smedley had really little to do with the day before them. In one minute the strained hush had evaporated, a schoolboy gabbling broke out, punctuated by a few whistles syncopated the hymn they'd just sung.

Guy Hudson stood against the corridor wall and let the mob press by him. But the boys stepped aside for Mr. Pilkey and the school chaplain to pass—a pretty farce indicating that undergraduates weren't worthy to touch the hems of the garments of these two Johns the Baptist. Guy Hudson saw that the expression on Mr. Pilkey's face was also changing as he emerged from church: he was rubbing his hands with fervor for the day's occupation.

When the chapel overflow had somewhat dissipated, Guy Hudson strolled down the corridor, skirting the desk of Mr. Pilkey. Out of the corner of his eye he saw the Principal answering his phone, dictating, and giving an audience to Mr. Philbrick Grimes, who was leaning intimately yet courteously over the desk. And Guy Hudson scorned himself for doing so; yet he lowered his gaze in passing. But he had the positive sensation that Mr. Pilkey was quite aware that he was going by, and had assessed him quickly and thoroughly, in much the same way that a mechanic on an assembly line checks the parts that are flying past him on a conveyor belt.

And before he got out of earshot Guy Hudson heard the quick conspiratorial voice of Mr. Grimes saying in the Principal's ear:

—I know I'm stupid even to harbor such a suspicion, but....

Although they were beginning a day of school, the hundreds of scholars floating through the corridors with books under their arms had a queer aimlessness about them. They seemed to be waiting for the bells to ring which would scoop them out of their idyll of the Natural Savage and into the classroom. On almost none of the faces did Guy Hudson observe the lust for learning that pictorial magazines speak of; nor was there any hint in their demeanor that precious scholastic hours were running through their fingers like golden sands, never to be reclaimed. He heard one indolent voice say:

—Say, Joe, I spent one hour on that goddam geometry and I'm handin in a blank paper. . . .

And another:

—Know what that bastard did? Made us memorize a whole sonnet. Creepers!

Now one of Mr. Pilkey's most ridden hobbies at The Academy was a period that lasted one half hour after the end of chapel. It was called Availability Time, and it had a prominent place in the catalog. The Principal told parents that it was even more important than classroom work because from it students could derive that vade mecum of finest American teaching—Individual Instruction. Every faculty member was expected (and Mr. Pilkey occasionally took attendance) to go to his empty classroom and sit there. This was Availability Time. It was supposed to combine the choicest features of the seminar and private tutoring (without, of course, the fee). Here students who were behind in their work could get Extra Help. The teacher simply sat at his desk, a passive purveyor, and his scholars came to him and asked searching questions about last night's homework. That was what the catalog said. But the only students who ever turned up at Availability Time were those thugs who hoped to wheedle their teachers into doing the homework for them.

But in accordance with the desires of Mr. Pilkey, Guy Hudson went to Room 18 and sat at his desk with folded hands. He was bursting with historical knowledge to impart, but no boy came near him. The classroom had a glass door. Outside in the corridor he could see students passing like Arabs in a market, whistling, reading their papers, and calling out witticisms to one another. And they seemed to find something humorous, these boys, to watch the faculty sitting in their little cells waiting, like fish in an aquarium pleading to be hooked. Guy Hudson wished he had something to read. He was being O, so available in the Availability Time, but no one was availing himself of his ministrations. Suppose a doctor, having hung out a sign that offered Free Medical Care, were to sit in his reception room twiddling his thumbs?

The bell rang for the end of Availability Time. There were five minutes before the first class. He wanted passionately the solace of a cigarette. But Mr. Pilkey didn't approve of smoking in The Schoolhouse. Guy Hudson knew of a broomcloset on the top floor. Thither he went and discovered half a dozen other faculty clandestinely inhaling.

—Well, he's finally found our lounge! a voice cried in the gray blur.

—God! sucking on nicotine as a dope against the morning tortures! said another voice, imitating the cadences of Mr. Pilkey.

In this closet, which was like a small telephone booth ablaze, Guy Hudson puffed on his butt. This ignominy was necessary because of an executive who didn't want his employees to be human beings. And the smoking teachers acted fretful, as though the eye of Mr. Pilkey was mounted in the wall of the closet. They all had a sense of guilt simply because they had pieces of paper and tobacco in their mouths. And the janitors would probably squeal to the Principal that the teachers were messing up their broomcloset. The consecrated profession! Consecrated to dust, ashes, and crud!

As he dragged on his cigarette, he listened to the voices coming from the bodies almost invisible in the jam and smoke. They were telling each other what they were going to do to their little bastards that morning. He was surprised, even after a month at The Academy, to hear American teachers express (not for the ears of Mr. Pilkey) a hostility between themselves and their students. Why? After a few years of teaching you seemed to resent going into your classroom and assuming the bardic pose. Why were teachers cynical? Were they speaking acidly of a love too deep to articulate? But it seemed to him more a case of chronic spleen, a distaste with life, with the whole business of imparting knowledge. During that privy smokefest in the crowded closet he seemed to be listening not to teachers, but to prostitutes bored with their trade. Now Guy Hudson was vindictive to the whole world; yet he still believed in redemption, which he could achieve for himself and for his students by a marriage of fact and wisdom. He believed that he could really *do* something on a high level of human activity: transforming himself before a class with the aid of his voice and a blackboard. He had suffered perhaps more than the owners of these voices, yet here they were, each proclaiming his own sophisticated brand of negation:

—American kids since 1941 can't grasp an abstract idea. . . .

—They resent the least attempt at discipline. . . .

—Popularity with your class is a form of prostitution. But by God I'm trying my damnedest to be a whore. . . .

Angry, he trod out his cigarette and went downstairs from the bilious symposium in the closet.

Every morning he went through four history classes. He believed that in these periods of concentrated fervor he was giving out the finest distillation of himself. There were twenty or so boys in each of his sections. (The catalog said that intimacy in classroom work was one of the Academy's strengths.) When he stood before a class, he was well aware that he carried with him his special brand of tension. He was goodlooking, except for his twisted mouth; the kids knew that he owned a Purple Heart, though that didn't mean as much as it would have a year or so ago. Nor did he wear his discharge pin from the army on his lapel, for he had a strange and quiet shame at owning to being a veteran. His mouth did that for him.

But occasionally he got returns from his teaching as only a young teacher can. He had moments when the whole classroom shot up like an elevator into such a heady altitude as is not found below Everest; when half his class lingered around his desk even after the dismissal bell; when individual boys suddenly at something he'd said looked as though lightning had struck them; when their *Look* magazines dropped unheeded to their feet.

But oftener he had spells of despair, the bottom falling out of everything, as it may with the artist or the teacher. What am I doing standing here beating my gums before twenty adolescents? Like all teachers I'm rationalizing my work from its barrenness into something heroic. This summer they will forget everything. And who am I to be standing here passing on the historical wisdom of Europe and America? The Messiah came once and was crucified for his trouble. Do I really believe I am making the world any better by standing here as a petty priest? Why am I not out Doing Things for my acquisitive sense and for the final glories of the capitalistic system? Do I *really* believe that I can have the slightest influence on these clever hard young minds? Am I not perhaps softening them up for life, destroying what originality they were born with? I am a Perverter, that's all, like those driveling old men who lure little girls into alleys with taffy candy. And who can prove that the lore I'm passing on may not be merely the accumulated fungus of centuries? Perhaps the twentieth century is right in being cynical about everything that has gone before. Perhaps instinctively these boys know more than I ever shall. . . .

Yet since Guy Hudson was no romanticist, only a sort of smashed idealist, he never expected, and never got from his students the hypocrisy of dewy eyes and:

—O thank you, sir, for the *good* you've done our souls! . . .

Though perhaps that was what Mr. Pilkey expected his teachers to angle for.

That year he had in his classes three students who gave *him* something to chew on. They were not that gratification which onanistic teachers seek; they were a spur and reflection of himself as he might be.

The first was a Jewish boy who oddly enough was President of the Student Council. Even Guy Hudson had to admit that there must be something great in Mr. Pilkey's Academy, if a Hebrew could rise to the highest office in student government. And he got there because he was loved by the students. Ben Gordon had that quality rare in any human being and almost unknown in very young men—compassion. He was a wondrous athlete, and if his duties in Student Government hadn't taken so much time, he would have been a magnificent scholar too. He was handsome in a shadowy Semitic fashion, and richly though quietly dressed. His mother was a vivid Chicago Jewess who espoused political and humanitarian causes, and occasionally descended on The Academy for an afternoon of tea-drinking and sparkling conversation. His father was a rich Chicago merchant who sent the faculty costly gifts at Christmas for their interest in Ben. But out of these two somewhat flashy people had come Ben Gordon. A quiet deep pool of gentleness and understanding, and masculinity of a sort that rarely coexist. He simply sat in class, a pencil in his mouth. He rarely said anything at all. His function seemed to *be* Ben Gordon. But sometimes Guy Hudson would look up from a piece of chalk in his hand, and there was the young Jew staring at him, with thousands of years of sadness in his brown eyes. And the teacher would forget what he was saying. The President of the Student Council overpowered him with a soft and intense richness; it was like wading in a warm pool. Ben Gordon *understood*.

And there was also a Negro boy, Tad McKinley, the first ever to be admitted to The Academy, though Mr. Pilkey hadn't shouted the fact in this year's catalog. It was an experiment, he told the faculty discreetly. The students treated Tad McKinley with kindness—a conscious kindness maneuvered by the Student Council, which had set out on an anti-prejudice campaign. But the Negro boy kept apart from nearly all of them. He was no whipped complaint member of the black race, humbly grateful to be admitted to the society of Whites. At seventeen he was a coiled avenger. He was out for everything he could get. Often Guy Hudson's eye was drawn to the Negro boy, who sat insolently in the front row of European History 2a. And the teacher was convinced that the boy hated him and was using him as a lever into something else. He never called him *sir*, but always *Mister Hudson*; and even this appellation fell like a stinger from his lips. Tad McKinley had the coiled pride of a rattlesnake. It wasn't so much courage that had dared him to be the one Negro at The Academy; it was homicidal disdain for the human race. Once Guy Hudson said to him privately:

—Tad, when did you turn on yourself?

—And when did you? the boy had said. During your *agony* in the war? . . .

And the third boy, who haunted Guy Hudson in a special manner, sat next to Tad McKinley and was his one friend.

This was the scholarship boy Ralph Du Bouchet, who with his long black lashes and response to Teecher without any attempt at flattery made Guy Hudson almost delude himself into thinking he was a Great Teacher. Sometimes (and he censured himself wrathfully) he caught himself teaching only for the response of Ralph. The boy lay open to him like a maiden. He had the reflexes of a lover in bed. Sometimes their rapport was so sharp that Guy Hudson swore Ralph knew what he would say in the next sentence. And when the teacher phrased something extremely well the boy would look at his notebook and smile dreamily, as though he was Svengali congratulating himself. Sometimes Guy Hudson decided he was a puppet in Ralph's brain. Outside of class they avoided each other; and when they did meet, there was an expression on their faces that said they had planned it this way. The arrowlike beauty of Ralph brought Guy Hudson back to those slim boys of Normandy who in 1944 had mascoted themselves to the American Army for food and security. And he himself had had a young friend, Marcel Bonne, to whom even now he sent CARE packages. But the repetition, the sense of déjà vu gave him many a troubled hour. He would examine his conscience as to his motives toward his most remarkable student:

—Listen, lad, if what I think is happening, *is* happening, you're a dead duck. Your effectiveness as a teacher will be sabotaged forever. Are you mad? . . .

—No, the other voice in himself said, it isn't *that* at all. It's just that underneath you're both very much alike. Attraction and repulsion between you are equally balanced. Each of you is sensual, with no true outlet for your desires. Neither of you is really sure of himself. . . .

Yet he got increasingly dismayed at the nuances between Ralph and himself. He ceased looking at the boy in class and went out of his way never to meet him in the corridors. But his teaching dropped into a vacuum if Ralph was ever absent.

Luncheons at The Academy were a ceremonial to which Guy Hudson never completely habituated himself. Perhaps Mr. Pilkey intended them to suggest a leisurely indoor picnic, prelude to a long lazy October afternoon. The menu never varied: macaroni with cheese, coldcuts, and milk. This order of things had been established twenty-five years ago at the Academy's inception by the Comptroller. And since it was possible to serve these starchy staples to five hundred persons at three cents per plate, the diet remained the same till today. Thousands of alumni remembered nothing else but The Academy's famous macaroni and cheese. It stuck to one's ribs throughout the afternoon; it suggested both heartiness and daintiness at midday. And Mr. Pilkey could boast in his catalog that boys put on weight. There was always more than enough of it; it came on the tables in green casserole after green casserole, encrusted with a smegma of grilled mouse-cheese.

Luncheons were also more decorous than breakfasts because, by order of Mr. Pilkey, the entire faculty and their wives turned up in the dining hall and sat on the dais which must be referred to as The High Table. Hence the Boys' School watched their manners. At the front table on the dais sat the Pilkeys (and sometimes Mr. Pilkey's ancient mother) eating away and exclaiming volubly on the merits of The Academy's cuisine.

Each day the faculty members were detailed by type-written roster to dine at the Pilkeys' table. The good thing about this command performance was that it went by rotation; Guy Hudson hit the Principal's table only once in two weeks. For to sit next to Mr. Pilkey meant that he had to listen to the old gentleman be an autocrat of Good Food and Good Table Talk, holding forth all luncheon long, his mouth full of macaroni, snorting on the excellence of the cookery, with flecks of lettuce on his massive chin. And when Guy Hudson had to sit next to Mrs. Pilkey, he had to be very careful not to brush her thigh under the tablecloth. Conversation with her was impractical and impracticable; the only topic was her pottery painting. And she was likely to be musing on some new problem of Her Art, and was most peremptory in snubbing loquacious young men. Only Mr. Philbrick Grimes knew how to draw out the Principal's wife. To him she sometimes said twenty words.

Or occasionally a Distinguished Guest sat at the Pilkeys' table on the dais—a retired State senator or some odd poet or diplomat whom the Pilkeys had annexed during their summers in Maine. When the tables were cleared, this celebrity (of whom no one had ever heard) would be asked to address the Boys' School. The signal for this was Mr. Pilkey's striking his water glass with a knife. Then a disconcerted and peevish hush would fall on the hundreds of diners and the Distinguished Guest would arise, reminisce on his rich career, and tell the Boys' School how *darn* lucky they were to be in so famous an institution.

This noon there was no speaker at the Pilkeys' table, Guy Hudson saw, with a sigh of delight. He sat down at one of the faculty tables with two teachers of Latin and Mr. Philbrick Grimes, who'd been attempting with greater than pertinent zeal to sit at the Principal's table. All luncheon long Guy Hudson watched Mr. Grimes watch Mr. Pilkey, sensitive for any reflex of displeasure on that lordly brow. If Mr. Pilkey fell into a tantrum during the meal (as he'd been known to do in the earlier days of the school) Mr. Grimes was ready to rush up with cold napkins as compresses. Guy Hudson ate his macaroni and listened to the two Latin teachers arguing about a genitive absolute in Macrobius. Mr. Grimes got more and more restless, for he believed that undirected luncheon conversation in an educational institution is dangerous and disorganized. He was one of the greatest living Shop-Talkers, and he couldn't afford to let his stretched elastic relax during luncheon. Consequently in the first breather of the grammarians' wrangling he said to Guy Hudson:

—You're not being amusing, Doctor.

—I'm eating. And I do it taciturnly, like an old Dutch patroon. . . .

But Mr. Grimes wasn't going to stand for any such nonsense as leisure time, and he goaded the two classicists and Guy Hudson into playing Ghost, a Victorian word game, in which the object is never to let the spelling of a word end on *you*. Now Mr. Grimes played Ghost with the passion of a huckster in a railroad smoker. He used every spelling virtuosity up his sleeve to impress the others at the table. He was pettish, raffish, and avid in showing off his vocabulary. And like the oldest child in a group of pretending children he decreed new rules to the game as they went along. And as each spelled himself out three times, he made a delighted incantation of the Ghost formula:

—Doctor Anderson is a Ghost, and as such must not be addressed. . . .

105

Guy Hudson was getting nervous; the contest narrowed down to himself and Philbrick Grimes. At last he spelled himself out on the word *zeugma* and threw down his napkin in a fury. Mr. Grimes waggled a finger:

—Naughty-naughty! Go out behind the barn and hide your head in shame! . . .

Then, eyeing the Principal's table, he trumped his own triumph by launching into a witty diatribe on the virtues, discipline, and vocabulary-building assets of the great game of Ghost.

—I've some acrostic books in my suite.

—*Hate* them, Guy Hudson said, surprised to find himself so piqued.

There was no dessert at luncheon since the Comptroller had long ago decreed that a sweet at midday was bad for the pancreas and the economy. The sign that luncheon was ended was Mr. Pilkey's suturing his mouth with a thorough swipe from his napkin, and rising from table after calling out to his wife:

—Ready, dearie?

Then the entire Boys' School and faculty arose in their places and chanted Grace After Meals, led by Doctor Smedley. The dining room was cleared in two minutes because they filed out in columns. Traffic was directed by Mr. Pilkey and Mr. Grimes with magnificent semaphoric signals. The Principal himself bellowed at boys (or faculty) who jammed the aisles by walking in the wrong direction.

There was now a half hour of leisure for meditation and digestion. After a month of teaching Guy Hudson discovered that life merely went underground for this period; the populous nervousness of The Academy never really let down from the beginning of a term to its end. And when the quadrangle was at its quietest the most singularly dreadful things were likely to be going on.

After lunch the Boys' School usually repaired to the chapel, where they held shouting caucuses of anarchy and remonstration which are called School Meetings. Here they protested everything that went on at The Academy. They drew up petitions against the faculty and against the length of assignments; under the gavel of Ben Gordon they aired all their gripes. Since the Academy, as the catalog said, was a democratic school, no faculty were admitted to these

School Meetings. Yet somehow Mr. Pilkey and his adjutant Mr. Grimes found out everything that transpired. And upperformers who had taken Freedom of Speech too rashly found that, next time they passed Mr. Pilkey's desk in The Den, a long arm reached out for their collars. But these were only whispers that Guy Hudson heard after a month at the school.

A more somber cabal than School Meeting, which took place after every weekday luncheon, was a ceremony known as Coffee For The Faculty. Each teacher and his lady were expected to turn up for a demitasse of jet molasses, whether or not he liked coffee or society. Guy Hudson suspected that it was Mr. Pilkey's way of checking on his employees at midday. As soon as the dining hall was cleared of students, the faculty (preceded by the Pilkeys, affectionately arm in arm) stepped down to a long planked table in the center of the dining room. Here was set up a silver urn (a relic out of Miss Sophia's Manse) and a battery of little cups in pastel colors. But now the Principal's wife was handed by her loving husband into a Regency chair. She Poured. In her absence this stately hostess-ship would fall to Mrs. Whitney, and so on down the ladies of the faculty, in order of precedence. Behind the coffee urn, beaming on teachers she liked, and just pouring coffee for those she didn't, Mrs. Pilkey under her white coronet braid and fantastic brocade gown looked like an old mandarin's wife shipping out poisons by commission. She never remembered how anyone took his coffee:

—Noir? she would say coyly.

Nor could she recall the names of most of the faculty. Mnemosynic excellence, she said when asked, is incompatible with the intense concentration required of the artist. Ladies of the faculty got their coffee first, each making a pretty speech to Mrs. Pilkey, inquiring about her Art or her arthritis. God help any gentleman who attempted to snaffle his coffee first, under tenure to some pressing engagement! He was swept back by the stout arm of the Principal:

—Chivalry won't be dead as long as *I* am Principal here, *sir*!

The ladies of the faculty, balancing their coffee, wanted to sit by themselves and have good hentalk about their chintzes and their children and the price of food. But this wasn't permitted. Mr. Pilkey was dead set against division of the sexes at any faculty function. His white locks flapping, he bumbled about, with his own arms bodily transplanting ladies and gentlemen, instructing them to make mixed conversation—or else. And Mr. Philbrick Grimes darted in and out of the bevy, carrying coffee to his favorite ladies, his ear cocked for a racy tidbit from their whispered prattle. He was, however, most obsequious to Mrs. Pilkey at the coffee urn. He treated her like a Great Hostess, murmuring compliments as he took the cups from her brown old hand. When the spigot stuck, it was Mr. Grimes who turned plumber and pried it loose. Or if the Principal's wife scalded herself on a jet of molten java, it was Mr. Grimes who got cold water for her flesh, amid many little nurselike cries of commiseration. Watching this comedy, Guy Hudson regretted that Mr. Grimes had been born in the wrong century; God should have assigned him as major-domo in the winter palace of a countess, some unspecified years before 1789.

As the Newest Addition he had to wait last of all for his coffee. Some of the younger ladies flirted heavily with him as he stood in line; jousting along Freudian lines was quite permissible to the wives of teachers:

—That handsome Titian-haired Mr. Hudson! Did you know there's always a pot of coffee on the stove at Our House? ...

—Mr. Guy Hudson! It *is* Guy, isn't it? They tell me you've had fascinating war experiences! Of course the war is over and done with now, and everybody's pretty well fed up with agony. But do drop in *any*time and tell us something of yourself! ...

Murmuring nothings to these ladies, with their bright eyes and nervous wits and calculating mouths, he found himself at last standing before Mrs. Pilkey at the coffee urn. Her eyes were a little bloodshot; she looked petulant and sorry for herself after squirting out seventy demitasses. Her white coronet braids were a dead wreath of snow:

—Speak up, young man! Who *are* you? An alumnus?

—I'm the newest teacher, he said, feeling like an orphan. We met last month, I think. ...

—Of course, of course! Mrs. Pilkey cried. I never forget a face. It's a game I play with everyone. I know *exactly* who you are!

108

Then suddenly the thin vibrating woman leaned toward him, grinned, and patted his hand:

—You shall sit next to *me*, young man.

And then the voice of Philbrick Grimes behind him:

—What an honor, mon vieux! Be *nice* to her. . . .

So Guy Hudson sat down beside the First Lady of The Academy. He sipped his coffee and tried to talk to her. The faculty weren't allowed to smoke at these coffees, for Mr. Pilkey feared that the smell of tobacco would put ideas into the heads of those scholarship boys who were waiters. But Guy Hudson balanced his yellow coffeecup and attempted to seduce the Principal's wife into graciousness:

—I hear you make lovely designs on plates, he said tentatively.

—Gracious, young man! You make me sound like a slavy at a sewing machine.

—The faculty say you're a great artist. . . .

—National Academy, she said gruffly. I don't know how I can do any better than that. . . .

Thus till the end of the constipated coffee he sweat every means at his disposal (and he loved to talk to women) to please this strange hag, with her twisted vivacity and perversity. He felt that she rather liked him, with the hopping tenderness of an old stork, unsure of which foot to stand on. Her glazed eyes said she wanted to be kind, but she didn't know how. She'd spent her life decorating crockery. She misinterpreted everything he said and turned it back on him. She wanted, he believed, to be elegant and sparkling, but there was some inhibition in her tired old mind that tripped her and sent her sprawling into gaucheries that would have made a millwoman blush. He wondered if all old women who were duchesses of schools blundered into this rudeness, a kind of aching Elizabeth-Tudorism. Finally Mrs. Pilkey arose from the coffee table and gave her arm to the Principal, who nodded frostily at Guy Hudson.

—This young man's got a lot to learn, she said. He doesn't know What's What, like most of our faculty. But we shall be happy to teach him any evening at our house, won't we, dearie? . . .

Mr. Pilkey summoned himself out of whatever pregnant design he'd been brooding on ($1,000,000 from the alumni?) and took over in his best strain:

—We like to have our faculty call on us. And we know they love to do it.

—Yes, do come, said Mrs. Pilkey. If I'm busy with my work I'll send you packing.... I'm an honest woman....

As she took his hand, Guy Hudson had a mad desire to bite it or twist it. She wanted so to be human!

—And you have red hair on your wrists, she added. That is offensive to an artist. Look how white Mr. Pilkey's hands are....

Then the Pilkeys went away, attended by Mr. Grimes.

—Sweet Jesus, Guy Hudson thought.

Herman Pilkey, only son to the Principal, stood drinking coffee, one hand caressing the melony breasts of his Georgian wife Nydia. In his intimacy with the whole faculty Herman paraded his exemption and privilege like a fat rind of bacon on the black market. As he toyed with his wife's appurtenances he bawled out a lewd joke at some of the Advanced Younger Ladies of the faculty. They tittered, blushed, and arose, pulling down their tweed skirts:

—Herman Pilkey, you're terrible! We don't know how you get away with it. But you're one helluva dear....

Most of the faculty were withdrawing now. They would go to their apartments, dissect the Pilkeys, and puff themselves blue on long-withheld cigarettes. Cliques sought one another out. Mr. Grimes came back and joined the most advanced of these little clubs. With little cries like a gull at lovemaking he sought out the slim icicle named Mrs. Dell Holly, also known as La Belle Dame Sans Merci. She and he governed a set that discussed drayma, books, and ideas, over sherry. Guy Hudson heard that this set ran the Academy, even to manipulating the Pilkeys.

—It's been *so* long, Mr. Grimes said.

—At least three hours, Philbrick, said the fair Mrs. Holly.

Mr. Grimes replied with his famous snicker and curl of the lip:

—Age cannot wither....

Soon there remained only Guy Hudson and the junior Pilkeys by the coffee table. Nydia Pilkey jiggled her sweatered breasts under Guy Hudson's chest:

—Hon-ey, Humman an me been discussin bout yo-all. Seems lahk you ain't happy heah no-how....

And Herman Pilkey took Guy Hudson's hand in his great

110

wet one, a clutch of raw hamburger:

—Listen, chum. As you probably know, I'm the Old Man's son. But don't you hold that against me. Not that I give a healthy crap. . . . Listen, you look lost here. You won't be able to make your way into any of these little cliques, see? Their doors were closed when Noah fell overboard from the ark, ha-ha. . . . But you come and visit with Nydia and me any time you feel like it. We got a kid and bourbon, but mostly bourbon. Nydia don't drink the stuff; she swims in it. . . . And listen, boy, if you got a belle amie within forty kilometers, why, bring her down too. We got a couch at our house. And during the war when I was a leatherneck, ha-ha, Nydia and me got used to foursomes in hotel bedrooms. Understand, chum? Anything goes at our house. Nydia and me are different from the other clogged arseholes Around Here. Don't trust any of em. . . . Pop's a good old goon once you know how to handle him. Being his son, I'm man enough to try. The rest are scared. . . .

—I may take you up on that, Guy Hudson said.

In spite of all that he'd known and done in his life, he found himself blushing. The picture of himself and some belle amie struggling together on The Couch while Herman and Nydia Pilkey went at it in the bedroom seemed to him sweaty and hammy. And now Herman Pilkey was flinging an arm about his shoulder. He heard Herman's friendly panting, spiced with the smell of macaroni and cheese.

—When, kid? Herman whispered hotly in his ear.

—O soon, Guy Hudson said, disengaging himself.

He hated to touch or be touched except when he intended business.

—Cain't be too soon! Nydia Pilkey gurgled. Hon-ey!

And rolling her breasts and hips, she jellied off with her husband.

As he walked in the quadrangle there ran toward him hundreds of students in revolt and dither; they were just getting out of their School Meeting.

—To hell with the faculty! a boy piped.

Seeing Guy Hudson, he hushed his mouth and turned scarlet:

—Hi, sir.

—Hi, Jones. . . .

Greetings sprang up here and there from those who knew

111

him. He knew. It was noised about that he couldn't be tortured like most new instructors, for he'd learned the ABC of sadism in the army. It was also said that he was horny, having led a less sheltered life than most young teachers. He knew that bets must already have been laid that he was committing adultery with some faculty lady. Adolescents love to think of their teachers as sexual athletes; much of their gossip revolves on this motivation. They forget that in a school like The Academy everybody knows everything everyone else does—even to that first creak of the bedsprings.

Still smiling with his scarred mouth, Guy Hudson ran up to his room, smoked a cigarette, and undressed. His corridor was rumorous with little boys preparing for what they called Sports. Jockstraps lay around; there was the flick of towels as kids filliped one another in sensitive spots. There was a clatter of cleated and spiked shoes, though this was a vandalism forbidden inside the dormitories.

Now it was the duty of every ablebodied male on the faculty, except Mr. Grimes, to do some coaching. Coaching meant that a man taught sportsmanship and the Will to Win every afternoon to a team of boys. The first teams of The Academy, by desire of her alumni, were entrusted to professional experts, but others (since every American boy must take exercise), called intramural or club squads, were chores doled out to all male teachers who were free from lumbago. Mr. Pilkey had announced in the catalog how rare a thing it was to see virile young men *playing with* their students. It encouraged male camaraderie and proved to boys that their teachers weren't just a bunch of bookworms. Mr. Pilkey envisioned something Spartan in his scheme of having all teachers take part in Sports. Privately perhaps it assured him of the masculinity of his faculty and saved untold expense in importing specialists in physical education. Guy Hudson had heard the bookish men on the faculty say that at The Academy your teaching wasn't really too important—what did matter was your ability at calisthenics.

So every afternoon he got into a spotted jersey, old baseball trousers, woolen socks, and cleated shoes. And hanging a whistle round his neck and taking a Spaulding Manual under his arm, he sallied forth to discipline his soccer team—twenty or so boys not good enough for first and second squads. It was called the Pequots. Other teams were known as Sioux,

112

Iroquois, Ojibways, Navajos—and so on through the Indian tribes. Thus at The Academy athletic combat was combined with a firm grounding in American aboriginal history. And every boy was on some team or other all year long, it being unthinkable that an American boy should not want to build up his body for some unspecified martial purpose in the world of the future.

In his loose athletic togs Guy Hudson jogged down toward the athletic fields among a spate of boys dressed for track, for soccer, and for football. The expressions of relief and pugnacity in these students' faces made it clear that this Exercise Period was what they'd really been waiting for all morning long. Some alumni believed that two hours wasn't long enough for the young male to build up his muscles, but play was here as rigidly controlled and regimented as everything else in American education. More virile students came to The Academy solely to play on her teams, get their names on sporting pages, wear letters on their wide chests, and be financed into college by some doting alumnus.

But Guy Hudson, running among them, noticed a few young men of decadent tendencies who were not happy as they rushed out to play in their armor. These, he guessed, were not the sort of boy Mr. Pilkey approved of. They were elegant and a trifle acid; their feminine beauty (or their thick spectacles) indicated that athletic costume sat sadly upon them, or that they felt childish and ridiculous. These held a little off from the other shouting warriors.

—Bessie, this football helmet, said a newly changed voice behind him. I'd like to rip it off and *spit* on it. I was writing the sweetest little cinquain you ever saw. Much too good for The Lit. . . .

—Never you mind, pet, said another, more studied, voice from Bronxville. I'll make it all up to you at teatime. I've a new album of Shostakovich. . . .

As he trotted along on his cleats, he smiled at this winsome exchange. He was too polite to turn his head and discover the identity of these plangent and precious voices. But America had made strides! Fifty years ago these arty children would have been done to death at such an Academy as this. Now, he supposed, they were uneasily tolerated, so long as they made the gesture of masculinity. Perhaps, he thought, Old Pilkey is right after all. They shouldn't be allowed to sit in their rooms all day long. Perhaps here Oscar Fingall O'Flahertie Wilde would have been captain of First Football. . . .

The athletic fields were the most farflung and notable landmarks of The Plant because there were so many of them, spread out like checkerboards or Chinese terrace farms. They were dominated by The Gym, given by a rich family whose sons had been killed in the First World War. Ah, yes, the playing fields of Eton. . . . There must have been twelve of these neatly gardened rectangles; some with football, and some with soccer, goalposts. And across the river Guy Hudson could see the Girls' School taking their exercise, playing softball and field hockey under the eyes of their mistresses. Was Miss Blanchard also coaching this afternoon? Not buxom enough. . . . The sluggish river must have been put there by the chaperoning geography of God, to keep the boys from going over to play in the girls' athletic fields. Shrill cries floated across the river from the girls at their scrimmage. Like a nest of robins fighting for worms.

Guy Hudson ran up to his team the Pequots. He took attendance, gave instruction in kicking, heading, field-running, and aggressiveness. He'd played First Soccer at Amherst, but that was nine years ago. Now he had only a polite enthusiasm. He stood near the goalposts and watched the little men of the Pequot squad play soccer. He was amused. The same personalities that stood out in the classrooms often didn't predominate on an athletic field. Sometimes quite the contrary. Brilliant students tended to be shy and unaggressive in team play. Brittle and clever little boys displayed to the coach's eye a subtle cowardice when combative boys bore down on them to take the ball from under their feet. Strange how, with the shinguards and metal jockstraps and all the armor of American sport, they were scared of having their shins kicked.

—For God's sake, O'Keefe, get in there and rough up that goalie a little!

It was his own voice saying this; he found that on such occasions on a chilly October field his shout was as raucous and bloodthirsty as a trainer's at the Y.

—But, sir! He *fouled* me!

Watching the play with an Olympian eye, he sometimes shrilled on the pompous little whistle that hung round his neck. For two hours this miniature slaughter went on, enclosed in a sixty-yard field. Gentle boys went to the infirmary for split shins and minor mayhems. But on adjacent football fields the wounds were even more serious. A crutch was a badge of dignity in the Fall Term at The Academy. When his own team of Pequots took a breather, Guy Hudson would watch the scrimmages going on in nearby football fields. He heard the crack of shoulderpads on hip pads; the delicious grunt of lineman against the proverbial inertia. These football Martians in their outrageous padded uniforms seemed to him the realized essence of the American Dream of Man—conflict well padded, and carnage politely enclosed on a gridiron. The grunts of the football men carried even over the screaming of the girls at their exercise across the river.

At four thirty o'clock the redheaded coach blew his whistle. And whistles were shrilling up from other fields too, except where First Football was practicing. By dispensation to sheer masculinity, and by insistence of the alumni, first teams practiced till darkness dropped. It didn't matter whether the warriors were exhausted and groggy till the season's end; the important thing was that each Saturday they must win games and put The Academy on the sporting pages. For that, after all, was the final index to the rating of an American school.

Guy Hudson and his soccer team of Pequots plodded toward The Gym. Everybody was tired, sweaty, and completely happy—except for those few elegants who played soccer because they had to do something; and it was a little less rough than football.

—Gee, sir, his fullback said, tottering beside him. Maybe in another year you won't have to carry your Spaulding Manual with you. . . .

—I'm waiting for that, Murphy. I study it every night. . . .

—Well, gee, sir, I'm not criticizing. It's just that you don't *enter in,* like other coaches do. . . .

Guy Hudson smiled and put a tongue in his cheek. He always chewed gum while coaching because it gave him a determined air. Now he spat it out and thought of the perspicacity of these children. You couldn't fool them. They saw everything. He knew the reservations they made in judging him. What they wanted—and what their parents

115

wanted—was a gee who entertained them in the classroom, who wasn't too tough a marker, who spoonfed them for the College Board Examinations, and who entered into their games with fervor. With detachment, scholarship, dedication, and solitary passion they tried to have as little truck as possible. But at twenty-nine he'd put an abyss between himself and these boys. He wished it so. He wasn't the sort of teacher who would ever be seen on the grass wrestling with his students.

The closest physical contact between faculty and students came in the shower rooms, where coaches and their teams boiled themselves out of their sweat and grime in tiled atria echoing with shouts and dewy with scalding water. Somehow he disliked the intimacy and the implication of democratic equality while he waited in soapsuds as a sixteen-year-old stood under the stinging needles, dousing his own body. Finally the boy would step out and he would step in.

—O hi, sir. Didn't know it was you waiting. Sorry to take so long.

In the enforced contacts of the army he'd developed all sorts of priestly tabus about being thrown with other men. To be seen naked by his students in the Turkish bath of the shower room was something offensive to him. It seemed more a Roman than a Christian laving, this elbowing of young bodies in the anonymity of steam and darkness. And newly matured boys would appraise everything he owned, sizing up his muscles and his maleness. Later that evening over their books, roommate would say to roommate:

—God, Hudson's as hairy as Esau. Got a neat build, though. Musta taken a course with Charles Atlas. . . .

He noticed too the epicureanism with which most students took their showers. They sopped up steam until they reeled dizzy and enervated. Perhaps a scalding shower followed by an icy douche was for them a sublimation of sex. Nevertheless he felt a certain malaise to have his own lean brown body, that had known love and war and death, weaving under a shower between white new ones, lately come into manhood. He remembered in his own function as a teacher that children must not look upon the nakedness of their fathers.

So he took a quick thorough shower, thinking more intricate thoughts than the other coaches, who would be getting home to their wives and their newspapers and their dinners. Then he walked up the gravel path from The Gym, wearing only a white twill bathrobe and his soccer shoes. The October twilight nipped at his bare calves. His soiled coaching clothes he carried tucked under his arm.

Students were on their way to afternoon classes, *post coitum tristes,* a little sad that the joys of physical expression were over. They were busy licking icecream cones and gnawing candy bars and cupcakes which they bought from a Good Humor man at the entrance to the quadrangle. After Europe Guy Hudson hated to see children nibbling sweets in public. He could never think of American boys without remembering that they loved Sports and ate constantly.

In his room he dressed and smoked a cigarette. He knotted his necktie and glanced at the pile of papers on his desk. These had to be corrected, but his lazy wellbeing impelled him to go visiting before dinner. Where? He had no friends on the faculty, and something told him that his solitude and bitterness would never permit his having any. He couldn't let this place become his life and his soul, as it had become to the rest of the faculty, since they'd sold themselves to Miss Sophia for the security of her salaries.

Then he decided in a burst of boldness and orneriness to call at that faculty house which was the Smart Set of the quadrangle, the salon ruled over by Mr. Grimes and the slim woman Mrs. Dell Holly. He thought he might enjoy their discomfort at the appearance of an outsider. He was curious also to learn everything about this Academy—especially by what rule one group of people sets itself off from all others, draws a circle about itself, and proclaims: We are the Saints and the Comedians.

So he left his room and walked across the chilling quadrangle, knocking on a certain door to a faculty house. It opened almost at once. Out came Ralph Du Bouchet, carrying a notebook. He was thrown offguard to meet this boy, who looked at him coolly, and, it seemed, a little knowingly.

—O, do you belong to the Inner Circle?

—Not for me, Ralph said, holding open the door. But they're all in there now, drinking sherry. . . . I sit with the kids for fifty cents an hour. . . . That's the union wage for baby sitters here, you know. . . .

Ralph went away into the October twilight. Guy Hudson tasted the reproach in his tone.

Mrs. Dell Holly greeted him. She extended her cool bony hand in a gesture of disdainful welcome. She was beautiful in a frosty and calculating way. A Lord & Taylor teagown accentuated her figure, unblemished from three childbirths. Her manner insisted that she belonged to a class more tony and leisurely than that of a schoolteacher's wife. Her laughter was a little spray of needles. She was pretending to laugh at the folly of the world. But he sensed also a certain chagrin at herself, which she would never understand and would resent having made manifest to her. There was no pleasure in her clasp; she gave her hand as an unwilling and sneering hostage:

—You're Mister . . . Hudson? How *nice* of you to come. So few of the faculty take us up on our invitations. For some reason or other there's a propaganda abroad that we are . . . well . . . rather stand-offish. It takes a brash new faculty member to overcome such sabotage, *doesn't* it! . . . Step in, please. A group of old friends are having a little sherry before dinner. Mr. and Mrs. Pilkey don't approve, but we do it anyhow. I think it makes a lovely little pause in the late afternoon. . . . Most of the faculty serve coffee because they can't afford sherry. But that simply puts them in the class with Mamie Mullins, doesn't it? When you come to think of it, there's so little that's truly distinguished Around Here. And while *we* aren't poseurs, we like to think we know how to live. . . .

The lovely creature in flesh and silk said all this without pausing for breath. It came out in a bored alto, as though she was relating a visit to a polo game which had failed to please her sensibilities. He felt that she was lashing him in a ladylike manner with all her little resentments. Following her scented wake and the swirl of her skirt (she seemed to have a board for a spine) he passed a nursery where three lovely little girls, the image of their mother, were solemnly and primly playing with blocks and a tricycle.

—O Mummy, one said.

—Not now, not now, dear, said Mrs. Dell Holly. Remember our *agreement*. . . .

At the door to her living room, she whirled again; even

118

her skirt seemed to be trained to eddy and settle according to a plan:

—Everyone is here, Mr. Hudson. That is, everyone who ever Had An Idea. . . .

As he entered, a trickle of unpleasant conversation was stifled. He knew at once that he was intruding. They didn't want him at all, for they'd been airing their souls in epigrams and mutual admiration.

—Surprise, surprise, the fair hostess called to her salon.

But her tone of voice was that repressed horror with which she would call the chief of police and report finding an abortion on her doorstep.

The salon sat around a bare living room that was supposed to be sleek and functional. They were all smoking and sipping sherry out of Smart Little Glasses. With liquid venom Lisa Holly introduced him around. She gave him to understand that he was nobody, but she would be quite happy to sponsor him in civilized society if he'd watch his manners.

—Doctor! Mr. Philbrick Grimes said, breaking off a narrative. This is the *only* house on campus. . . .

—No, there are other houses, Lisa Holly said. But in them the ladies do their own work because they're too *mean* to pay an accommodator. And all they talk about is the price of *food*. . . .

There were present Lisa Holly's husband Dell (his true name Adelbert, shortened by her because it sounded so chic) who was in charge of Alumni and Testing at the Academy. He was a tall thin earnest man, pockmarked and platitudinous. He seemed to have been bitten about the soul by his beautiful wife. At every tentative thing Dell Holly said she shot an arrow out of her gray eyes as though to say she would settle *him* later.

There was, of course, Mr. Philbrick Grimes, the intellectual moderator of all good conversation.

There were a gentleman and lady of the faculty whom Guy Hudson had never seen before. He was a teacher of advanced math, and puttered dreamily to himself about the ultimate reality of mathematics. No one listened. His wife was the powerhouse of the League of Women Voters (Republican) and played with political ideas as with jewels. She was dressed like something out of Siena in 1299.

Then there was also Mrs. Launcelot Miller, a pimply

faced lady of no age who announced she'd just given herself a permanent with a new two-dollar liquid. Her hair looked like French fried potatoes before the grease is drained. She wore a sweater suit, never listened to what was said, but took out of her mouth a smoking corncob pipe to insult whoever said it. She said she painted On The Sly.

Guy Hudson sat down uneasily, lit a cigarette, drank his sherry, and listened. They veiledly ridiculed other members of the faculty, reciting little limericks and referring to them by code names. They even trampled on the Pilkeys, though Guy Hudson knew that this was the circle which manipulated the Principal. And Lisa Holly nodded her head in sneering approval, dropped aphorisms which she'd been rehearsing to herself all day, and served sherry, though he noticed that she refrained a niggardly fifteen minutes before refilling an empty glass.

But they all admired one another tremendously; each was unique in his or her field. After them there would be no Brilliant Conversation left in the world. Sometimes Lisa Holly's three little girls peeked into the room and were shooed away to their supper by the icy alto of their mother. Mr. Grimes recounted the exhaustions of his day, diffidently insisting that he was only a cog in a great school.

Guy Hudson fatigued rapidly with their persiflage. They seemed to be attempting to stiletto one another out of boredom. In their talk he heard no happiness, no peace, no play of reason. Each had an attitude which he or she struck as insistently as a tuning fork. Then the pimply lady with the corncob pipe reached over and took his hand for an instant:

—Don't forget me. Mrs. Launcelot Miller. I too have a salon. Not so brilliant as this, of course. We need these little gatherings to keep out of *ruts*. . . .

—All of society, said Mr. Grimes, boils down to those one goes to the movies with, and those one doesn't. . . .

—I read something like that in the latest *New Yorker*, Lisa Holly said.

But Philbrick Grimes shut her off to relate what John Gielgud had told him backstage. They listened and agreed that Mr. Grimes was a mousetrap for all sorts of interesting lore.

—You *can't* go wrong here, said Mrs. Lancelot Miller,

bending her rugose face toward Guy Hudson's.

Then she told him she was sterile and treated him to all the arid intimacies between herself and her husband. She said she didn't know whose fault it was she couldn't have babies. She spoke in a hideous whisper, like a little girl in confession to a deaf priest.

—Mr. Hudson hasn't said a word, the hostess said, laughing sharply.

—They never do, Mr. Grimes said. Not till they've been here ten years. Then you can't shut them up. . . .

Guy Hudson wondered what The Circle said of each other when they weren't together. He could guess. There was no person in this room who could ever be trusted. But he watched their spastic and guarded love. For such is the palsy of closed little clubs.

That evening about ten he sat in his chilly room, mobilizing himself to correct the papers which had come in during his morning classes. He'd told himself that this going-over papers with a blue pencil was almost a touchstone of a good teacher. Yet Mr. Pilkey in the regimen of his Academy had arranged it (perhaps intentionally) so that teachers would have little leisure in which to grade their papers. Consequently they did it, if they did it at all, after the Boys' and Girls' Schools had gone to bed. When all other workers—janitors, doctors, lawyers—might devote themselves to some pleasure, the teacher must settle down to that solitary work which is characteristic of him alone: the penciling and the rages and the despairs of anyone who truly tries to teach a class.

Guy Hudson insisted to himself that this paperwork was a stimulus and a check to any honest teacher. He prepared his classes; then he stood before them and gave them the hypodermic of his own personality. Then to see whether the shot was positive or negative, he gave them daily written work. The quiz. What had been written in ignorance or wisdom on these small sheets of ragstock was the measure of what he'd accomplished. They hated these daily tests. He hated them too. But he thought it was as necessary to his job as sharpening a pencil or bandaging a cut.

And now his corridor of lowerformers was going to bed. He sat in his chair under the reading lamp and listened to the welter of boys taking their last showers of the day, fuss-

121

ing with one another, screaming out in unchanged voices their own brand of watered-down obscenities, hitting one another with pillows. There was something lonely in their boisterousness. Perhaps what these little boys—no longer children, not yet men—really wanted was to be home with their mothers. Yet these same mothers were hundreds of miles away, settling down to another rubber of bridge, or ordering another Alexander at the country club, secure in the conviction (if they worried about it at all) that their offspring were being tucked in bed by those foster mothers, male and female, who are also incidentally teachers in their spare time. He smiled. He would have scoffed as a second lieutenant of infantry. He too was a mother, a dry one, with neither milk nor comfort for these children of other people, who would never thank him nor understand what he was trying to do for the sons whom they themselves were too lazy or too rich or too neurotic to discipline. The American school supplements the American home, Mr. Pilkey had announced in his catalog. But after a month of teaching Guy Hudson wondered if there was any such entity as the American home, or whether the schools of America were trying to do everything that the home should, but didn't, do.

He smiled to hear these little boys calling each other by their last names and threatening each other like gangsters in the movies. Poor little kids! They believed themselves mature! Their lives were bounded by sailing in the summers, by their fathers' incomes, and by their own view of life, which was to adore the big athletic heroes of the school and bide their time till they too should come into the upper hierarchy of The Academy. Little Men! ...

—Pierpont, get the hell out of my closet. ...

—Didja see the first team scrimmage this afternoon? Cripes!

The lights on his corridor were turned out every evening at ten by a master switch from the powerhouse. In the catalog Mr. Pilkey boasted that lowerformers got nine healthful hours of sleep every night, and they would awaken at seven the next morning refreshed for a new day of Christian energy. It also saved electricity. But the final ritual of the evening was the rounds of the Student Council, coming like bellmen to see that lowerformers were in their beds. This was one of the responsibilities of Student Government, and they carried if off with a mixture of cynicism and tenderness toward the little boys, who lay rigid in their cots waiting to be wished Goodnight by those who were already men.

There was a tap at his door.

—Come in, Guy Hudson said.

The President of the Council stood smiling on the threshold; he wore a heavy bathrobe; there was a numeral cap askew on his dark face. The young Jew looked at him wistfully; Guy Hudson again felt like wanting to cry for no good reason.

—Do you want help in your work, Ben? he said.

—No, sir. . . I thought you might like to be wished a goodnight too. . . .

—Thank you.

The door shut, and he fell to brooding on what makes the difference between the sweetness of real human beings and the jangling of phonies. There was plenty of both here. Where did the wonderful kindness and dignity of a Ben Gordon come from? And where the inscrutable excellence of a Ralph Du Bouchet? It was all the more moving because they were on the threshold of their lives, which could never possibly be worthy of them.

He cut off his thoughts. Must be the frost of an October night. Down the corridor he heard unchanged voices replying to greetings of the older Councillors; he heard those almost-soprani trying to hide their worship of the eighteen- and nineteen-year-olds making the rounds:

—Night now, Pierpont. Don't let the bedbugs bite. . . .

—Gee, Ben! You were neat today! . . . the way you carried that ball. . . .

—Ah, skip it and drop dead. . . .

Then the corridor quieted by degrees, as though a blanket had been drawn between Guy Hudson and all sound. Ben and the other Councillors went downstairs, jesting to one another in an intimate and masculine manner:

—This babe named Fay writes to me today, see? . . . I'm slippin the green banana to three at once. Broth-er. . . .

And the soft voice of Ben Gordon:

—I've got a jug of cider freezing on my windowsill. . . .

Then Guy Hudson, his stack of papers still in his lap, sat listening to the little boys going to sleep, turning in their sheets, which were coarse and longwearing because they

123

were bought by the Comptroller. He noted the rustle of a boy turning in his cot. He believed he heard a muted sobbing from a notorious one who was always homesick and took out his longing in nightly bed-wetting. And through the thin walls he heard a chuckle, as of two boys initiating a third into mysteries untaught him by his mother, now seven hundred miles away.

—I'm gonna cover my ears with my blanket, a protesting whisper said.

—Sissseeee! Ho-mo! another voice said, on the grating change between childhood and puberty.

He was aware of a longing and a plaintiveness riding the still October evening. There was the soughing of thirty or forty forms wrestling with their bedclothing. And now and then the suspect rhythmic creaking of an Academy cot, pausing in its beat to ascertain who was listening to its clandestine enjoyment.

Here maternity was impersonal and vested in extensions of the personality of Mr. Pilkey. At an age when they were still attached to the umbilicus, most of these boys had a need for something they couldn't frame in words. Was it for their fathers, thinking of their next day's forays in factory and office? Or was it for their mothers, to come and kiss them goodnight? Guy Hudson didn't know. But he did know of an emptiness and indefinable pain (such as Mr. Pilkey or Mr. Grimes would never have admitted) which might make for trouble as the school year piled up in tension. He knew that the collective energy of these students would wax strident because it had no real outlet—only books and athletic fields.

—This place is a combination prison, library, and gymnasium, he said, and took up his papers.

Then for many minutes he gave himself up to that peculiar introverted mystery known only to teachers and proofreaders.

Finally he threw down his blue pencil and stared malevolently at the scrawled follies in his lap.

—What in the name of hell am I doing here? What has all this got to do with anything? . . .

There was a kick on his door, which flew open. He jumped to his feet, holding his papers in both hands. In the aureole from his reading lamp stood that blond god from European

History 2a, smiling and bowing to his teacher in a broth of deference and arrogance.

—Hi, Buddy Brown said.

Guy Hudson throttled an impulse to walk over and kick the boy, who was wearing a yellow lounging robe, figured pajamas, and sheepskin slippers.

—Brown, he said quietly. I didn't hear you knock. Get out and enter properly. . . .

—Gee, sir, I had an idea you were different from the rest of the stuffed shirts Around Here.

—Did you hear what I said, Brown?

The boy paled in a sickening but not humble manner and retired.

There was a gentle knock, and Buddy's head reappeared prehensilely around the edge of the door. He had now shifted to the Coy Approach, which to Guy Hudson's undeceived eye was as revolting as a parrot playing peekaboo with an old biddy.

—Is that better, sir? Buddy said, gliding into the room.

His voice drawled insidiously over the *sir*. Guy Hudson thought of taking one of the fencing sabers over his fireplace and lathering the kid's shoulders. But then he sat down by his papers. He tried to keep from clenching his hands so that this eighteen-year-old might not see the force of his fury.

—May I sit down now, sir? Buddy Brown said, half-closing his eyes.

This purring froze Guy Hudson. Instinctively he knew that Buddy was a swaggering turd with boys his own age, and a bully to younger ones.

—Yes, if you park your gum. . . .

Buddy removed a wad that bulged his cheek, placed it behind his ear, sighed, and sank into a stiff chair opposite the easy one in which Guy Hudson sat. Then he proceeded to accommodate himself in this seat in much the manner of a gorgeous model touching herself up for a photographer. The reading light spangled his blond close hair. His pajamas fell open at the throat, baring the glassy whiteness of his fine big chest. And he raised one of his thighs, delineated in his tight silk pajamas, until his knee was two inches away from his teacher's. There it swayed softly up and down, like a bough in the wind. Guy Hudson moved his own knee; he'd passed now into the glacial stage.

125

—Make it snappy, Brown, he said, oscillating his blue pencil like a metronome. I'm doing papers.

—Look, sir, Buddy said, smoothing his thigh. I just don't *get* this history stuff. . . .

—Then what right have you to call it stuff?

—Anything you say, sir. . . . But I thought from what you said in class that you were always willing to give extra help.

—I can always be found at Availability Time . . . by those who first try honestly to do their work themselves.

Two tears sprang into the brilliant blue eyes:

—But I *do* do it, sir! Two hours a day. Honest to Christ! . . . I thought that if I came up here for a little session every evening, you could. . . .

—The tutoring charge is three dollars an hour, Guy Hudson said.

—Well, gee, I guess my dad can afford that! But that isn't just what I mean, sir . . . I just thought . . . maybe . . . we could visit together each night after your corridor goes to bed . . . and you could sorta *hint* to me what tomorrow's test will be on . . . Look, sir, I'm slow at books. I was cut out to be an ath-a-lete. But I remember anything anybody tells me. . . .

That knee came so close that Guy Hudson stood quickly up. He got a feeling of relief from oppression to be towering over this boy, who looked up at him in violated innocence. Then Buddy Brown's voice came forth in a stylized whine, one he must have practiced since babyhood:

—Christ, sir . . . I hate to say this to you cause you'll say I'm brown-nosin. . . . But I said to myself that you're the only teacher I can talk to Around Here. . . . I know what you did in the army, sir. You're different from most of the fairies they've got on this faculty. . . . I thought maybe you and me could be friends . . . real friends. . . . Listen. I know what the score is. When I'm not at this dump, don't think for a minute I spend my time readin Shakspere. No, sir! I may be only eighteen. But I bet I know a lot of the things *you* know. . . .

Guy Hudson often dreamt of the niceties of seduction. It was one of his favorite fantasies on lying abed in the morning when he had no one sleeping beside him. In Europe he'd become expert at them. In seductions, mental and physical, you had to play all at once the serpent, the toad, the lion, and the turtle-dove. But what was going on here in the name of scholarship was quite the most epicene thing he'd seen yet. The muted voice of Buddy, the stagy sprawl in the chair, the pajamaed body—all sickened him. He felt as though lizards were running up and down his spine. And again he had an impulse—this time to slap the no-good and handsome boy across the face. But then in a certain sense he would have capitulated, and Buddy would leer like a crayfish every time they met.

—Brown, he said, get out. Go to your dormitory and open your history book. And God help you if you're unprepared in class tomorrow.

Buddy rose slowly from the stiff chair. The sleazy pajamas rustled into place about his body. He buttoned his tunic, modestly averting his eyes, which were streaming with tears. His sobs were soundless. And Guy Hudson remembered the hysteria of a young SS captain at Bolzano in April, 1945. For an instant he paused on the slippery course of his anger and disgust.

As a teacher what was he doing to this boy? Were these tears perhaps real? Was he perhaps closing forever some chink in the handsome hard boy's armor, which might have been vulnerable to himself alone? Was he perhaps already so cynical that he'd mistaken and treated roughly that honest cry for help, to which a good teacher is ever susceptible? He was on the brink of relenting and pressing Buddy Brown's shoulder when the boy sniveled again:

—Gee, sir . . . I never expected this of you, of all people. . . .

Then Guy Hudson stiffened and froze forever; he wasn't mistaken.

—Brown, I consider you the pimple on the arse of this school.

The boy, padding in his sheepskin slippers, head bowed, sniffled his way out the door, leaving it open. He continued down the stairs till he was lost to Guy Hudson's eyes and ears. Finally the teacher sat down again to his papers. But for five minutes he couldn't lift the blue pencil. Something obscure was working within him, that he didn't wholly understand because he was afraid to. Presently he laid down pencil and papers and went to his closet. He took out the pornographic etching he'd looted from Berchtesgaden. He looked at it critically. This picture had always amused and excited him and his army friends. And examining it from several angles he discovered what he had imagined—in the tangle of three bodies writhing together, one of the faces was a blond man, horribly distorted with his bipartite delights. And it was like the face of Buddy Brown snorting and crying.

—O my God, he said, setting down the etching on his desk.

Hearing a noise, he looked through the reading light to the illuminated door. There stood the faunlike boy Ralph, carrying his history book. He too wore pajamas, but they were cheap cotton ones. On his feet were scuffed moccasins. His calm black eyes went from his teacher's face to the large etching in his hands. At the distance between them every detail of the three naked bodies was apparent to him. A surge of cringing sheepishness swept up through Guy Hudson. He felt as though he himself had been surprised in the flagrant madness this picture detailed. He flushed. But he also refused to turn it over, as most men would have done. An idiotic question burbled from his twisted mouth:

—You wanted to see me, Ralph?

—I guess you're busy. Tomorrow morning maybe, at Availability Time. . . .

The slender boy turned in the doorway to go. He seemed to move in a dignified and restrained sadness, rare in one who was of the same generation as Buddy Brown. And though Guy Hudson wouldn't have cared for any student or faculty member to see the etching, a fever of affinity and kinship made him loathe himself that Ralph had been the one to see it. For of all the Boys' School there was something between himself and Ralph that had leaped like a spark across the gap he'd set up as a teacher. And now that crackling void had been blotted out forever. Ralph *knew*. Guy Hudson's regret was a sheet of scarlet. Something in both him and this boy had been wedded and divorced by the ring of this pornographic picture. Perhaps now they saw themselves as one and the same—Adam and seraph, both together and apart.

—I stole this in Germany three years ago, he muttered.

—I thought there was something nazi about it, Ralph said quietly. . . . Goodnight. . . .

Then he turned and skipped softly downstairs. Guy Hudson picked up his noisome treasure and laid it away in the closet.

6

At The Academy the fall weather deepened and purpled and coldened in October and November. The damp green fields turned to rust and rime; every morning there was a caul of frost on the grass; pumpkins stood stacked in rows like heads after a cold guillotine. And Ralph Du Bouchet continued to share the double room on the floor of Hooker Hall with Buddy Brown. In two months the hostility between them muted into a cool defiance, a surface-tense film of hatred almost cherished, like that of two cellmates doing a life stretch together. Ralph had taken down the barrier of darning thread that separated his part of the room from Buddy Brown's. Yet their respective zones of occupation were plainly demarcated by the effluvial deposits of their personalities. The room was still split diagonally, like those rooms in House of Fun which are painted in two colors to bemuse and dizzy the spectator.

Buddy Brown's area was streaked with banners and glossy prints of pinup girls, openly offering their charms, since these were made impregnable by the separation of the camera. Lying around too there were mouldy jockstraps and wet towels, unmated pairs of shoes, pieces of football equipment, pointless signs of prohibition from lavatories and railway stations, and a radio-phonograph combination as blatantly enameled as a jukebox, with piled chipped discs of canonical hot jazz.

Ralph's bed was pushed into the opposite corner; it had a virginal air, as though it was never unmade or slept in. Near it leaned his violin case, a plain table he used as a desk, the closet containing his few clothes. He usually dressed in slacks and a worn green coat of velveteen. Whereas Buddy had eleven suits of clothes and odd jackets of plaid

129

and pastel colors which called attention to themselves by their trick collars and calculated negligence. The schoolbooks on Ralph's table had often been touched with the sifting reverence of an intense and good student. Buddy Brown's were always leaning against one another like fraternity drunks. Over Ralph's bed were a Picasso reproduction and a photo of his mother looking tired and imploring. These were all the things he owned in this world.

These November mornings he awoke in frosty air before the first rising bell pealed. He slept only in pajama trousers; the cold air struck his nude chest with a sensuous pleasure that only Spartans know. He'd lie in bed for a while, one arm under his head, trying to finish a dream he'd been dreaming. And he knew with his sly smile that this passionate dream had wrought a physical reaction on his new manhood, for his bed was swampy. Ralph lay there in the relaxed contentment of subconscious expenditure, yawned, and thought of the Biblical story of virile waste. And he tried to reconstruct the details of his dream that had awakened him to a tremulous climax. He looked over at Buddy Brown's bed. His roommate still slept snoringly, blond hair matted, a trickle of saliva dribbling down his jaw to the pillow. Then Ralph got out of his cot and shut the window; it was the one service he would perform for his roommate. Outside on the quadrangle the sun was brilliant; the hoarfrost looked like a brocade. Then the bell in the corridor outside rang, and Buddy started up in bed as though he was a child screaming out of a nightmare:

—Sonofabitch! . . .

—That's the only morning prayer you know, Ralph said.

Then Buddy Brown looked at the moist map on his roommate's pajamas:

—Boy, you have em so often . . . nearly every night. . . .

—Vissi d'arte, vissi d'amore, Ralph said.

—The hell you say, Buddy said, rubbing his eyes and scrabbling about for his drawers.

While Ralph dressed quietly and dreamily, Buddy blundered about the room, cursing for the whereabouts of his clothes. Upon awaking he was always sullen and hazy, as he was loud and profane later in the day. In the course of their weird marriage Ralph thought of some ten years hence, when Buddy would be living with some girl infatuated by his good looks. Then she too would be doomed to these cold surly awakenings which the roommate already knew too well. She would beseech her husband to return to bed, and he would repulse her with an oath.

—I'm going to allow you to bring me two cups of coffee, Buddy said.

—Thank God I'm not waiting on *your* table.

Scholarship boys arrived early at the dining hall to eat their breakfasts before they waited on the richer fellows. In the pantry Ralph buttoned on the white coat that was the sterilized livery of his embarrassment and servitude. Then he sat down with the other menials and ate his cornflakes and milk. The dishes were cold, the cereal was cold, and the milk bottle clotted with cold sweat. The other scholarship boys took advantage of their slavery (there were no faculty in the dining room yet) to act like gardeners or grooms at a swill bucket. They cursed at one another in the confraternity of galley slaves, for they were outcasts in this aristocratic-democratic setup. Mr. Pilkey in his catalog had never described these ribald breakfasts of the scholarship waiters. They pushed one another hoarsely as they sat eating; they spilled milk and snickered hoarsely. Ralph alone ate silently, hunched a little unto himself. Other waiters nudged him and tried to draw him into their play.

—Smatta, Paganini? Get outa the wrong side of the bed?

They believed that he considered himself above them, though he was of their level. He too was poor. It wasn't just being a scholarship boy that caused him an acute malaise when he was with the other waiters. It was the knowledge that he lacked the tough-grained extroversion to clown like them and thumb his nose at a hypocritical system that called itself an educational democracy, a classless society. It was the knowledge that he, one of the few at The Academy, had every qualification for what she offered her students in her catalog. Education was his birthright, and he was earning it by wearing a white starched coat and carrying trays and setting out food before other eighteen-year-olds. Their fathers were rich; his was not. Thus especially at meals he burned with a cold abhorrent fire.

—Paganini's thinkin, one of the waiters called. Bet he had a dream. . . .

131

—He always has em, another waiter said, who had once wooed Ralph without success.

Paganini. They seized on a trait and let it stand for the whole. They'd heard that Paganini played a violin; so he was Paganini.

When the slavish business of carrying on trays and mopping up the dining hall when the swine had charged out after breakfast, leaving cornflakes all over the cork floor, was done, Ralph hung up his white coat for another five hours. In the pantry by the dishwashing machine the dietitian was cussing out her husband, the chef, in Polish. On duty she wore (by order of Mr. Whitney) a white prophylactic uniform like a trained nurse's; her hair was done up in a bandeau. She stopped eating out her spouse when she saw Ralph, and called him over to make the Old Man jealous. Each mealtime Ralph had to go through this farce of desire, for every year the chef's wife had her favorite among the waiters; and this year he was it. She ran her hands through his hair and sometimes tugged his slender body to her meaty one, kissing him about his neck. This process, like coition with a raw steak, excited and revolted him at the same time. Was it this Polish slut of whom he'd dreamed this morning?

—You're going to make some woman mighty happy, darlin, Mrs. Miekiewicz said.

And the chef, seeing his wife and Ralph swaying in an embrace comic and lecherous, waved his meatcleaver at them:

—You hunky whore! Robbin the cradle!

She screamed back:

—The kid's more of a man than you are! Come over here and feel. . . . Then Mrs. Miekiewicz called after Ralph:

—I'll give you somethin nice in the root-cellar after lunch!

His cheeks blazing and his blood excited, he went back to his room to make up his bed and sweep. Buddy Brown lay on his cot, popping bubblegum and reading a comic book. He paid a little lowerformer fifty cents a week to do his housekeeping, and now this worshipping and frightened kid was furtively wielding a broom and mop. Every so often Buddy, without looking up from his Superman, would give him a kick to hurry up. He called this Keeping Underclassmen in Line.

—Got any you-know-what yet? Buddy Brown said to the kid.

—No sir, the kid said blushing.

Well you just keep working on it. . . .

While he made his own bed and swept, Ralph looked out of the corner of his eye at this plump pink little boy bustling about his master's business. And he wondered why he himself seemed so unpredatory, compared to everybody else.

In the nonsectarian chapel upperformers were privileged to sit in the rear pews. Perhaps by this Mr. Pilkey meant to imply that those graduating in June would soon be out of the clutches of religion. They were ranged in alphabetical order, as though worship was a bureaucratic thing. Ralph sat beside a fat-thighed boy named Desmond, who drew moving pictures in the margins of his hymnbook throughout the service. The upperclassmen sat at rigid attention, or else assumed the bored militancy of those who have just discovered that they are atheists and are subtly broadcasting the fact. These refused to bow their heads during prayers—except when they saw the gray eye of Mr. Pilkey peering at them from the rostrum. Then their heads went down as from a samurai's sword. At eighteen Ralph saw through the flimsy fabric of passive resistance. He knew how few schoolboys (or maturer individuals) would dare to stand alone in the pinch.

He hated The Academy chapel services. It wasn't that he was irreligious, for he took out much of his spirituality in his violin, his books, his flushed dreamings of a distant love-to-be. But he found the worship of God irrelevant to readings from Scripture by unctuous voices. And all this was supposed to derive momentum from nineteenth century hymns about blacksmiths and striving from morn till even. (Who indeed wouldn't strive for something he really wanted?) Ralph, listening to the new baritones and monotones of the upperformers and the shamed treble of the lowerformers knew that there was nothing here they really desired. It was an interlude their parents had prescribed.

Now began a morning of classes which Ralph, almost unique among the four hundred in the Boys' School, loved, as most people love games or the theater. He relished learning from the voice of a teacher and from books. Each day of merely *learning* something was a deep adventure to him.

Sometimes he laughed and told himself that he was unnatural, for American boys are supposed to hate school. They followed a pattern of Redblooded Masculinity, set up by traditions of hookey and Mark Twain. But he had no resistance whatever to his studies. He took them supine and with gusto, with the receptivity of a girl whose desires have been aroused by loving blandishment. Those four or five times a morning when he entered a classroom, he got a fuzzy thrill like a low voltage shock. Yet he was free from any banal desire for Self-Improvement, such as immigrants and clubwomen know. He knew that the things he heard in the classroom were His Meat; he absorbed them effortlessly, and with an almost holy joy of recognition, as though a curtain was being rung back on something he'd known dimly since his birth. School certified his intuition.

Thus, without sycophancy or girlish eagerness, he was Teacher's Pet of the Boys' School. He would sit in every class, his legs crossed relaxedly, his notebook open, running his tongue over his lips, his black eyes shining. They never left the face of the teacher. He was never the little smarty-pants; he didn't laugh too hard at Teacher's stories. Yet nearly everything struck some chord in him. Rarely did he volunteer an answer; but when called on he would answer perfectly in his low hesitant voice. Even other students didn't resent him, for he was always ready to do their homework for them. Nor did he ever laugh in a superior way at their mistakes.

—That Paganini is a genius. We'll hear from him. . . .

And Ralph, when he thought about it at all, guessed it was because his brain lay open like a sunrise to anything new. Besides having an almost flawless memory, he thought more than eighteen-year-olds do. His reasoning and power of relating things was as logical as the bubble in a plumb-level. Only in class did he ever forget the poverty of his mother and father, the ignominious white jacket he wore as a waiter, and the ugliness of spirit he noticed in boys at The Academy. They played with vice, sticking a toe into an icy bath. But these memories vanished in learning. Ralph thought everything in life worth knowing.

In class he seemed to be watching a didactic comedy. Nothing that his teachers did escaped him. He saw all their tricks, as sharp eyes see the wires that pull a puppet. In class he was visited with a kind of clairvoyance: his brain, better than that of the men who taught him, called all their shots. Yet his humility thanked them for showing him certain things.

There was the English class of Mr. Philbrick Grimes, who, as all but the literalminded knew, was Mr. Pilkey's white-haired boy. But Mr. Grimes was an excellent teacher for all but those who saw through him and his mechanics. He would frisk into the room like a braked mouse, wriggle his hairy wrists, and at once proceed to do with the class exactly as he pleased. They were like tame birds; the nervous little man had them hopping up and down in his palm. Only Ralph didn't suffer himself to be fastened on the jess; he soared beyond Mr. Grimes. The cynicism of this English teacher seemed the bitter tea of one who has never really known life except from books. Mr. Grimes's great moments in class were full of a sophisticated idiocy. Cocking an eye on his class, he no doubt believed himself superior to any boy in it:

—Gentlemen, gentlemen! Think of the unhappy plight of Othello! Imagine yourselves a muscular Negro, married to a lovely blonde Venetian . . . babe. . . .

Or there were the clammy classes of Doctor Sour, the plump head of the French Department. Ralph found them experiments in eschatology, as well as firm groundings in the limpid tongue of Paris. The upperformers, who knew more than they guessed, called Doctor Sour Auntie, but Ralph savored him the way he would a ripe oyster. Doctor Sour was fifty, fat, and unmarried. He wore a girdle, which still didn't prevent his stomach from bulging through his dove waist-coats. His eyes were frequently discolored, his breath raging with drink. Yet he spoke excellent French, and there was no one who could pound in the paradigms of the preterit more painlessly than Doctor Sour:

—Boysss! Boysss! Don't sneer at Prousssssst! Il est fort bien formidable! . . .

Doctor Sour handed back papers by a personal delivery system. He would sashay about the classroom, patting the wrists of those handsome and hulking boys he admired. When he administered warnings or discipline, the desirable ones got shaken till their teeth rattled, or smacked on their derrières. For some intuitive reason Ralph had never been patted by Doctor Sour, who also told his class (in idiomatic

135

French) of weekends in New York with demoiselles élues. Few were fooled. And Ralph, a little chagrined to see teaching and pathology so intertwined, knew well that big tough boys of the football team could always help their French by sessions in the apartment of Doctor Sour. Buddy Brown often went for Extra Help. The whisperings about Doctor Sour's soirées had reached all ears but Mr. Pilkey's.

Ralph had also classes in physics and advanced math. These subjects were taught by rote from the mouths of bespectacled earnest young men. They sneered at all other departments and prefaced curdling remarks by the shibboleth:

—Science tells us. . . .

They implied that *their* subjects were the only utilitarian ones for Americans to study. They said that the key to technology and mastery of the modern world lay in science and math. They roared at culture and at the humanities. They promised in Their Fields a new Utopia of Progress for America. Ralph wondered why it hadn't come yet.

But the teacher whom he found most to his liking was the redheaded and intense Mr. Guy Hudson. Feeling the secret and ambiguous waves that were forever traversing the interstellar space between them, Ralph would sometimes at midnight twist on his cot. That twisted mouth too often said privy things for *his* benefit; those eyes too often sought out his own. But he was grateful that their affinity was a little too tenuous for any other student in The Academy to notice and kid him about. There was always something working between them. He remembered, with a flush he couldn't interpret, the night he'd caught Guy Hudson with the etching. What it showed! And what was this yeast? Outside of class they deliberately avoided each other. Why? Was there some precipice of loneliness or understanding upon which they were mutually tottering?

—Let me read to you what Rare Ben Jonson said about Queen Elizabeth, Guy Hudson would say to the class in his angry grating voice.

Sometimes, piercing the irate rush of words which he too perfectly understood, Ralph believed that Guy Hudson saw a potential in him. Then again it might be their two unconfessed lonelinesses that prowled each other. For Guy Hudson was different from everyone else on the faculty. He walked alone. Ralph believed that this teacher was wretched. He'd come back from war, against everything. Perhaps he was outside the pale of pity, love, or friendship. Yet his cold savage mastery thrilled Ralph at eighteen. This man was a free man.

Or at noon, when his classes were done, Ralph walked alone through shrill stamping corridors where four hundred boys jostled and ran and whistled because their true work for the day was over. He was alone because he walked slowly and musingly, digesting and filing away all those unrelated facts he'd learned that morning. It was like stringing an incomplete necklace on further pearls.

These corridors in The Academy schoolhouse were every hour filled with the exodus from classrooms. They would be silent for fifty-five minutes; then they would burst with a riotous stream of life. The hallways were vaulted, hung with many pictures supposed to keep the student's mind on the stream of history into which his education was indoctrinating him. Few but Ralph had ever paused to look at these framed reproductions, or knew what they concerned. They were pre-Raphaelite aquarelles of vignettes from history: King John signing Magna Charta on Runnymede; La Pucelle kissing a crucifix at the stake; the execution of Charles the First. These lined the walls, which were dark and airless; the figures in these paintings looked too jaded or saintly ever to have made history.

Detached still from the throng hurrying to lunch with books under their arms, Ralph entered the Hall of Trophies. Here in an alcove known as The Den was the desk of Mr. Pilkey, whence he could review the whole pageant of the Boys' School passing in front of him. There was a portrait of old Miss Sophia, foundress of The Academy; there was an American flag limp on a polished standard. And here were medals and cups and loot won by the athletic teams of The Academy. Ralph often wondered at the bias of the artisans who had fashioned these mementoes. Winged god-like young men of bronze were forever standing on globes, waving wreaths of laurel or marathon batons or lyres or even footballs. They were Old Greece directly transplanted into an American school. They were gladiators announcing their victories in an embarrassing and Peloponnesian manner. Ralph was puzzled. Did such athletes ever exist outside the minds of the sculptors, or the parents of dead boys, who had paid for these trophies?

In the alcove he shifted his books to the other hand. Mr. Pilkey was just rising from his desk and dismissing the epileptic Miss Pringle, who was shutting her dictation notebook. Mr. Pilkey looked for someone to Go To Work On. Seeing Ralph, he bore down upon him with a jovial waddle. Though the Principal was generally nonpartisan to his boys, preferring to remain suspended over them all like a Damoclean sword, Ralph had a good idea that he himself wasn't Mr. Pilkey's Ideal Boy, a Lovely Fellow. Wasn't he a little too brilliant as a student? Didn't he play the violin? And perhaps there was something dark and brooding in his face which would make Mr. Pilkey a trifle uneasy—if he ever thought about it.

Nevertheless, the Principal laid a hand upon his shoulder. Ralph took the caress for what it was—a Victorian and fatherly gesture. Mr. Pilkey's mane of white hair was above Ralph's head; the old man was tall, though a bit stooped. The hand rested the appropriate five seconds by Ralph's collar, then sheared off to his waist. This was a mark of favor and regard. It was evident that the Head intended to walk with him to the dining hall.

—And how are things going, young man?

It was his usual question to his boys; the answer was prescribed. After that, if you felt subversive, you might complain about a teacher whom you didn't like.

—Just fine, sir.

—I've been reading your reports with pleasure. Your parents must be mighty pleased, mighty pleased. . . .

—That's one reason I'm here, sir.

—*One* reason? Mr. Pilkey cried archly. Name two better ones, my boy. . . .

Conversation with the Principal was the most delicate social problem at The Academy. Few but the chosen athletes and mimes ever bridged the gap between them and Omnipotence. The wiser merely listened to the old man think out loud. His conversation was an airing of things which had been on his mind that morning, genial and noncommittal, except when he launched into politics. For Mr. Pilkey was a Republican of the vintage of Abraham Lincoln. Students

138

were expected to consider themselves privileged to hear him hold forth on whatever interested him. But you couldn't go off into a haze, saying yes and no at pauses. Every so often Mr. Pilkey would ask you a question. He never seemed to hear the answer, but you had to mutter something courtly. He listened to his boys only when they came forthrightly to his desk with some gossip, scandal, or gross complaint against the faculty.

Ralph and the Principal walked arm in arm toward the Dining Hall. The old gentleman leaned affectionately on him, talking in oracular fashion. And passing students, seeing Ralph in a confidential position ordinarily enjoyed only by Ben Gordon and Mr. Grimes, made little sucking sounds with their lips. Not loud enough for Mr. Pilkey's ear, but quite audible. He blushed and smiled guiltily, for every student knows the meaning of that quick puckering intake of the breath. Ralph might hear more of this little walk later in the afternoon.

Near the entrance to the dining hall Mrs. Pilkey was awaiting her husband. She liked to lunch in the proximity of students, having once gone on record as saying to a parent that schoolboys keep artists (and teachers) perennially young. Today against the November chill she was wearing her battered fur coat and a cloche hat of the style of twenty years ago. Her white hair wisped out from under it. Rumor said that she was older than Mr. Pilkey. The school said many cruel things about their king and queen. The consensus was that they ruled by senility. Together, Ralph saw, the Pilkeys made up a mutual admiration society something like those pitiful staring old people who look out of rotogravure sections on the celebration of their golden wedding. The school saw the Pilkeys as a pair of old buzzards sitting on a dual nest, The Academy. But Ralph saw them as two lonely old people whose artificial and sanctimonious authority had taken them out of the world and given them no real kingdom to be at home in.

The Principal loosed his arm from Ralph's and kissed his wife with a queer mixture of ornate devotion and display before the passing schoolboys, as though he would show them what a perfect marriage was.

—Hullo, dearie. How did The Art go this morning?

—O, she answered sighing. Not too well. This cold gets in my joints. I did only two plates. . . .

For Mrs. Pilkey spent her days in an attic painting designs on crockery. The students said that she gilded old chamberpots. In their public utterances the faculty said that she was the singlehanded reviver of a great and ancient art.

—Do you know this young man, dearie? Mr. Pilkey asked his wife.

Ralph felt like a doll squeezed by an auctioneer. Mrs. Pilkey peered at him from her kind scared rheumy eyes. She tried so fiercely to like people and act like a Principal's wife! But she could never remember names, and her brain was glazed from licking the tips of little brushes with which she stippled eagles and gryphons onto old china. She took Ralph's hand into her leathery one. It felt as though a passing owl had stroked him.

—Well, she said. He must be a nice boy because he has lovely eyes!

Ralph flushed again. Two passing students entering the dining hall caught the remark and snickered. Later that afternoon he would hear:

—Hey, Paganini with the *love*-ly eyes! . . .

Mrs. Pilkey, clutching at her fur coat, rallied to what for her was an exquisite cordiality:

—Won't the young man have lunch at our table?

—I . . . have to wait, Ralph said. I'm a scholarship boy. . . .

The strange, somehow still-womanly old creature turned to her husband:

—Dearie . . . can't you waive his waiting . . . just for one meal?

Mr. Pilkey's shrewd gray eyes shot around at the mobbing schoolboys from under his bushy white brows. And his rehearsed graciousness suddenly clotted and froze:

—Dearie, I'm afraid you don't understand. The other waiters would be demoralized by the exception. . . And what would the school say?

—O, Mrs. Pilkey said, subsiding and taking her husband's arm.

Then Ralph bowed to them both. He went into the pantry and put on his crisp coat. Mrs. Miekewicz stopped her screaming at the other waiters long enough to give him the wink. She said something enticing in Polish. Ralph noticed that they were having macaroni and cheese for lunch. He himself would eat after the school was fed.

After the digestion time that Mr. Pilkey and the human body demanded, Ralph got into his soccer uniform—a canary yellow jersey and a little pair of purple felt pants with piping round the edges. On the jersey were the taped letters of The Academy. Thus it seemed to him that he was forever taking off or putting on some kind of livery: his snowy waiter's coat, his frayed velveteen jacket, or this soccer uniform. It was a strange bondage in order to be educated.

Slim and supple he stood up before the mirror on his dresser. His roommate watched him from the bed where he lay chewing gum and snapping a slingshot at a fly that buzzed around the ceiling. Ready to Buddy Brown's hand was a purple yoyo, with which he played when he did his math or wrote his illiterate themes. He had the scorn of a football prince for anyone who played soccer. His particular derision was reserved for the shinguards Ralph was donning:

—Smatta, sweetheart? Fraida gettin kicked?

One of his roommate's BB pellets caught Ralph on the thigh as he went out the door. It stung.

He was a fast and catlike soccer player. He loved the game, for it was swift and tangentially aggressive, as he suspected love to be. And he had a delicacy of playing all his own, which perhaps no football player ever knew. His skill at soccer had done more than anything else at The Academy to preserve him from the clandestine persecution meted out to the fruits and the arty clique. Soccer was the only physical contact he had with other boys, because he held aloof from those dormitory wrestling parties which are known as Dicking. But on this field, racing, zigzagging, kicking, and heading, Ralph oxidized completely whatever meanness and violence there was in him. And this afternoon when the teatcleats on his shoes tore the calf of the goalie, he looked down at the muddy bleeding gash with surprise and delight. Even in him the tendency toward legal murder wasn't quite atrophied.

Winded and tranquilly delighted in the peace that comes

141

after combat, Ralph took his shower. Across the tiled room at another jet of soapy water he observed his redheaded teacher Guy Hudson soaping his groin in the tender abstraction which athletes devote to their bodies. The air was murky with heat vapor and fragmentary singing. Ralph continued to soap himself but turned his back, lest Mr. Hudson or himself should feel the urge to speak. It was odd: mornings he would hear that twisted mouth dissecting the Thirty Years' War; afternoons he saw that whiplike hairy body naked and bathing in an echoing cavern. The priest became a troll.

—Hi, boy, a voice said.

There was a black body in the shower next to him. Soapsuds in those hands looked like creamy flowers in a glove of black velvet. It was his friend Tad McKinley, the only Negro at The Academy. Ralph got a voluptuous pleasure in being addressed by Tad, who never spoke to anybody else. He liked also the flow of Tad's muscles, corrugations in the ebony sheath of his skin.

—Why did you turn around just then? Tad said, soaping his kinky hair.

—My modesty, I guess.

—It wasn't that at all, boy. Don't try to kid me. . . .

The shower room began to clear of boys and coaches; Tad McKinley surrendered himself to the hottest shower he could find. Ralph had finished his cold one and stood aside to watch his friend. The Negro boy went limp in the iridescence of the scalding spray; his white teeth grinned with the effete pleasure of having his flesh soaked through with live steam. He gave out groans:

—O my God, my God, my God. . . .

—Easy now. You'll faint from ecstasy.

In the anteroom beyond the locker stalls they whipped at themselves with Academy-issue thick-napped towels. Tad flickered about like a black perch, fluid as those strange sonnets he brought to Mr. Grimes's English class.

—Tell me, boy, Tad said, do you feel The Urge?

—Why, yes, Ralph said, dropping his voice.

—Same place, same time?

After they'd dressed beside their respective lockers and put on their leather windbreakers against the November afternoon, they approached their rendezvous by devious and separate routes. Ralph could see Tad working tortuously around the side of a hummock of grass, looking back over his shoulder, lest Mr. Grimes should be out doing detective work. Ralph in quiet gusto caressed a cellophane packet in the breast of his windbreaker.

Finally after doubling back on their own footsteps, they met at an old tobacco barn by the river—its side jutting on hinged slats. In this barn the one unpardonable crime against Mr. Pilkey's administration was committed by three quarters of the students. They were going to Smoke Cigarettes. It was the only infringement of The Academy rules that Ralph perpetrated; the Negro boy broke many others. On a sheaf of drying broadleaf, in the autumnal cold, Ralph and Tad enjoyed their mortal sin, which entailed the surest damnation from the fold of the elect. At The Academy you might be discovered in sodomy, in frottage, in theft, or in fellation—but you would be surely expelled by Mr. Pilkey's own hand is you were caught smoking. For to the Principal's and the faculty's mind there was an arbitrary date fixed to the use of tobacco. That date was always at some unspecified time *after* graduation from The Academy.

Ralph offered a cigarette to his friend and lit it for him. Then they lay down flat on the tarpaulin atop the broadleaf and let out smoke toward the ceiling of the old riddled barn.

—O my God, my God, my God, Ralph murmured, parodying Tad.

—I like the way you put your mouth around a butt, Tad said. You're going to be plenty sexy one of these days, boy. . . .

—I am already, Ralph said. What do you advise me to do about it?

—O, I'll show you sometime.

They lay side by side dizzy and exalted from the first cigarette in two days. They hadn't much to say to each other. They never needed to talk. The aloofness of the Negro thawed in the sadness of Ralph Du Bouchet. For they gave each other that masculine love, best tasted before twenty, which vests itself in respect, disinterest, and understatement. They never quite knew what they meant to each other—but they knew that it was something cool and devoted. So without a word they had another cigarette. Then Tad began to articulate the slow fury that gnawed at him all day long:

—They have me here because the catalog says this is a democratic school. . . I'm one of their showpieces. Something for the catalog: see? we've jumped the color line Around Here. . . . Pilkey is a hypocritical old turd. . . . But I'll show them. You will too, boy. . . . So what difference does it make what goes on here at this goddam school now? . . . those condescending chapel talks . . . those meaningless cups and trophies . . . the fascist cheering at football games . . . the other day a cheerleader bawled me out because I wasn't putting my heart into it. Christ! . . . We're here only to get something, aren't we, boy?

Ralph sat up in the loft of broadleaf; he was stirred:

—Mr. Pilkey says we have to do things we don't like. Says they're good for us. I guess that's the Puritan spirit. I do them. Not that I think they'll make a man of me—the way Mr. Pilkey means. But I'm learning what Other Things are like. I have a range of possibilities to choose from. . . . Otherwise you and I would be just like those perfumed kids who write for The Lit. . . .

—Yes, boy. But I don't want perfume. I want to fool around with crap and make that smell sweet too. . . .

After a while of silence and smoking they left the old barn and walked back along the river road, though it was imprudent to do so together. The time was close to sunset; a foggy cold wind was ruffling up the stubble left in the fields. Goalposts raised their bony white arms against the yellowing sky.

They passed the white clapboard buildings of the Girls' School, where Daygirls were shrilling around the buses that were to take them home. At the sound of the whirring soprano voices Tad McKinley stopped in the road.

—C'est une école des femmes, he said pompously. You know what I've always wanted to do? Walk into their locker room some afternoon. Naked. I'm so black I'd scare them out of a week's growth. . . .

Ralph saw a beautiful woman staring at him out of the third floor of the house of the Directress of the Girls' School. Did she teach here? She looked lost and lonely. Then a car skidded up behind them, a Packard convertible coupe. In it sat Mr. Philbrick Grimes returning from the village. He had in the back seat a host of brown paper bags containing his Shopping—delicacies which he cooked in his suite for those little dinners he gave the Pilkeys and the Inner Circle.

—Bet you he'll stop and speak to us, Tad McKinley whispered. He has to know the whole score, the toad!

And Mr. Grimes did stop his Packard and lean out at them through the window. His bright eyes pored excitedly over their faces, for like a literary hawkshaw he was always on the lookout for secret vice.

—Have we been good all afternoon? *Extra* good?

—O yessir, they answered, smiling their sweetest schoolboy smiles.

Mr. Grimes reached over into his back seat and took two pretzels out of one of the bags:

—Then here are goodies!

Then he drove away, spraying them with the dust of the road.

—He makes me want to puke, Tad McKinley said, throwing the pretzel into the road.

—O, he makes *me* laugh, Ralph said.

The rest of the afternoon and evening Ralph spent in various ways invented by himself for the spare and sweet delight they yielded him. They weren't devices known to most American students. He might read in the school library, which Mrs. Pilkey had designed more for looks than for books. The Library Fund was spent—not to buy new volumes—but to keep a fire in the grate (Mr. Pilkey said a library should be cozy) and flowers in bowls by the windows. Ralph was one of those boys who read everything, cultivating taste and catholicity by browsing. At eighteen he was in the Aubrey Beardsley-James Huneker-Max Beerbohm-Norman Douglas stage.

Or if it was Monday he might take his weekly violin lesson from Mr. Schmidt, an old Kraut who came out from the city to instruct those students who thirsted for what the catalog called Instrumental Instruction. Mr. Schmidt was interested only in the mechanics of music, but Ralph knew this. He was a martinet for technic. But Ralph needed a grounding in these aridities if he was ever to do anything with the

145

golden instrument that he held smilingly under his arm as he waited for Mr. Schmidt to finish a harangue on the Weimar Republic. Then he would put his fiddle under his chin and play something of Handel or Vivaldi or Corelli, and Herr Schmidt might weep a little:

—Gott, boy! You may yet haff somtink da rest of us need! . . .

Or after supper (having laid aside his white waiter's coat for the third time) Ralph sat over his textbooks. Much of the time he spent in doing the homework of his roommate. And here was the secret of his growing ascendancy over that blond mastiff. They sat with their desks back to back under their reading lamps. Ralph did his work with despatch, in a passion of concentration. Buddy Brown paced the floor, fingered his pinup girls, and popped bubblegum. Sometimes he would play his radio with the volume down, quenching it when he heard footsteps in the corridor outside their door.

—Listen, Buddy said, hurling his book on the bed, I've decided that this snatch Desdemona married that big black dinge for one reason only. . . .

—Oversimplification, Ralph said.

—And by the way. I've been noticing your bunghole buddies with the one boog in this dump. You know who I mean. Tad McKinley. Someday me and my gang are gonna form a KKK and lynch that jig. He's got no right here anyhow. The Southern kids are plenty PO'd. Doesn't your flesh c-r-a-w-l?

—No, Ralph said. Listen to this: She lov'd me for the dangers I had pass'd. And I lov'd her that she did pity them. . . .

—Shakspere was a fag, for Chrissake.

And often, when the lights were about to go off in the dormitory till morning, Buddy in pajamas and with toothbrush in mouth would decide to wrestle with his roommate. Ralph rarely resisted. Buddy was strong: he would bend the slender boy's neck back till it all but cracked. He would force Ralph back to the floor and sit on his chest. He would stay there on top of him longer than his triumph warranted. And Ralph, smelling the harsh youthfulness of his roommate's embrace, would wonder why he himself had never really been young.

146

7

Like a physician who watches the creeping paralysis of his own disease and reaches out to take his pulse, Miss Betty Blanchard observed herself in a soft but not birdlike agony. She'd taken to spending late November afternoons leaning out the window of her room in Mrs. Mears's house. She knew well what it was drove her to the window. It was substantially the same force as pulled housewives to their tenement balconies and made birds spar against the gratings of their cages. And although the November wind was chilly it gave her a sort of surgical relief when it knifed her bare throat. Sometimes she was halfway out over the windowsill in a frenzy of peering. She saw the whitesteepled church and the browning graveyard where Miss Sophia lay buried. And in the twilight she would watch the progress of cars on the road. These bore insurance girls and telephone operators on their way home from work. But they were all freer than she was. Sometimes, as when she leaned out of the WAC barracks in Algiers and Naples, she had to stifle a hoyden impulse to call out a greeting to passersby. They might understand her imprisonment and come up to fetch her down.

From her window at Mrs. Mears's, Miss Blanchard noticed the movements of masons and painters and garagemen in their loose overalls, going home to families and hot suppers. Her spirit whizzed with the jolting motorcycle riders, racing in pairs, or with their girls behind them clasping their waists. These were the maddest and freest of any who passed. They awoke an ache in her; for she was an arrow unable to shoot into the air. She envied the thoughtless vulgarity of the costumes of the motorcyclists—flapping windbreakers and windrippled trousers about their taut thighs, gaudy shockbelts, which they wore as lasciviously as sailors,

147

crusted with fake jewelry and curved with leather over their kidneys.

She stared too at boys and girls coming home from the public grade-schools of the town, playing incredible games (with penalties) on the concrete sidewalk. Her eyes glistened in the cold air as she joined these games vicariously. She was sad because she realized that the girls *she* was teaching were no longer like these independent calloused children; they believed themselves to be young ladies a-finishing. Her duty was to give them the final flick of the chamois. As a teacher she would be their last abrasive, the last person they would have to put up with before they emerged as young American ladies, ready for dances and brilliant marriages.

—Come, Blanchard, she said to herself, do you fancy yourself as a nun leaning from her cloister window? Well, you *are....*

She had just about decided to pull in her neck lest Mrs. Mears or one of the British accents on the faculty should catch her gawking wistfully at the Great World Outside. Just then two boys passed under her window. And since they were the strangest specimens she'd seen that afternoon she followed them with her eyes. A certain sauntering elegance of manner told her they came from the Boys' School. Then she gasped, for she noticed that one of them was a Negro. She had heard how Mr. Pilkey had flown into the face of tradition this year by permitting the enrollment of a black boy. That must be he. But as one who had looked on many men in her time, Betty Blanchard was struck even more by the other boy, the companion of the Negro. Did they really have boys like that at the Boys' School? He was delicate and intense, like the entering of a wedge of velvet. And then she smiled, for she guessed what the two boys had been up to. Smoking in that abandoned tobacco barn up the road. She blessed them both.

Noiselessly she shut her window. The expression on her face was complacent and listening, like the pleased expression of a pregnant woman. She shut the window with great care, lest a slam attract the attention of the meandering boys. Something cruel in them would have gloated to catch her spying on them. Something maternal in her rejoiced at having seen, as a mother learns some dirt on her son and treasures it up in her heart.

148

She walked briskly to her desk and picked up two test papers that had been separated from the main pile. She knew exactly what she was going to do, though the flagrance of what she'd discovered and the dread of the forthcoming ordeal had made her hyperanxious all afternoon. She folded the two papers in her hand and marched downstairs. She heard other mistresses getting ready for supper: Miss Demerjian singing in the style of Lucienne Boyer, Miss O'Leary wrestling with her undies on a drub board in a sink. The house was teeming with its usual irrelevant bustle—of women just having done something, or just about to do it. Betty Blanchard went into the cold twilight. The air had the tense foreboding smell of November; the earth was taut and frozen under her feet.

Outside the Ionic temple of the main building of the Girls' School Daygirls were bustling into their vehicles. They carried home books to con (unlike their sisters at the town high school) and they were chewing their gum so efficiently that their bandannas jiggled. They were planning jokes to play on the driver of their bus, who, they said, was young and strictly from hunger. At the approach of Miss Blanchard the clucking hysteria ceased. They called out to her in their dutiful classroom soprani:

—Night now, Miss Blanchard! Don't work to haaaaard!
—Goodnight, girls.

Abstracted and nervous, she entered the lighted corridor of the school building and stalked past the bulletin board, which was in its usual disarray, with giggling notices of the fall prom. She walked into the locker room, where panties and bras were strewn about in a chorusgirl wurra-wurra. She stationed herself at the entrance to the showers, blind with steam as from a volcanic cave. Because she wore low brogues with rubber heels, she made no sound. Inside girls' voices were harmonizing on the School Song, written by none other than Mrs. Mears, with technical hints from the music mistress. It was full of cloying thirds and sixth; its sentiment mixed American virginity with the Do-or-Die of polite heroics:

—Alma mater, at your behest,
 Brightest, noblest, bravest, best. . . .

Miss Blanchard's voice cut across the harmony and the steam:

—Girls! Is Midge Mears in there?

She appeared, a rubber bathing cap over her platinum pageboy bob. Her rich body was pink from steam and hot water. And strangely enough she covered her breasts with her forearms. It was these renowned tubers that had the Boys' School leching after Midgie.

—You wanted me, Teech?

—Yes. Get dressed at once and report to your mother's office. And if Joanie Dorchester is in there, tell her to come too.

—Reet, Teech, Midgie said, turning and disappearing into the steam.

Even as Betty Blanchard walked away from the fulsome air, all singing in the shower stopped. There was a smothered scream and a lot of whispering. At the door to Mrs. Mears's office she paused and collected herself. She noticed that the rope of pearls over her sweater was befogged from steam. She was oddly frightened, though she knew that from any ethical basis she'd no grounds to be. Yet . . . was she perhaps brewing up a tempest in a teapot? Should she perhaps drop the whole business? Then she decided that, if she did, her last prop as a teacher would be kicked out from under her. So she wiped off her pearls, straightened her shoulders, and knocked—louder than necessary.

When her knock was answered, she entered the office of Mrs. Mears. She was aware that she was marching stiffly, much as if she was reporting to her major in the WAC. But this was better than slinking in. After all *she* wasn't the culprit. The Directress of the Girls' School sat behind a mahogany desk. In the mild fluorescent light she looked like one of those smart women executives who appear regularly in ladies' magazines to assure the sex that, goddam it, they can hold their own with men. She was wearing a tailored suit and some chaste jewels. Her braided white hair gave off austere lights; her ruddy wrinkled face looked pleased and easy. Her great breasts within the mannish jacket hulked over some reports she'd been studying. Altogether she seemed like a genial and jaded Great Dane wearing a peruke. Near her on the lowboy in a flat glass bowl there floated flowers, which gave the office a woman's touch. Otherwise it might have

150

seemed dictatorial. Mrs. Mears arose, showed all her teeth, and put out her hand. She was evidently in A Good Mood:

—Betty, my dear! This is the first time you've come to see *me*. . . .

Mrs. Mears motioned her to a chair and took off on a purring little speech about how happy it made a Directress if her teachers sought her out daily. But teachers were busy, alas, and she hoped she was big enough to understand that. Still. . . .

—Mrs. Mears, I have a piece of awful news for you. . . .

Mrs. Mears made a stately wipe at the air, as though to indicate that *she* at least had everything under control.

—All young teachers think that anything out of the ordinary is bad news. When you are as old as I, my dear. . . .

—Well, I never dreamed that anything like this would happen with the sort of girl we have here. . . . Mrs. Mears, brace yourself. . . . I've caught your daughter Midgie and Joanie Dorchester in a flagrant case of cribbing. . . .

There was a silence so sudden that she could hear the girls on the road getting into their buses. The twilight of November seemed to have been struck by lightning.

Mrs. Mears closed her eyes and put her forehead in her jeweled hand. Then she offered a cigarette to Betty Blanchard, took one herself, and lit both. This was something she rarely did. She leaned back in her chair, seeming to have fallen asleep or died. Yet obviously she was prepared to fly out the window, shattering the glass and carrying the rent body of Miss Blanchard in her tushes.

Finally she blew out a puff of smoke, opened her eyes, and looked straight through Betty, who could have sworn that now a bonfire had been ignited back of those hard eyes. The she leaned forward and blew another puff of smoke right past Betty's left ear:

—My dear young lady, this is a serious charge to make. *Our* girls cheating? On written work? You *must* be mistaken, my dear. . . .

—I'm not the sort to destroy my evidence, Mrs. Mears. . . .

After her unreasoned shame and pity and fear Miss Blanchard was beginning rather to enjoy herself. With a definite gesture she planked down the two papers on the desk.

—Those Spanish themes are alike, word for word. They've even made identical errors. . . .

Dragging too hard on her cigarette, Mrs. Mears cushioned her leonine white head in her hand and leaned over the evidence. Her eyes darted from paper to paper, comparing, contrasting, collating. And in one minute's time she passed from a virile roaring dame into a tottering old woman. Her bosom collapsed. Her ringed powerful hands clenched and unclenched. And something inflated collapsed into something groveling. Betty Blanchard felt rotten. She was *almost* sorry she'd brought up this case. And the look that Mrs. Mears shot her now was beseeching, like a dog with distemper:

—My dear. I . . . just don't believe it. I won't believe it. My own daughter. . . . My own little girl. . . .

Betty Blanchard charged in, a little starchily and officiously:

—I believe, Mrs. Mears, that cheating on written work is the most serious sin a student can commit. If a teacher can't trust what she gets on papers, what *can* she trust?

Something of the old tigress struggled and revived in the Directress:

—My dear, please don't babble like a Normal School Graduate.

—But it's the *truth!* Why, if these girls aren't dismissed from school . . . I . . . I think I'd resign my job. Why, Mrs. Mears, it's simply inexcusable!

—You're hysterical, my dear. It's such a teeny and human thing to do, after all! When you were a girl in school, didn't you *ever* . . . ?

—If I got caught, I knew perfectly well what would happen to me. . . . Mrs. Mears, don't tell me you're condoning this filthy business? . . .

There was a knock on the door of the office; Midgie and her sidekick Joanie Dorchester minced in. From their showers they had a fresh and innocent air, like babies presented to kiss the company before being whisked off to bed. They were wide-eyed and maddeningly uncomprehending. They were dressed almost identically—the sweater, the pearls, the plaid skirt, the bobbysocks, the loafers. In her clairvoyant rage Miss Blanchard guessed that they'd parked their gum on the doorjamb before entering. It was inconceivable that

152

any girls who'd done what they had could look quite so cherubic and puzzled.

—Midgie and Joanie, said Mrs. Mears in a throttled voice. I have something to say to you both. . . .

—What, Mom? Midgie asked, disguising the throaty quality of her voice into the squeak of a rodent.

Miss Blanchard couldn't stand it any longer. Taking the bit into her teeth, she leapt to her feet. She felt triumphantly righteous. She didn't care if Mrs. Mears sent her packing tonight.

—I've caught you two cribbing! Redhanded. Now what have you got to say to that?

—Miss Blanchard, please, Mrs. Mears said in her best Assembly voice. Anyone is innocent till she's proved guilty. . . . That's what the Charter of our school says. . . .

—*Proved* guilty?

Joanie Dorchester, being the weaker sister of the two, and the sillier, hid her face and burst into tears. But in the eyes of Midgie Mears Betty Blanchard saw the same lurid gleam she'd observed in the mother's. Midgie turned brick red, swallowed hard, pouted, lowered her eyes, and began to poke at the nap of the rug with her moccasined toe.

—Midgie, you're President of the Student Council, her mother said. You couldn't do this to me . . . to the school. . . .

—We . . . we were rushing for time, Midgie said. Miss Blanchard is terribly strict with us . . . so . . . I looked a little over Joanie's shoulder, and she . . . looked a little over mine. . . .

—O, by the way, Miss Blanchard, said Mrs. Mears, squashing out her cigarette, I *have* heard complaints that your examinations are too difficult and too long. . . .

Betty Blanchard's spine prickled; her hair wanted to rise:

—Then you're offering irrelevancies as any excuse for cribbing?

—Why, none whatever, my dear, said Mrs. Mears with Old Testament briskness. But any fool knows there are always extenuating circumstances. . . .

The girl teacher was about to scream *Name two!* Instead she clenched her fists. For now Midgie had dropped down on the floor beside Joanie and was sobbing her heart out. Joanie's father was Governor of the state, and Midgie's mother was Directress of the school. It was touch and go which girl was the more untouchable. The sobs now filled the office.

—My God, the scandal, Mrs. Mears murmured to herself.

—Condoning it in an educational institution seems to me a greater scandal, Betty Blanchard said.

She felt moral and thrilled and charged with a great cause —all at once. And she was angrier than she'd ever been in her life. But suddenly Joanie Dorchester began to fumble with the hem of her skirt. Betty Blanchard tried to get free of the gooey clutch, but she backed into a windowseat.

—Miss Blanchard, we're so soooorry! Honest to God we are! We'll never do it again! . . .

Midgie followed suit. There were now two of them, practically pulling the teacher's skirt off:

—Yes, we've learned our lesson! We'll never be so stupid again.

—Stupid? Miss Blanchard said. I call it *evil*. . . .

Their moans were so loathsome that she thought she was going to vomit on the huddled keening forms at her feet. Mrs. Mears arose at her desk and assumed a beatific and prophetic pose, just as though she was saying grace after meals in the dining room:

—There, you see? Penitence! They're not really *bad*, you know. It's the sort of mistake anyone is entitled to make. . . .

And to the girls she added, filing her voice to stern kindness:

—Go out now, my dears. Miss Blanchard and I must discuss this serious matter at greater length. . . .

Huddling together, the two crawled out the door. Betty Blanchard could have sworn that the gleam was returning to the damp eyes of Midgie Mears. Their sniffles wafted down the corridor, the plangencies of violated wood doves. The Directress sat down at her desk and contemplated her rings:

—There, my dear. Aren't you satisfied? We've caused enough suffering for one day to their little hearts. We've made them nerrrvous. . . .

—Is your daughter to be cashiered from the Student Council? And is Governor Dorchester to receive a sharp note? . . .

A smile of the most ghastly sweetness-in-suffering transfigured the face of the Directess:

—My dear . . . mountains out of molehills . . . the scandal . . . it would make the whole school nerrrvous. And I assure you that a second offense would be more crucial. . . .

—A *second* offense? Then, Mrs. Mears, you're taking no action?

She felt her own hot tears coming, and a desire to claw.

—My dear. Listen to reason. Let us talk as woman to woman. . . . Forget I am your superior . . . Miss Blanchard, I'm a poor woman. . . .

—What has poverty go to do with it?

—Just this, my dear. I can't afford to call in a psychiatrist for my Midgie. . . .

—Did you say . . . a *psychiatrist*?

Mrs. Mears nodded sweetly. Betty Blanchard rushed out of that paneled office. She ran into the chilly November cemetery. She sought out the grave of old Miss Sophia.

8

By early December Mr. Guy Hudson was reaping a harvest he hadn't dreamed existed outside of seed catalogs. As the last month of the year came on and the sunsets got purpler, he was astonished to find that he contained in himself the pathetic fallacy. He was growing older and mellower. The war hadn't aged him; it had only roughened and coarsened him. But here at The Academy, with the days getting shorter and a pattern of routine to guide him, some of the seeds sown in him by the war had begun to sprout. Some of his bitterness died like a weed; in its place shot up an agnostic wisdom. Sometimes he was almost glad he'd taken up this teaching job, instead of installing himself in some bar, drawing his twenty dollars a week, and gradually eating out his own insides. For here by teaching he'd had to drive outward all his own gnawing. By extroverting his deeper sadnesses, he'd pulled away a lot of the old scar tissue. And he was surprised to observe that under the epidermis of his cynicism fresh skin had been growing all the time. Thus he came to realize the recreating therapy of action after a long time of thought and melancholia.

The boys liked him—or better, respected and trusted him. Guy Hudson knew that popularity for a teacher in the sense of a Gallup poll is vicious and meaningless. Good teachers never seek favor with their classes. But it soon became clear to his students, to the boys on his team the Pequots, and to others whose paths crossed his, that he would never betray them, that he was in this school to do something with and for them. And, since élan and purpose are always respected in America as the mark of a man who knows what he wants, he slowly overcame the inertia of the boys he worked with. He knew instinctively the cardinal function of a teacher— which is a stout lever to raw mass. He knew also that no teacher ever accomplishes as much as he thinks or hopes to do. He never settled down into the fat complacency of: God, how my pupils love me! Nor did he ever capitulate entirely to that sin against the Holy Ghost which says that knowledge can never be transmitted except by direct experience. He spanned these dual abysses with a bridge of his own devising and walked between them, silent, a little bitter, but satisfied, like a good general, with small advances and no retreats. Finally he found that good teaching is a process of insinuation, though he was wary of playing the hypnotist or ventriloquist. And when most of those lacquered hard little minds opened an inch to his seductions, he knew that the wedge must never be pushed in too far. He was not to be their father, priest, or lover. The most delicate of all the teacher's inhibitions is learning to keep his oily fingers off the souls of the young. Strong and sinister is the temptation to play God or puppeteer, since the teacher is the stronger man, particularly in working with unsure minds. He is likely to find himself training up the young in the image of himself. Guy Hudson knew that no narcissism could be more ugly than this.

Although Mr. Pilkey and Mr. Grimes and other hirelings didn't approve, he never entirely sacrificed himself to The Academy. He reverenced any institution for what it could do by its organization, but he wouldn't fall in love with anything so impersonal. The longer a teacher remained here, the more he tended to melt his own personality into the crucible of the school. Guy Hudson wouldn't allow himself to be thus castrated. If going his own way should eventually cost him his job—why, well and good. It would be better to be disgorged into the world an intact personality than to have Mr. Pilkey geld him by blocks and duplicities.

Guy Hudson believed himself to be sailing a course midway between sanctimoniousness and ethical diarrhea. But against the Pilkeyan thesis that teacher must be always Doing Something to be effective, he reacted with his own brand of passive resistance. Quietly he refused to play a part in everything that went on at The Academy. He preserved some small leisure in every day for himself. That was His Time. How else was a man to keep from growing stale and robotish in a term of three months, in which he had no peace from seven in the morning till ten at night? Factory workers had their eight-hour days and a union to watch out for their interests; but the teacher's day is never ended, and all's to do again tomorrow. Mr. Pilkey had said that teaching was a labor of love. But Guy Hudson knew from his own experience that even love sometimes entails satiety and boredom. The Principal's faculty never talked back to his sophistries. Guy Hudson did, in a negative sort of way, by omitting to live up to certain sacramentals of The Academy.

—I didn't see you at the football game this afternoon, Mr. Grimes said one Saturday.

—I was walking in the woods.

—Zut alors! Around Here we expect you to get out and root for our teams. . . .

Mr. Grimes pretended to satirize the idea of the Old School Tie, but Guy Hudson guessed that he was really rather disturbed when a teacher didn't surrender his whole time to the school. From morning till night Mr. Grimes was about his Father's Business; his nervousness went into a crescendo as the term progressed. Whereas Guy Hudson got cooler and more detached as the pressure waxed. A constant pouring forth of energy, without knowing where the refueling would come from, seemed to him a business for lemmings only.

—Why don't you ask the Head to put you on a committee? said Mr. Grimes.

—*You* are happy on committees. . . .

It was true. When there were pots to stick a finger into,

Mr. Grimes was as happy as a witch in cauldron season.

But the oddest benefit to Guy Hudson was the enforced celibacy of the unmarried instructors. In Europe, off the line, he'd never slept alone. Now he did every night. It wasn't that he'd become sexless; he was always as randy as a javelin. But the chastity belt buckled on him by Mr. Pilkey made him hurl himself at goals, rather than at the center of another's body. And he thought that in such abstinence man is luckier than woman. He wondered how the mistresses at the Girls' School made out. Sometimes in the village he passed, and nodded to, Miss Blanchard, whose mouth was getting drawn and whose shoulders were beginning to droop. Why didn't he take her out some evening? Was American convention closing about him at last? All the fables about candles and obelisks came back to him, and he laughed a little ruefully.

In spite of that undeclared war between student and faculty that is the internecine factor of American education, students and their teachers sometimes overflowed into one another, like neighboring pots boiling on a stove. Boys had favorite teachers whom they sought to know more intimately than was possible in class. The process of getting to know a teacher as a man was furtive and coy. They would call on the idol-confessor; the calls would become more frequent. And by this process of attraction and seepage there grew up in the course of the Fall Term those salons which are stalactites of educational life. Every unmarried teacher had a salon sympathetic to his own vibrations. And ladies of the faculty, imagining themselves bluestockings, would also invite in students for amusement, for baby-sitting. They vied with one another in luring campus notables to their tables. Mrs. Launcelot Miller copped most of the athletic lions. She ran a cutthroat business, like a Washington hostess scheming up a dinner party.

Guy Hudson had heard most of the blazing coterie of Doctor Sour, a closed corporation with entree by invitation only. Here came boys not yet sure of their sex, athletes desirous of raising their grades, and those young bullies who rejoiced to have a motherly and fussy ear bent to their experimental thuggeries. Wearing a silk mandarin lounging robe over his flabby hips, Doctor Sour served tea, played the piano, and patted them in tempting places. Guy Hudson had heard tales of nude parties in the suite of Doctor Sour, of hard cider and beer, of chases and titterings in his darkened study. Here too came all the subversive elements of The Academy's student body, fastened to Doctor Sour by that umbilical cord which no teacher should ever tweak. And he held them to him, concealing all the malfeasances of his proteges and whispering sibilantly to them all the peppery gossip of the faculty.

And Mr. Philbrick Grimes had a small but choice salon. Because he was himself a wit, he could tolerate only those students whom he considered Amusing. Mr. Grimes's idea of a gifted eighteen-year-old was one who talked like the prose of Katharine Brush. His boys were expected to be brittle and disillusioned. They wore glasses and identification bracelets (fashionable in America since the recent war), mewed out epigrams, and read Wolcott Gibbs. In the suite of Mr. Grimes over iced tea and polite glassy laughter The Academy's Literary Magazine was cooked up monthly. Needless to say, The Lit talked like Mr. Grimes and thought like him, for nothing got into print without his imprimatur. Consequently he though himself as much a literary dictator as John Dryden or any New York editor.

Guy Hudson saw that the professional coaches had salons too, though perhaps they should be called gymnasia. The burly cigar-smoking coaches were frequented by those boys who would never dream of being seen in the company of most teachers. These graduates of Springfield College entertained nightly the sweet and coordinated athletes. In these smokers-without-smoke the children sparkled as they did in no classroom. They discussed Big League scores and standings and boxing and hockey and track records till their tongues were dry. And here many a musclebound coach, who considered the faculty-proper a bunch of Commie intellectuals, would snicker mellowly and tell reminiscences of his boyhood around the crackerbarrel. These sessions were golden with Boy Scout humor, backslapping, and feats of strength.

Guy Hudson alone kept no salon. It seemed to him a little unfair and more than a little incestuous for a man to surround himself with a circle of doting boys half his own age. These salons were an unconscious cry of protest against the social ostracism and the false security of the American teacher. It was as though the faculty was saying defiantly: Well, their parents have no time for me; so I'll retaliate by snaring the children. There was no doubt that many a fading wistful man got a sense of bigness and conquest by surrounding himself with handsome boys, who treated him like their uncle and their pal. To Guy Hudson's eye all these faculty cliques with students had an air of repressed vampirism. They were a phenomenon not to be seen in the outside world, where men must keep company with their equals and contemporaries.

One night in December Ralph was sitting in Guy Hudson's room making up a history map on the Partitions of Poland. The boy's forehead was furrowed under the reading lamp; he bit his full red lips as he colored in crayon and inserted mutable boundary lines with heavy dotted lines. Guy Hudson sat opposite, correcting papers, aware of that slender brown hand going over the blank map with slow precision. He was now at the point where he disliked any meeting with this boy outside of class. Something in each was always watching the other, their minds pussyfooting. It was now much more intimate than those very salons that he didn't approve of. They needed each other secretly—and that was bad. It was madness to think that a boy of eighteen and a man of twenty-nine had really anything to say to each other. And yet it was there, this constant prowling.

Ralph, without looking up from his mapmaking, said:

—When do I get another look at that etching you've got in your closet?

—Never.

—Why?

—I don't know....

—I'm glad you didn't come out with some fake remark, like my not being old enough....

—Let's not talk about it, Guy Hudson said, laying down his blue pencil.

—I want to tell you the truth. Yesterday afternoon when you weren't here, I came up and cleaned your room. You're very messy in your personal habits. There was dust all over the place. And I took that picture out and looked at it to my heart's content. There's a copy of *Psychopathia Sexualis* floating around school. I've read it, like everybody else. But that picture you have makes it look tame. Wow!

Guy Hudson stood up and opened the door:

—Goodnight, Ralph. . . .

The boy stood up, holding his unfinished map. Guy Hudson had never imagined how Ralph would look when surprised. Now he saw. He looked almost like a girl on the wave of her delight. Ralph paused at the door:

—Why do we have to act so foolishly to each other?

—I really don't know. But I'd rather you wouldn't visit me again.

—Perhaps you're right. . . . I've thought about it. . . . Yet I think we're both acting very silly. . . . Goodnight. . . .

—Goodnight. . . .

He shut the door and sat down in his chair. He felt as though there were claws in his chest. Gripping the arms of his chair, he thought: Jesus, *that* was a subdued battle! But it seemed as though a piece of himself was walking downstairs in Ralph's moccasins. And in horror he realized that for the past five years he'd never allowed himself or been allowed leisure for the more delicate emotions. He'd known only hate, sex, disgust, boredom. And recently there'd been a little fume curling inside him that had all the provocation of incense. . . . Cleaned my room, did he! His privacy had been invaded by that boy, but he found no resentment. Only a weak and giddy delight. He ran his hands through his thick red hair and kicked out his legs in a spasm of trying to get free. From what?

—This school is driving me as nutty as the rest.

There was a knock at his door. His thought was that Ralph had come back again, and the whole cat-and-mouse comedy was to be played over with different nuances. But the door opened and Mr. Pilkey walked in. His long white bangs were in his eyes; he was puffing from climbing two flights of stairs. It was the first time the Principal had ever called on Guy Hudson; malcontents said Mr. Pilkey had only two virtues as an executive: he never invaded their classrooms or their quarters. Guy Hudson jumped up, feeling awed and childlike.

—Just had a yen to see how you were making out, Mr. Pilkey said with heavy jocosity.

He seated himself in the best chair in the sparely furnished room, put his feet up on an ottoman so that his garters showed, and lit his pipe. His small pot jutted under his vest; the fine nest of lines crinkled as he looked over the furnishings of the room. Probably pricing everything. Mr. Pilkey's labored breathing continued during his survey. Then he settled back, more at ease than Guy Hudson had ever felt in his own room. But after all the old man was merely feigning to visit a peasant sharecropping on his land.

—No folderol here, Mr. Pilkey said. When I was a young teacher. I lived almost as simply as you do. I commend you. With your permission I should like to bring Mrs. Pilkey up some day, if her heart will stand the climb. She might care to make further suggestions about your room decoration. . . .

—Thank you, sir.

It was the way his grandfather had dictated the accouterments of his room at Amherst. Mr. Pilkey emitted several clouds of pipe smoke and opened his heavy jaw:

—In general I am pleased with your work here. I have heard several flattering comments from your students. Perhaps you haven't as much zest as an old hand like Philbrick Grimes, but then you're a war veteran, and I expect it will take time for you to learn how we do things here. . . .

In the sonorous condescension of the old yet vigorous voice Guy Hudson felt that he was being beaten over the head with a velvet truncheon. The Principal thought for a moment, then gathered himself:

—My intention was to pay you a purely social call. But while I am here, I might as well mention that this morning I received a letter from Mr. Marlow Brown. I think you teach his boy? . . .

Guy Hudson nodded. Something was cooking.

—Buddy Brown?

—Exactly. The father seems to think you don't understand the boy.

—I dislike him intensely. Perhaps I show it. . . .

—No question but what Buddy Brown is a Lovely Fellow, Mr. Pilkey said. I've been watching him for almost three months now. And the father is a high-type business executive. The mother is one of our nobler ladies. . . .

—I hadn't heard that. I know only that the kid is cheap, spoiled, and brutal. . . .

—Pardon me. When I was a young teacher, I tended to go

off half-cocked on my judgment of students. But forty years of experience at schoolmastering have mellowed me. You're young yet. . . .

—In years perhaps.

—You have also a quick temper, Mr. Pilkey said smoothly, biting the stem of his pipe. My grandmother Bowditch had red hair too. She was a firebrand. But she improved with maturity. You too, I think, will get yourself in hand. I try by example to show my young teachers that moderation is the best policy. Mr. Grimes, for example, has learned that truth. . . . Well, to make a long story short, Mr. Brown writes that you use the manners of a drill sergeant on your classes. Does that strike you as quite proper? I know you're enthusiastic and only recently separated from the army. But after all in this school you're dealing with the cream of young American civilians. Every boy at this Academy has been carefully screened. I have always maintained that love works more miracles than hatred. I wish you'd try it on your classes. . . .

Guy Hudson was appalled to find himself taking up the defensive position. There was bubbling in him now a slow rage. For Mr. Pilkey was spanking him, slowly, lovingly, and thoroughly. He clutched at his trousers to ascertain that they were still buttoned, and himself not bent over a barrel. The Principal's voice ground on in dreadful urbanity:

—Since you admit that you do not like the boy, I must take the liberty of asking if you have been quite fair to him. It's so damnably *easy* to dock a few points from the paper of a boy one doesn't like. And one *thinks* one is being just. . . . As a young teacher I experienced the same temptation myself. So I solved the problem by bending over backward to scale my grades up the other way. . . . So many teachers, I find, are poor mathematicians. Perhaps you've made a small error in computing the monthly average? Small, of course, but it would mean much to Buddy Brown. Students never think of questioning the accuracy of their teacher's grading. . . . I wonder if I might trouble you for a look at your gradebook. . . .

—My *gradebook,* sir? Guy Hudson said.

He was vermilion with anger and shame. Mr. Pilkey, observing his perturbation, withdrew his foot from the breech a fraction of an inch:

—Yes, your gradebook. The merest formality. It is some-times advisable for an old hand like myself (he chortled richly) to give a new one a few tips on grading. Let us put it this way. I am merely calling your stewardship into ac-count. Like the parable of the talents in Scripture that I read in chapel this morning. . . .

Guy Hudson walked to his desk. A quilt of the richest hue had seeped up his cheeks to the roots of his red hair.

—This means, sir, he said quietly, that you don't trust your teachers in the administration of their classes or of justice? . . . My *gradebook*! Why that's as sacred as my diary . . . if I kept one. . . .

Mr. Pilkey poured a little more mazola on the waters:

—If you are a truly honest man (as I believe you to be) I don't see how you can possibly have any objection to my asking to see . . . the ledgers of your business. . . . Think of me, if you please, as a bank examiner. . . .

In his screaming degradation Guy Hudson was still ob-jective enough to see the false analogy here. What was really happening, however, was that the Principal, for all his affa-bility, was putting him in the stocks. It was as though a pa-tient, receiving a doctor's prescription, sent it out to get it tested for poison. And here he was, supposedly an expert, being challenged in his own field. Was there no end to Amer-ican cynicism, even in education? He'd been entrusted the teaching of these boys, and here was the executive whom fate had placed over him vitiating his every dignity! For an instant his scarlet anger whispered to him to tell Mr. Pilkey to take his goddam school and shove it. But an ounce of discretion left in him also whispered that a roar of outraged honor would only further befool him in the Principal's eyes. Any man so calloused as to ask for a look at a teacher's gradebook certainly wouldn't be impressed by a stand of outraged idealism. His protest would be as futile as a virgin covering her pudenda before a Moroccan, intent on her spoliation.

His hesitation didn't escape the Principal, who recrossed his bandy legs and said smoothly:

—Mr. Philbrick Grimes, you know, often shows me his gradebook for suggestions on marking. As a young teacher I learned many shortcuts, which I am delighted to pass on to interested parties. . . .

164

The more whore Philbrick, Guy Hudson thought. But in these past instants the idealism and humble noblesse that had flowered in him this autumn were blasted on the stem. What little respect he'd ever had for Mr. Pilkey withered forever. So this was the way American teachers were spayed! A little sabotage here, a few direct insults there, and the bravest motives were frozen into compliance. He'd fought his way through a war, but it was never so dreadful as this hour. There remained now only the desire to hurt Mr. Pilkey as he himself had been hurt. But how? This old gentleman was really a whited sepulcher, with walls of complacent lead. For the first time since combat in France and Germany Guy Hudson thirsted for murder and revenge.

—I beg you not to be angry, said Mr. Pilkey. I know that young teachers are sensitive. Too much so. But remember, I have a right to know what is happening in my school. Do you blame me? I get a letter from a parent, and I'm in duty bound to find out what's at the bottom of it. I have nothing against you personally.

The fine fallaciousness of that reasoning! Guy Hudson thought. This man has the conscience of a squid. He's too yellow round the bunghole to back up his teachers against the parents. But naturally. In American education the customer *must* always be right. . . .

Mr. Pilkey was asking with cunning archness through his pipe smoke:

—Can't you find your gradebook? Or is your marking perhaps like what Mrs. Pilkey calls the impressionism of nineteenth century painting? . . .

Had he been a woman, Guy Hudson would have screamed at this point. There was something in the Principal's voice that had taken twenty-five years to achieve—a kind of wheedling glaze muffling the undertone boom of authority, as ripples mask the expanse of a cesspool when ordure is dropped in. And in a final twinge of perception he saw that Mr. Pilkey was happiest in those moments when he could bully his staff, subtly or openly.

So Guy Hudson rummaged in his desk drawer. There, among unanswered letters, a metal box of condoms, and some postage stamps his hand fished out the little book, held shut by an elastic band. It was larger than an address book and smaller than a ledger. But here, in ruled columns, was exactly entered by his pen the day-by-day progress and record of some hundred boys at this Academy. Across the pages marched small neat figures of that percentage system used in American schools. And trying hard not to slap it into Mr. Pilkey's palm (as a nurse lays a clamp in the hands of a surgeon), Guy Hudson placed his gradebook in the Principal's outstretched hand—a strong horny old hand—the same that had smacked recalcitrant boys, the same that had paddled the breasts of Mrs. Pilkey O so many years ago. It was the hand of a schoolteacher, white and a little flabby; yet it had always about it a suggestion of discipline and the shape of the invisible reins it was used to holding.

Then he sank moodily into the chair behind his desk. Mr. Pilkey put on his reading glasses and scrutinized the gradebook. He looked now like a genial old lawyer preparing a brief. But those gray eyes missed nothing.

—I will concede that you're very workmanlike. But perhaps you have *too many* grades here? Do you exhaust your boys by testing them too frequently? As a young teacher I discovered that one weekly quiz was sufficient check on their progress and my success. . . .

—They get a daily test. You suggested it yourself in Faculty meeting. . . .

Strangely he was fighting an impulse that would drive his chin down onto his chest. And this sinking of defeat he wouldn't have the Principal see for the world.

—Well, said Mr. Pilkey, I don't believe in dictating classroom procedures, understand, but a test a day seems to me too much to expect of adolescents. What would happen if every teacher here gave every boy a test a day?

—Nothing. It would probably be good for them. . . .

Mr. Pilkey now began to show the first querulous signs of his own anger. He had a kind of Old Testament rage reserved for inferiors, or for children caught masturbating. He took off his reading glasses and stared at Guy Hudson. His mouth worked like the maw of a devilfish:

—Really now? Goddam it, sir, why are most of my teachers such prima donnas? Everyone thinks that the class he happens to be teaching is the only important thing in the school! . . .

—That seems to me the only way to get results.

Mr. Pilkey subsided sulkily:

—They fail to consider the health and the span of attention of the students under them. No boy can possibly keep up with all you . . . you fellows expect of him here. . . Why, when my son Herman was a student here, he told me that his instructors ran him ragged. . . . Yes, I can really understand the plight of that Lovely Fellow Buddy Brown. . . . Goddam it, man, haven't you got a heart?

—I have never asked for more than the traditional one-hour preparation, Guy Hudson said doggedly.

Then came another nick from the razor. Mr. Pilkey took out his fountain pen and tallied up all of Buddy Brown's grades. While he was adding and dividing the old man chuckled dismally:

—Even in grade school I was a great hand at totting up averages. . . .

Then leaning forward, scratch paper in hand, his glasses generously misted, the Principal set his latest trap:

—I don't suppose you happen to remember Buddy Brown's average for last month?

Guy Hudson was ready for this one. He answered out of a fog of weariness and disgust:

—Fifty seven-point-five per cent. I was bighearted and called it fifty-eight. Wouldn't you say that was an E by all announced standards of this Academy?

Mr. Pilkey hurriedly consulted his own average:

—Numerically yes. But I must say some teachers are awfully picayune about one or two points. Why, I still remember the June Herman graduated from here! What a to-do there was about passing the poor boy in French IV because he had a fifty-nine average! . . .

—I understood that the passing grade here was sixty per cent, Guy Hudson said in a rattling whisper.

—Quite true, quite true, the Principal said, folding his hands judicially. But goddam it, man, life is never so cut and dried as all that. What difference will it make ten years from now whether this boy got a fifty-nine or a sixty-one in European History 2a?

—None whatever, Guy Hudson said truthfully.

But then something being garroted in him gave one more kick at life, like a strangling marionette:

—But I do think, sir, that when you make a rule, you should abide by it. . . .

The violence of Mr. Pilkey's response to this was altogether out of proportion to the stimulus. His old eyes suddenly got bloodshot. Dropping pipe and gradebook, he lurched to his feet and toward Guy Hudson, sullen at the desk. The young man thought for a moment that the old one was going to attempt to thrash him. Mr. Pilkey's voice filled the room; it was like his roaring reading of Saint Paul in chapel. This bellow would awaken every boy on the corridor:

—Goddam it, man, do you presume to tell me how to run my school?

—Not at all, sir.

And he meant it. His rage and shame had leveled off now, there remained only a scorn that a man in such a position of moral authority should so bully his subordinates.

—You should take a leaf out of Philbrick Grimes's book! cried Mr. Pilkey. He's not much older than you, but he knows what's what!

Guy Hudson refused to answer. He was choking on some hellish oyster lodged in his windpipe. The Principal sat down and tried to put his pipe back in his mouth. The old man's great chest was panting, worse than when he'd climbed the stairs. For a moment the teacher wondered if his superior was going to have a stroke. But Mr. Pilkey was subsiding. His breath came in sobs. He wiped his glasses. Had Mr. Grimes been there, he would have cried *Fie* on Guy Hudson for getting the poor old man so worked up. Then Mr. Pilkey crossed his legs, showing his garters and the mackerel flesh on his calf. And his voice came out again, now sinuously reasonable:

—That poor boy Buddy Brown must have extra help, of course. I want you to give him one hour of time outside of class every day.

—Very well, sir. Shall I mail the bill to the father?

—*Bills*? I'm not speaking of *tutoring*. I do not approve of tutoring at three dollars an hour in my school. I do not think it looks well when my teachers, with their more than adequate salaries, go scrounging money from parents. I am asking you as man to man to give this boy extra help. Without charge. . . . Obviously you have failed as a teacher where Buddy is concerned. You just haven't *got* to him. As a young teacher I considered it my *moral obligation* to give my students extra help outside of class. When a teacher has *failed* with a boy in the classroom, he must get to him elsewhere. . . . Besides, it's no chore to teach the highly selected group we have here. As Mr. Grimes told me only the other day, the test of Great Teaching is the dull student. And we have none here that I know of. . . . Now I'm sure that you will take up this challenge that I throw down to you. I know you want to redeem yourself in my eyes and in your own. Besides (and Mr. Pilkey lowered his voice to a knowing whisper) I have reason to believe that Buddy Brown has . . . certain psychological troubles . . . his father is taking him to an analyst during Christmas vacation. The Browns can well afford it, you know. . . .

With a valedictorian beam Mr. Pilkey arose from his chair, knocked out the heel of his pipe, and moved toward the door. There was majesty in his mien and walk, like a crotchety and aloof old god. At the door he put out his hand to his subordinate, who was still hunched at his desk. Guy Hudson took no notice of this disarming gesture. Mr. Pilkey waved:

—Thank you for your hospitality. . . .

(O my God! my God! Is there no finale to this ballbreaking? Get out, you old fart of brimstone!)

—I really believe, Mr. Pilkey continued, that you and I understand each other a little better now. I hired you with many grave doubts, but I did want to give a veteran a chance. That's the least a grateful country can do, as I said in my catalog. I think you will work out all right when you get yourself in hand. . . . These little talks between a teacher and his boss are like a PTA, don't you think? Teachers tend to run a little wild when they are young. They need a guiding hand. My fault, I fear, has been to err on the side of laxness. Now if you had to work for *some* principals. . . . O, by the way. . . . In his letter Mr. Brown also said that you had used disgraceful language to Buddy. Do you care to tell me what you said? Does it bear repeating? Or perhaps you don't remember? . . .

Feeling faint, Guy Hudson stood up at his desk. He had some deathlike desire to slither down to the floor. He heard his voice slip out, high, white, and meaningless:

—Yes. I called the little squealer the pimple on the arse of the school. . . .

There was a silence. At the door Mr. Pilkey took off his glasses, wiped them, and put them on again.

—You did? You said that? . . . Dear me. . . . I am not amused. . . . Well, Mr. Brown insisted that I fire you. But I always stand behind my faculty. I said that you were new here and possibly raw from overseas. Of course in my public school system I should *have* to dismiss you. But I give any young man two years to make or break himself. . . . Such language as you have used is intolerable. To the ears of an innocent boy it is inexcusable. I am ashamed of you. Goodnight. . . .

A tall corpulent ghost, Mr. Pilkey faded out of the lamplight in Guy Hudson's room. The old man walked slowly downstairs. Guy Hudson stood a long while at his desk. Something in him had suddenly grown old and beaten—a wisp in the wind, like all the rest of the faculty. He wanted to vomit, to kick, to punch, to make the air violet with curses. He picked up all his day's papers and tore them to ribbons.

Then he put on his hiplength army coat and walked over to the village. In a bar with assorted druggists, mail clerks, and tobacco workers he got silently and stinkingly drunk. At one o'clock the bar closed and he staggered out into the cold December streets, colder because no snow had yet fallen that year. In prim salt-shaker houses townspeople had gone to bed. Farmers and hardware workers lay beside their wives without ecstasy or abandon. Out of such beds came frozen little children into the world, cramped children with no desire to learn of life what Guy Hudson and his kind knew. Future generations of teachers would struggle with their chilled little hearts, with the same net result as all teachers in all centuries. . . .

He was sloppy-drunk. He wavered from lamppost to lamppost. The little diamonds of the stars high over his head in the December sky seemed those asterisks with which obscenities are indicated in genteel novels. In a gust of maudlin affection he stopped to pat a dog that was watering itself on the curb. He fell on the dog and befouled himself. The gay green corduroy hat with the little goose feather skidded from his head, where it had been clapped at a drunken angle. Then lifting himself out of the dust and the urine he raised his gritty voice in song, an American college

170

song composed by dead carousers of a more relaxed era of capitalism, when scholars took college as a maudlin country club:

—We are poor little sheep who have lost our way. . . .

Blurting this out and almost weeping, he tottered along the river by the dormant classic buildings of the Girls' School. Some hectic and lachrymose gallantry, forgotten during the war, made him lift his singing in a braying cadence of courtliness. A window on the third floor scaled privily up; there looked out at him in a pink housecoat that lovely remote girl whose name, he remembered, was Betty Blanchard. Her voice came clear and low down to him in the December night:

—Mr. Hudson, you aren't in the satchel by any chance?

He replied, swaying below her in the frosty moonlight:

—My dear, close that window! Your re-pu-ta-tion! . . . O bro-*ther!* Don't ever teach school, my dear. . . .

The window slammed shut. He made it an unsteady bow. Again his green velveteen hat fell off. He groped for it, then wove off along the river toward the Boys' School and to bed.

9

Except for poets who write for greeting cards and merchants who turn an honest penny out of tinsel and jollity, Mr. Pilkey was the last surviving American to plump for an Old Fashioned Christmas. By this he meant the sort of merrymaking he'd known as a boy. Nothing since made any sense to him. He decreed at term end time that Christmas should be kept at his Academy, and keep it his five hundred students and faculties did. His idea of Christmas was founded on the poem Ring Out, Wild Bells, and Dickens's *Christmas Carol*, which he read aloud on the twenty-fourth of every

December by the hearth to his wife and to his old mother.

The Sunday before the Fall Term ended, both Schools were put through an orgy of feasting, carol singing, and sanctity as would have prostrated the hardiest Santa Claus. Mr. Pilkey staged everything but The Birth. Unfortunately that happened two thousand years ago, and even he couldn't trump up a repeat performance. But no one knew better what true heartiness was.

The liturgy of this yearly festival, probably the last great noncommercial splurge in the United States, had been drawn up in the first year that Mr. Pilkey was Principal. It had been repeated every December for twenty-five years. And since nothing is to be gained by the improvement or alteration of traditional ceremonies nothing had been added or subtracted to the rites since that first Pilgrim Christmas at the new Academy. This December too boys and girls would fulfill to the ruddy letter the fetes that their fathers and mothers had enjoyed before them. The Order of the Day was typed on mimeographed sheets by Miss Pringle. In charge of executing all the prescribed minutiae were Mr. Philbrick Grimes, and a small committee of the Principal's elect henchmen. They were stage managers to the only indigenous miracle play in America.

Mr. Pilkey had nicely allotted and parceled out the separate Christmas responsibilities of the Girls' and Boys' Schools. The girls took care of the Gentler Facets of Christmas. At eight o'clock on that Sunday morning all boarding girls were ravaged from their beds by the powerful hand of Mrs. Mears and several muscular mistresses.

For Christmas breakfast the girls descended to the dining room in Mrs. Mears's cellar. Their privilege was to go down without getting dressed. They appeared in wrappers and slippers. Many wore their hair in snoods; a few arose with the curlpapers in which they'd slept. As they lit into the warm nourishing breakfast of hot oatmeal and hot milk, they murmured to one another like peevish nurses evicted at midnight from their hospital. Indeed in the dining room there was a subdued snarling—not the tinkle of talk and laughter such as filled the air at noon meals. A hundred girls in kimonos, gouging at their hickies or plucking winkers from their eyelids, glared at the steaming bowls of cereal.

In token of the loving informality of the Christmas breakfast Mrs. Mears was wearing a flowered lounging robe and furlined stadium boots. She was wider awake than most, for she'd spent the past hour working out her déshabille to perfection. She looked like a prosperous widow surprised at her lounging by a vacuum cleaner salesman. She was vexed that such a lamenting and sour spirit hung like a miasma over the dining room.

—Girls! Merry Christmas! Don't act so nerrrvous!

Then pumping the joviality into her voice, she uttered a special Christmas morning Grace. It was like all her other Graces Before Meals except that she rang the Virgin and Saint Joseph into it, along with a special citation (almost like a singing commercial) for these grateful rolled oats they were about to ingest. Then the Directress rang her famous bell and one hundred girls drearily plunked themselves down to eat the scalding oatmeal. Student waiters stood ready to refill the bowls, but there were no calls for seconds. Only the steaming milk went inside the girls.

Miss Betty Blanchard sat at her place at Mrs. Mears's table, staring in nausea at the wholesome old fashioned breakfast. Only Miss Demerjian was stowing it away. And Mrs. Mears was setting an example to her girls by shoveling great spoonfuls of the awful paste inside her wide mouth.

—Girls! she cried from her place. Eat up every bit of these tasty morsels! We need strength for The Ceremony!

And the Girls' School shuddered in their chairs and buried their faces in the saucers of slop. A bright and pretty senior whispered to her roommate:

—I feel just like Jane Eyre. . . .

Next to Betty Blanchard was the mistress of music, Miss Carpenter, an aging virgin with steelrimmed glasses, the frames of which were fogging up with the oatmeal steam.

—God, when can we have a cigarette? Betty Blanchard said.

—Not till after The Ceremony, Miss Carpenter murmured.

—Girls! cried Mrs. Mears. You're not having *fun*! Relax!

A windy sigh passed over the dining room. A few flabby freshwomen ate their oatmeal and clamped their lips, lest they regurgitate the scalding gruel. Then Mrs. Mears arose and intoned another Grace, in which she evoked piteous pictures of Roger Williams and his little band of exiles freezing to death in the wilderness, because they had no turkey to eat. Then she rang her little bell, which was the signal for the entire Girls' School to get dressed for The Ceremony.

Half an hour later they all issued forth. It looked rather like a junket of nuns off for a day of mountain climbing. The Directress led the way, waving her arms and shouting encouragement. She was wearing her astrakhan coat and a fur hood. Many of the freezing girls wore fur capes of cony or marten. They huddled together for comfort; the snow was two feet deep. Then Miss Carpenter, gasping from the intake of icy air into her lungs, blew on a pitchpipe. One hundred and twelve voices struck up most dolefully the carol We Three Kings.

—Louder, girls! Mrs. Mears called, hurling into the monophony her own sure alto.

The already numb little procession halted at the edge of the road while a snowplow passed. The driver, a fat man in a sheepskin coat and heavy gloves, leaned out of his cab and waved at the women and girls, singing disconsolately away on the shoulder of the road. The hymn became a wail. The plow turned up a wave of snow that all but engulfed those standing nearest the road.

—You-hoo! the driver of the snowplow said.

—Don't answer him! Mrs. Mears screamed, dropping out of the stanza.

Then the entire Girls' School and faculty, leaping snowdrifts and dropping here and there a dainty rubber boot, hurtled across the now cleared road and catapulted themselves into the snowy cemetery by the white church, lacy with ice and snow. In the churchyard the blanket was incalculably deep. The hymn was now punctuated by shrieks of surprise as the snow filled the shoes of the girls leading the rush. But the singing kept bravely on: Star of Wonder, Star of Light. There was now a great deal of hopping about in the graveyard, trying to keep from getting buried in the drifts or from breaking a leg on the concealed tombstones. Many a schoolgirl barked her shins on old marble underneath. Had the man in the snowplow looked back, he would have seen a spectacle like a hundred rabbits in wild rout.

—Here we are, girls, cried Mrs. Mears, stopping at the river side of the cemetery.

—Has she a divining rod or is she traveling by azimuth? Betty Blanchard said to Miss Demerjian.

—Hush, baby.

Then The Ceremony began. As President of the Student Council, and wearing a kolinsky jacket that must have cost her mother a month's stipend, Midgie Mears stepped forward with mincing reverence. She was carrying an ordinary heavy-duty shovel.

—Ready, Mom?

Betty Blanchard thought Midgie was going to roll up her sleeves like a washerwoman. The fur cap slid back over her bleached pageboy bob. Then Mrs. Mears made a signal to the mistress of music, who clapped her hands three times. And from a hundred freezing throats came an agonized cheer:

—Merry Christmas, Miss Sophia!

—Louder! said Mrs. Mears. How do you expect the poor dear to hear you under all that snow?

The greeting was repeated, in precisely that frenzied shriek with which the girls delivered their basketball cheers.

—School spirit has fallen off sadly this year, said Mrs. Mears to the mistress of gymnastics.

Midgie shoveled some snow off the grave of Miss Sophia. She put her buxom shoulders behind two or three loads; then she turned the shovel over to the lower-ranking Councillors. Soon the grave was clear, down to its withered grass. There came into view that small plat under which lay all that remained of Our Gracious Foundress. A spoonshaped stone of white marble said that here was buried Miss Sophia Abercrombie, who was gathered to her fathers in July 1867. The stone notified all concerned that the deceased was a maiden lady of untarnished reputation, and there was a verse from the Magnificat:

—Henceforth all generations shall call me blessed. . . .

Mrs. Mears observed this minor exhumation with pleased absorption. Betty Blanchard saw something almost like necrophily in the eyes of the Directress as that modest little grave came into view from under the snow.

Well, she thought, shifting from one foot to the other in her icy galoshes, all education is a pact with the dead; and here we are in covenant with the bones of an old virgin whose revenues pay my salary. But must we be reminded quite so literally of our debt to the charnelhouse? . . .

Some of the younger members of Girls' School watched

the snow being dissipated with popping eyes. The young are queasy in the presence of death; to them all tradition is a return to the womb from which they have recently escaped, with no hard feelings. Suppose that shovel should dig in a foot too deep? Would the ghost of Miss Sophia arise from her grave? Or would the digging excavate a skeletal old hand, or one of Miss Sophia's femurs?

When the grave was uncovered on that bitter Sunday morning, Mrs. Mears took into her gloved hands a typewritten sheet of paper. It was prepared by Miss Pringle and dictated by Mr. Pilkey. It was the yearly homily on Our Gracious Foundress. It never varied in content; every girl heard it four times during the four years she was at The Academy. Mrs. Mears read this eulogy in her clear hard voice, often glancing over her pince-nez to see that girls and teachers were paying attention. The prose of Mr. Pilkey was stately and mellow. Though Miss Sophia was already long in her grave when Mr. Pilkey was born, he wrote as though he knew her personally. All the girls had seen Miss Sophia's portrait, peering and a little confused in her shawl and kerchief. But from Mr. Pilkey's sermon on her virtues, as read by Mrs. Mears, she emerged as a gracious lady of Civil War vintage. Betty Blanchard found herself wondering if Miss Sophia hadn't been a virtuous and baptized Scarlett O'Hara.

Mrs. Mears read with great emotion. Her favorite mistresses nodded their heads and occasionally sniffled, like close relatives at a wake in hope of a legacy. Only Miss Blanchard exercised her fingers in their gloves and thought that this was all pretty ghastly nonsense—lip service to a heritage. It might even cause pneumonia in some of the more delicate girls. The exordium clattered along the railroad track of a double metaphor:

—Our Gracious Foundress sleeps here forever. But her spirit is a torch that will light, a trumpet that will resound through America . . . .

—Amen, said Betty Blanchard.

Miss Demerjian looked at her in horror.

Then the snow was shoveled back into place. Two pretty maids from the freshman class came forward and laid a wreath on the snow, a coronet of artificial poinsettias. Their teeth of blood glittered. And Miss Sophia was left to her repose for another year.

Betty Blanchard ended by being touched in spite of herself. She wondered if that ancestral dust and lace under the counterpane of snow heard these impatient feet trampling above her, who was eighty-one years buried. She wondered if the strange idealistic old woman, wherever she was now, suspected how few of these brittle little girls had caught any of her own fierce spirit. And in spite of the brilliant folly of Miss Sophia's idealism the young woman teacher marveled at a tired, possibly cantankerous spinster (for she must have been, in spite of Mr. Pilkey's portrait of her in lavender and old lace) who would leave money for a school. And each year girls cold and resentful had to come out and pay her homage. The tribute was outrageous, but possibly the idea behind it wasn't. . . .

Mrs. Mears spoke with a certain relief:

—Now girls! You have all morning free. But I don't want you to make yourselves nerrrvous. . . . Why don't you make snowmen? That's what I used to do as a girl. I'm sure Cook will let you have some raisins for the eyes. Won't that be *fun*?

—*Mad* fun, said the pretty senior to her roommate.

Miss Blanchard went back to her room to thaw out. She built a fire in her fireplace and served hot buttered rum to the music mistress. Miss Demerjian tried to horn in, but was brutally snubbed. And after a while the music mistress got a little high. Her glasses slipped down on her flat breasts, and she confided in Betty Blanchard. Once, twenty years ago, while on a walking trip in the Italian Alps, Miss Carpenter had been loved for one night by her guide Lodovico. Ma che uomo! Betty Blanchard sighed and stretched her fine legs to the blaze. She considered that to this pass she herself would come twenty years from now. An old hen burbling of the one cock in her life.

At noon both schools of The Academy observed Christmas in the chapel. There the old head of the Classics Department conducted a brief but telling service. Doctor Hunter was the only surviving member of the faculty who would have reminded anyone of what American teachers were like in the Golden Age. He was a tall stooped octogenarian with a mustache and Van Dyke beard. He walked in the courtly dignity of one brought to maturity in 1885, when there was still style and longevity to life. In those times it was believed

177

that America might produce an aristocracy of brains. Old Doctor Hunter spoke a measured and lovely English, different from that spastic thing on the tongues of the younger faculty and students of The Academy. He was born the year in which Miss Sophia died.

Since 1900 he'd had no truck whatever with the world, withdrawing to his library to read and read again his Homer, his Horace, his Virgil, and his Catullus. And once a year, at the Christmas service, his voice came rusty and humane to the boys and girls of The Academy. They revered him almost as a memory without quite knowing why. To read the *Aeneid* under Doctor Hunter was a moving and tender experience. But now only four boys out of four hundred took Latin IV. Why should they? There were technological skills now to be learned by bright young Americans; Latin was a stupid old vermiform appendix that had lingered on because no one quite dared sever it. Doctor Hunter was unique on The Academy faculty. He'd taught here twenty-five years, and elsewhere for another twenty-five. The boys still felt he had something to teach them—but what? Even the roughest were somehow touched when that slouched old man rheumatically crossed the quadrangle. Such teachers, human and leisurely and wise, would never come again in America because the matrix which had stamped them was now forever cracked.

As he conducted the Christmas service, everyone realized Doctor Hunter's wife had committed suicide, and that the old man now sat every night in his rooms, drinking himself into a stupor among her faded relics. With her death his last hold on life went. Criticism was muted. To him was granted all that affection in which teachers were once held, centuries ago. It was obvious from him that there had once been illusion and grandeur in America.

In his Christmas service, the only time he appeared yearly before the entire Boys' and Girls' Schools, Doctor Hunter wore his black gown with the revers of red satin. Over this his white hair and goatee made him seem a weary and ascetic old prince. For once Mr. Pilkey and Doctor Smedley didn't sit on the rostrum.

His service itself was a melee of styles, rubrics and dispensations, strangely sad and intense, as Protestantism sometimes is when it strives to rise to the level of true ceremonial.

178

It was a spawning forth of all the things ever said on the Birth of Christ. But only the Catholic and Jewish students noticed how hybrid were the roots of its inspiration.

As a note of extra pomp the Boys' Choir had been joined by the Choral Society of the Girls' School. They all sat in the Choir Loft, giggling surreptitiously to find themselves a mixed company. By order of Mr. Pilkey (and under protest from Mr. Amos James) they were all wearing rented choir gowns, which to the religious experience of most of them were like the smocks a barber throws over his clients. Yet on their faces sat that pure washed intensity which leaves most members of the human race by the age of twenty. The boy and girl students had obligingly adopted a holy, not sanctimonious, air because their elders wished it. Had their parents seen them at this Christmas service, they would have said:

—Why, how *sweet*! They never look like that around the house. . . .

This mixed chorus sang of Israel's longing for Emmanuel, to the air of the aching old Hebrew chant. And they sang Adeste Fideles in Church Latin. And they sang Stille Nacht in German. Few would have found this mixture of tongues unorthodox. And they sang The First Nowell and This Endris Nyghte. The pure young voices soared in the chapel. Mrs. Pilkey wept in her pew. No one would have dreamed that this wonderful singing came from American boys and girls, none of whom was over twenty. For a little while as they sang, these young persons became timeless, stirring even the cynical men and women who taught them and knew them too well. Was it possible that this flood of gorgeous sound came from boys and girls who made demons of themselves all term long? Perhaps there was something in the rejuvenating and revitalizing idea of Christmas after all. . . .

Then old Doctor Hunter arose in his scholar's robes and read aloud the Christmas story according to Saint Luke. And finally the dreadful heart-breaking tale of Christmas came alive as it did at no other time on that Sunday. Doctor Hunter understood Christmas. The old Latin scholar brought to his reading a world of regret, jubilance, and comprehension, for he knew at eighty the reason Christ was born. His voice hesitated on the words:

—Because there was no room for them in the inn. . . .

And there could be heard throughout that sunlit chapel the sobs of boys and girls, of men and women. Emotion, which students cunningly mask, trembled there in The Academy's chapel.

Then the entire Boys' and Girls' Schools trooped into the dining hall for a monstrous dinner. The menu was prescribed through Mr. Pilkey's memories of Dickens. Five hundred and seventy people sat down to a feast of roast goose. Any other Principal would have settled for turkey, but not Mr. Pilkey. The Comptroller had for weeks scoured the markets to buy enough goose to feed the two schools. Student waiters and waitresses squirmed in the costumes of Bob and Martha Cratchit, with gay ribbons, and collars bent down to simulate an 1840 cravat. The faculty didn't sit on their dais today: at every table on the main parquet sat a gentleman or lady teacher struggling with a goose for his or her pretended family.

The dinner began with a contest. The teachers had to see who was briskest in carving up the goose for twelve plates. The last twenty-four years Mr. Pilkey had been allowed to win the goose-carving race by tacit permission of both faculties. But today a redheaded teacher of history, named Mr. Guy Hudson, dismembered his goose and served his entire table, which applauded him wildly. The Principal was so angry that he sulked all during the dinner.

—Do you want to lose your job, sir? one of the boys said to Guy Hudson.

For dessert there were fruit and nuts and coffee. Americans don't ordinarily care for this sort of chaste sweet. But that was the way it was in Dickens, and that was the way it would be at The Academy.

Some of the lowerformers were really sick after all this. But the day was only beginning. Mr. Pilkey planned no lull in the festivities. His wife and the faculty ladies hung wreaths and poinsettias in every empty nook of the main school building. Mrs. Pilkey forced the ladies to climb stepladders and place lighted candles on red and green velvet. in every niche she could find. Here too she was a tigress for effect.

Meanwhile Mr. Grimes and his salon of bespectacled epigrammatic boys were accomplishing their own secret. It was a daring innovation in a non-denominational school. He'd been mulling it over for weeks. It was so rakish and chic that he hadn't even dared to ask his Principal's sanction. It was to be a Surprise. Jabbering to one another like a Left Wing Theater Group, Mr. Grimes and his satellites locked all the doors to The Academy chapel and sealed all the windows. Then holding their breaths for various reasons, they lighted sticks of Roman Catholic incense all over the chapel. This sacramental Mr. Grimes had wheedled (with dark hints of becoming a convert) out of Father Fogarty, pastor of St. Lucy's in the village. As the holy and spicy odor permeated every corner of the huge white-walled chapel, he thought himself swooning with a priestly gladness. For many years now he'd had yearnings toward Rome or at least toward Canterbury; he told his salon that he was in need of the steadying pattern of scholastic philosophy. Soon the chapel was smelling like a cathedral during Solemn Mass.

—O Caspar, Balthasar, and Melchior! Mr. Grimes cried.

For shortly to be staged in this now stinking chapel, by a handpicked cast from Boys' and Girls' Schools, was the first performance of an English miracle play from the Coventry cycle. It had been Mr. Grimes's very own idea; he'd coached and cast and mounted it. He was quite nervous; he wasn't sure exactly how Mr. Pilkey would take it—not to speak of the Calvinists and Marxian-Socialists of the faculty. Directing draymas was Mr. Grimes's most visible contribution to the life of The Academy. Here he put his whole soul on a stage for the rabble to look at. He was a good dramatic coach. He had a way of turning ordinary boys and girls into actors, forging them to their parts till the whole play shone like a jeweled vase.

The allotting of parts alone had been handled most raffishly by Mr. Grimes, with many a Machiavellian consultation with Miss Demerjian, who was in charge of dramatics at the Girls' School. Mr. Grimes had to *handle* Miss Demerjian without allowing her to have any part in the play. He was all for awarding the parts on ability and looks. But Miss Demerjian (after consulting Mrs. Mears) was inclined to the belief that fat speaking parts should be given as consolation prizes to girls who weren't outstanding in their studies or in field hockey.

—I must have a Jewess for the role of Mary, my dear, Mr. Grimes had said.

—Why, Philbrick! Don't be sacrilegious!

Miss Demerjian was at that age of startled virginity in which she construed everything either as an invitation to bed or as blasphemy.

But by ductile applications of his own persuasive powers on Mrs. Mears and Miss Demerjian, Mr. Grimes had brought his miracle play to ripeness. A Jewess, the daughter of a prominent delicatessen magnate in a nearby city, *was* to play Mary. Mrs. Mears had been placated into coos because her daughter Midgie, minus bobbysocks and hairdo, had won the part of the Angel Gabriel. Last month over a cup of tea Mr. Grimes had whispered to the Directress that Gabriel was much too *ethereal* for a boy to play. Privately he didn't approve of anybody from the Boys' School appearing with wings on a stage to declare the Annunciation to Mary. He was most touchy about such things. . . .

The light of the December afternoon dropped into a rosy purple, precisely as if Mr. Grimes himself had regulated a sunset from a theater switchboard. But no, it was only the chapel of The Academy brought by his magic closer to his dream of medievalism. What had the Coventry guilds that he and Miss Demerjian didn't have?

Presently, still turgid from their roast goose, the casts of the Boys' and Girls' Schools arrived to put on makeup and costume.

—Here are the mummers, Mr. Grimes said stylishly to Miss Demerjian.

—Tee-hee, Philbrick, the Syrian virgin replied, thrusting her mustache at him.

For ten years now she'd been trying to make him. She figured it would be better married to this queen-bee than to no one. Mr. Grimes, however, tolerated her only when they were Doing A Play together. Otherwise he ruthlessly truncated all her invitations to dances and to suppers cooked on the chafing dish in her room. And to his charmed circle of the faculty, the salon of Mrs. Dell Holly, he said that Miss Demerjian was a nymphomaniac from Aleppo.

By order of Mrs. Mears those occasions when the Boys' and Girls' School came together to Do A Play or to have a dance were heavily chaperoned. Mr. Grimes aided this surveillance, for in his small head he foresaw everything that could possibly happen, and he forestalled it. If Mrs. Mears and Mr. Grimes had their way, no two people from the Boys' and Girls' Schools would ever be left alone together. Consequently the small cast of the Miracle Play was rigidly policed by the Misses Betty Blanchard, Habib Demerjian, and Marian Carpenter. They weren't just around by accident; Mrs. Mears had detailed them to this duty weeks ago. And in the little closets where visiting ministers vested, boys and girls were putting on cold cream and rouge and mascara. Mr. Grimes did the makeup himself. Darting back and forth between dressing rooms, he noticed Miss Blanchard:

—Nice to see you here. You must criticize my play. But ruthlessly. . . .

—It's nice to be here.

She was all but choked on the fruity attar of incense which filled the chapel with a blue haze of piety.

—Philbrick's gone High Church, whispered Miss Demerjian, who was busy ogling the hairy legs of the boys as they climbed into the tights and jerkins of shepherds.

Under the powderpuff of Mr. Grimes, Ben Gordon, laughing and protesting a little for the effect on the girls, was transformed from President of the Student Council into a glowering Herod. Ralph Du Bouchet had his face stained umber and became one of the Magi, under a little gold crown that looked like a polished cuspidor. Betty Blanchard, who loathed touching the girl, was helping Midgie Mears into the costume of the Angel Gabriel. Midgie wore a long tunic of white samite that buttoned up the back, huge gauze wings, and a shimmering halo fastened like a boating hat to the back of her head. Tongue in cheek, Miss Blanchard laced and buttoned her pupil, for Midgie was assuming an air not angelic, but like the vision of a chorus girl in levitation during an attack of the DT's.

—This is strictly out of Alice in Wonderland, you know, Midgie said.

—Never mind that. Do you know your lines?

Midgie climbed up on a low step, flapped her wings, shook her halo, and said in her sultry voice:

—Hail, Mary. . . .

—That's quite enough, thank you.

Then Betty went to work on Judith Strauss, daughter to

the rich delicatessen mogul. She'd heard that, next to Midgie, Judith was the hottest snatch in the Girls' School. Yet with her pale blue gown and the fillet in her hair, the lovely Jewess became something modest and abashed. It was the way Mary *might* have looked. Miss Blanchard mused on the ironic perfection of Mr. Grimes's casting.

Now both schools and faculties were filing into the chapel and coughing on the incense. Till now the doors had been kept shut, lest any of the myrrh leak out. Mr. and Mrs. Pilkey, in company with the Principal's saurian mother, took pews close to the dais and looked complacent and pleased. A Miracle Play in their chapel! Such imagination! Next year Mr. Grimes would have a raise in salary. Mr. Pilkey told his mother that he wished every New York drama critic could be here. The talent he had on his faculty! . . .

Then the Miracle Play began with boys' voices in the dark fragrant chapel singing the Gregorian chant Omnes De Saba. There were few in the audience captious or historically minded enough to wonder what such music had to do with the liturgy of The Academy. Only Guy Hudson sat crossing and uncrossing his legs. He thought that all this was pretentious and meretricious nonsense. Four years ago he was fighting in the snow at Malmédy. He looked at the Pilkeys up front, peering at this charade. They looked like Tudor burghers at an execution. Holbein might have painted them with flatulent expressions on their fat chins and gold chains round their necks.

The Coventry Miracle Play was in blank verse. The students proclaimed it lovingly and rhetorically, with the same ringing passion they brought to their winter debates on Shall Russia Be Atomized? And the audience sat watching this starched old piece of five hundred years ago with the same stifling reverence one brings to Shakspere. It was a nice handsome old bore, and soon they would be away from these artificialities on their Christmas vacations, skating, dancing, and getting expensive gifts from their parents.

The staging and acting were polished, for Mr. Grimes knew what he was about. He hadn't been in Mask and Wig shows for nothing. His actors fell into stained glass attitudes; there was something deliberately Gothic about the whole thing. Most of the action went on around a tryptich built like an altar. And Mr. Grimes, having studied a thing or two about modern dramatic art, had the three kings come right out of the audience. He liked plays to be in three dimensions.

—So precious! Betty Blanchard whispered. Just like Little Theater movements we had at Wheaton. Once we did Sophocles in an amphitheater. It *reeked*. . . .

—Why, it's lovely! Miss Demerjian whispered back, rallying to the defence.

Mrs. Mears was sitting in the pew in front of them.

It was the moment of the first apparition of the Angel Gabriel. Midgie Mears glided out on stage to bring her tidings of great joy to Judith Strauss, kneeling in prayer. There was an intake of breath from the audience. Her blonde hair glimmered; her wings shimmered in the yellow spotlight that picked her out. She looked like Venus stepping from the pages of the New Testament. Even the lowerformers of twelve and thirteen awoke from their postgoose sleep. And hearing the gasp, Midgie smiled at her audience to placate them. It wasn't the smile of an archangel sent from the Holy Ghost; it was a leer that some of the older boys in The Academy had seen in a parked car by a lake under a moon. Perhaps they remembered that their mouths had been smooched in non-Biblical passion against the rouged lips of this very Angel Gabriel.

Like a match to dry shocks, a snicker scratched up from somewhere in the darkened chapel. The spark was contagious. There was a draft of giggles and finally a whole blaze of whistles. Soon the chapel was roaring with laughter. The religious fabric was rent for good. Midgie Mears turned her back on the audience, her wings shaking with hysteria.

Then Mr. Pilkey vaulted up from his pew, spewing with rage. He turned and faced the entire chapel; the spotlight picked him out. He was a Principal in apoplexy. His voice roared louder than Ben Gordon's as Herod:

—Goddam it, shut up, all of you! This is a sacred thing! If you don't appreciate it, get out of my school! . . . I'll . . . I'll lop three days off your Christmas vacation! . . .

The catcalls and laughter stopped as suddenly as though the entire school had been asphyxiated by his blast. Student Councillors ran up and down the chapel aisles, spying out the headquarters of this subversion. The audience were frozen in their pews. Mr. Grimes, who'd been as nervous as any first-night playwright, seemed to have been struck with paralysis, except that he kept fanning himself with his mimeographed program. All the art and craft on which he'd lavished a month of rehearsal and plotting had been dashed to earth by the laughter of American Philistia. The spruce little man looked ready to weep. Even Guy Hudson was scarlet at the outrage of the school's ill manners. For the first time he pitied Mr. Grimes.

The Nativity Play ground to a close with the Flight into Egypt. But the pieces of the shattered chalice couldn't be put together again. It became a Black Mass. The actors had been demoralized. They showed a tendency to burlesque their roles. The whole piece became subtly distorted, like reading the New Testament in a whorehouse. Everything ended with what Mr. Grimes had calculated as his tour de force: the choirs marched around the chapel with lighted tapers singing the Halleluiah Chorus. But they marched so fast they tripped over one another's gowns. After the late fiasco this procession of triumph looked like a torchlight procession of drunken revelers at the Mardi Gras. The afternoon ended in a rout of sacred love by the profane.

The decent students got out of the incense-smelling chapel as fast as they decently could. The meaner ones were unabashedly laughing as they straggled out. Mr. and Mrs. Pilkey were purple with chagrin. It was good the New York drama critics hadn't come after all. And old Mrs. Pilkey said she was going home and to bed for the rest of the winter —possibly forever.

—Just goes to show you what happens when you aim too high! Doctor Sour chortled to his cronies.

He'd laid bets that morning that it would stink.

Miss Demerjian stormed up to Midgie Mears, who was sobbing in the vesting room and still wearing her wings:

—You nasty little girl! I'll never speak to you again. . . .

—Gawd, Midgie bawled. It wasn't my fault! . . .

—Go home at once, Midgie, Mrs. Mears said.

Betty Blanchard thought this was the tone the Directress should have used on her daughter seventeen years ago.

In the corridor outside the chapel Guy Hudson went up to Philbrick Grimes, standing limp and disheveled. The little man kept staring at the floor, as though it should open and encave him. All the bustle and merciless enthusiasm had died out of him. Guy Hudson, touched, took his hand:

—Hell, I'm sorry. . . .

—It's nothing, doctor, Mr. Grimes said, shaking his shoulders. Nothing at all, mon vieux. Just one of those things. . . .

And since he was filled with a rare access of sentiment, Guy Hudson went back into the chapel and approached Betty Blanchard and Miss Demerjian, who were even now chaperoning the girls' getting into their furs. The Virgin Mary was crying bitterly:

—I'll scratch that Midgie. . . . Spoiled my scene. . . .

—Hush, Judith, Betty Blanchard said. Don't step out of character quite so fast. . . .

Among all this frenzy of sobbing and recriminating girls' voices he hesitated. Then he went up to Miss Blanchard and touched her lightly on the shoulder. It was a way he'd approached WAVES and SPARS and crying French girls:

—May I walk you home?

She turned and stared at him. He noticed that her eyes were as lovely as the rest of her:

—No, thank you. I'm On Duty. . . .

—Then may I wish you a Merry Christmas? he said shrugging.

—Thank you.

Still her remarkable eyes were fixed on his sunken sad ones. He walked away, tingling a little. Behind him he heard Miss Demerjian go all to pieces and twitter:

—Well, my dear, all I have to say is a great big Hmmmm! What an *interesting* combination!

And he thought he heard Miss Blanchard answer:

—O don't be a nitwit. Mr. Hudson was drunk under my window a week or so ago. . . .

He stopped walking, but didn't turn around. She'd hurt him and she'd meant to do so. And her voice seemed more edgy and constricted than when he first heard it in September. She too was growing claws.

The remaining two days of the Fall Term were an orgy of distraction and lunacy in which schools and worlds end. No further work was done. Discipline spattered like a thrown inkbottle. The corridors of the Boys' and Girls' Schools clanged with trunks going off by express, taunts as to who was going to have the wildest vacation. The virgin boys swore they were all going to lose their cherries. Those already initiated said that there was nothing they weren't going to try this time.

Guy Hudson had no home. He was going to New York and take a hotel room for three weeks. There he would carouse with his old army pals. He was going to make up for three months in which he'd been a model for youth. He would cease being the priest and revert again to the satyr. Perhaps he could slough off this skin of hypocrisy which he was beginning to accept as natural. The fictions of American education were becoming too real to him. He would be away from the eye of the Principal, in a world that knew not Mr. Pilkey. It was a world that was dishonest, but threw up no duplicity around its dishonesty.

Only Ralph Du Bouchet was dejected. In this nervous and unnatural life of school he'd flowered as most boys did not. Now he must go home to his tired mother and try to lighten her work. For him there would be no round of parties such as the other boys bragged of.

—Will you come and have dinner with me some evening during vacation, Ralph? Guy Hudson said.

—Do you think we'd have much to say to each other off this quadrangle?

Thus they parted for three weeks with a vague hostility on the part of each.

Special trains bore hundreds of boys and girls all over the United States. For an artificial and exigent reason they'd come together in a school that Miss Sophia had built for them. They carried back to their homes a resentment of a tyranny she'd never planned. And she remained under her snow in the churchyard. All seasons were alike to her.

III

The Book of Winter

1

At the end of the year the unfettered wind from river and unfenced fields heaped the snow high in the graveyard. It drifted up against the side of the whitesteepled Meeting House like a concave awning. All the ragged tombstones were buried under two feet of white meal, with a gleaming crust on top so that one could scud across it and never know that the dead looked up at him as he skated. Thus Miss Sophia and her ancestors and the departed untouchables of the town lay bedded below a blanket of glaring cruel white. In early January the sunlight in this cemetery bounced off a screen lucent with a million diamonds. It was bleak here now, a desert of winter's own making. Sentimentalists would find their teeth chattering to think of the dead lying under this icy shroud.

Now and then in the graveyard the purity of the heaped snow had been defiled by little yellow burrows, drilled by incontinent dogs and rabbits as they skidded across the pane of snow. Here and there were the marks of a scurrying hare or of the wedges made by snowshoes. But winter was in general for the refrigeration of the graves; the field was undisturbed by the feet of those mortals who used it as a shortcut in more genial weather. Thus, a cemetery powdered with snow, bent over by husks of frozen trees, is the very realization of death itself: a chill of piercing sweetness, a white of utter oblivion.

On New Year's Eve a Negro tobacco worker, leaving the tavern at one o'clock, staggered along the river road near the Girls' School. He was singing Calypso songs of Trinidad, which he'd left under fabulous lures of a tobacco company to work in America. White rum was flaming in his stomach, and he lost his way in the cemetery. He sank down to the voluptuous death of freezing in the snow right over where Miss Sophia lay buried. He was found at dawn on New Year's Day, seeming to be in a drunken sleep, his head pillowed on his reclaimed army overcoat. Did Miss Sophia hear his resistless death of cold above her? Did she, always tartly merciful, thrust out a little jeweled hand from her coffin to push away, in fastidious maidenliness, his black and gamy body, out of which the heat slowly passed into her mound? Nevertheless the death of this anonymous Negro put a certain curse on the austere burial ground, and the ebony ghost might return to it in greener seasons. Betty Blanchard would be wise not to look from her window in the late evenings.

On New Year's Day Mr. and Mrs. Pilkey, in keeping with the raw murder of the season, gave an eggnog party in their Cape Cod house. Almost no one came, since both schools were practically empty. Mrs. Mears was there, and the Comptroller and his wife. The Principal made a brave show of toasting dead alumni and faculty in hot buttered rum, but it didn't quite come off. He made a mental reservation to order back the entire faculty early for next New Year's. After the eggnogs Mr. Pilkey commanded his sparse guests to go skating on the hockey rink, remembering that in his boyhood he'd loved Hans Brinker. His daughter-in-law Nydia fell through the ice and wasn't revived till she'd drunk half a bottle of whisky the Principal had been saving for purely medicinal purposes.

At this time too another child was born into the faculty. He came squalling and uncalled for into the diamond winter scene because his father and mother, being underpaid by Mr. Pilkey, had little else to do but go to bed soon after sunset. The Principal stood godfather to the frozen little creature, the mother hoping that through this compliment he might increase the father's stipend for teaching smelly chemistry to boys. And at the christening Mr. Pilkey got well oiled on the mellow lethal rum he so loved, and preached a sermon, drawing parallels between the birth of his new godson and another Little One born amid the snow of winter. For his Christmas spirit lasted on into January, when economy and the laws of vegetable decay forced the Pilkeys to take down the Christmas tree in their drawing room.

Furthermore Mr. Pilkey was casting auguring eyes on the

swelling chassis of his Atlantan daughter-in-law Nydia. Herman had been up to the old doings of a studhorse again; and Mr. Pilkey, counting on his fingers, reckoned on another grandchild in the spring. Thus the dynasty of The Academy was being secured even to the third generation.

During Christmas vacation that little club of octogenarian janitors, presided over by Mr. Twarkins, went into action and cleaned all the school buildings. Except the dormitory rooms, which boys did themselves. And the head janitor dug up scores of complaints against the slovenliness of the faculty. He told them all to Mr. Pilkey, who listened and approved. This winter the Principal was really going to Bear Down.

Strikes in the mines of Pennsylvania threatened that there would be a coal shortage soon. Mr. Pilkey rejoiced at this tightening of the belt in prospect. He'd outlaid $12,000 more than he intended on the remodeling of his son Herman's bungalow. Here was his chance to make it up, since the school wouldn't be able to buy coal. It meant merely that the Boys' and Girls' Schools must do with fewer of their enervating hot showers. Bathing once a week was sufficient for young Christians anyhow. As a boy Mr. Pilkey had contended himself with a tubbing on Saturday night, his mother soaping his back. His boys and girls would be happier if they bathed less and ate more frugally.

And while the legacy of Miss Sophia's four million was safe as long as the American system of capitalism should endure, the entertaining possibility of being able to pull a poor mouth before his faculty, students, and parents was relished by Mr. Pilkey as a Spartan and by Mr. Whitney as Comptroller. And there had been in the Fall Term a few instances of what the Principal indulgently referred to as His Extravagances. For example he'd bought for the school library several thousand dollars worth of Wedgwood plates, decorated by Mrs. Pilkey with scenes from Shakspere's comedies. All of his wife's talents as a miniaturist had been lavished on these lovely things. They were at least as fine as Coptic urns and vases. What boy so crass as not to rejoice while looking up from his book in the library, and seeing on rare china a scene from *As You Like It*? It was also Practically Useful in the teaching of English. Every English class would be made to come to the library and view the newest specimen of Mrs. Pilkey's genius.

If necessary, Mr. Pilkey told Mr. Whitney, with his arm reassuringly around the Comptroller's shoulder, they could also cut down on the heinous waste of food in the Boys' and Girls' Schools.

—It's going to be a tough winter, Herb. In the next few years the American Independent School is going to have to justify its existence . . . or else. . . .

Little Mr. Whitney shuddered, partly from the icy weather, partly from financial implications undreamed of by Mr. Pilkey. When he got to his house, the Comptroller wept quietly, as he always did when the squeeze was on. For Mr. Whitney was a graduate of Roger Babson's. Suppose the United States were to go Socialist in the next few years, the way so many nuts and veterans were demanding? Thank God that Mr. Pilkey, for all his lack of financial sense, was a Republican! . . .

The Principal's old mother viewed the New Year with a bilious eye. Perhaps, she said, it would be the last she would ever spend at that Academy her son had brought into being. Now, tended by Florinda, she spent most of her time in bed under an electric blanket, with the heat control turned on full. Yet Old Mrs. Pilkey had been born into this sort of cold —in Vermont, ninety-three years ago. It had conditioned her gray old gums. She saw life as a struggle between the heathen Indians and the loving Pilgrim Fathers.

And how had the boys and girls and the faculties of The Academy spent their Christmas vacations? For now they were on trains and in cars and planes, returning to this damp frozen valley, with sunken eyes and curses for the brick buildings where more culture was to be medicine-dropped into their closed lips. The vacations of Americans are as varied as the country and the people.

A few, like Ralph Du Bouchet, had really rested and read and loafed, longing for the resumption of the academic year. A few pondered on what they had learned (if anything) during the Fall Term—went to concerts, and exhibited to their delighted parents that they were now a little closer to those ladies and gentlemen on whom $1800 a year was being expended.

The younger boys and girls had passed their vacations at home in what Mr. Pilkey called upholstered idiocy; they went skating and played with their electric trains and evening gowns, and went on visits to their relatives.

And the older boys and girls experimented in Growing Up —the painful way. They were subjected to tribal adolescent tortures. They got drunk in or out of their own homes. They went to the theater and rolled the names of plays and actresses on their tongues in a prickly critical style which would perhaps admit them to the salon of Mr. Philbrick Grimes. And a few made dates with their teachers in Boston, New York, and Philadelphia. These were the children from broken homes, who thought more of the men and women who were teaching them than they ever would of their separated parents. And to these boys and girls three weeks' separation from the teachers whom they loved with uterine passion was unthinkable. Mr. Pilkey would have been startled to see Doctor Sour drunk and pawing three upperformers in the Bacchante Room in Providence.

Most of the upperformers of the Boys' School sought out the pleasures which in an earlier age were believed reserved to grown men and women. They toyed with booze and carnality, guessing that a rubbing knowledge of these would give them more than books ever had. Such as these wallowed like damp little pigs in their first hangovers or in their first experiments with the body of a waitress. At The Academy they would talk all winter long of these accomplishments:

—Bars? I did a million of em. On Eighth Avenue I met a snatch named Stella. Stella by Starlight I cailed her. . . .

Tad McKinley thought of withdrawing from school. He met a dancer in Detroit, a high yaller with a purple housecoat, who was so taken with his verses that she installed him for three days in her hotel room, where the walls stank of light housekeeping. Even as he thrashed about in her musky arms on New Year's Eve, Tad wondered what his friend, Ralph, was doing. Probably not this. And when the octoroon had fallen asleep, the boy wept against her flank, wishing he was back with Ralph, smoking cigarettes in a tobacco barn and talking, just talking. . . .

Mr. Pilkey didn't say so in the catalog, but perhaps it isn't in schools that American children grow up. Their stumbles toward orientation of themselves with their hard racing world are more likely made during their vacations. Perhaps the schools don't offer them anything commensurate with the reality they suspect all about them—the fierce reality of American life. Mr. Pilkey, never admitting this, always wondered why his boys and girls returned for a new term so fagged and jaundiced-looking. Most of them had been experimenting with life far more earnestly than they ever did in a chem lab.

The Academy reopened for the Winter Term on the sixth of January. Boys and girls came back with skis and skates and snowshoes and trunks—a little like ghosts checking in for a sojourn in hell. There was none of the noise and excitement with which they'd left these cloisters three weeks ago. In the winter twilight most looked with dying eyes on a liberty they were quitting for another two months and a half.

The Pilkeys were never happy during vacations, since they never knew what to do with what Mr. Pilkey called God's Gift of Time. The Principal, like a businessman returning from a fishing trip, looked forward with piteous intensity to the opening of each new term. He said to his wife during his morning calisthenics in front of the frozen window:

—Dollars to doughnuts they're happy to be getting back. They don't really know what to do with themselves when they're home. . . .

—We've given them a second home here, his wife sighed.

There was a shriek in the next room as Old Mrs. Pilkey's crêpy flesh got singed in her electric blanket. Florinda could be heard soothing the old lady.

—Poor mother, Mr. Pilkey said.

—I think she's in her dotage, dearie, his wife said.

Like all artists she never parleyed with the truth.

The Principal Made It a Point to greet all returning scholars of the Boys' School. He liked to think of himself as a father welcoming home four hundred prodigal sons.

So at five o'clock in the afternoon he stationed himself at his desk, The Den, under the shadowy primitive painting of

Miss Sophia. There every boy (and girls if the spirit moved them) came to shake his hand. Missing this ceremony meant an Unexcused Absence, as serious as cutting a class or athletics. The powerful old man bent over each boy, looking into his face and calling each by name. This cordiality masked an attempt to ascertain whether his students had been smoking or drinking on their way to school. He would say jovially to each one:

—Nice to have you back, sir. Now you can buckle down to business.

No one would deny that in his twenty-fifth year of incumbency as Principal of The Academy Mr. Pilkey didn't work just as hard at his job as a president of a big corporation or the Chief Executive of the United States. He'd never been a lazy man, and in his old age he still exacted that merciless adherence to Duty that had made him and his school. Like his faculty he was on call twenty-fours hours a day. He was directly responsible to God and to their parents for the lives of almost six hundred people. This accountability didn't sit lightly on his shoulders. Often he compared himself (at meetings of the Headmasters' Association) to Old Fezziwig in Dickens. No. Mr. Pilkey worked hard. If in his school he was an absolute dictator, he told himself that there were few miscarriages of justice or abuse of his authority. As a young man he'd thought out carefully just how the Principal of a school should act, and he'd lived the role for twenty-five years. He loved the part. He would play it till he dropped dead; he would die in harness.

When his school was in session and things were going well, Mr. Pilkey was the happiest of men. He was old and still virile. He loved the combination of kingship and ministry which his job, unique in American life, demanded. And in a sort of steely benevolence he'd actually come to believe that he could do no wrong. Only the smartest of his faculty and student body ever questioned whether his pose—indeed his whole school—were worthwhile in modern American life. Not that their dissenting voices ever reached his ear. The Holy Ghost is immune to the capital sin of Doubt.

And so in the January twilight the proud old man, pitiful to some, noble to others, stood at his desk welcoming back students and faculty. He floated on the tide of their reverence—real or feigned. But after shaking hundreds of hands he tottered a little. For the first time in his life he realized that he wasn't so young as he used to be. He was dizzy; his ears sang.

—I think The Head's going to pass out, an observant upperformer whispered.

—Not a chance, said a member of the Student Council, whom Mr. Pilkey called a Lovely Fellow.

Holding a battered suitcase and a valpack, Guy Hudson presented himself in the reception line. As his hand was shaken, he thought for an instant that the Principal was genuinely glad to see him. But he remembered the incidents of last term. Yet it was odd that this school and these children, whom he sometimes hated, had a clutch on his heart. Sometimes he almost looked forward to the slow death of teaching here forever, of being revered as a dinosaur's tooth by generations of Academy boys, with that cynical deference which successful Americans mete out to those who have labored to teach them. . . . No, never! . . .

—How's that temper of yours? Mr. Pilkey said loudly, pressing Guy Hudson's hand.

—Somewhat calmer, sir, he answered, picking up his bags.

In a way he was gladder to be back at the school than he'd have admitted to anyone—least of all to the Principal. He'd spent his vacation in that same riot of debauchery he'd learned overseas when he was out of combat. He'd been drunk and profane and lecherous every night. He was disturbed by the nervous exhaustion of postwar America. So for three solid weeks he'd joined in the Dance of Death of other young men, who could never quite forget that they'd just come back from a war, that the economic system of the United States was out of control, that perhaps another war was already brewing. And he, the paragon for the young, had gratified every desire, in that same numb seeking after sensation he'd known in Europe, when he'd believed that every night of leave would be his last. All the significance had fallen out of life in New York. Everyone outside this school was empty and aching; they drank too much and slept with anything they could lay hands on. Only here at this Academy, for all the duplicity of the faculty and Mr. Pilkey, was there any pattern like what he'd known before the Second World War. It was a pattern of bourgeois morality and reasonable economic security set by Mr. Pilkey and many Calvinistic worthies dead and gone. This scheme of things, of thinking of tomorrow and the day after that, of believing in the integrity of capital, was a concept that was perhaps dying in postwar America. But Guy Hudson returned to it this January with something like relief. He felt like a wayward nun who slinks back with sour mouth to her convent and resumes her habit. For three weeks he hadn't slept alone. Now he almost looked forward to the isolation of his narrow bed after those tumbled apartments and wrestling hotel rooms in New York. . . .

As he was walking back down the reception line, he saw Miss Blanchard standing her turn. She was wearing a caracul coat, open all the way down, and a fur hood over her hair like a wimple. Her color, gray in December, had returned. Her fine throat sparkled in the half light. He determined to speak to her, not forgetting the snub she'd dealt him three weeks ago. So he set down his baggage and went up and shook her hand, which was cold, loose, and reproving. And he imitated the sardonic voice of returning students:

—Dja have a nice vacation?

—I went skiing in the Adirondacks, she said, not looking at him.

Her smile was still as prim and her voice as needled as a librarian's. From her impersonal tone he decided that she'd spent her holidays in black goggles and blazing snow, eating her heart out with a lot of other hens, who were each doing the same. Ah, she *mustn't* sit nights looking out of her window! He thought of the contrast between his unbridled debauchery in New York, meaningless and orgasmic, while she, fair and cold and chaste, had continued to turn on herself. And he guessed that she was surrendering faster than he to this matriarchal and disciplined society that had brought The Academy and Mr. Pilkey into existence. She was forgetting faster than himself that there had ever been a war, during which people like themselves had decided that there should be a new liberty and freedom from the nonsense of centuries. . . .

He picked up his baggage and walked on, hearing her sharp intake of breath as he left her. She had determined not to like him. Was it the system or himself?

199

2

Each January Mr. Philbrick Grimes told his gossips that he went into his own brand of private delirium, like a dutiful bloodhound sniffing for corpses under the snow. He agreed with the Principal that there was a great deal more to keeping school than just teaching classes. Somebody had to do the dirty work of organization. And Mr. Grimes, sensitive as a weathervane to the winds of authority, supposed it might as well be himself as another.

After two highballs in the salon of Mrs. Dell Holly he would admit with a diffident titter that he was one of those born to be a petty functionary, a big frog in a small puddle. Father Grimes had been a Baltimore politician, Mother Grimes a Baltimore clubwoman. Thus Philbrick had been exposed to machinations at an early age—the talk of his parents at their dinner table. It had early been scarred into the little boy that the world was too filthy for his talents—that is, the world of action. His parents' solid bellies under checkered waistcoats, fortunes to be made, the sherbety myth of Good Women. But in his dreaming boyhood little Philbrick had been buffeted between the bullying of his father, and the prayers and sighs of Mother Grimes, who sang the songs of Carrie Jacobs Bond in her best conservatory voice.

—There's a mouse in that boy's veins! Father Grimes had shouted.

—He's got the artistic strain of *my* sisters! Mother Grimes had whimpered.

The thin bright little boy lived in an overstuffed Baltimore house. The political machine of Father Grimes kept rare roast beef on the table. Mother Grimes went in for Wallace Nutting watercolors, read aloud from Owen Wister, and played Ethelbert Nevin on her rosewood piano. But she'd seen how precocious her offspring was, and soon she was begging off from the strenuous games and chores Father Grimes had prescribed to make a man of his son—a man in his own image.

In the first twelve years of his life Philbrick Grimes read everything in his mother's chintzy library, wih the bust of the Gibson girl on top: the Yellow and Green Fairy books, Alice, The Wind in the Willows, the mythology of all nations. He tinkled on the piano too; but not so well as Mother Grimes suspected, for he did his practicing by turning on the player attachment and pumping like mad on the pedals. No, the genius of little Philbrick was ideological rather than musical. And he was delicate, suffering from asthma like Marcel Proust, though Mother Grimes had never heard of this Frenchman, and wouldn't have approved if she did. This disease was a useful out from many unpleasant impositions from Father Grimes, and Philbrick retained its symptoms long after he'd outgrown the smothering torment.

Consequently he was free to play with little girls. At twelve he was already improvising for them dreadfully imaginative games. He made slaves of them, as only a bright and pretty boy knows how to do. One day just before his thirteenth birthday he discovered how girls are different from boys. They were acting out Lamb's Tales from Shakspere one rainy afternoon in the Grimes attic. Jennie Myers was taking the part of Perdita. Philbrick was wearing a gray Eton suit and an Eton collar (Mother Grimes always dressed her darling to the hilt). And something Jennie Myers did or suggested that afternoon gave the little boy a trauma from which he was never to recover. This shock closed the little brain to sex. The whole trope was so horrendous that thereafter Philbrick Grimes elevated woman to her only permissible place in the scheme of things—as hostess in a salon. Even in his thirties Mr. Grimes retained a frigid distaste for that means through which children are conceived and by which crasser members of the human race take much of their pleasure. A thirty-seven he'd never known woman.

In this thirteenth year her Philbrick was so pale and bookish and asthmatic that Mother Grimes decided to send him away to school. After deliberation and catalog reading Father Grimes chose a new academy that was making quite a name for itself in its ten years of existence. It had been founded by a spinster named Miss Sophia and was headed by a driving man named Mr. Pilkey. The Grimeses read the catalog with critical ardor. At this new school children of all strengths and religious denominations lived and played and learned together in perfect harmony. Little Philbrick Grimes was packed off to this school. The night he was to leave Baltimore he nearly strangled of asthma, but it did him no good.

Awaking the next morning in a cell with three demoniac little roommates, Philbrick sustained the second major trauma of his life. He couldn't have expected anything better of his politician father, but he'd never quite forgive his mother for thus summarily detaching him from her. And for four years at Miss Sophia's he was tortured exquisitely by the other boys. He walked about in knickers and a bow tie, a hand on his hip, for it was here that he cultivated the habit of moving disdainfully. His slender asthmatic little body sustained more cuffs and fiendish initiations than any other child in school.

Yet like turtles he had his compensations. Unable to play on any team because of his asthma, he spent his time with books or with the ladies of the faculty. By fifteen or sixteen he was as accomplished a connoisseur of the plumbing of the feminine heart as Dorothy Dix or the late Samuel Richardson. None learned faster than he how to turn a phrase of gossip; none knew better how titillate (mentally) a newly married teacher's wife. He became superb in the more feminine side of school politics. As an Academy upperformer he was president of the Dramatic Club. He whipped up soufflés for his little friends. And best of all he won the heart of Mrs. Pilkey by telling her stories in those long hours during which she decorated that crockery which had won her a national reputation as a plate painter.

By the time he was ready to graduate, none dared to torment him because he was patronized in high places. The Pilkeys said that the jittery boy was the loveliest and most gifted fellow in school. All but a few of the faculty, obedient to the propaganda of the Pilkeys, considered young Philbrick Grimes a genius. Others said secretly that he was a waspish dilettante who'd managed to survive by developing a nice case of protective coloring. That the flutter of his wings fooled most people into thinking he was really flying, instead of buzzing. He heard these rumors. They hurt. He would get *them*. And he went on developing a coat of enamel three layers deep, remarkable for its hardness and sheen.

Highly recommended by the Pilkeys and the College Board Examiners, Philbrick Grimes zoomed into Princeton at seventeen. Here he passed four of the happiest years of his life. His asthma left him. He spent his time sneering at his professors, for after those hours of browsing in the library of Mother Grimes, he knew that they had nothing to teach *him*. At Princeton the money from Father Grimes's political machine made it possible for young Philbrick to live well. He dwelt in chambers hung with The Correct Things, and every afternoon served tea to other elegant young men like himself. They sneered at everything and at one another. They claimed they were imitating English university life around 1890, when people ate cucumber sandwiches. They read George Moore and Max Beerbohm aloud. They cornered the Literary Magazine and wrote marvelous things in the style of Pound and Eliot. They were effecting an American renascence (Mr. Grimes preferred the English noun to the French). At nineteen he created a sensation by appearing in a violet toga in *The Frogs* of Aristophanes. Two Princeton professors committed suicide out of sheer envy of these brilliant undergraduates.

By his senior year the incandescence of his spirit was almost too bright to look upon. He graduated Cum Laude. He might have done even better, but he'd been too busy leading a combination Victorian and Hellenic life. Away from Nassau at twenty-one, he was convinced that life offered no more flowers for him to sip.

What to do? He was already probably one of the most refined and clever young men of his generation. He thought of going to Europe and storming Paris. But he didn't approve of the Left Bank. He thought of going on the stage, but he had too raffiné a manner for Broadway. Congreve was the only thing he would dream of appearing in.

Then came the crash of 1929 and three horrible years of debacle. By 1932 Father Grimes was laid away of arteriosclerosis, his casket covered with sprays of wreaths from his political machine. Mother Grimes took nervous prostration. There remained only for that glittering being Philbrick to find a job and support himself. Father Grimes's fat allowance was gone; and his son, with all the Manner in the world and a Princeton diploma, realized that there was nothing in this world he was really prepared to do. To his friends he'd once said that they'd be happier under a benevolent despotism than under American capitalistic democracy. For they'd been born to lounge and to entertain. But now he had to do *something* to keep himself and Mother Grimes off relief. What?

Just as he was prepared to pull a Thomas Chatterton by swallowing an overdose of veronal, he received a letter from his old Principal. It offered a teaching job. So when some young men of his generation were jumping off the Empire State Building or selling apples on streetcorners, Mr. Grimes went back on the faculty of that school which he'd left as a student seven years before. It was his last brush but one with the outside world. He returned to the uterus of American education which, as cynics know, is walled with quicklime. His starting salary was $1100 a year, with room, board, and laundry. Thus did Mr. Pilkey snare promising young men from those three American universities of which he approved.

Mr. Grimes's first years as a young teacher weren't easy. He had to turn from the cool epigrams of his salon at Princeton to a hectic nursery and playground for the sons and daughters of the well-to-do. He saw The Academy as he'd never seen it as a student. Now he had to instruct and police those hoodlums who seven years ago had flayed him alive. And this time the flaying began again, on another level. The way of student with student is cruel enough, but the way of student with a new teacher of no definite athletic tendencies is crucifixion. In his first years he had on his hands study hall riots, landslides in his classrooms, and the pushing of his esthetic hands into bowls of chocolate blanc mange by husky upperformers.

But after three years of assorted hell he came into his own. He saw with his quick eyes that he would never be the Great Teacher, the Great Disciplinarian, the Great Coach. So he decided to become one of the Greatest of Living Operators. He learned the hard way. He learned how to master his classes by shock treatment, which is more theatrical than French tragedy.

Better still, he learned to study his students. In every adolescent there is an abyss, a soft spot of the soul that will later close with his maturity. Mr. Grimes exacerbated this Achilles Heel; he wouldn't suffer it to close. Thus he tortured his students in a far more metaphysical way than he himself had been tortured. He kept raw the souls of every boy and girl with whom he had to deal. On some he left a mark for life, shriveling them forever with his pose of omniscience. He would trap boys and girls into confiding in him during some hour of anguish. Then he would hold over them as a sort of celestial blackmail whatever it was they told him. Thus he had many in his power during their residence at The Academy. All he needed in his maturer days to reduce a recalcitrant boy or girl was:

—Well, aren't we getting just a tiny bit off the beam, eh? It seems to me I remember the time. . . .

Outside of class he consolidated his beachhead by capturing the highest headquarters of The Academy. He cultivated the Pilkeys until they were lost without him. He entertained all distinguished guests of The Academy with a tour of the grounds. He read aloud to Mr. Pilkey's aged mother. He gave Intimate Little Dinners. He entertained only those boys who were sympathique to him, but he managed to persuade Mr. Pilkey that he did more for students than anyone else on the faculty. If any calamity struck The Academy, Mr. Grimes was there before it happened. He specialized in telephoning the parents of boys dying in the Infirmary:

—Don't get alarmed, but. . . .

Mr. Grimes never visited them, but there were a few idealists on the faculty who murmured that he'd sold down the river the dignity of the teaching profession. He'd turned in fifteen years from a water lily into a spiked sea urchin. And thus he would continue at The Academy till it failed financially, or till Mr. Pilkey dropped dead and a new Principal came to sweep out the faculty with the broom of a reformer.

This January Mr. Grimes was leading the life of a Cistercian monk, without the vow of silence or the duty of copying manuscripts. He had a sumptuous apartment on the third floor of Hooker Hall. He lived in greater style than any other unmarried man on the faculty, for he'd gone way beyond the salary of $1100 with which he'd begun. Only Mr. Whitney knew exactly how much was the emolument of Mr. Grimes. But rumor said he was making almost as much as Mr. Pilkey.

He usually awoke about six thirty, feeling metallic and jaded from the veronal that was his nightcap. And he would lie in his bed, his brain dancing with those schemes such as children know after sleeping. Although he was only thirty-seven he never came to himself in that tension and potency with which young men awake. The discipline and horror of his masculine tendency had been so long practiced that whatever vigor he'd once possessed had atrophied. He was safer from passion than most eunuchs.

He arose in his bright pajamas and skipped about his suite, much like a little girl taking inventory of her dollhouse. His taste ran to cream Venetian blinds, Japanese screens, and Chinese scrolls. Some said that his living room seemed to be the abode of a spinster with satiric and eclectic tastes. His library was enormous. Though he read nearly everything, he loved books for the sake of owning them. He was a gull for those odd publications which are announced by London firms in snobbish little brochures. He thought of himself as town crier for Little Gems he'd discovered himself. He liked to drop into the salon of Mrs. Dell Holly in the late afternoon with a slim volume in his hand. There he would engineer the conversation in order to read aloud from his latest expedition into the realms of gold. He would force his favorite book on anyone he met. Next week he'd have a new enthusiasm; the old would be forgotten. Since Mr. Grimes's life outside The Academy was nothing, he had to enlarge it by reading. The books he liked were not those fierce and terrible ones which are the masterpieces of the human race. No, he found the Greeks too naked, the Russians too stark, and the French too precious. He preferred little tooled gems, originally phrased and witty, which had sold one hundred copies from a bookstall in Oxford.

Smoking a cigarette, Mr. Grimes pulled a volume from his bookshelves. He wanted something witty to give his classes and his salons. He found a spicy snack in this book on witchcraft, an anecdote about Old Mother Leslie, who was burnt as a witch in Sudbury in 1674. Here was sufficient material to get him through his morning's classes. He didn't stick to the texts his students were reading, preferring to give them what he called Background.

He had a little kitchen, completely accoutered; a little stove on which he brewed his famous coffee, a little frigidaire in which he kept his famous icecubes. You hadn't lived until you'd tasted a Grimes Old-Fashioned. Since long ago he'd been relieved of the onus of going to breakfast in the dining hall with other unmarried teachers, he now set about concocting a delicious little bachelor breakfast of orange juice, eggs benedict, and spam. Thoughtfully he drank two cups of coffee, although it made him ready to fly. And he reflected that no woman could ever get a breakfast like this. . . .

Then he sat down in his lushest chair, crossed his wispy knees in their tweeds, and began to skim the morning papers. He had five minutes till the chapel bell. This would be the last leisure he'd have till he went to bed tonight. Mr. Grimes was a living illustration of the horrid modern fact that only to teachers, artists, and burglars is there left any love of, or pride in, craft.

In these five minutes he skimmed three complete newspapers. He recognized only the *Times*, the *Tribune*, and the *Monitor*. The larger canvases of his ideas were blocked out by *Time* magazine and *The New Yorker*. He read nothing else but books. Believing himself one of the better-informed men of his day, he drew most of what he called his Banter or Topical Conversation from this five-minute reading. He didn't really enjoy finding out what was going on in the world, for his world was The Academy. But he hated to be caught without a current allusion at his fingertips. So in these five minutes before chapel he performed an incredible feat of day-to-day education: he memorized out-of-the-way facts and headlines. Sometimes he told the salon of Mrs. Dell Holly that one contaminated oneself by reading newspapers. But he did it grimly, for he was no Ivory Tower Kid.

A perusal of the journalism at the end of the first half of the twentieth century always aroused in him a horrified fascination. He read at terrific speed, giving out little whimpers of disapproval and incredulousness. The world was a frightful place. But half the time he suspected that the stories and pictures furled before him on the ragstock were purest propaganda, inventions of columnists and editorial writers to keep the world in a stew. Why, it couldn't be as horrid as the headlines were saying! The only truth, the only peace were to be found serving Mr. Pilkey at The Academy. And the jeerers had said he was leading a sheltered life! Who was right—he or they? As he read account after account of bloodshed, rape, divorce, murder, eviction, and every conceivable and inconceivable vicissitude and tragedy, he often assured himself that his own life was closer to what God had intended for man. Mr. Grimes decided that current events and history were a painful, heartbreaking, and bloody circus. A war in which millions of men lost their lives was mere proof of the orneriness of the uncultivated human spirit— which was what he was fighting against as a teacher, wasn't he? And those ghastly movements in which the so-called Masses tried to rise and level the privileged and responsible— they were to him just another proof that the artist and teacher is justified in distrusting the canaille. No, he had faith only in the creative minority—a phrase he'd culled from some historian. Shyly he told himself he was a member of this vanguard. Why, most people rushed about city streets and lived from hand to mouth! He was an aristocrat. A humble one, though, he said.

Thus for five minutes he Caught Up with the News. Sometimes he sipped from a coffee cup; sometimes he passed a hand over his eyes; sometimes his heart ached at the perfidy and futility of all history—especially contemporary history.

Mr. Grimes had had a brief brush with what is known in vulgar parlance as Reality. In the year 1941 there'd been a lightning moment in which it looked as though he was going to leave The Academy. He'd received the usual summons from his draft board. He was terrified at the prospect of leaving his gown and books. Yet the terror of being drafted was in a way so hugely cathartic that he found it almost delightful. Hitherto his life had been lived in little spurts of detailed and nebulous ecstasy, like a Henry James heroine on a bender. Consequently the days before his induction physical were the most high keyed he was ever to know. He permitted himself a greater flamboyance and swagger, not unseemly in one about to become a private in the Army of the United States. He began to think almost with pleasure of dying on some far field of honor. In those days there

208

cropped out in him a frenzied despairing courage. At last he'd have to rub elbows with soldiers immune to the siren spell of his teaching: taxi drivers, union organizers, bartenders.

But the Principal, who'd permitted several of his stronger teachers to be raped by the draft board without so much as a murmur of protest, balked. He could patriotically spare everyone except Mr. Grimes. In fact all the other young males who had gone into service were a brilliant advertisement that The Academy gave her all in war as well as in peace. If any teachers or students got killed in action—why, Mr. Pilkey and the trustees were only too glad to put up a plaque in the chapel; and Mrs. Pilkey would take time out from painting her china to design it.

But Mr. Pilkey paled at the prospect of losing Mr. Grimes. He personally appeared before the draft board to plead a case of irreplaceability:

—Goddam it, gentlemen, I swear it's not lack of patriotism! It's only that this fine young man is to my school what a skilled technician is to a munitions factory. . . .

The aging Principal was magnificent as he stood before the elders of the draft board. His white mane glittered like ermine under the shaded lights of that upper room in the Town Hall. But the old men, chewing tobacco, were unmoved by Mr. Pilkey's oratory. It was one of the few times he'd ever come out into public from the fortress of his school. It was said in the town that his faculty were Commies, that free love was practiced by faculty and students in the school's precincts, that An Unknown God was venerated in The Academy chapel. These old chieftains of the draft board listened to Mr. Pilkey plead the case of Mr. Grimes. They whispered among themselves cruel, irrelevant, and jealous things special to the solons of small towns. Town and Gown! They were a grocer, a postmaster, and a lawyer-politician. They hated Mr. Pilkey and they hated his school. They hated the memory of Miss Sophia with an eighty-year-old incrustation of myth and intolerance because she'd left her fortune for education, not to the town. Thus the case against Mr. Grimes was as open and shut as the processes of the Spanish Inquisition.

The old men were in a position to strike back virulently at the generosity of Miss Sophia and at the tradition of private education. For the first time they were able to focus in one act of vitriol all their odium—and they did it on the slender flinching person of Mr. Philbrick Grimes. Furthermore, hadn't the sons of two members of the board been expelled from The Academy for being morons or kleptomaniacs?

That night in 1941 in the musty rat-trodden Town Hall there was fought another round in the battle of democratic mediocrity against private excellence. Smiling mournfully and sympathetically, the draft board decreed that Mr. Grimes should go through with his physical examination for induction into the Army of the United States.

And so he did, with admirable braggadocio. He didn't sleep for three nights before his physical, no matter how much veronal he swallowed. But he turned up punctually in the queue of other stinking candidates and suffered the embarrassment of standing naked before a jesting country doctor, who roared at the undeveloped state of his Equipment. He showed also high blood pressure and mild hyperthyroidism. Mr. Grimes endeavored to joke feebly at the probings and the Wassermanns. Everything went well till his bout with the psychiatrist.

This specialist was one of those indeterminate persons who in another age would have gone into the Church; but now with the new techniques of the twentieth century he'd made it his profession to terrorize the souls of others by his peculiar and recondite jargon, much as unscrupulous medicine men have been known to do.

—Tell me all about sex, brother, he said clammily to Mr. Grimes, who sat opposite him stark naked.

But Mr. Grimes had already doped out this character with the swift hawklike swoop of appraisal that every teacher acquires. He looked at the hornrimmed spectacles peering at him; and, elated at having emerged so well from the rest of his physical examination, he decided to play with the psychiatrist much as he toyed with his classes—ironically. He'd sized up this smirking creature as one of those plump aging men who devote themselves to charitable and social work involving the rehabilitation or salvation of muscular young men. And since Mr. Grimes was at least as well read as the psychiatrist (who that day was especially bored at trying to pin neuroses on sodajerks and tobacco workers), he decided to give him a dose of his own medicine. He knew

Freud and Jung and Kierkegaard as more than names. A cat and mouse game got under way. The psychiatrist leaned over and laid a pragmatic sweaty hand on Mr. Grimes's feathery knee:

—How do you react to that, my boy? Get something other than a reflex, hmmmm?

—O, don't be silly. Let's not play pat-a-cake. . . .

Yet he flinched, a fact that the psychiatrist gloatingly marked down on his report. And for another half hour they had a sprightly conversation, couched in all the clichés and latter-day Torah of psychoanalysis. Mr. Grimes enjoyed himself thoroughly.

But a week later he learned from his draft board that he'd been classified as 4-F. His relief was enormous, yet he was in a pique to know exactly why the army was rejecting him. He called at the Town Hall and saw written across his form in a bold medical hand:

MILDLY PSYCHOTIC—OLD BIDDY TYPE—EXTREME ANXIETY STATE—NOT TO BE INDUCTED FOR ANY REASON WHATEVER

He left the Town Hall in a state of purple chagrin. He *had* pulled the wool over the eyes of that muzzy psychiatrist! Yet he never told Mr. Pilkey nor the salon of Mrs. Dell Holly exactly why he wasn't to be drafted. The Principal breathed a sigh not to lose his right-hand man. The whole of his faculty might go into the army, navy, and gyrenes—just so long as he could keep Mr. Grimes.

And all over the United States millions of young men were dragged into the armed forces. Many never came back: their bodies lay in Africa, Italy, France, Germany, on Pacific atolls. But Philbrick Grimes never went to war. He sat it out on the faculty of The Academy. He advanced higher and higher in his department, in the graces of the Pilkeys. He followed the headlines and read Housman to his classes. But sometimes a skewer would go into the dominie's heart when one of his students, bullied by mob hysteria, would ask:

—Why aren't you in uniform, sir? . . .

And he would bury his face in his hands and murmur about his asthma and his responsibilities. . . .

The bell for chapel rang. Mr. Grimes laid his three newspapers on an ottoman and arose. His day was beginning. He could leave behind him the grotesque world that the newspapers were screaming about. He would now enter a higher reality—the sphere of Truth and Bureaucracy in American education.

Before he could take his seat in the Choir Loft of the chapel, he had to go through several maneuvers to insure his peace of mind that all was running well. These were strategic compulsions, imposed by his function as The Finger of Mr. Pilkey. First he went up and checked the gladioli bosoming forth from a vase under the rostrum: they must retain the symmetry ordained by Mrs. Pilkey. Then he closed all doors that were ajar, for Mr. Pilkey disliked the symbolism of apertures in the House of God. Then he looked at the Principal's face with earnest scanning, to discover whether his boss had slept well last night. Then he sped about the filling chapel and whispered to various schoolboys taking their places; he always had little deals on with half the student body—that was why they imposed in him an enormous trust.

Mr. Grimes was especially assiduous in paying court to undergraduate Big Wheels, like the President of the Student Council. He knew better than to fawn on Ben the way some teachers did. He treated the young Jew with a handsome and witty intimacy. They were like two sages swapping stories in a coffee house. He thought Ben a Darn Good Guy, and hoped Ben thought the same of him.

Doctor Amos James was beginning the organ prelude; so Mr. Grimes stole smilingly to his place in the Choir Loft. It was a shy and secret smile, worn by girls in the Middle Ages who made church a trysting place. His expression changed to accord with wherever he was: in chapel he was scrubbed and boyish, as though the word of God was a personal treat to him; in class he was satirical; in the salon elegantly dictatorial. He took his place in a pew beside a young history teacher whom he called doctor out of affection. Privately he thought of this redheaded man as an enlightened ruffian. Ten years ago, before the war, such parvenus were not hired to teach at The Academy. But the past few years had decimated the young teaching blood in America. Mr. Grimes guessed that Guy Hudson was a little in awe of him, the way an elephant is of a brainy mouse. He'd tried, God knew, to bring this veteran out of his shell, but Hudson was surly and emotionally removed. Which proved another thesis of Mr. Grimes's; that war made a man crass. *He'd* been spared that. But as usual he was gracious:

212

—Have a good breakfast?

—Blueberry pancakes and tender little link sausages, Guy Hudson said, staring with those hollow mad eyes.

Mr. Grimes felt hurt and said quickly:

—Zut, alors, vous avez bien mangé. . . .

And he whipped out his little wallet that bulged with secret documents and began to take attendance of the rows beneath him on the floor of the chapel. He was precise: no boy who slipped in late to his pew ever escaped a tardy mark. Fifteen years ago wasn't someone sitting up here and marking *him* absent?

The period after chapel was a time that Mr. Grimes loved best of all his day. He rushed to it like a maiden to her assignation. For in that time he had his daily appointment with Mr. Pilkey, giving into the old gentleman's ear a full account of his stewardship of the preceding twenty-four hours.

Students choked the corridors. They squared their shoulders like Little Men as they strode past The Den, Mr. Pilkey's desk. The Principal was dictating a letter to Miss Pringle. Last night she'd had one of her epileptic fits, but this morning she twinkled like a cherry behind her glasses. She thrust into Mr. Grimes's hand a translation she was making from Sappho, for her hobby was The Classics, which she read as most women play bridge. Her knowledge of Greek and her maidenhood sat strangely on her. Her hair was pulled back from her forehead in the style of college girls of 1899. Her merry eyes feasted on Mr. Grimes, whom she considered the one young man Around Here not tainted with fleshly flaws. Mr. Pilkey looked up from reading his mail and said Hullo:

—Our Muse dashed off another last night. I find her poetic diction quite as fine as her shorthand.

Mr. Grimes skimmed through Miss Pringle's translation of Sappho. It was full of pantings, and he felt a little giddy. He returned it to her:

—Lovely! I don't know why they bother to publish Edna Millay.

Almost ready for another epileptic fit, Miss Pringle scampered off to her cubicle and her virginal typewriter, to peck off the morning's letters. And Mr. Grimes went into conference with the Principal. It was a touching and reverent thing, this colloquy of the old man with the younger. Occasionally the Principal leaned an arm on Mr. Grimes's shoulder and listened hard. Out of all this would come new classroom procedures, new disciplines, new committees. Between them they kept The Academy in a constant furor of change. For they were determined that nothing in the institution should settle down to stagnation or quietism. In fifteen minutes they hatched enough plans to keep a government busy for a generation. There must be more entertaining of students; there was too much leisure for teachers. Thus Mr. Pilkey could boast in the next edition of the catalog that they were toiling up Parnassus.

—Well, good morning, sir, Mr. Grimes said. You've cleared the cobwebs out of my brain. . . .

—And you're my calisthenics for the day, Mr. Pilkey said fondly.

But the happiest secret times were in the evenings when students had their noses in their books and the rest of the faculty were up to various domesticities. He knew how to utilize those still cold January evenings. He spent them in his rooms. He would rearrange his furniture and play all sorts of quaint games with himself—actors and authors would come to call upon him and find him immersed in their new book or play. Thinking in long Socratic dialogues, he'd rehearse all the lightning things he'd say to The Great. He would offer them little amenities and criticisms from a Well-Wisher.

To be sure, every so often his eye flirted with the stacks of his papers that raddled up higher every day. But tonight he simply couldn't bring himself to correct them. His head was too full of coups, which he toiled over like Gladstone dictating his memoirs. He felt more like browsing through his own library, pretending he was a rustic strayed into a bookstore. Cunningly closing his eyes, he'd snatch down a volume at random from his shelves. He'd look at his own bookplate and wonder what sort of man could possibly own such a varied and intellectual library:

—My, what a well-read fellow! Sure would like to meet *him*! Maybe he'll happen in any moment if I just stand here and pretend to be nobody! . . .

And like a total stranger to himself Mr. Grimes would examine the marginal glosses in his books—notes and exclamation points where he begged to differ with the author, or called him an egregious ass. Then he would say aloud:

—Mon Dieu, what a critical sense I had then! . . .

On these January evenings he would also send out his bulletins to the outside world. He composed during this winter term some of his rarest distichs on human experience. He sent little squibs to *The New Yorker* (always for some snotty reason rejected by the editors). He penned little gossipy notes to his mother on monogrammed stationery, beginning Ma chère Mumsy. And in his noblest moments he favored the editors of the New York *Times* with elaborate syntheses on the state of the world. But he liked best of all to write letters to the publishers of books and dictionaries, pointing out to them the tiniest errors in format, spelling and footnotes. These helpful and courteous letters always began:

—I am an anonymous friend who prides himself on being a perfectionist. . . . Don't think me sniveling, but. . . .

And while he kept up his extensive correspondence with editors and alumni of The Academy, he turned on his little radio, housed in a polished Jacobean commode. Soft chamber music discoursed to him and lubricated his charming prose. He was a master in the use of the semicolon. He did his writing in dressing gown and slippers and imagined himself Alexander Pope at Twickenham. He knew himself to be essentially a satirist in an age of historical novels written for clubwomen.

And at ten o'clock, just before they went to bed, Mr. Grimes reviewed his corridor. He saw to it that they didn't coagulate too long in the lavatories, brushing their teeth. He frowned on adolescents taking warm showers just before bed, since such ablutions set up languor in a boy. Or sometimes students came to him for help with their work, but he didn't care to have his mellow creative mood shattered:

—First thing tomorrow at Availability Time. Tonight I'm simply snowed under with my paper work. . . .

After the Boys' School had gone to bed, he looked from his windows at the moonlight monking it up with the breast of the nunlike snow on the meadows, the icy brilliance of a winter night. And though he was snug and safe in the crib of this Academy, there would come to him in little wintry weepings the gusts of sadness and desolation. Even here the Teacher (who is the Second Person of the Blessed Trinity) kept a controlling hand on Mr. Grimes's nostalgia. There passed before his mind a frosty landscape of all the life he wasn't enjoying and didn't quite understand. Then a January wind would frost up the glass of his clear vision, like his homesickness for Mother Grimes when he was still a small asthmatic student at this very school. At such moments of slackness he would think that after all he was only a poor pointless squirrel gathering up little nuts and laying them away. And no one would care where the nuts were hidden. Then for an instant he would sympathize with all these hundreds of nice boys being trained up to take their place (wherever *that* was) in a dizzy world, which would one day destroy them. Why *shouldn't* they hate school? Why shouldn't they resent the Christing tyranny of the faculty, himself included? Didn't his students perhaps see through him, and simply play him for what he was worth, giving him enough rope to hang himself on? They would go out into a world he had never known, get married, make money, and get knocked off in war. Yet they would send their children back to this same Academy for more doses of pseudo-knowledge. Thus the pattern would slink on to world's end. The Philbrick Grimeses were only its silly perpetuators—for their own security and interest. At such moments he almost believed that the teaching profession is just another type of modern medicine man. . . .

Then he would pass a hand over his eyes and over the svelte reading stand that held his book:

—Mon Dieu, mon Dieu! That way madness lies. . . .

Or like a Jesuit at his Spiritual Exercises (for Mr. Grimes was in a perpetual novitiate) he would force his mind back to convenient rationalizations such as teachers are expected to think in, for parents have corseted teachers into an image of themselves. And he would draw a little comfort from the prose of Mr. Pilkey's catalog:

—We believe our faculty does a superb job . . . in an age when young people are quitting the teaching profession by the thousands . . . the courage to stick at the helm . . . responsibility for generations yet unborn. . . . Plato . . . Aquinas . . . Erasmus. . . .

The heat would finally go off even in the apartment of Mr. Grimes, by order of the Comptroller. And then in the descending chill and the scrabble of mice in the wainscoting, Mr. Grimes could never quite believe his own arguments.

And the cheek of the snow outside mirrored his own blanching emptiness with the sardonic eye of unfulfilled white paper. At thirty-seven he should have had a wife to talk to! It was already too late for that now, though. The cords at the back of his neck nagged him onto stratagems no wife would have dreamed of. . . .

When the probing of the winter evening became too great for him to bear (he told his classes he cherished solitude), he would start telephoning. He might call the Pilkeys in their house, where they passed January evenings at backgammon or Chinese checkers. And forcing a businesslike rasp into his voice, he would speak to the Principal of new schemes for the glory of The Academy. Mr. Pilkey loved to be phoned at home; it swelled his paternalism to have his teachers lay projects in his lap.

—Sir, I couldn't sleep. A wonderful plan just came to me. I just had to get out of bed and tell you. . . .

—Twenty-six hours in a day wouldn't be enough for you, Mr. Pilkey replied.

—And how is your mother? Was her electric blanket repaired?

—Snug as a bug in a rug. . . .

Sometimes realer needs of his nature asserted themselves. Philbrick Grimes would make himself a toasted cheese sandwich on his little stove. At such times a frostbitten hospitality would peek out of his soul; he really wished he had a friend or mistress to share it with. Or he might call up Miss Betty Blanchard at the Girls' School and describe to her over the wire all the erotic details of what he was putting in the sandwich and how it felt in his mouth. Or he would read her aloud, the telephone against his chin, a passage from some mild old essayist. He would hear her brittle but comely laugh through the receiver, and he guessed that she too was lonely and grateful for his ringing her. He saw her sitting in a kimono on her chaise-longue, dying for a drink, poring over her next day's Spanish. All the while the winter moon would be scoring curlicues on the naked snow and making mockery of all warmth except a marriage bed.

Half listening to Betty Blanchard's voice at the other end, Mr. Grimes would reflect on what a poor gnat of a man he was at thirty-seven. What had singed his wings? He resolved to invite her to the Spring Prom. Yet even to *her* voice there was the crisp and professional veil of the woman teacher. This was no girl he was talking to, but a machine. Both had their guards up in those January evening conversations by phone. Even when they fooled wittily, they were only quoting at each other. Nothing came from the heart. Mr. Grimes knew well enough that the usual conversation of a man and woman teacher is that misty talk of two shepherds under a cliff during a cloudburst.

—What are you doing, my dear? he would ask.

—Just exactly what *you* are. Looking at the moon on the snow and wondering. . . .

There: the caul had begun to rip, and he hung up as fast as he decently might. For he knew that his age or his teaching or the January night had made him frozen beyond any dream of his youth. He didn't really want emotion tonight or any night—just a sort of assurance of his own identity and a woman's voice saying it to him. He could see Betty Blanchard slowly replacing her phone in its cradle and lying back on her bed while the snow cast a crystal screen on the ceiling of her room. What *was* this repressant agent? Was it the cold cemetery where Miss Sophia lay, keeping watch over the legacy of all her vicarious children?

After midnight he made ready for bed. He took his veronal. He examined his conscience as he brushed his teeth. He took finicky care of his body; his medicine cabinet was battalioned with tricky medicines. He'd already settled into that deliberate process of fossilization that hits spinsters and teachers (male and female) at uncertain ages. He knew that he'd live almost forever, slowly subsiding into the tomb of himself, too polite to bang the door of his vault. The dreams of his young manhood were now receding points of glister, like the merciless facets of that snow outside. What had he done today? He'd been in constant motion. He couldn't persuade himself, though, that the heart of one single student had opened to him. Though the response of his classes were always a glassy perfection, like a fine recording of the roulades of a piccolo. And there were two weeks' back papers to be corrected. Well, tomorrow was another day. . . .

Philbrick Grimes got into his elegant little bed, purchased from the honorarium of an article he'd published five years ago in *Cosmopolitan* magazine on The Teacher as Priest and Prophet. He wore silk pajamas over his grasshopper joints.

Beside his bed was a sparkling new book, but tonight he wouldn't turn on his overhead light to read. As he lay waiting for his twitching and shallow sleep to come, he wondered if peace was what mankind really wanted. He was supposed to enjoy it here at The Academy. But it was the peace of an autopsy on a corpse, with the guts dangling out like balloons at a country fair. Not far from the simulated peace of this school there were cities. This very midnight men like himself were drinking and plotting for someone to sleep with—even now making overtures undreamed of by Mr. Grimes in his cool little bed. Again there came to his mind the vision of Miss Sophia's graveyard, where she lay close to the road and the river, near that human life which passed her by all unmindful. At such moments it seemed to him that the dreadful and Christian old woman had laid her bony finger on the lives of everyone in this school—himself most of all. She'd invited them into her charnelhouse in the midst of their young life. That was what education was: a visit to a cemetery made holy through tabus. He himself must be a commissioned caretaker of graves.

3

On February afternoons Ralph was aware of a death in life. He moved concentrated and whirring on his skates over the glassy table of the hockey pond. He felt the warmth of his uniform and shinguards; he heard the whizz of the puck as it skittered over the ice, scratched up from the inflection of the razored runners of skates. There were shouting players dancing up and down in the penalty box. He flailed his hockey stick before him like a broom; it whispered on the crust of the shaven ice. He couldn't really feel the textures of things through his heavy gauntlets; through canvas and fur he had the grip of one frozen to death.

Darkness was setting down on the hockey rink like a douche of cold ink. The shouts of his teammates hung on the air in stalactites. Often there was a thud as cold body hit cold body, the crunch of opposing players in high words or a fight. He was aware of all this, yet really there was only himself skating intensely in this winter world of darkness. He heard the sigh of gelid reeds striking the blades of his skates if he skidded near the margins of the pond. Then the coach blew his whistle, and Ralph skated into the boards that fenced the rink into a rectangle. He took off his gloves.

—Ya gettin aggressive as all get-out, the coach said, clapping him on the shoulder.

On the shore of the hockey pond a faculty lady was dispensing hot chocolate to the warriors on skates, become little gentlemen now that they were out of the arena. Walking on the toes of their skates, the team minced up to her and her steaming milk can of cocoa. Ralph didn't really want to ask her for her bounty, but he was frozen, and he welcomed the relief of having his throat scalded. He let her fill him a paper cup. The chocolate was so hot that the wax ran off into his roughened hands.

The lady who was doing the ladling was a wispy pimpled person in a fur coat and the astrakhan fur shako of a moujik. She was smoking a corncob pipe. Every day, though no one asked her to, she appeared at the end of hockey practice with a hot drink for the players. Her voice was a tremolo of worship for all athletes. She was married to a big fat man who taught biology and spent his time encouraging tadpoles and students in experiments. Since they'd never had children, the barren womb of Mrs. Launcelot Miller had exploded into an umbrella open to catch all comers. Therefore she took out all her yearnings on the athletes and Big Wheels of The Academy. She was in a perfect position for a lady with ambiguous desires, but too ladylike to indulge them except by her own brand of mental frottage. Ralph had just finished reading of the court of Queen Anne. And he decided that not since the eighteenth century have ladies, except at schools, been able to surround themselves with handsome lusty boys, who pretend to be eating out of their hand. Such was Mrs. Launcelot Miller. Since she was the daughter of a minister, she was forced to take out her lusts in a saintly mothering of those young men she liked. Sometimes she

220

went so far as to lay a hand on their arms. This year her passion was Ben Gordon. She entertained him lavishly in her house. She loved all athletes and active manly boys. Ralph thought of her as a sort of stultified and whining Pompadour. There was no boy at The Academy who wasn't aware that Mrs. Launcelot Miller was a harmless mystical nympho. They took her meals and her graciousness, then talked about her behind her back, as students do.

Holding his paper cup, he listened while she made much of Ben Gordon. She asked pointed and personal questions about his family and his girl friends, to which Ben, standing kingly and humble in his hockey uniform, answered demurely and sweetly. Ralph admired Ben for the unspoiled dignity with which he held his high offices at school.

—O Ben, you're a perfect devil! screamed Mrs. Launcelot Miller.

Ralph saw that her whole body in its fur coat seemed to shiver with delight, as though she imagined Ben loving her up.

—Yes indeed, mam, Ben said.

Out of the corner of his eye he kept looking for his roommate Bill Hunnicutt. Then Mrs. Launcelot Miller, for want of somebody better, noticed Ralph. She spoke to him in her self-pitying auto-enthusiastic voice:

—I'm so glad *you* came out for hockey! I never dreamed. . . .

—Thank you, Mrs. Miller, he said.

He dumped the grounds of his cocoa on the frozen ground, thanked her and walked pigeontoed toward the gym. He never quite shared in the afterscrimmage jubilance of the rest of the team. He amused himself by thwacking the macadam road with his hockey stick. A few boys remained behind to fight over the honor of carrying Mrs. Miller's milk can to her house. Tonight they would tell their roommates how she screamed with delight over their politeness, like a girl drowning for the pleasure of having a lifeguard save her. Ralph knew. She would coax the huskiest into her apartment for tea, where she would wrest from them with delighted little screams stories of their exploits with girls. She was the only woman at The Academy who knew the scores of every game played there. She maintained a fervid correspondence with past favorites who had graduated. Her salons were conducted from her bed, where she lay, complaining of spinal trouble, and surrounded by her favorites. Her husband countenanced his odd cuckoldry, serving tea to the boys. Ben was even allowed to light her corncob pipe.

After violent exercise on February afternoons Ralph was relaxed and sad. He suspected that these wintry vistas of melancholy would deepen as he grew older. He entered the gym, took off his hockey stuff, and took a shower alone, speaking to no one. He thought his friend Tad McKinley must be still up in the fencing room, whipping about at the white boys with his deadly épée.

Now in the shower room Ralph noticed a tension, an expanding awareness of boy with boy that had been absent during the Fall Term. Perhaps it was the ice outside, and now this arousing and lulling steam on their bodies. Many hadn't seen a girl since Christmas vacation. But there was certainly a crescendo in crudities, frankness, and grossness. Roommates under the showers were forever crying out for their *wives* to come and soap their backs. There was a great deal of irrelevant bumping and jostling. If anybody bent to pick up his soap, the whole shower room roared with laughter. There was something restless and unsatisfied here, and all sorts of odd suggestions, made half in jest, half in earnest.

Someone hurtled against Ralph, who was soaping himself up:

—Mind if I share your shower? said a voice, proud of itself for being a bass.

—Next one's empty.

Then the voice of a lurid upperformer:

—I just *love* to put the lowerformers to bed! Just like little girls in their cots! So helpless too. . . .

—Ah, dry up! another voice called. I've read books about *your* kind. . . .

There was a midwinter fever behind all this boasting. Ralph had seen how during the Winter Term the whole Boys' School had ranged itself into two groups. The maler boys had turned to giggling and passivity; the wiry primping ones were now taking the aggressive in everything. There was also a great deal of courting of little blond boys, and meaningless fights breaking out in the dormitories for no apparent reason. The members of the Literary Magazine were in a tizzy of pleasure over these new developments and commented on it to one another with lisped quotations from pertinent classic writers. He finished his shower and left the gym, making his way through the snow to the dining hall.

He buttoned on his white waiter's coat and ignored the blandishments of Mrs. Miekewicz. He sat down at table with the other waiters.

—Pass the Mung, Paganini, an upperformer said.

—There's Mung in the cauliflower, another said.

Mung. That was The Academy's name for the food they ate. The group mind had chosen it for its sound, suggestive of protein and protoplasm.

All through the ritual of waiting on table (he was serving the Pilkeys on the dais) Ralph thought of sex. He went through all the motions of bringing on platters, removing plates, crumbing. He thought how all this food would be converted into jellies and plasmas inside their bodies. Watching Mr. Pilkey wipe mint jelly from his chin, snorting as he ate, Ralph for the first time realized that the Principal was a sexual man too. This drive—what was it but the humming of phallus and scrotum, sublimated into a prong (deified by education) which prodded the whole school?

Outwardly as obsequious as a good butler, Ralph ran riot with his fantasies of sex. Until now it had seemed incredible to him that Mr. Pilkey had ever been astride his wife. And those ladies of the faculty at the High Table—why, they were all there for variants of the same power!

Finally Ralph brought on the dessert, a cherry-quivering blob of red jello. His excitement knew no bounds as he laid the ruddy quivering mammal before the serving spoon of the Principal's wife. So this was all there was? Quiverings and spurtings and snortings? It seemed the jest of a satiric God, who, to humble man in whatever dignity he had attained, forced him down again to make love on all fours. . . .

—Pass the cream, dearie, Mr. Pilkey called out to Mrs. Pilkey.

Ralph heard it clearly as he stood at his serving table with his arms folded over his white jacket. Suddenly at eighteen he knew what made him different from all other boys at The Academy. It was his fastidiousness. Why else did he play the violin and love the idea of love, which he'd never yet known? It must be that his own desire was a vine which he'd

223

never suffer to be dragged in the dust and empearled with the spittle of frogs.

In the evening of that February the snow outside the dining hall was a swamp of aloneness. But these sophisticated children didn't run out and play in it. Snow was something they pushed people into whom they wished to torture and humiliate. No, the hour after supper was passed in the dormitories. There they wrestled together for various purposes. Or they broke things their fathers could afford to pay for. There were perhaps a few in school who went to read or examine their souls. But for most it was a time of rout, since most American boys aren't capable of entertaining themselves, except by the destruction of limb and property. Anything else would have been sissified or lower-class. Hundreds stood in their doorways, loafing and inviting trouble. Insults and obscenities were exchanged, for the hour after supper in schools is traditionally a time of expansive rowdyism, of unbuttoned masculinity. These boys at The Academy were merely taking a leaf from the chivalry of their fathers, home from the office with their feelings raw, taking out their nerves on wives and children. Few there were among students or faculty at this school who imagined that this hour after supper on a chill February night could be pleasant with warmth, song, and true leisure.

This was the hour of the Bull Session, in which congenial seventeen- and eighteen-year-olds gathered in the rooms of Student Councillors and carried on conversations with philosophic overtones. They sprawled on beds and in jagged cacophonic phrasing held forth in imitation of males of maturer years. They talked on three subjects, and three subjects only. Sex (what they knew and what they guessed). Sports (an analysis as exhausting and exhaustive as a statistical report). Cars (alluding either to their father's or to a jalopy they hoped to purchase this summer). These boys had identified themselves completely with the sleek machines whose original function was to transport them over the roads. Each tenderly described his Dreamboat: its whitewalled tires, its motor, its accouterments (which consisted of all possible chromium). To hear them discuss automobiles an outsider would have thought they were rhapsodizing on sex; to hear them talk of sex, he would have imagined that machinery was their topic. But of these three themes their shouted, impolite, and platitudinous conversation never wearied.

When he first came to The Academy Ralph had tried to enter into these Bull Sessions. Not to curry favor, but simply because he thought he ought to share the life of an American student. It wasn't enough, he told himself, to have his violin and his thoughts. But one week was all he could tolerate of these evening gatherings of young masculinity. The others noticed his withdrawal and resented it. For he was eligible to be One of the Boys. And he'd turned it down. It was almost like telling society what it could go and do to itself.

Thus he found himself seeking out the Untouchables and Pariahs. And he was a little startled to discover (for every eighteen-year-old passionately wants to conform) that he found the outcasts better company. Still he went through the bitter little hypocrisy of avoiding them on the quadrangle. It hurt him and hurt them, and he itched under his own dishonesty.

So this February evening, after taking off his waiter's jacket and submitting to the caresses of the Polish dietitian, he found himself knocking at a door to which no one came, except charter members of an exotic little club, as esoteric and restrictive as only young men know how to make it. Everyone in school knew that he'd become intimate with the Dreeps, the Fruits, and the Awfuls, but he still maintained a polite fiction that he only *happened* into their room.

Elsewhere in the dormitory there was the sound of squirting waterpistols as the Normals had their bullish fun. There was the sound of smashing furniture. And downstairs shouts of disemboweling as one husky sixteen-year-old sat on the chest of another and beat the daylights out of him to prove to applauding onlookers the manliness of both.

But behind this door where Ralph was standing he heard a scuffling and a tittering. Out came Doctor Sour, the only faculty member to fraternize with students in their rooms. Caught offguard, he looked right into Doctor Sour's mouth, past the pearly-blue false feeth. The doctor laughed in fellowship; for the first time he frisked him ticklingly about the ribs. Ralph had seen it done to many others, but now he felt as though somehow he'd lost caste and pedestal. He stepped out of the way of the little man's paunch.

—Good evening, sir. . . .

—Good evening, my grandmother! Doctor Sour said, puffing out his sherry breath. Say, lissssen, when are you coming up to play Mozzzzart sonatas with me? I take it very ill, very ill indeed that the only decent violinisssst in thissss school doesn't let me play for him. . . . God, I'm no tyro, kiddddd! Played the organ at the Military Masssss in Notre Dame in 1919. What more do you want . . . aspidistras?

—I'll be up soon, sir.

—O, *good!* Doctor Sour said, tweaking him again. Don't think I haven't been watching you! . . . I said to myself I said: That One's got something better than a brain for Frenccccch. . . . And by the way, wait till you see their new décor inside . . . simply screaming!

Doctor Sour whisked off, whistling a serpentine tune about doings in Budapest in the early twenties. And Ralph, biting his tongue, turned to see a tall blond boy in ballet slippers regarding him quizzically and affectionately in the doorway.

—Hmmmm! How long have *these* assignations been going on?

—Hmmmm yourself, Ralph said waspishly.

This boy was known as The Abbot. His blond hair was swept up in a finger wave; his delicate hands wore natural-toned but glistening nail polish. His willowiness had caused him to be tortured as a lowerformer, or invited to all sorts of body-service by older more crass football players. But now that he was an upperformer, The Abbot was left strictly alone with the other monks and nuns of what he called His Abbey. His mother was rich and psychotic, having thrown him down a flight of stairs when he was a baby. Each year she made munificent grants to The Academy's endowment, out of the fortune of her husband, a Greek who had owned a gambling boat outside the twelve-mile limit. And now in his last year at school The Abbot reigned in sylphlike splendor, inviting whom he would to his Little Evenings At Home. He had as much freedom and debauchery as the catalog would permit. Mr. Pilkey probably thought of him as a rather silly little esthete. By students and by some of the faculty he was known as Homo.

Yet The Abbot, with his ecclesiastical sense of the fitness

of things, didn't put his arm around Ralph's waist. He simply bowed low and said:

—Come in, you Delectable Mountain. We've done over the Abbey.

Ralph greeted the other roommate, known as The Abbess, who was distractedly bustling about with pins in his mouth, fixing crepe paper over one of the room's double windows. The Abbess was a dark and gibbering plump boy who couldn't grow a beard. In his closet he kept a sailor suit, into which he slipped with modest titters when the demure festivities of the Little Evenings At Home reached their climax in Brilliant Talk and innuendo.

—Why, Ralph, The Abbess said, fussing with crepe paper, may we consider this a *social* call?

—What else?

—You're *mean*, The Abbess said, making a moue, I thought it might have other *ends* in view. . . .

—For heaven's sake, reverend mother, The Abbot said. Renew your vow of silence for the next twenty-four hours. . . .

The room was full of ottomans and whimsical loveseats. Ralph sat down on one of them and surveyed the decorations The Abbess was puttering with. His social life was always a choice of evils—here he felt prickly; with The Boys he felt like a living yawn.

Each week The Abbot and The Abbess did over their room. In the village they bought rolls of crepe paper and satirical junk from an antique shop. Stepping into their room was like entering a bower in which two pixies and two upholsterers had gone mad with tape measures and frou-frou.

All the windows (which Mr. Pilkey in his catalog said admitted health-giving light and air) had been covered over with masks of building board cut into Gothic arches. Behind these had been tacked façades of crepe paper, back of which electric light bulbs burnt. Thus the whole room was suffused with a pious glow of sunset streaming through fake stained glass. In front of each window was a Victorian divan, with springs falling out and trailing on the floor, like somebody's bowels. The Abbot and The Abbess called these their Ecstasy Seats. There was always a smell of incense in the room—jasmine or bougainvillea which suffused every crack. It even permeated the cubicles of other students on the corridor, causing complaints to the Principal and a periodic raid on the décor of the room, in which football players tore down and threw out into the quadrangle.

The walls were peppered with Currier & Ives prints; with framed neumes of Gregorian chants; with pictures by Alma-Tadema and Watts (notably Hope) turned upside down; with playbills and programs of the ballet. And in amusing little niches were enshrined jockstraps holding fig and acanthus leaves, Greek statues with significant parts chipped off them, and tennis rackets strung with artificial flowers.

—Say that you *like* it! The Abbess said, plaiting crepe paper.

—Not particularly, Ralph said.

—But you *will* like it, The Abbot said, after you've had some of our rich crumbly cake and wintry wine. . . .

Then clucking to each other like old biddies and old room-mates, The Abbot and The Abbess proceeded to brew green tea on their electric stove. This regularly blew all the fuses on the corridor, resulting in disciplinary action and the enraged screams of the Comptroller.

Ralph picked up some of the books lying about and stud-ied them. They were slim tomes on the ballet, some poems by Rimbaud, and a Bible with naughtinesses in the margins. There were also the *Journals* of André Gide and horrible woodcuts by Dürer.

—May I put on my tutu? The Abbot whispered in an ecstasy.

—Not yet, child, The Abbess said, playing with the teapot. Not till I get my sailor suit out of the mothballs. . . .

Ralph, pretending to read, sat watching them. He felt aloof and amused and a little puzzled. The hot water began to burble in the teapot. The Abbess, waddling slightly to suggest that he was seven months enceinte, set out Mexican plates and put creampuffs and eclairs on them. The symbols were nearly ephemeral in the pastry.

—All *sorts* of little persons are coming tonight! The Abbess whispered, bending low to Ralph's ear.

It seemed as though the plump boy's tongue lingered on the whorls for a moment.

In order not to make The Abbot and The Abbess think he was watching them through spyglasses in their boudoir,

Ralph never looked directly at them. He did this although he knew somehow that nothing could ever embarrass these torpid twins. He scanned their books and fingered their record collection, though he knew by heart everything they owned. He was rather like an uneasy dog sniffing out a new hearth, turning around before he lies down. All the books had an air of recondite and febrile smartness bound in limp leather. Within the covers of their books were the hectic things these boys would have liked to say, had they been born fifty years earlier.

Even odder was their large record library, a pastiche of tastes and styles. Only at The Academy could American boys of seventeen and eighteen have developed such dainty palates for music. Ralph guessed that all the record albums were there for two reasons—their rarity and their esoteric impressiveness. This Winter Term he'd listened to and assimilated in his own passionate skepticism such works as Das Lied von der Erde and Gurre-Lieder and Bachianas Brasilieras and Belshazzar's Feast and somebody's sonata for harp and ocarina. After he'd got attuned to the strange brilliance of these things, he fell out of sympathy with the Bach and Handel that his taste had absorbed before he knew The Abbot and The Abbess. Or sometimes by candle-light his hosts played recordings of harpsichord and viola da gamba. They approved of nothing after the death of Beethoven. The whole air of their salon was of Taste tuned up so high that her pegs shrieked like a violin about to snap. Ralph wondered whether the affectations of The Abbot and The Abbess weren't those nebulous refinements of artiness which hit all young Anglo-Saxons of sensibility. He belonged to an older, cooler tradition. But Americans artistically aware beyond their own intelligences take the gestures of art for the real thing; they babble of Black Masses before they can spell the name of God. He thought that the pattern of chi-chi followed by these boys was somehow intrinsic to young men desirous of raising themselves through Art above the sordid materialism which had made their families money. Buddy Brown was a truer pattern of American boy. The Abbot and The Abbess were already in the sink of decadence without the intervening stage of true culture. They were in the senility of youth which has never known a wayward childhood. . . .

The chief fear of this salon was not that it should be raided by burly upperformers, but that Mr. Pilkey or Mr. Grimes should Break It up.

—Mr. Grimes, said The Abbess tidily, was just Like Us, I hear at Princeton. . . .

But now as mentor of upperformers Mr. Grimes looked with a liverish eye on any manifestation of estheticism. And so far the Principal had no idea of what went on in the most recherché undergraduate cult of his school. The Official Art of The Academy was hymnsinging and the decorations made by Mrs. Pilkey on dinner plates. Nor was there any objection to the *National Geographic* being read. But The Abbot and The Abbess didn't delude themselves. They knew what would happen if the Principal ever discovered (or the athletic coaches for that matter) that within the walls of This Academy American boys of seventeen and eighteen were really practicing ballet positions and listening to music in which the singers *talked* in scabrous German! . . .

There was a knock at the door. Quick like a ballerina The Abbott flew to the phonograph and removed the needle from its groove. The Abbess covered up the green tea simmering on the hotplate with his portly buttocks. Ralph watched the door, fascinated to be caught in such a stew. Both roommates genuflected:

—This may be curtains for us, dear. . . .

—Nibble-nibble-mousekin! cried The Abbess.

—Hmmm, The Abbot said. Such ugly imagery. . . .

The durable school door was kicked open. In it stood two young men whom Ralph had never suspected of frequenting the Little Evenings At Home. One was a handsome blond upperformer known as The Body, editor of *The Academe*, the school newspaper. He wore dungarees on all possible occasions. And now for the first time Ralph saw a connection between the tight pants on the haunches of The Body and those sailor suits that The Abbess whisked into when the salon really got going.

—Damn it to hell, you bitches, The Body said in his choice baritone.

—Hmmmm, said the Abbot, shut the door quickly, chickie. . . .

With The Body was his roommate, a pockmarked muscular Alabaman referred to (outside the salon) as Mung. He was a guard on the football team. And socially conscious faculty members, aware of a certain perception and disillusionment on Mung's themes and history papers, called him The New South, and agreed that Birmingham was way ahead of what liberal magazines said about Dixie. Mung bowed to The Abbot and The Abbess and sat down softly on an ottoman. He sniffed at the incense, which was now going like a conflagration in a joss factory.

—Ah thot fo shooah yo-all had a Nigress in heah, Mung said. But no mattuh. . . .

—Hmmm, said The Abbot and The Abbess together. *We* do have a Negress who does our chamber, but she only comes on Tuesdays. . . .

—Goddam it, The Body said, also sprawling into a seat. The two of you are so arty I don't know why the hell I come here. You must have *some*thing. . . . Yet you're both as queer as all get-out. . . .

—Well, hmmm, the two roommates said, looking at Ralph to see whether he Got It.

The Body reached over and cracked Ralph's knee with his sneering noisy good fellowship:

—Goddam it, Du Bouchet, I had hopes for *you*! But you come here too. . . . My last illusion gone. . . .

—I like it here.

—Hmmmmm! Will you listen to That One! said The Abbot and The Abbess together.

—Buddy Brown's your roommate, Du Bouchet?

—Yes.

—I hate his guts, The Body said. But *he* thinks I'm his arsehole buddy. . . .

—O shut yo big mouth, Mung said in his tired voice.

On his ottoman, pretending to be absorbed in *Theater Arts Monthly,* Ralph peered at The Body and at Mung. Mung he could account for easily, for the Alabama boy had that quiescent sensuality that invests most Southerners by the time they're five. But he was still puzzled by the presence of The Body, flaunting everything he had in blue dungarees. The Body was the best undergraduate executive at The Academy—a tycoon at eighteen. He ran the school paper with radical insouciance. In it he weekly published editorials libeling the food in the dining hall and exposing the incompetence of half the faculty. And each Monday after the

231

paper's appearance Mr. Pilkey's hand reached out from his desk in the school corridor, collared The Body, and shook him. Once a term the big blond boy got suspended from school for practicing the freedom of the press that Mr. Pilkey spoke of in his catalog, saying that *The Academe* was comparable to the New York *Times*. . . .

And yet till tonight Ralph had been aware of The Body only through the glass door of the Press Room. There, his feet on a desk, he drawled out orders to his editors and viciously exploited the little lowerformers called Heelers, who were trying to get on the paper. The Body made them perform during their apprenticeship jobs more menial than a janitor's. He was also an Inner Wheel of the Student Council.

Tonight Ralph *saw* The Body for the first time. There was an enthralling coldness and cruelty in that fine face in repose: the lips too red and pouting; the use of blasphemy too grating and obvious. Ralph decided that The Body's mother nineteen years ago had prayed for a girl. She'd got a phoenix.

—Well, goddam it, The Body said. Do we get Kultchah or do we not? Put on some Puccini. . . .

Though Puccini was against the artistic code of the salon, The Abbot and The Abbess rushed to do his bidding, squealing with delight over his abuse. Tugging over record albums like two ravens for possession of an elastic band, they found and put on the turntable the air Non Piangere, Liù from *Turandot*. The sinuous fragrant music, with its Italian Neo-Orientalism, had a disintegrating effect on The Body. His last pose as a young American executive went out the window. He lolled wantonly on his ottoman, his mouth open to convey that he was in dire physical transport. Then he knotted up his fist and made motions along his belly as though he was jerking up and down an invisible cocktail shaker.

—Darling, I'm coming!

He intended to give an impression that he was at home in orgies. To Ralph his performance was somehow ugly. The Abbot and The Abbess watched with appreciation:

—Hmmm. Did we put any cantharides in our green tea today?

The boy Mung from Alabama eyed his roommate with

weary aristocracy, as though all this was a pretty stale and adolescent fiasco. He arose, and in his dark rich tweeds (got from his father, a Birmingham cotton broker) he walked lightly over and sat down by Ralph, who was beginning to feel that he ought to have qualms about this, but instead felt only boredom. In the Alabama boy he found something eminently nice—the crisp hair, the great strength relaxed.

—Ah gotta say somethin, Mung said tentatively. Ah lahk yo vahlin, but not the company yo keep. And ah would lahk fo yo-all to play me a sonatah one of these days. . . .

—Thank you, Ralph said, reaching for the green tea in the cup of Mexican pottery.

—Don't run round with nigguhs, heah?

—I hear you. But I'm running just the same. . . .

Mung sighed and settled back, almost putting his head against Ralph's shoulder.

—Kin ah heah yo play? With yo puhmishun?

Ralph nodded, a little weakly.

—Ah heahbah invaht yo to Bumminham nex summah, Mung said gently, taking his arm.

—I can't. I have to get a job teaching people sailing, off Cape Hatteras. . . .

Mung went on in his dreamy voice, that concealed its urgency:

—In Alabam ah got a little ole gal. An yo know what, boah? She looks lahk you. . . .

—Hmmm! The Abbess said, overhearing as he made a fresh pot of green tea and added a new stick to the incense burner.

—A *lovely* salon! The Abbot said, looking unselfishly at his roommate.

There was another knock at the door, the same scrambling furtiveness to make the room look respectable.

—Goddam it, The Body said, coming out of his Puccinian trance. If it's the Principal himself, I will beat the shit out of the old bastard. . . .

Without invitation the door flew open. Standing on the threshold was an episcopal panoply that seemed to have come straight from Rome—from the tomb of Cecilia Metella. The tallest and beefiest boy in The Academy, six and one-half feet tall and weighing two hundred and fifty pounds,

stood panting with his asthma, his thyroid, and his avoirdu-
pois. On his head he wore a miter made of cheesecloth. In
his puffy hand he gripped a pastor's crook. About his frame
was closed a cope of gaudy cloth.

—Dear Bishop! screamed The Abbot and the Abbess,
kneeling to kiss his ring. Dooooo bless our house!

—O goddam it, here we go, The Body said, falling on his
knees.

The Bishop roared forth, parodying Doctor Smedley and
all Sunday speakers in The Academy's chapel:

—Good evening, my friends and my parishioners! There's
a great deal that's wrong with this world! . . . I repeat . . .
there's a great deal that's *w-r-o-n-g* with this world. And
what are you doing about it? Brethren, you aren't doing one
. . . single . . . damn thing. . . .

Everybody knew where The Bishop had just come from.
Each evening after supper he retired to his room and vested
himself in this priestly garb he'd stitched up. Thence he went
on a solemn progress to that corridor where the lowerformers
slept. He wrestled for the soul of Mr. Guy Hudson, the
heretic, who, The Bishop said, was the reincarnation of
Judas Iscariot. Then he visited his diocese—all those underclassmen whose voices hadn't changed. He told them he was
Bishop Coadjutor of the State. He knelt on them individ-
ually with his two hundred and fifty pounds till they squealed
out that they embraced Sweet Jesus as their savior. Then
The Bishop gave lollipops to all the converts, smacking them
on their little-boys' rears.

Or on clement evenings (if Mr. Pilkey and older faculty
members were off campus) The Bishop might ascend to a
balcony on the second floor of a dormitory and preach a
sermon to the entire Boys' School, milling and cheering below him. Though he was but sixteen, he looked fifty in his
vestments. His voice issued straight from his navel, tired
about with doughnuts of muscular fat. He preached on Sin,
Franklin D. Roosevelt, and Communism. His organ of a
voice would rebound from the brick buildings of the quadrangle. Even literal-minded athletes found it hard to believe
that The Bishop's sermons weren't the highest satire The
Academy offered. He was also one of its brightest upperformers, the ward of two maiden aunts from Oklahoma.

Sometimes in the privacy of the salon, The Bishop cast

aside his vestments. He put on the smock of a Shakeress and a gray poke bonnet and gave imitations of the Principal and Mrs. Pilkey about their conjugal duties. He took the parts of both, and he looked like a large maternal sow caught in a typhoon....

But now he stood in the doorway of The Abbot and The Abbess, blessing his flock and rolling his saintly eyes to heaven, bellowing:

—This place is inimical to true sanctity! But I will consent to walk among the unwashed, like my Master before me. ...

And he billowed into the room, smelling of sweat and vestments, for he rarely bathed, lest his pores contract iniquity as most people do a cold. He squeezed his girth into one of the divans with the dropping springs and was cajoled into taking a dish of green tea and some eclairs. He beamed on his hosts:

—Bless you, bless you, my children. For this, three indulgences....

Then it was observed that The Biship's train was being held by his page, a plump little redheaded upperformer called The Beetle. This little person was also puffy; he was the jest of The Academy in the showers because at sixteen his testicles were as yet undescended.

—Attend to the comfort of my curate, The Bishop said blandly, waving a fat hand loaded with glass rubies. Whatsoever ye do for him, ye do also for me....

So The Beetle was also served green tea and eclairs. He was a droll acidulous little boy with eyebrows always raised, and he peered at everything and everyone as though they were beneath his wit or his notice.

—Of course I hate everything here, The Beetle said, grimacing his pink face.

The Bishop cuffed his stooge roundly:

—Silence! Silence. You live under perpetual threat of excommunication....

The Beetle put a tooth into an eclair and spat out the whole thing:

—Tastes just like that mung they feed us in the dining hall...

—What, suh? the boy from Alabama said, starting up. What did yo-all say, suh?

—Hmmmm, cried the hosts, separating them. Do you want

235

our Little Evening At Home raided?

—It is an abomination before the Lord, The Bishop murmured.

And after he'd made a frugal repast of three cups of green tea and a dozen eclairs, and when the hosts had piled on more incense, the salon settled down to its main function, which was brilliant conversation, to counteract the Philistia of the rest of The Academy.

Then The Abbot and The Abbess locked their door by inserting a knife (stolen from Mr. Whitney and the Dining Hall) across the jamb. Other than by this means it was impossible to lock a dormitory door. Then the floor was cleared of ottomans. The Abbess reappeared in a salior suit, The Abbot in a Taglieni tutu. Suspended over his naked flat chest was a bra, which he called his myàh-hah. Mung rumbled deep in his throat.

Reading out of De Blasis' pamphlet, The Abbot and The Abbess gave everyone a lesson in The Dance. The phonograph played Maurice Ravel. Everybody pointed, jetée'd. leapt, and entrechated like stinking.

Then they settled down to a square dance, locking and loping, clapping and flushed. The Abbess listened at the keyhole out into the corridor. Only The Bishop refused to dance in the figure; it was beneath his priestly dignity. Holding up his cope, his miter askew on his huge fat head, he circled by himself in a corner of the room, grunting in Latin as he improvised a saintly sarabande.

When everyone was panting and hectic and flushed, The Abbott and The Abbess put out all the lights behind the crepe paper and lit candles in dripped-on sconces. In the center of the floor they set a chamberpot. On it were stenciled a crowing rooster and the motto:

—QUANDO QUESTO GALLO CANTERÀ, IL MIO AMORE FINIRÀ.

Everyone, including The Bishop, who was muttering about choirboys, sat down in a closed circle about this Accommodator.

—God, I'm hot as an alleycat, The Body said.

—If ah change mah expression, ah pay a fahn. . . .

There was a pause in which Ralph heard the breathing and the panting and the tension and the madness.

Ready, dears? cried The Abbess in a shrill whisper. One . . . two . . . three . . .

4

Like nuns huddled at the South Pole The Girls' School in February drew closer together for survival. The air was frosty and shrill. Outside their feline insularity of February lay only the graveyard and inhospitable fields of snow. And the souls of the girls and of their mistresses took on scars, much as if they'd been raked by icicles.

After her disillusionment with the fall, Miss Blanchard had sworn to keep aloof from everyone. She would go to classes and be chillily polite to Mrs. Mears. Yet she pined for the first shiverings of spring. Then she would go to a Teachers' Agency and hunt herself up another job—preferably teaching the Bible (in Spanish) on an atoll where American virginity had never been heard of.

That winter too, when she'd have liked to be alone, she had the enjoyable rape of a new friendship. It had been happening since her days at Wheaton, when bepimpled smelly girls had attached themselves to her cool beauty for solace and for foil. By February unmarried ladies at Mrs. Mears's settled down to relationships as intimate as before they'd been jangling. In the drawing room after supper women teachers took little turns, their arms about each other's waists, cooing and rivaling the very schoolgirls. There were ripe secret whisperings in the house till bedtime. Even Mrs. Mears took up a friendship with The Sex, repairing across the street for soul-searching talks and teas with another widow, who owned a drygoods shop in the village.

Betty Blanchard shivered with a pneumonia of disgust. Intimate friendships among ladies snowbound! The white seventeenth century house quivered with a February suffocation. She thought herself caught in a cattrap for fur and felt, with lacquered springs. Every night she sat in her room with her Calderón or wrote letters to teaching agencies. Next year she was determined to teach in a public school. She would be happier to have a football coach (whose first name was sure to be Russell) throw himself at her in the janitor's room of a high school in Wilkes-Barre.

The Directress watched with delight the friendship between Miss Demerjian and Betty Blanchard. She'd been uneasy about her pretty new teacher of Spanish. She figured that the lonely tense girl was heading for a breakdown or something. So she used every means in her power to throw the two mistresses together. She even contemplated hinting that they move in together, just like college roommates.

Tonight Mrs. Mears brought the Two Chums together. She detailed them to joint responsibility for decorating the Girls' Assembly Room. Betty heard the prescription and paled with anger. But she and Miss Demerjian, who was prattling away in French, turned the Assembly Room from a sexless white study hall into a toothpaste advertisement, such as would look happy in a drugstore window. On the dais at one end they hung curtains for Miss Demerjian's play *Try We Lifelong*. It had been written five years ago. Everybody said it was at least as funny as those off-color Broadway comedies.

They surveyed their handicraft. The floor was covered with thumbtacks and hammers and squirls of crepe paper. Miss Demerjian put her arm around Miss Blanchard's waist and endeavored to buss her.

—Baby, how beautiful! You're an artiste! Next year you can design new sets for my play!

—Thank you, Betty Blanchard said, removing The Arm. And I've asked you not to call me Baby. . . .

Since a school must constantly give laymen proof-positive that it is up to no nonsense with the young, each term the Girls' School gave a party for parents. Mr. Pilkey (and by emulation, Mrs. Mears) solved the Integration Problem of Parent and Teacher by spectacular means. Mothers and fathers of the boys and girls at The Academy were bidden to spectacles put on for their benefit. The purpose of these educational Open Houses was to prove to the parents that their children were absorbing no lasting harm from books, that they could do useful things as well.

The Girls' School called this intellectual rummage sale a

Midwinter Bazaar. Nothing was sold. In the Assembly Room mothers and fathers of the girls were served coffee and sandwiches, economically limited to wafery bread and micrometer-sliced spam, by order of Mr. Whitney. Then the parents would sit down to watch Miss Demerjian's comedy. Then they'd go home again, convinced that the school really put on a show, didn't it? Such an evening was merely an extension of Latin debates and orations delivered in the nineteenth century by promising students. At The Academy, under the cunning showmanship of the Pilkeys and Mrs. Mears, the evening had something modern and sophisticated about it. But nothing suggestive. O my, no! . . .

Mrs. Mears trundled into the Assembly Room and appraised the decorations. On state occasions she wore a lorgnette, for that was what parents would expect as a scepter of her dignity. In her moire evening gown she looked like a combination of Carrie Nation and the prophetess Deborah. Her shrewd eyes took in all the prettifying. She was so gratified that she kissed both Miss Demerjian and Miss Blanchard. Her piled white hair shook as she shrieked:

—Run and dress, my dears! *Scads* of cars are pulling up outside!

Shortly (for schoolmistresses may not take time for refinements of the toilette, yet must appear decent in public) the Misses Blanchard and Demerjian re-entered the Assembly Room just as girls began to arrive, shivering in their party dresses. Betty wore a black gown that had cost her a month's salary; there was a gardenia in her hair.

Miss Habib Demerjian had on a formal frock for which she'd spent two months' salary, plus a few dollars wangled from her friends the rug merchants. This gown looked as though she'd wrapped the American flag around her body. In her hair were two gardenias. Swelling up from her neck was something meant to be a mantilla, but had collapsed into a broken weathervane. She'd plastered her brown face with a deadwhite cream rouge, which not only hid her mustache but gave her the appearance of a corpse fresh from embalming.

They took their places in the reception line, but low down, far from Mrs. Mears's left. Above them stood the older and more bitten mistresses, in order of seniority.

—Mrs. Mears! cried Miss Demerjian, wouldn't it be fun if I greeted the parents in French?

—My dear, no! You'd only make them nerrrvous! . . .

The Academy girls who were to act as waitresses (by typewritten roster from Mrs. Mears) took up their stance behind the coffee tables. The boarders were happy to emerge from their nunnery into an hour or so of evening dress. The Daygirls were furious to be herded out to school on a weekday night. The fun they'd passed up for this tomfoolery—the lovin in parked cars at Howard Johnson's, the cigarettes! . . .

—Girls! Mrs. Mears cried from the reception line. Stop giggling! If you get nerrvous and spill coffee over the hands of your dear parents, they'll pull you right out of school!

First to arrive were the Pilkeys, who took up their places in the reception line next to Mrs. Mears. There were kissing and handshaking and charitable screams from the Directress, who said she hoped she was giving a good account of herself and her school. Betty Blanchard dated Mrs. Pilkey's evening gown at 1922. The Principal's wife had had one of Her Bumps this afternoon; she tottered a little and fixed a smile on her face. Old Mrs. Pilkey was home in bed under the electric blanket and the care of the Negress. Miss Blanchard observed that the Principal took in every detail of her; tonight he looked tired but determinedly social.

The Assembly Room began to flutter its streamers of crepe paper as it filled up; warm air arose from bodies. There arrived now the faculty of the Boys' School and twenty-five upperformers, ordered by the Principal to put in an appearance.

There came by the Principal's son, Herman, and his Georgian wife Nydia. He paused before Betty Blanchard in her black gown. His form was swaying genially; he sprayed her liberally with the bourbon on his breath:

—Well, now, look at this! Why don't we meet more often?

—That's not up to me, she answered.

—Don't hold up the lahn, hon-ey, Nydia Pilkey said, urging her husband on.

She gave Miss Blanchard the once-over, calling her hon-ey also in a different tone of voice, possibly cracker-white. Betty observed that Nydia's second child was well along.

There was also Mr. Grimes. Immediately he had the ear

of Mrs. Mears. Possibly he'd discovered that one of the Daygirls was about to have an abortion? The Directress nodded her white head:

—No, Philbrick! Don't tell me! . . . O, I don't believe it! . . . She's just nerrrvous, that's all. . . .

Mr. Grimes bowed over Miss Blanchard's hand:

—If there's anything I can do for you. . . .

—It's all done, Mr. Grimes. . . .

What was it? It was dressed like a man. Was it a praying mantis?

—Oooh, baby, he likes you a *little,* Miss Demerjian whispered, nudging her in the ribs.

—I'm so glad.

Other persons of the Boys' School faculty came by and shook hands—the Comptroller and his wife—he estimating the waste in crepe paper, she shoe-horned into a violet gown that bulged with her fat, an orchid on her breast to show that *she* was Second Lady here. She gave out motherly hoots to everyone, and a rich laugh such as she imagined typical of a dowager hostess.

Miss Blanchard shook hands with fat Doctor Sour, who seemed especially interested in what the boys were doing. Later tonight he would twit his favorites, half-aroused and not satisfied with mere ogling the girls.

Miss Blanchard pulled herself up even straighter, for she had to face the scrutiny of Mrs. Dell Holly, who was sizing her up with merciless suavity. Perhaps Lisa Holly was thinking that five years ago *she* had been the beauty here. She spoke in a languid drawl:

—Betty, that gown! I wanted it when I saw it in *Vogue* . . . before Lord and Taylor marked it down. . . .

Betty murmured something and took her hand, squeezing it with the injunction that Lisa Holly should pass on. But before she slipped past with her thin haunted husband, the cool woman let fly again:

—I thought that as an expert on female education you'd have called on me and my three little girls. . . . You should *see* their watercolors! They really express themselves. As I told Dell, we're not bringing them up to be just *ordinary* children. That's too easy. Soon, Betty, you'll be teaching them. . . .

—That's what I'm waiting for, Mrs. Holly.

She smiled listlessly and Lisa Holly glided on, exclaiming

to her husband on the banality of the decorations. Miss Demerjian whispered:

—It's so stimulating when we get together with the faculty of the Boys' School!

—We're like teams from rival orphanages playing hopscotch. . . .

Her spine like a ferrule in her black evening gown, Betty stood at attention while the reception line crawled by. Most of the teachers at the Boys' School were just faces to her. Yet she observed a kinship between them and the mistresses under Mrs. Mears. All were marionettes jerked by executive fingers; all were Punch and Judy idealists twitching in rigor mortis. All looked at the Pilkeys and at Mrs. Mears out of a corner of their eyes for confirmation that they were really Doing All Right, like children at their first party, to be later thrashed if they didn't behave. These were grownup men and women—American teachers and their wives. The women especially chilled Betty Blanchard. She now saw that if she didn't get out from under soon, she'd end up a teacher's wife. Or worse still, an unmarried schoolmistress, all her lusts and individuality splintered into a piece of Sèvres china. She studied these men and women passing before her, with the absorption of a dissecter of cadavers who pauses long enough to reflect that she too will end up on this self-same table.

Most of the younger women felt it their duty as teachers' wives to put on an act. But there wasn't sufficient income to support their little theatricals. They tried to be brittle and witty, like heroines in English novels. Or else they looked washed out from struggling with too many kids on inadequate funds, and trying to rear them in the traditional pinafores of Campus Children. Betty found something grinning and horrible in the whole parade—the teacher class making a stab at being aristocratic. Actually they were only sextons and vestals to a shut-church society. Tonight she fathomed the true tragedy of a teacher's life: this shining-forth of light onto barren ground, this constant underpaid and pathetic expenditure of self in the vineyard of a world that cynically crushes the grapes of idealism into a paying proposition.

Twenty-five of the Boys' School were passing down the line, resentful and obviously on their party manners. Miss Blanchard liked most of them. There were the burly, the beanpoles, the handsome, the splotched with acne from chocolate munching and adolescent inner battles. Her brain hummed under her gardenia as she pressed their hands. There was something sweet about these boys, sweeter than girls of the same age. They had dignity. So far they hadn't been perverted—much. She did observe, however, that the sexual segregation of the system had made them churlish in the presence of women. Later that night in their dormitories, she knew, they would speak of her with wolf calls. But now, shaking her hand, they were tense or abrupt or just plain silly. And she knew that in spite of her good looks, she was no longer a woman to them. Not because she was twenty-five, but because she was a teacher. She was a smiling ramrod of an ideal already dead. Yet if she passed them in front of a drugstore, they might whistle. But as a beautiful girl who was also a teacher of Spanish, she was no more flesh and blood than a statue of the Virgin Mary. . . .

Miss Demerjian on her left gave out a stifled whoop and clapped a hand over her whitewashed mustache. Betty saw approaching in the reception line that Negro boy she'd watched from her window last November. Now this boy was in evening dress; there was a lurid mahogany grin on his face.

—O, aren't you shaking hands with me? he said to Miss Demerjian.

—Why, of course! she babbled. I've been reading all sorts of books on the problem. . . .

Betty Blanchard, reddening, lurched forward and grabbed the cold dry hand of the boy:

—Nice of you to come. . . .

—I think it was a ghastly idea, don't you? he answered.

He passed up the line. Behind him came the other boy she'd seen from her window. His melancholy fine face reared like a flower above his evening clothes. They were clean and brushed, but the pattern of their lapels told her that someone else had worn them fifteen years ago.

—You'll be Ralph Du Bouchet? she said. How are you?

—Well, thank you, Miss Blanchard. . . .

He too passed by; she was surprised and thrilled that he knew her name. She'd seen him three months ago, and now the low softness of his voice impinged him further on her reality. She thought that he must be a lovely person, and

243

regretted that there was no way she could ever know him better, or at all. . . .

Miss Demerjian leaned over and whispered:

—What I've seen of the Boys' School, baby, leads me to believe that they're really nicer than our girls. . . .

—Poor things, she answered, more swiftly than she could check it.

But now she truly braced herself, for she saw coming up one about whom she'd been repressedly thinking all evening long. There he was, redheaded and slender and ironic in his evening clothes, which from their very casualness she guessed he hated to wear—he who had once worn combat boots and a shirt open at the throat. In a flash of knowing she guessed that he too was much aware of her presence in the line, for he stood talking to Miss Demerjian longer than was necessary. She felt a sort of apprehension. She observed that Guy Hudson's eyes were taking their own brand of fun, for they lingered quizzically over Miss Demerjian's mustache and mantilla, as a child's fork deliciously hesitates before attacking his favorite dish on the plate. In this privileged instant of anonymity Miss Blanchard looked at him harder than she ever had before. She was for the first time completely aware of that scarred mouth, which must once have been rich and mobile. She saw the shadow of his close-shaven red beard under his clear white skin. She watched the intense carriage of his curly head as he said impossible party things to Miss Demerjian. Worst of all she admitted to herself that there was something sparse and thrilling about Guy Hudson, a weasel on the prowl. His edgy voice was saying:

—Miss Demerjian! Dear God, you look like something out of the Song of Songs! In the Bible, I mean. . . .

—Oooooh! De blague, monsieur! . . .

And for the first time in her winter's trance Betty Blanchard was touched by the way he played up to the Syrian mistress of French; he was aware of her greasy and screaming hunger. The man had tenderness. Perhaps a horrific and fierce tenderness, but it was there. And he pitied Miss Demerjian. She saw that Guy Hudson hated everything that went on at The Academy; but instead of drawing into himself, as she was doing, he was retaliating with a porcupine of irony. And suddenly she was ashamed of the way she'd treated him. Then she began to tremble and got hold of herself, for he'd finally taken her hand, as he did after Christmas vacation. It was an absolutely impersonal clasp.

—Miss Blanchard, Guy Hudson said, good evening. Are you keeping up your skiing?

She looked over his shoulder at the snowy cemetery outside the windows.

—I'm afraid the crust is too hard for skiing right now. . . .

—O, there's a hard crust everywhere, he said. But it *could* be broken. . . . Things are tough all over, they tell me. . . .

And giving a wiry little laugh, he moved up the line. She took her right hand into her left. Miss Demerjian murmured:

—Baby, don't say a word! I *saw* your eyes! That *mouth* of his. . . .

—Hush, Habib, please. Not another word. . . .

She had an impulse to run from the Assembly Room in panic. But almost immediately, arriving together fully mobilized, the parents of the girls descended on the reception line. There were at least a hundred of them: sleepy insurance actuaries, bitter doctors, the mayors of nearby cities who sent their girls here as a convent from that world they knew too well. With the fathers (and far more twittering and competitive) were the women to whom they'd been yoked. These mothers were got up to within an inch of their lives. Betty Blanchard's eyes missed no detail of their costly dresses and warpaint. They were going to *show* the Girls' School tonight. Some looked almost as young as their daughters, except that the shrillness of the girls had frozen into bitchiness in the matrons. But the traits were the same: The Girl would be Mother to the Mature Woman. There were society ladies and Presidents of Leagues of Women Voters and those rich females who lay all day long on chaise-longues, arising at teatime to force their exhausted breadwinners out to cocktail parties and suppers. The mothers' eyes darted about with a wicked gaiety as they thought of how they were going to make the Girls' School teachers dowdy by contrast to their own fine feathers. Their laughter was the silver tinkling of women on the make, elbowing their way into a cloister for the express purpose of embarrassing the nuns.

Betty greeted them all, casting her eyes down modestly, as though she was a poor relation. The fathers were affable and retiring as they shook her hand; and some gave her the twice-over of delighted surprise, expecting to find a tired little wren, like Miss Carpenter. But the mothers barged right in and took over. Their huge ornate bosoms lunged close to hers as they clamped her hand in their ringed wellgroomed fingers. These mothers didn't miss an inch of her beauty, nor of her black evening gown, nor of the gardenia. On the breaths of some she smelled martinis:

—So *you're* Miss Blanchard! I declare! From what Emily says about you, I'd expected to find a dried-up old prune! . . .

—Miss Blanchard! What *does* a girl have to do to get good grades in your class? I'll have you know my Martha is *any*-thing but a moron! . . .

—Miss Blanchard! We've been planning for months to have you out to our house for supper! But I know how tied-down you teachers are. . . .

—Miss Blanchard! Have a heart! I think you're *much* too strict on Eleanor! Don't you realize she had a mastoid only last spring? . . .

There was only one tired Irishwoman to whom she was grateful:

—Miss Blanchard, I'm only a trained nurse. I don't know anything about this education racket. All I can say is, you've got to my Norah as I never was able to. Been too busy. But I'm grateful to you. You must have lots on the ball. And I never expected a woman teacher could be pretty too. Most are such old hens. . . .

—Thank you, Mrs. Donahue. . . .

But in shaking the hands of the men and women who had brought into the world the girls bad and good, stupid and bright, trullish and sweet, who were enrolled in the Girls' School of The Academy, Betty that evening certified what she'd always suspected. The attitude of a parent toward a teacher is a broth of humility and truculence, of envy and admiration. If only parents and teachers could sit down to a highball and a good heart-to-heart talk! But such sim-plicities of conduct would never be permitted by Mr. Pilkey nor by Mrs. Mears. The parent was always right, and the teacher only a salesgirl plying a customer with intellectual nylons. . . .

In the middle of the greetings and the Hampton Court etiquette Miss Blanchard decided that *she* was the butt of all this rigamarole—that none of the men and women in this room cared anything for her as a young woman, as a human personality. She was mentor to their young, to be kept backstairs and out of sight as long as she was suitably and daintily cringing. Did she ever step out of line to insist on excellence from her girls? Did she ever seek to teach them anything out of the dictates of her heart? Did she ever attempt to lead a life other than that of a fading spinster in lavender? She knew what would happen. The wrath of all these good solid people would break over her head. She'd be called unfit to teach the young. She saw it all now. Those same matrons who on committees and civic affairs were loudest for democratic justice would unite in crying for her scalp if she ever stepped outside of what *they* saw as the line. All this she perceived, and she trembled. She wondered how teachers have permitted themselves to become the puddle for all social classes to step in. Herself and thousands of others declassed, abject, unhonored, and screamingly futile. Pallas Athene with a mouthful of sawdust. . . .

The Assembly Room was now full. The crepe paper decorations gibbered with the rising hot air. This evening Mr. Whitney had doubled the steam in the radiators, just to prove to parents that their girls weren't being frozen at school.

Mr. Pilkey got political tips from all the fathers in public office—such innocuous gossip as Mayor This or Governor That saw fit to hand out to the Old Boy. Twenty mothers were kissing Mrs. Mears for all she'd done for their daughters. And other mothers were working off private grudges with the mistress of music, the mistress of gymnastics, the mistress of art, or the mistress of French. The air was molten with flattery and bullying.

Then the Principal clapped his hands several times and, flushed with the pleasure of consorting with the near-great and the well-to-do, stepped into the center of the Assembly Hall:

—Attention, please! . . . I don't want to interrupt the jollification for more than a moment. After all, I'm only the stage manager who brings all you good people together. . . . In the name of Mrs. Pilkey, Mrs. Mears, and myself, I merely want to welcome you on your winter tour of inspection of the Girls' School. . . . You know, I often tell Mrs. Pilkey that

247

we can't do enough for our parents. We *like* to have them look us over. For they come to us with the realistic and critical attitude of people making their way in the world. We like to have parents point out our faults . . . if any. (Laughter.) Sometimes I'm afraid we schoolmasters and schoolmistresses tend to grow a little impatient of the outside world. And that's too bad, because we jolly well have to put up with it. Doesn't it pay our salaries? (Laughter.) But I think you good parents know by now that an old dog like myself tries to stay liberal by keeping an ear open for criticism. Your suggestions for improving my school are always welcome. . . . That's why we like to keep close to our parents. Some schools tell parents to keep their hands off. That's not healthy, and it's not modern, is it? . . . Besides many of you unselfish men and women had dipped most generously into your own pockets to swell the Endowment, left us by Our Gracious Foundress. . . .

Here he paused for a moment. In a touching way his gaze wandered to the snowcovered cemetery where Miss Sophia lay buried. A mother murmured appreciatively to her husband; her eyes filled up with tears. Mr. Pilkey continued:

—Enjoy yourselves tonight! There's coffee and cake (we try to be both generous and frugal in these days of food shortages). No lady or gentleman here present would, I know, want us to spread a Lucullan feast when Europe is hungry. Besides, you've already had generous suppers in your own gracious homes. . . . And after the refreshments we invite you to see that famous comedy, written and coached by our own Thespian, Miss Demerjian. We repeat it every year, at your very own request. . . . After all there's not much on the modern stage that would be a fit vehicle for the talents of your daughters, who we believe . . . we know . . . are young ladies. (Laughter.) Our emphasis here is on wholesome living and wholesome entertainment. Every mother here will, I hope, concur with me. And now I invite you to an evening of innocent merriment. . . .

There was applause for the gracious old man as he stepped back to join Mrs. Pilkey. Betty Blanchard felt ill and ashamed, as though the Principal had set her up in a pillory and invited the rabble to throw cream pies at her. But the faculties nodded approvingly.

Coffee and sandwiches were served by upperform girls

from tables dripping with Mrs. Mears's own damasks. The fathers took their refreshment in a beaten-down and submissive manner, their eyes constantly beseeching some of their menfriends to come and lift this weight from off their shoulders. Betty Blanchard found something elephantinely dainty in the way brokers and lawyers in evening dress held their coffee cups and nibbled their Spam-wiches. But lurider was the fiction of the mothers, who expressed pretty surprise at seeing their daughters as waitresses—or pretending not to recognize them at all. Soon the mothers entered into the spirit of things. After pummeling the women who had taught their girls, they turned the party into their own private affair. A lady executive shrieked an anecdote at a plump flower-toqued mother across the room. And a committee-woman was taking to task the mistress of music for her lack of civic spirit:

—We have so little time! Miss Carpenter said in a whisper. She was fearful of the ear of Mr. Pilkey or of Mrs. Mears.

—*Time!* the mother caroled. If you teachers would get your noses out of your books and try to find out what's going on in this world! . . . No wonder you get old so quickly! . . .

Finally the strong coffee was drunk, and there remained only breadcrumbs sprayed about by some mother in crusading argument. Girls of the lower forms brought in metal folding chairs. The parents seated themselves to view Miss Demerjian's comedy *Try We Lifelong*.

A baby spot picked out the improvised stage. The mothers set up coos of expectancy; the fathers wondered if the theater would be dark enough to nap in. Everybody knew the play, since Mr. Pilkey ordered it done every year. The parents settled down with that fond complacency with which one views the dramaturgy of one's own offspring. No one was going to be critical.

Betty sat in a back row. She found her eyes going down front, to where Guy Hudson sat joking with Ralph Du Bouchet and the Negro boy. But she quickly reclaimed her wandering and anxious glance, for Miss Demerjian sank into the folding chair beside her. Each year she went through the anguish of a playwright at an opening. Her mashed mantilla waggled with her despair; the two gardenias wilted with sweat from her tresses. She smelled a bit gamy:

—O baby, tell me they're going to like it. . . .

—Don't be silly, Habib. They have no choice. . . .

The makeshift curtains jerked back to reveal an English drawing room. Over the audience floated a little hiss of gloating from the teeth of Mr. Grimes. He always came to assure himself that he was still a better dramatic coach than Miss Demerjian.

The parents talked audibly to their neighbors when their own daughter wasn't on the stage. Miss Blanchard watched with the morbid fascination of one who sees a baby burying itself alive with its little shovel. She wanted (tonight somehow especially) to pity, to feel sorry for Miss Demerjian and the whole business. But *Try We Lifelong* was even awfuler than she could have imagined. In her first and last play the mistress of French had thrown together all the elements of *Charley's Aunt* and pre-1900 British comedy. Even the slapstick was gangrenous, and the lines couldn't conceivably have been uttered by anyone outside of Godey's Ladies' Book. For a generous moment Miss Blanchard permitted herself the hope that Miss Demerjian had intended to write a Marxist parody of that very society seated in the darkened Assembly Room. Not so. As the hideous thing ground on, she realized that Miss Demerjian just wasn't very bright. But the parents laughed and applauded in the right places, and the Boys' School shouted with delight at the sheer corn. Sighs of relief wafted up from the musky bosom of Miss Demerjian, who was mouthing to herself all the lines as the actresses said them:

—Sir Marmaduke, I shall see you outside. . . .

—Our hostess Lady Plumley invites you all to drink something cool with strawberries in it. . . .

Far more epicene to the eye of Miss Blanchard was the indisputable and uncamouflageable fact that all the parts were taken by girls. Now a boy actor may give a tolerable imitation of a girl. It may even be *too* good. But no girl since Sappho's time has ever succeeded in disguising her walk, or in convincing an audience that she's cut off her breasts. Therefore it was startling to see Midgie Mears prancing about the stage in evening clothes, pretending to believe that she was the Aryan and muscular hero of the piece. It was doubtful if even the parents accepted this transvestite illusion. There were also bits of lovemaking in which girl made up to girl: in their chaste embraces it was all to obvious that their little breasts were snuggling. Here the guests from the Boys' School began to chortle softly. Mr. Pilkey stood up in his chair and glared out into the darkness. He intercepted the beam of the baby spot; and presto, there was his leonine silhouette imposed on the stage action of *Try We Lifelong*.

Late that night, after the mumming had stopped and the Boys' School had returned across the river and the parents had gone home in their Cadillacs, Betty heard Miss Demerjian sobbing in her room. She arose, put on her kimono, and knocked at the door, intending to ask for a mouthful of Syrian fudge.

—Baby, Miss Demerjian said. It wasn't *too* awful, was it?

—Not *too*. Will you tell me how Mr. Hudson looked at me tonight? . . .

5

That February he was reminded of the raggedness of his mouth. The cold burned into an orifice with more than a hint of pain. Winter hit the twisted edge of his lips, and he knew at last the meaning of the saying, to have one's teeth on edge. When the medics had stitched up his wound in France, they'd sewn up also the plasticity of his face, as dead people who die cursing are frozen in a sneer. Most of the quality of Guy Hudson's expression was conditioned by the red rip at the left side of his mouth; forever now there would be a grin, hideous, when it once had been slack and amiable. Therefore when he smiled now, he seemed austere and refrigerating, like a smile smashed on a satyr centuries ago. It was a mockery and a satire on the twentieth century. Sometimes he thought of himself as a male Mona Lisa, with the reverse of her provocativeness. Now he was rather like a lascivious attitude caught undressed.

As he shaved that morning, the brilliance of the sun on the snow outside refracted a clinical floodlight on every detail of his expression. At such moments when he peered into his own tortured looks, he felt the disgust of watching a suppurating wound. His red hair, his white skin—all had their focus in the menace of his mouth. Whatever charm there had once been in him was now like sin seared into the flesh as a warning to all. He listened to the grating of the razor on his cheek; he heard the icicles fall tinkling from the eaves outside.

And as the water swirled the myriad clipped red hairs out of his razor, he thought of his experiences in New York last vacation, of the remarks of his bed companions for the night, who were intrigued by his broken mouth:

—Oooh, brother! ...

—Kiss me that way again. Haven't felt like that since a lobster bit me. . . .

—Put that mouth of yours against my neck and draw blood. . . .

He wondered if his technic as a lover had also been wrenched by his scar, for now his was a mouth more meet for prayer than for caresses. He dried his face and sopped on after-shave lotion:

—My God, Hudson, you ought to go on tour as an example of the power of gunpowder and metal. The final product of the Industrial Revolution. . . .

He thought especially of Miss Betty Blanchard as he'd seen her the other evening at the Girls' School reception. First that mustached mistress of French had lingered on his deformity; then he'd taken Blanchard's hand. It hadn't felt quite the same as those other times. And for the first time they'd really looked at each other. That beautiful bitch! She was like an orchid taken out of an icebox and propped up on a grave! Most of all he remembered how her mouth had twisted in a fashion complementary and concave to his own, almost as though he'd laid his lips on hers. The red softness of her mouth was beginning to tighten down into a disapproving hyphen, like the late George Washington's. He fell to wondering how it would feel to dash his lips against hers. Spikes perforating fragrant watercress?

He'd thought several times of phoning her and asking her to go to the city with him. But she'd refuse. Her façade as a teacher. And he would be hurt again, as he'd been hurt many times in New York at Christmas, when he always imagined he might find love with his lovin. He couldn't waive the assumption that Blanchard liked her men (if she liked them at all) whole, and rather after the pattern of an Arrow Collar ad. He might have passed as such before the war. Now his face, he admitted, had an obscene and rakish quality, goatlike, which could only serve further to wind up her tension. Yet, he thought, if the world should end tomorrow, I'd go over to the Girls' School and muss her up. Her goddam primness! All that richness going to waste! I'd like to shatter her somehow. But I'd end by shattering myself. She has an iciness which would cut me to pieces by degrees. That's the way they all are—little edges that tickle us into illusion; then stab us down for life. . . .

The February sunlight went on and on, merciless as a teacher in introspection. His cell of a room shone forth in the bare cold sheen, as though spotlights had picked it out, and he was a convict scampering through the freezing daylight. He put on his jacket and went downstairs.

The corridors were alive with students, for once wearing an air of intensity. This was examination time, which is portentously called Mid-years. And these four hundred boys were at last worried. The anxiety lasted only a few days. But after months of torpor and of braking the school down to the pace of their own inertia, they now had aroused themselves. They had a few hurdles to leap. They were in the crisis of firemen who've forgotten how to slide down poles. They sat asking one another review questions in alcoves:

—Hey, what's the French for *saliva*? . . .

—Canya take ya logarithm book in withya? . . .

—O swear not by the moon, the inconstant moon. . . .

This morning Guy Hudson was a proctor. He was to stand by in Study Hall, look severe, and see that no one copied from his neighbor. Once, when Mr. Pilkey was younger, the Honor System had been tried out at The Academy. It was discarded when teachers found similarity in examination answers.

He tugged at his jacket, threw back his head, and marched down three creaking steps into the Study Hall, where fifty students sat at their desks. Like all teachers he entered proudly and a little disdainfully, for only on such occasions does the American Teacher strive to preserve that last touch of majesty which remains to him in a leveling world. As he took his place at the desk, the hubbub died down, and those who sought to curry favor shushed their neighbors.

—Put away all books and papers, gentlemen. . . .

—Aw. . . .

He didn't respond with any of the coy wit that an older teacher would have pulled out of his bag of chestnuts. He simply tightened the edge of his mouth, which gave him a glare of ferocity. By this little tic he could be sure that every boy in the room was staring at him. A dead silence fell over the brilliant room, glaring down from the snow outside. Before sitting down, he opened a window. The bitter February air streamed in to freshen the musty place, paper-and-ink smelling. There was a chorus of protest:

—Aw, *sir*! . . .

These same boys who whipped themselves into madness at hockey and basketball resented any intrusion of the dry wine of winter upon their steamheated consciousness. Curling his mouth sadistically, he opened more windows, dashing about smartly as when on parade as a second lieutenant.

—Sir! Aw, *sir*! . . .

—This place stinks, gentlemen. Smells like a laundry hamper.

Then he sat down at the desk, his chest rising softly as he inhaled the stabbing new air. The boys shivered and made droll gestures in pantomime of freezing to death, of Saint Bernard dogs coming to succor them. He was unmoved by the charade. He folded his hands on his breast and stared like an ogre. The candidates drummed with their fingers. The Study Hall was filled with a little whirring nervousness, like machines long untried testing their gears. Some of the faces were blank, some in travail, some red and defiant. They would crack this one, by Jesus! Only the blond boy Buddy Brown in a front row shifted his gum from one jaw to the other. Mockingly he whistled a Re-Bop tune.

—Brown, shut up!

—Sure, coach. . . .

With some embarrassment and a certain slinking sense of importance, Mr. Dell Holly entered the Study Hall, his arms pregnant with professional impedimenta. The students burst into applause. Dell Holly's nut-brown canopener face flexed

254

into a grin. He bowed like an old actor at a benefit. Was their applause ironic? Or was this really a tribute to himself? He was sheepishly pleased. After all, it was recognition of *some* sort; and as Guy Hudson saw it, Dell Holly sought favor with the boys almost as much as his wife curried it from the wits of the faculty. Blushing and perspiring, he laid his burden down on the desk. The students watched with alarm. Mr. Holly was tall and wrapped in tweeds furled like a flag on his beanpole body. His wrists, his hips, and his shoulders made angles showing even through his suit. Even his tiny skinny stomach was so tight in his tweeds that one all but saw the little navel between his congested flanks. He looked like starvation in a Brooks Brothers window; Lisa Holly had seen to that. Two generations ago he'd have been a clergyman. He spoke to the proctor in his nasal psalmy voice:

—Hudson, hadn't you better go get a stopwatch?

—Look, I have a sweephand . . . red too. . . . See it move?

—Please be serious. These tests are primed to the fraction of a second. Any laxity in their administration will raise Old Harry with the percentiles all over the country. . . .

—Wouldn't that be tragic? Then we wouldn't get our norms and our medians and our quartiles and our raw scores right for the year, would we?

—All right, all right, Dell Holly said. But just lay off me. I didn't set these tests. . . .

And he dumped on the desk a hundred mechanical pencils of graphite, a hundred answer sheets prickly with dotted lines, and a hundred question books. For these were The Tests. They were machine-scored examinations, made up on a multiple-choice and true-false type of knowledge. Guy Hudson hated and distrusted them. By them were measured the Intelligence Quotient of the student, his knowledge of foreign languages, and his spelling and reading ability. At first every teacher at The Academy had protested them. But their champions were Mr. Pilkey and Mr. Holly—who by his fussy efficiency in administering them hoped eventually to work himself into a job as Principal somewhere. These tests were rammed down the throats of the schools of America by the Educational Records Bureau. What they claimed to be doing was rating every boy and girl in America on a Long Curve. They didn't test feeling for abstracts, nor the power of sustained thinking. They were as spastic as a radio quiz program. Guy Hudson believed that their ultimate aim was mechanistic and fascist—to strap up American education in a straitjacket of conformity. This year their power over teachers was already considerable, so that those teachers whose students did poorly on the mechanical tests were called into question by Mr. Pilkey for the efficiency of their classroom work. It was in vain that such teachers cried that they were unwilling to teach bloodlessly for an objective machine-scored test. The claws of the machine were now reaching into education, with emphasis on fact (and *that* rigidly controlled). Perhaps even now, Guy Hudson thought, the Educational Records Bureau was developing a super-machine that would scuttle into classrooms and take over the teaching too in a gramophone voice. Mr. Pilkey was hipped on machine-scored testing because they showed himself and his patronage exactly how his boys and girls stacked up beside thousands of others in other schools. They gave him statistics he could conjure up and wave in his salesmanship of his Academy:

—You see? This is a democratic school. Even our examinations are given democratically . . . like a presidential election. Why, taking an examination in this modern age is practically like pulling the lever on a voting machine. . . .

Guy Hudson trembled. The old type of written examination still survived at The Academy. But creative teaching was already a bit suspect. Except for himself and a few humanitarian die-hards, more and more teachers taught with the ultimate goal in mind of what their students would get on the machine tests.

And seeing those mechanical pencils and those blue answer sheets which were as close to electronic death as good teaching is to life, Guy Hudson let out a little wail to Mr. Dell Holly, who was assembling his tools with the devotion of a mad scientist in pulp magazines:

—God, man. How can these tests test a feeling for history? Or the ability to marshal facts? Or the ability to reason? How can they judge intelligence, as distinguished from recognition and sheer bright doping-out?

—The Tests are still new yet. But they're constantly being improved. When they've had years of trial and error behind them, they'll be just as accurate as—maybe even more so—than we fallible human teachers. . . .

—And when that day comes, . . . Guy Hudson said.

Angry and depressed at the thought of the coming new world of collators and correctors and checkers of metal and tubes, he distributed mechanical pencils and answer sheets and question books to the students. He looked at their hands playing with the graphite pencils dubiously, shaking them and listening, as to a time bomb fuse. Poor kids! Just adolescent guinea pigs for education in a democracy! He slapped down the answer sheets on the desks. Why did they have to experiment on schoolchildren? And he pictured himself in a losing judo battle with a Mechanical Teacher, in which the machine finally swallowed him as a devilfish would, and digested him in its chromium hopper. And all these children would be crotched up like clothespins on the clothesline of the Educational Records Bureau. And finally this line of plotted and graphed mediocrity would sag to the ground, where they would let it lie in a clatter of scaled scores and raw scores and percentiles and medians and quartiles. . . .

Back at the desk Dell Holly said, squinting religiously at him:

—Hudson, I'm afraid you don't take The Tests seriously. . . . Think of it! For the first time a complete standardization of results and grading is possible in America! Every boy and girl knows exactly where he stands in relation to every other boy and girl in the United States! . . .

—My. How Jeffersonian.

Dell Holly prepared to withdraw, pussyfooting on to another examination room, where his hypnotized bureauphilia would dole out hundreds more of the mechanical pencils:

—Please observe the timing schedule, he warned.

Guy Hudson sat down and unbuttoned his jacket. He spread his knees open and began to read aloud to the examinees from the mimeographed sheet in front of him. No deviations were permitted: this morning a hundred thousand students all over America would hear the same words from the mouths of thousands of boiling-mad teachers. How should he read them? Perhaps what the Educational Records Bureau wanted was the studied brightness of a radio announcer burbling of a new hair rinse? His harsh voice shredded into a monotone as dreary as the glacial prose from the offices in New York:

—Now have you filled out *all* lines on the cover of your

answerbook? The test which you are about to take is called The American Council Psychological Test . . . You are not expected to finish any one section of it. . . .

—I don't believe a word of it, he heard a voice say under his desk. But it sounds wonderful, doesn't it? . . .

Looking down, he saw Ralph Du Bouchet looking up at him from a desk and imitating his peevish expression. He pulled himself together and shouted *Go!* when the sweep-hand of his watch stood at twelve. It was like a potato race on the Fourth of July.

Giggling a little, the students inched down their answer sheets, cautiously blackening in little spaces which would be scanned by a photoelectric cell in a machine in New York. Later other machines would type out rosters, saying that Susie Golden and John Maginess were in the 88th percentile (national) of reading comprehension. This meant that they could understand anything except the novels of Franz Kafka.

The Test was divided into several parts, each testing what was called A Skill. There were vocabulary words. There were matching and disparate figures of circles, blocks, and trape-zoids. There were cubes to be counted. There were missing words to be filled out from the context. There were darling little arithmetic problems to be totted up on special scratch paper (provided for the purpose). Each section had a time limit, at the end of which the Proctor, leaning his head in in his hand, scarcely muffling a groan, would call out:

—Go on to Section Three. Remember that you are *not* to turn the page until you are told to do so. . . .

—O, that's *nice*! said the soft voice of Ralph beneath the desk.

The boys whipped over the pages as directed. Some of the brighter ones began gurgling to themselves, as at a risqué show. They saw through The Test. It was like playing with an erector set and doping out which part fitted where. They saw, those quick ones, how the dignity of the classroom had been perverted by statisticians with no sense of humor.

While reading the instructions, try as he might out of a sense of fair play, Guy Hudson couldn't keep out of his voice a certain goody-goody quality, as of a fairy god-mother giving a recipe for poisoned gingerbread. Mr. Pilkey

258

and Dell Holly would have been wild with rage to hear that The Tests weren't being taken seriously. The sense of humor and the sense of humanism were being sucked out of American education. In their place would remain only an encyclopedic and lexicographical perfection—all scored by machine.

—Go on to Part V, Guy Hudson chanted. Do not turn back. . . .

—I won't, massa, said the voice below him.

And in that frantic Study Hall, with privileged and intelligent boys matching themselves against the literalminded of America, he found himself pondering on the difference between the Teacher and the Executive in education. The latter was becoming more and more the businessman—out for exploitation and plunder. What was so horrid about actual teaching that all its bright young men tried to Get Out From Under into executive jobs? There they would soon lose all touch with the reality of classroom work. They would sit in their offices and think up schemes to keep their teachers busier and busier about nonessentials. Already they'd espoused the machine-scored tests, on the assumption that the human touch, that individuality of approach and results, were quite the worst thing that could happen in a school. Eventually all young Americans would be taught to think alike, interchangeable brains on an assembly line. Finally all teachers would have nervous breakdowns (to be scored by machine). Then the Executives and their machines would reign sole and undisputed. The children would be sucked into the machines too, leaving only them and the executives, playing machine-scored pingpong in an airconditioned office.

—Stop! Guy Hudson read aloud from his sheet. You must remain in your chairs till the papers are collected. . . . Don't forget to turn in your mechanical pencils, for they're expensive. . . .

—Mayn't I *please* keep mine for a souvenir? Ralph begged.

Guy Hudson smiled. He gathered up the answer sheets with their little hieroglyphic scratches and put them in a neat pile on the desk of Mr. Dell Holly. Then he went up to his room, lit a cigarette, and wondered how long it would be before a new way would be devised to do away with such primitive Skills as reading and writing.

6

Mr. Pilkey had himself an afternoon. Sometimes he said that he loved the month of March; it reminded him that good Principals are like lions in their roaring.

At two o'clock he was to attend a meeting of the trustees of The Academy. Now they didn't convene as often as they did in the early days of the school, but that was the way it should be, for institutions work up their own momentum. Mr. Pilkey jestingly referred to his trustees as his Supreme Court. The reason for today's meeting had been a sharp note from Judge Hopkins V in New York. Two of the oldest members had died, and Judge Hopkins had suggested there'd better be a meeting or else. The Principal chuckled, as he did at all peremptory utterance other than his own. For Judge Hopkins had been speculating in the Chicago wheat pit; he seemed to think that he could also speculate in a great American school. Mr. Pilkey knew differently and meant to prove his point.

He arose from his desk, The Den, and walked painfully to the second story of the schoolhouse. He walked slowly and a little worriedly, for in the past few days he'd been aware of something going on in his left side, like the subdued buzzing of a well-mannered telephone bell. This ringing in his breast disturbed him. Except for his dizziness at the opening of this Winter Term, Mr. Pilkey had never been ill a day of his mature life. And now this muted tremor. He hadn't spoken to Mrs. Pilkey about it, nor to his personal physician, who was also honorary school doctor in the catalog. Wasn't he a mere sixty-five? Yet he remembered how his grandfather, Eliphalet Pilkey, had felt just such a jangling one afternoon in Vermont. And Grandfather Pilkey had lingered on for a year of complete paralysis. The Principal knit his snowy brows and flexed the fingers of his left hand, which were numb, as though he'd hit his funnybone.

Miss Sophia's trustees met in the Biology Laboratory, which was set up like a medical amphitheater. The walls were strung with cages in which fretted or ran living fauna experimented on by boys under the supervision of Launcelot Miller. White mice and guinea pigs and salamanders and hamsters lived in drawers or concealed hutches; so the Bug Lab always smelled of fur and trembled with a murmur of little living things caged. Also on the walls were graphs of weather pressure areas in Omaha, mounted butterflies and stuffed birds labeled in Latin by botany and zoology classes. Mr. Pilkey presided over his trustees from behind an onyx-topped laboratory table into which were inset sinks, with running water and gas jets. And if he became too impassioned with his trustees while promulgating a pet project, he was likely to turn on a gascock accidentally, and the meeting would be edified with the saccharine fumes of escaping illuminating gas.

Slowly and with some effort at breathing deeply he neared the Biology Lab. But by its glass door Herman was waiting for him. This afternoon his son would attend his first Trustees' Meeting, for the Principal believed that the time was ripe to baptize his heir in executive matters. Herman's hands fidgeted in the pockets of his doublebreasted sack suit. His mane (like Mr. Pilkey's, only brown) was in his eyes. He was red and perspiring. The Principal took a manly and affectionate swipe at his son's jaw.

—Go in, go in, son. They'll be waiting. . . .

—I think they'll hate my guts for coming, Herman said uneasily.

—They'll resent nothing! They're *my* trustees, aren't they? But comb your hair out of your eyes, son. . . .

The aging father locked fondly onto the arm of his sturdy son. Together they pushed open the door of the Bug Lab. There was a sound of rising as nine trustees paid tribute to their Principal. Only Judge Hopkins V, Chairman of the Board, remained in his seat. Mr. Pilkey was delighted and beamed at his son. There were only three members of the board who never rose: Judge Hopkins V and two old bankers. And now the two old bankers were dead. The nine trustees junior to Judge Hopkins V were all alumni of the

261

Academy. And they still held Mr. Pilkey in that awe they'd felt when they were students here.

—Good afternoon, gentlemen, the Principal said, taking his place behind the gas jets.

—Good afternoon, sir! cried all the trustees.

Judge Hopkins V merely nodded.

Mr. Pilkey surveyed his trustees. Except for the Judge, they looked like a classroom of men a little past their first youth. Mr. Pilkey'd known them when they wore knickerbockers as students here. The gesture of his paternalism kept them even now in thralldom. They were successful businessmen, doctors, lawyers, bankers, and a cousin of Mrs. Pilkey's. There was a football captain of the class of '25, now a chubby investment counselor. And the wrestling captain of the class of '29, now a lawyer in Orange, New Jersey. And the president of the Student Council of the class of '33, now a surgeon famous for his lobotomies. But they were all Mr. Pilkey's boys. All except Judge Hopkins V, who now rose, truculent and accusing in a pinstriped suit:

—Do you think it advisable, sir, for your son to attend a meeting of the trustees? He couldn't stand up in court as a witness without prejudice. . . .

There was silence from the other nine trustees, shocked that their Principal should be called to account. Mr. Pilkey heard the melting snow and the whirring of the animals in their cages. He leaned against a gascock:

—Isn't it a father's right to teach his only begotten son some of his tricks?

—I'll go, paw, Herman said blushing.

—Sit right down, my boy. Take that seat right next to F. Wainright Carter, whom you already know. . . .

Judge Hopkins V subsided rumbling in his jowls; Herman took a seat among the trustees, to a sprinkling of cordial applause. The Principal was delighted. No, they hadn't changed since they were boys at this Academy.

Cigars were passed around, for this was the only time that there was legal smoking in the Bug Lab. The Principal leaned on the onyx top of the experiment desk and folded his powerful white hands:

—There's not a great deal on the agenda this afternoon. We may, with your permission, even call this a Bull Session between the Head and his committee. . . . As you all know, from following our athletic records in the papers, we've been having a wonderfully successful term. Our hockey team has won six out of seven games. . . . The ice has been favorable to us . . . and the wrestling team. . . .

Judge Hopkins V asked to be recognized. He arose, turned his back on Mr. Pilkey, and addressed the other nine trustees. He was the oldest and most authoritarian of them all.

—We can all read athletic scores in the Alumni Bulletin, he said brusquely, clearing his throat. I don't know about our honored Principal, but there are two things very much on *my* mind. . . .

—Let the Head go on speaking, several trustees said anxiously.

—I have the floor, gentlemen.

—So he has, Mr. Pilkey interjected graciously.

But the buzzing in his side, he noticed, had resumed. . . .

The voice of Judge Hopkins V rang through the laboratory. Mr. Pilkey was aware that any Student Councillors eavesdropping in the corridor outside would hear it too. But he kept his urbanity. He'd faced worse things than a chairman of the Board of Trustees with a bee in his bonnet. But it was too obvious that the Judge wasn't purring, as when he ran for Republican party office.

—I desire, said the Judge, to protest a growing tendency by the Principal to pack the Board of Trustees with men who are exclusively alumni of this Academy. It doesn't look good. It is, in fact, incestuous. . . . And don't say that I've got a case of sour grapes! . . . Fortunately or unfortunately, I am now the only one left on this board who is not a graduate of this school. . . .

There were horrified murmurs from the other nine trustees. Mr. Pilkey was growing a little piqued too, but he called out in his choicest Assembly voice:

—Gentlemen! Listen to your chairman! Parliamentary procedure! . . .

Judge Hopkins V continued:

—We all know as business men that it's perfectly natural for the president of a big corporation to play ball with his stockholders. Similarly, what principal or headmaster doesn't dream at night of having his trustees under his thumb? . . .

263

—I protest! Herman Pilkey said, jumping up.

—I'll thank you to take a seat, Judge Hopkins said. You're here on sufferance. . . .

—If you were my size, or a few years younger. . . .

—Herman! the Principal cried.

But he was mighty proud of his son. . . .

Judge Hopkins V continued, now with his famous understatement that had fried murderers in the chair:

—It is my considered opinion, as an attorney of some standing, that Mr. Pilkey intends to replace the two late trustees with two more alumni. I am protesting it to the last breath of my body, and I still have quite a few left in my lungs. Any cretin knows that the only purpose of a Board of Trustees is to be a check and balance against any dictatorship by the Principal. . . . And gentlemen, how can a Board of Trustees be wise and disinterested if they are all alumni of the school concerned? . . .

Mr. Pilkey concealed his annoyance and said jovially:

—Alumni trustees will love their school all the better!

—Hear! hear! cried the younger trustees.

—It's not a question of *loving* the school, Judge Hopkins V said. We are here to see that the will of Miss Sophia Abercrombie is interpreted in perpetuum, and in the spirit and letter that the old woman would have wished. And I don't think that the little lady would be any too pleased to have her Board of Trustees a caucus of stooges. . . . No, I'm sure she would have wanted prominent men from the *outside* world to keep a benign but critical eye on how the school is run. . . . With all due respect to our Principal, I charge that he is attempting to make his school a charmed circle, a closed corporation. For instance, I find it both cynical and insolent that he has invited his own son to this meeting. Why? Because he contemplates his son as our next Principal. I for one flatly and virulently disapprove. . . .

Nine trustees were now leaning forward excitedly on those same armrests on which bored students listened to biology lectures. Mr. Pilkey smiled broadly on the agitation:

—Doesn't any father cherish hopes for his son?

—What does your faculty think about all this? the Judge cried suddenly.

—They're a happy and contented group, the Principal answered. Why, only yesterday, Mr. Philbrick Grimes told me. . . .

The Judge interrupted him:

—I sometimes believe that we trustees should hold a hearing open to the entire faculty. . . .

—Ah, they don't know beans, Herman muttered, still pink.

—Really? said the Judge. I wonder. Well, I've given out a piece of my mind on *one* subject. . . .

—You *are* clearing the air, the Principal said blandly. Please go on. . . .

He took out of a drawer in the lecture table a legged lectern (fashioned by Mr. Launcelot Miller) and leaned upon it judicially.

—Here's my other blast, the Judge said. I think that the Alumni Bulletin should publish an itemized budget of the school's yearly expenditures. In these days when everyone is being asked to kick in to the Endowment Fund of a so-called charitable and educational institution, they have a right to know exactly how these sacred monies are being spent. Charity and education are two of the greatest rackets in twentieth-century America. . . . For example, it's not sufficient to list the lump sum of $126,000 for teachers' salaries. Be explicit. Who gets what?

The pain in Mr. Pilkey's left side was a true threat now. In his mounting anxiety his senses magnified the sound of the experimental animals scrabbling in their cages. His voice became patient, expository, and long-suffering:

—Our books are always open to inspection by the trustees in the Comptroller's Office. . . .

But the voice of Judge Hopkins V went right on:

—O really? I've looked at them. And there are two items which seem to me to be highly irregular. . . . First, there is the little matter of several thousand dollars for plates, decorated by Mrs. Pilkey, to be installed in The Academy library. Now I know nothing about art. But is such an expenditure justifiable in these times?

The trustees now were openmouthed. The Principal smiled and waved a dispelling hand at the chairman of his board:

—According to the charter, when your grandfather chose me Principal, I was to have the right to make appropriate

265

expenditures for the educational advancement of my school. . . .

—True, true. But you're also providing a fat little nest egg for your wife. . . .

Several trustees rose to their feet. Herman clenched his red fists. The Principal signaled for order in the uproar:

—Judge Hopkins, if you are intimating. . . .

—I am only calling things into question! And as Chairman of this Board I believe I have that right. . . . The second thing which bothers me is the $12,000 you spent to have your son's bungalow remodeled. . . . Among local contractors and architects, Mr. Pilkey, you have the enviable reputation of being a wasteful and extravagant builder. If you don't like the wainscoting or wallpaper, you have it ripped out. *After* it has been installed. And I think also that your wife meddles too much in designing of Academy buildings. . . .

—She is known in our catalog as the Official Artist of the school, the Principal said.

—I have said my piece, the Chairman of the Board of Trustees said, sitting down.

Something seemed to have aroused even the mice in their cages along the walls of the Bug Lab. The place squeaked and rocked. Never at student school meetings had there been such pandemonium. Those younger trustees whom Mr. Pilkey had educated as boys were pallid with rage and horror that he should be so addressed. Football players and heroes of twenty years ago stared at the Judge, who was examining his nails. The Principal leaned forward and said in a choking whisper:

—Well, gentlemen, you've listened to the Chairman of the Board of Trustees. . . . He accuses me of mismanagement, incompetence, and gross dishonesty in the disbursement of the Endowment. . . . Shall I go . . . shall I go to my office now and have the indefatigable Miss Pringle type up my resignation? . . .

Nine trustees rose to their Florsheimed feet and shouted:
—No!

Mr. Pilkey breathed heavily and stared at his only son:

—I'm no longer a young man. Sometimes, I know, I *am* a little too generous with money. But remember that I built this school up from an idea and four million dollars. I've always felt that Miss Sophia's spirit was in sympathy with me. Only Judge Hopkins seems to disagree. . . . If I ever err, it's on the side of generosity. . . . I believe that I've made this Academy into a great school. And if so, *I* have made it that way. With the help of an excellent faculty, of course. . . . In the future I shall be more careful of how I spend and what for. . . . But gentlemen, you can't run a school on a shoestring! You will allow that as an educator with forty-five years' experience in back of him I know what it is expedient to spend! An American school can't stand still, gentlemen! When it does, it is finished. I've tried to found a tradition here. I think I've been successful. And not to sound vain, gentlemen, I think that *I* am a large factor in that tradition. It stems from me. Gentlemen, when you think of this Academy, of whom do you think first?

From the throats of nine trustees:

—Our Principal, Mr. Pilkey! With a ti-ra-ra!

It was an old Academy football cheer. Mr. Pilkey looked expressively at the Chairman of the Board, who sat tracing and doodling on an armrest, already initialed and carved by twenty-five classes of boys:

—You see, Judge Hopkins?

—I'm afraid I do, the Judge answered.

In Mr. Pilkey's eyes he was now as sullen as a flunked student.

The Principal discovered that the disquieting buzzing in his left side was abating with his triumph. From the pocket of his gay blazer he took a sheet of onionskin typed by Miss Pringle. On it were two names and addresses:

—And now, gentlemen, to more serious business. After canvassing you all by letter last week, I have here the names of two boys to fill the vacancies left by our two late lamented trustees. The first is Dick Fremont of the class of '36. Many of you will remember him. First Football. Student Council. A genuinely Lovely Fellow when he was here. He's now a buyer in the delicatessen department of Macy's. Lives in Scarsdale with a wife and two pretty daughters. A Mason and a member of the Rotary and Kiwanis Clubs. The kind of young man who's going places. . . . And the second is Tom Wallace of the class of '23. One of our first and most renowned alumni. An editor of *Time* magazine (good publicity for the school, you'll agree, in a national periodical of solid reputation).... You older trustees will recall Tom, what an eager and studious little fellow he was when he was here. Comes to every alumni reunion we hold in New York....

There was a burst of filibuster cheering from the younger Trustees. Judge Hopkins V again asked for recognition from the chair; Mr. Pilkey gave it blandly.

—This is my last protest. You do *not* want an all-alumni Board of Trustees. Your school will die of stagnation in no time at all....

—O for God's sake, Herman Pilkey bubbled through the uproar.

The two new trustees proposed were elected by a vote of 9-1, Judge Hopkins dissenting. Fresh cigars were lighted; there were backslapping and wishes that the Principal would attain his hundredth birthday. Then the trustees dispersed, taking rail and air back to their private enterprises in all parts of the United States. Ah, they were still, though graying and paunching, those fellows whom Mr. Pilkey'd admired as students, ten, fifteen, twenty years ago. To him they were the spine of America: the small business man, the civic leaders, the clearheaded. There wasn't a radical among them. And they were so because they'd been tempered in the tender mercies of this Academy. He waved to each of them as they went out of the Bug Lab. There remained behind only Judge Hopkins V, bristling by the gascocks, with one of which Mr. Pilkey toyed musingly.

—Well, the Judge said, putting on his gloves, you're a shrewd article, sir. My grandfather said so too when he engaged you thirty years ago.... And now you're absolute despot here. I doubt that you'll use your power wisely. I have no use for absolute rulers. And in America they positively stink. For a year or so now I've sensed something putrid in this school. I think the putrescence is *you*. Twenty-five years is too long for any man to reign unchallenged over anything without its getting to smell like old mackerel. You've become both senile and dangerous.... But no matter. The last link with old Miss Sophia is broken as of today....

—Why, what do you mean, sir? Mr. Pilkey said glancing up from the gasjets.

—Simply that I hereby resign as Chairman of the Board

of Trustees. From now on you can run your own school. And my opinion as a lawyer and business man is that you'll run it into the ground. You have delusions of grandeur, I guess. You think of yourself as an honest and pious man. But I disagree with your estimate of yourself. . . .

Mr. Pilkey's white eyebrows jumped several times; he pursed his thin strong mouth:

—Won't you reconsider? I suppose you'll give a statement to the press. The papers have tried many times to smear me. . . .

Judge Hopkins smiled acidly and tapped his cigar into the laboratory sink:

—I shall say nothing. Your corruption would take a more idealistic muckraker than I am. I know the world. No, sir, I shall simply watch you and your school with the amused detachment of one who is in the know, with the Olympian shrug of a former lover watching an ex-mistress go to seed. . . . You had the possibility of doing something wonderful here. In the first years of your administration you made something very fine out of this Academy. That was what old Miss Sophia wanted. But now you're superannuated and doting. And like all silly and self-deceiving old men, you'll end up with a mess of pottage. . . .

Mr. Pilkey's left side was afire with this reproach, the vilest he'd ever received in his sixty-five years:

Goddam it, sir! What does a country lawyer know about running a school? You've thwarted my every move! . . .

Judge Hopkins V reached for his Chesterfield and his Homburg:

—The last block in your way is now removed. From now on you can go on like a steamroller over your own particular cliff. . . . But remember that posterity will judge you as I am judging you now: as a foolish and rather dishonest old Brahmin who's been too long out of the competition of the world. I have to hand it to you. You have that supreme ability to rationalize any evil or injustice you do into a virtue. . . . But don't be afraid that I'll talk and cause a scandal. I know that expediency has always been your ethical touchstone. No, I shall tell the world (if it cares at all) that I resigned from the Board of Trustees for reasons of failing health. . . .

And the Judge withdrew from the cigar-smoky Biology Laboratory, walking in the stately and disdainful manner he was famous for in court. To the sound of animals running in their cages, the Principal and his son looked after the Judge.

—Gee, pop, Herman said. If you were ten years younger, you'd have laid him out on his arse. . . .

—The man's a maniac. It's probably just as well he resigned.

—I think I'll go see Nydia, his son said. She's taking her second pregnancy mighty hard. . . .

—Do that, my boy, do that. And give me more grandchildren . . . and great-grandchildren. . . . Herman, you and I know what this school needs. Better than anyone else in this world. It's in our blood. . . .

—Bro-the*r*!

The Principal walked brooding and alone back to The Den, flexing and unflexing his left hand, for the tingling had begun again. With the Judge he'd worked himself up to a passion such as he hadn't known since two lowerformers, ten years ago, set fire to a dormitory. From the onslaughts of the late chairman of his trustees, Mr. Pilkey saw with clarity the plight of the idealist-strong man in America. Now he was an enlightened liberal of the late nineteenth century ilk. Like Oswald Garrison Villard. But Judge Hopkins V was an old Tory. Only in himself did some of the old Whig vigor survive. He was a latter-day prototype of that fine old democracy set up by rugged men like his grandfather Eliphalet on his farm in Vermont. He answered only to the Constitution of the United States, to his conscience, and to God. . . .

He sat down at his desk in The Den, and Miss Pringle came pattering in to take dictation in her laced boots. She appraised him over her spectacles:

—And what's the good word on the Trustees' Meeting?

He put his forehead in his hand, the first weakness he'd ever manifested before her:

—O, we cleared some dead lumber out of the attic. . . .

—There's plenty of that Around Here, she said, playing with her memo pad. But trust *you* to clear it out. . . .

—Thank you, my dear Miss Pringle. If everyone was as loyal as you. . . .

—I love the school, she said tremulously, and everything about it. *Every*thing. . . .

Then, as though she feared she'd said too much, she went into a little paroxysm of giggles and whipped her pencil out of her hair, which she wore up on a rat of wire. O, Miss Pringle was wonderfully devoted to himself and to his school; but sometimes the Principal found his thoughts wandering to the beauteous Miss Budlong. But Miss Budlong, a recent graduate of the Girls' School, wasn't so accurate in taking dictation. . . .

With Miss Pringle making henpecks and scratches of Gregg phonography he began to improvise the genial prose of his March Letter to Parents. She took it all down with sighs of bluestocking approval. He'd developed his Addisonian style even at Dartmouth, when he wrote home to his mother.

This was what the parents would read in a few days:

—When I wrote you last, dear friends, the December snow was rich and high outside my office window. And now I note that the snow is still there, though it is March. Let us hope that this is the last snowfall of the year. When I was a boy (I was known as Jellybean) we used to make our March snowballs extra hard, for we feared it would be our last opportunity for a battle royal that winter. I often think that the children of today have no idea of how to enjoy themselves in the snow. . . .

Miss Pringle interrupted:

—I know the parents love your seasonal opening paragraphs. They're just like the Farmers Almanac. . . .

—I come from a healthier and more primitive epoch, he said meditatively.

Miss Pringle didn't transcribe this into shorthand. She was versed in distinguishing between the Principal's dictation and remarks addressed to herself for her personal edification. He sighed and resumed his soliloquy to the parents of his students:

—With this casual winter's end greeting from me will go the term end reports of the Boys' and Girls' Schools. We are including also a mimeographed sheet chillingly labeled Distribution of Grades. Don't be alarmed. It simply shows you where your boy or girl stands in relation to the whole of his or her class. I believe that this sort of rating is more meaningful and democratic than the old-style letters: A, B, C, etc. Teachers tend to be dry-as-dust perfectionists in their grading. One of mine told me only the other day boastfully that no boy would ever get an A in *his* class. But I put him right on *that* score.

—There is, I fear, a growing anarchic tendency among American teachers (as in labor unions) to regard themselves as apostles to, rather than servants of, society. But here at my own school I modestly endeavor to keep my teachers from such feelings of superiority and from pure tyranny over their students. If you, dear friends, have any complaint about the report cards of your boys and girls, I hope you will write to me directly, as well as to the teachers involved. I see to it that my faculty takes time out to answer your communications promptly and in full. As I said only last week to my wife and to my dear mother: if we don't have good public relations, we are falling down in our functions as a school in a democracy. Even a great Academy can't afford to cock a snook at the public. . . .

Miss Pringle rolled her eyes and gasped at this euphemism. And the Principal, remembering that he'd once been a teacher himself, became didactic with his secretary—but delicately:

—Do you mean to tell me you know the meaning of that phrase?

—Heavens, yes! It means . . . to thumb . . . the nose. . . .

—I should never have dictated it if I had dreamed. . . .

Miss Pringle adjusted her spectacles and sniffed daintily:

—I read a great deal. In Latin and Greek, of course. . . .

—Of course.

He found himself thinking that, had she been the luscious Miss Budlong, he might here have patted her knee in a fatherly and pedagogic fashion. He continued:

—I now come to the delicate question of finances. The American independent school is at the crossroads of crisis. But it will survive. The first democratic education was given by independent schools, and I fondly believe that they have *not* outlived their function. They never will, as long as they continue to justify themselves. Now, as all parents and patrons know, we have not raised our tuition. We have sought to make up our deficit through voluntary gifts from parents and alumni. I am asking you to continue your openhandedness. This sum will be added to the Endowment, and used exclusively for teachers' salaries. While all my faculty are well paid, you know as parents and breadwinners that the cost of living has gone up because of our fear of Russia, though Communists ascribe it to the selfishness of those classes that control supply and distribution. But the central cog in our academic system is probably the teacher. Now it is my desire to reward especially teachers who have grown spiritually and educationally in my service. I have in mind, for example, the establishing of a Shakspere chair of comparative literature. Its incumbent would be Mr. Philbrick Grimes, known to you all for fifteen years of faithful service. . . .

—A lovely person, and worthy of every honor, Miss Pringle said, looking up from her notebook.

The Principal nodded and continued his dictation:

—But all this will take money. And there are a few other teachers here who perhaps deserve something extra for their stipends. Do not misunderstand me. It is far from my intention to give indiscriminate salary raises to everyone on my faculty. I refer only to those who have matured in my service. Here, as at every other school, I am sorry to say that we have drones, who do no more than is expected of them. And now may I wish you all the jolliest Easter?

—They'll *love* that, Miss Pringle said, scampering to her typewriter to prepare a mimeograph stencil on this Letter to Parents.

Presently Mr. Twarkins arrived, and began to sweep round The Den, talking to himself about the hope of the world and the Republican party. The Principal pretended not to notice until the head janitor whisked a feather duster over his papers and muttered something horrible.

—What's that? what's that, Twarkins?

—I said you've got enemies on the faculty, Mr. Twarkins said. Perverts and Communists. . . .

Then plying his broom, the head janitor shot down the corridor as though he was pushing a scooter.

—Eyes and ears open! Mr. Twarkins called back with hideous significance.

Mr. Pilkey was now aware that he was no longer A Well Man. Forty years he'd taken his calisthenics and coached football and roared through the corridors of schools. But something ailed his whole left side. Inside his massive virile old body a volcano was brewing in readiness. That numbness was increasing. To distract himself from this feeling of creeping palsy, he signed several dunning letters to parents and several recriminatory notes to lax members of his faculties.

Outside, the slush and snow of March lay in arid dreariness; he heard boys coming up from the gym. Tomorrow he'd consult the school physician. Just then the President of the Student Council passed like a cat before his desk.

—O Ben, by the way, Mr. Pilkey called out easily.

The young Jew, still wearing his hockey uniform, turned innocently. Mr. Pilkey had done everything (short of stopping the elections) to keep Ben off the Council. He was happy, of course, that his school was democratic and nonsectarian. But a Hebrew as leader of the undergraduates! It would give alumni and parents clammy ideas! Now he was determined that this Academy shouldn't become a fashionable ghetto for well-to-do Jews. He'd never had a quota at his school before. But perhaps there might have to be one soon.

—You called me, sir? Ben Gordon said.

Mr. Pilkey rejoiced that the boy didn't *look* Jewish. He might have passed for a Brazilian or an Italian. But to the Principal's Vermont taste there was something languorous about the President of the Student Council. He sensed a negation of everything in Ben, for he preferred the roaring extroversion he'd known at Dartmouth in 1900. . . .

—Ben, It's far from my mind to make a policeman or spy out of the President of the Council. . . . But just what has been going on in Hooker Hall after lights? . . .

The boy looked at the parquet:

—Boys will be boys, sir. . . .

—Unsavory rumors have reached my ears.

Ben Gordon hesitated again:

—It's the fag-end of the Winter Term, sir. What do you expect to happen when you shut up four hundred boys for three months?

—Goddam it, boy. I didn't expect to hear that from *you*. . . . The pattern of my school was set up before you were born. What gives you the presumption to censure it?

—Times have changed, sir, Ben said steadily.

—Not so far as *I* am concerned. A Christian gentleman is still a Christian gentleman. . . .

Then he remembered to whom he was speaking:

—Or a Jewish gentleman....

Ben Gordon leaned on his hockey stick and bowed without answering.

—I'm going to ask you a question, Mr. Pilkey said, coughing delicately into his palm, because of the great trust I and the student body repose in you.... What is your frank opinion of the faculty?

The handsome dark boy made a little swipe with his hockey stick:

—That's a big order, sir.... In general I like them.... I think they work hard....

—Do they say they're persecuted? the Principal cried.

Ben Gordon's yellow eyes wandered uneasily to the muddy snow outside the window:

—They've never said so to me, sir.

—Just as well. You will, of course, agree that Mr. Grimes is the finest teacher we have here?

The boy creased his hockey gauntlets:

—I don't believe *my* opinion matters, sir.

—It matters a great deal. Let us think of you as the knight errant of the entire student body. You are, you know.... Have you read the Idylls of the King? Every boy in a responsible position should. It was *my* favorite as a lad. Listen: I made them lay their hands in mine and swear to reverence the King, and their conscience as their King.... Why are you smiling?

—Because when Mr. Hudson wants to show us in class that something is mystical nineteenth-century corn, he says it's Alfred Lord Tennysonish....

The Principal started up from his desk:

—He says *that*? Such cynicism to a class of young men? Did you say that Mr. Hudson makes fun of the Idylls of the King in a history class?

—I shouldn't have said that, sir. I don't want to get anybody in the doghouse. Least of all Mr. Hudson....

—My boy, I am merely finding out what goes on in my school.... Tell me more about Mr. Hudson's classes....

—He's the best teacher in this school, Ben Gordon said softly. And also the nicest guy on the faculty....

—How can he be if he makes fun of the Idylls of the

King? Do you mean that Mr. Hudson is a better teacher than Mr. Grimes?

—*We* think so, sir. Mr. Grimes . . . is always putting on an act. . . . He . . . tries to impress us. Mr. Hudson pulls no punches. He gives us the stuff straight from the shoulder. I and most of the other kids feel that Mr. Hudson has . . . really *lived*. . . .

The buzzing in the Principal's side turned to a humming. He stared over his spectacles at the President of the Council:

—What do you mean, *lived*? Is there . . . is there sexual discussion in Mr. Hudson's classes?

Ben hesitated again, kicking his toe against the cork floor. Mr. Pilkey saw struggling within him Jewish subterfuge and duplicity:

—There's no smut, sir, if that's what you mean. But if there's sex in our history lesson, Mr. Hudson doesn't gloss it over. He's a very frank man. I like that. Most of the other kids do too. Except the prudes. But they're always the biggest hypocrites anyway. . . .

Mr. Pilkey simply stood and stared at the tall muscular boy. His pet peeve was the Jewish liberal. Here was one ready made. The Principal's granite Puritanism found nothing but decadence and subversiveness in Jews who pretended to be intellectual and progressive. They set on edge his Republican teeth. For such liberalism (it was really chaos, a lack of sense of values) always led to free love and Communism. So he raised his voice to Ben Gordon:

—I thought it was clearly understood at the first school meeting last fall that sex was the province of our chaplain, Doctor Smedley. . . .

—He's an old man, sir. . . .

—I too am an old man!

—Sorry, sir. You asked me what I thought. I think that Mr. Hudson is a much finer teacher than Mr. Grimes. Because he knows what life is all about. . . .

—Then you've been seduced and suborned! I'm ashamed of you! . . . You are excused! . . .

The President of the Student Council bowed and walked away, treading in his lithe manner, the muscles in his shoulders corrugating the canvas of his hockey jersey, which was stained with sweat and The Academy's colors. Mr. Pilkey sat down, breathing hard. He saw now that there was an intellectual ferment in his school which would be more appropriate in a Warsaw Ghetto. Ideas! Plots! Radicalism! Something putrid had been wafted into his nostrils. In his catalog he was fond of speaking of freedom of research and inquiry in American education. But in his own school, he saw, his fine tolerance had been interpreted in certain quarters as laxness. But he was no jellyfish! To Mr. Pilkey the great historic cataclysm of modern times was the decay of the Puritan tradition. He still read the wonderful sermons of the Mathers and Jonathan Edwards. O, that there were still a check to keep dissenters in line in twentieth century America! For the Principal had been reared in the stern commercial sobriety of John Calvin. As a young man he'd declared war on fruitless speculation and Bohemian leisure. And now his school was a hotbed of Jewish intellectuals and a redheaded history teacher who'd picked up dangerous ideas as an infantry lieutenant! Making fun of the Idylls of the King! Why, there was none of the old tenderness, such as he felt for Mrs. Pilkey, left in America! The country was like a coiled steel spring. He would preach on this text some Sunday soon. . . .

Faculty meetings were held in The Academy chapel. Mr. Pilkey preferred to hold them here rather than in the Faculty Room. In the chapel he could require his teachers to sit up and look alive, like undergraduates at vespers. He stood at the rostrum and took attendance of his employees as they entered. He knew, of course, of some Principals who held faculty meetings like socials—even serving cocktails before and cigars with. Not he. That was an index of the degeneracy of the age. *His* faculty meetings, from the inception of The Academy, were more like Quaker Quiet Times. It was proper that any conclave so serious and highminded should be held in the automatic reverence of the chapel.

He decreed a faculty meeting for every Tuesday at seven o'clock. He chose this time because he knew that bachelor teachers liked to go into the city to opera and concerts and the theater. By putting faculty meetings on Tuesday evenings he spared his young men from wasting their money on frivolity. Each Tuesday morning a typewritten note from Miss Pringle reminded the faculty of the Boys' School that they had an infallible appointment with their Principal:

—Tonight we will discuss a few urgent matters that have been troubling my mind. . . .

So Mr. Pilkey arrived first after an excellent supper and sat on the platform. From this point of vantage he could watch the entrance and demeanor of every one of his faculty. They usually arrived five minutes early, carrying copies of that picture magazine known as *Life*, of which he didn't approve, since it put a minimum premium on reading. He was also vigilant lest they peruse this magazine in their pews while he talked on subjects near to his heart. Picture magazines in the house of God! Next week he'd have Miss Pringle type up a note. . . .

Always the first to arrive was the only lady on the faculty of the Boys' School. Miss Hendrickson taught a subject very dear to Mr. Pilkey. Remedial English. She was bosomy and sprightly in an aggressive manner, like public school teachers of uncertain age who scintillate at the drop of a hat because they've renounced all hope of marrying. He was proud of her and of the whole educational concept of Remedial Work. There was an extra charge of $500 a year for this priceless course. Mr. Pilkey explained Remedial English this way in his catalog: grade school teachers were no longer instructing children how to read; so boys came to The Academy unable to get anything out of a printed page. Or at sixteen years of age they saw backward and couldn't spell. Miss Hendrickson was in sole charge of this corrective therapy. She taught phonetics. Under her zestful ministrations, upperformers were known to pass in one year from third to sixth grade reading proficiency. It was one of the boasts of the catalog. Now Mr. Pilkey was fully aware that his faculty (except Mr. Dell Holly and Mr. Philbrick Grimes) thought that Remedial Reading was the biggest racket yet in American education. They said sullenly that secondary schools now existed merely to repair the defections of the primary ones. But Mr. Pilkey saw far more deeply than this. His sort of education (as he said in the catalog) must adapt itself to the needs of its patrons. He was fed up with wildeyed impractical idealists who lamented the decay of Homer and Virgil. . . .

—Good evening! cried Miss Hendrickson, plumping herself into a pew. And how is our Head tonight? . . .

278

The Principal arose and bowed. Miss Hendrickson licked her lips and adjusted a vast chrysanthemum in the button-hole of her pinstriped suit. She crossed the nylons on her huge calves. These Steinway legs proved that she was a teacher with Drive. Nor was she long at a loss for conversation. She was as militant about her profession as a fashion stylist. She insisted on Stimulating Talk. . . .

Shortly she was joined by a musty young man from the Classics Department. Mr. Pilkey had little use for Doctors of Philosophy—other than honorary degrees; he'd only an M. A. from Dartmouth himself. But Ph.D's *did* look magical in his catalog. Doctor Anderson knew more and more about less and less. In the *Journal of Classical Studies* he was forever publishing learned dissertations on the use of the vocative case in Etrurian inscriptions. Then he would dedicate the article to his Principal. Whenever possible, Doctor Anderson spoke Latin. He'd even tried to organize a Mensa Romana in the Academy dining hall, but Mr. Pilkey had vetoed the project as a trifle q-u-e-e-r. What would parents think visiting the Academy if they saw their sons lying at table wearing wreaths and nibbling on nightingales' tongues?

Dr. Anderson called out a greeting to his boss and to Miss Hendrickson:

—Ecce quomodo moritur justus!

Mr. Pilkey, who'd found high school Cicero tough sledding, waved genially and returned to his meditations.

—There's starch in medieval Latin, my dear, said Doctor Anderson to Miss Hendrickson.

Then they began an avid and naughty conversation in French, just to keep up their feeling for the tongue between their summer excursions to Europe. Mr. Pilkey didn't approve of this pedantry. But he watched Miss Hendrickson's bosom heaving as she emphasized her nasals, while Doctor Anderson gleefully waited to pounce on her for any error in sequence of tenses.

Other faculty members sauntered into the chapel. The Inner Circle sat in the front row of pews, tacitly reserved for them. Mr. Philbrick Grimes and Mr. Dell Holly carried clip-boards of reports they intended to make to the faculty. The Principal beamed on them and they on him.

There came in old Doctor Hunter, who took a pew far back, and laid his head in his hand, through which his white goatee stuck. He seemed in prayer or travail. And there was also Doctor Sour, simpering to his acquaintances. Mr. Pilkey watched his faculty with an aloof amusement. All strolling players of a sort! It was his hand, and his hand only, that could transform these unruly players into some kind of symphony. Otherwise they'd be soloists crying in the wilderness. Each of these persons believed himself to be doing the only important job in the school. Mr. Pilkey allowed them their delusions. Principals and orchestral conductors know how to flatter their instrumental components —up to a point....

The noise in the chapel rose to a rasp of chatter. Special homage was paid to Miss Hendrickson as the only woman present—florid salutes and European hand kissings. Mr. Pilkey thought ironically that all these people had read little somethings in textbooks and, to edify the others, held educational irrelevancies up before their personalities, as a woman tries on a dress before a mirror.

But he stiffened at the arrival of Guy Hudson, who swaggered in with a curl of his wounded mouth and took a pew by himself and stared coolly at everybody. Well, The Principal gave his teachers two years in which to make or break themselves....

Finally the youngest teachers (who'd been sucking cigarettes and swallowing enervating coffee in their apartments) arrived and took their places. Last to appear was the Comptroller, who came with an aggrieved look from the Bursar's Office. Mr. Pilkey took a rapid census of his faculty, and nodded to an aging man with cropped hair and an English accent:

—May we have the minutes of the last meeting, Mr. Clowes?

The Recorder stood and cleared his throat. It was his only chance to shine intellectually before fifty other intellects:

—Last meeting was held Tuesday, March first. A committee was formed to investigate student smoking on the second floor of Sophia Hall. A committee was formed to inquire into the culprit who inserted white flour into the organ pipes, sprinkling the officiating minister of two Sundays ago. A committee was formed to look into the possibility of lowering the level of the noise in the Dining Hall. A committee was formed to ascertain The Academy's liability for the broken legs of two upperformers who fell from a gutter on the southeast end of Hooker Hall. A committee was formed to track down charges made by Mrs. Miekewicz, the dietitian, that profanity is being used in the pantry by undergraduate waiters. It was voted that Harry Reynolds, a lowerformer, be allowed to remain at school on the threat that his mother would commit suicide if he was expelled for theft. . . .

—Strike that out, Mr. Pilkey said testily. It mars the dignity of our records. . . .

Mr. Clowes made a pass at his notebook and concluded:

—Meeting adjourned at nine forty-five.

The Principal nodded and recovered his suavity:

—Are there any additions or corrections? If not, the minutes may stand approved. . . .

—Yes, a voice said.

Guy Hudson, recognized, stood up in his pew. He thrust a hand in the pocket of his plaid jacket and leaned indolently toward the faculty. His cleft chin jutted and his red hair glowed in the light of the chandeliers.

—I'd like to move that we hold fewer faculty meetings. . . .

The buzzing revisited Mr. Pilkey's left side. In the front pew Mr. Grimes jerked his head around and stared in astonishment. There was a gasp from the entire faculty.

—I don't hear that motion seconded! the Principal roared.

No voice was raised. Dell Holly gritted his teeth and wrestled with his tobacco-dyed fingers on his skinny knees.

—May we ask Mr. Hudson's reasons for this extraordinary motion?

—I give them gladly. Faculty meetings at this Academy are merely one of many devices for frittering away a Tuesday evening. I don't know about the others, but I have a stack of papers to correct. . . . Look objectively at those minutes of last week's meeting. Was one single worthwhile thing accomplished by sitting on our tails for three hours and beating our gums about petty disciplinary matters? Everyone knows that not one of those committees that was appointed last time will ever bring in their findings to the faculty. And nobody cares whether they do nor not. . . . In the seven months that I've been teaching at this school I haven't heard one worthwhile bit of educational philosophy

281

discussed at these faculty meetings. Are we teachers or a bunch of nuns playing politics? I've heard nothing brought up that merits the dignity of the entire faculty sitting on it. These administrative details could be settled outside of caucus with the individuals involved. The only important matter that ever came up for faculty vote in these seven months was a flagrant case of cribbing and a disgusting piece of dishonesty by half the Student Council. But that was shoved aside or hushed up as though it was unimportant. . . . So I repeat my motion that there be fewer faculty meetings. . . . I think, sir, that you have faculty meetings just to see that no one gets off the quadrangle on Tuesday nights. Or else you use us as a sounding board for your own ideas. But after we vote, you go ahead and do as you please. Of course, it's *your* school. . . .

Mr. Pilkey's voice cut through a blanket of wintry silence. He leaned as heavily on the rostrum as he leaned on his irony:

—The young veteran doesn't like the way we do things here. Does anyone second his motion?

The silence was now like glacial velvet.

—A great many here feel the same way I do, Guy Hudson said. But none of them has the guts to stand up and say so. . . .

Goddam it, sir! . . . Pardon me, Miss Hendrickson. . . . I've never ejected a faculty member from our little meetings before. But I think I'll start on you. Leave the chapel, sir! And I'll see you later. At my house. . . .

The redheaded teacher of history buttoned his sloppy jacket and tramped out of the brilliantly lighted chapel. Off its whitewashed walls bounced a purple brouhaha of mixed sensations. Mr. Pilkey was dizzy with rage. He all but fell into the chair behind the rostrum and took several deep breaths to recover himself. He crossed his knees, panting, and the garters showed above his fine-woven socks. At last, seeing Miss Hendrickson eyeing him maternally, he spoke wearily:

—Has any of those committees we appointed last time anything to report?

None had, and the Principal felt even dizzier until Mr. Grimes mercifully arose, ruffled through the papers on his clipboard, and announced that he would report on a Teacher's Convention held last week in the grand ballroom of the Hotel Commodore in New York. Everyone was grateful for the change of tempo and mood, for Mr. Grimes made his report a charming little comedy. He read his notes, facing half toward the faculty, but deferentially never turning his back on the Principal. It was a national conclave of teachers of English, he announced, simpering satirically. He made the three-day affair (with chicken dinners and speeches) sound like a husking bee of peasant bumpkins. He ridiculed delicately the public school teachers he'd met, calling them gripsies and grimsies. He added titteringly that of course these faded men and women deserved a *heck* of a lot of credit for the work they did, in spite of overcrowded class-rooms and Iron Maiden lesson plans. He gave a sibilant imitation of an old virgin called Minerva Pennypacker, who taught Ivanhoe and Silas Marner in Pensacola. And finally he described a verse-speaking choir from a Chicago high school declaiming the poem about the Raggle-Taggle Gypsies, O. Then he sat down to applause from the faculty. Mr. Pilkey was pleased with the information and the diversion. He asked studiously:

—Then we have nothing to learn from the public schools?

—In my opinion, nothing, Mr. Grimes said delicately. We're several light-years ahead of them in the teaching of English. And in the teaching of everything else, I presume. . . .

There was another round of applause; Miss Hendrickson beamed around at everybody. The Principal nodded in the direction of Dell Holly:

—Dell? Will you give us the good word on The Tests?

Mr. Holly arose in his pew, tugged at his tight tweeds, and rustled and unrolled sheaves of graph paper.

—The Tests, he said in a consecrated voice, have finally been machine-scored, and I have in my hand all the returns. Of course by themselves Raw Scores mean nothing, and neither do Scaled Scores. But I must say that our school's percentile standings are most heartening. Three quarters of our boys and girls rank above the national median. Though of course we have a highly selected and screened student body. But the percentage of our boys and girls who lie within the ninetieth percentile speaks volumes for the excellence of our teaching. . . . I would only venture to suggest that next year *certain people* would administer the tests without their tongues in their cheeks. . .

—Who dared make a farce of The Tests? Mr. Pilkey cried.

—I'm not naming names, Dell Holly said darkly.

Mr. Philbrick Grimes nodded chipperly in approval. Then Miss Hendrickson asked for the floor, was recognized, and bulked to her feet in her pew:

—I know I'm only a woman. . . .

—And as such merit our chivalry, Mr. Pilkey said sweetly.

—I'm only a woman, but I do want to say to this faculty that there's altogether too much sneering at Educational Psychology. It's the very *newest* thing, but I say to you all that it's going to displace much of the old superstitious mumbo-jumbo nonsense about teaching that's been rampant for centuries. Yes, centuries! I work in Remedial Reading, and I'm *darn* proud I do! But let me tell you, I've taken many a dirty dig from subversive elements on this faculty. They say that I'm merely duplicating the work of a first-grade teacher! And I want to tell you that it hurts my feelings! . . .

—Who has dared hurt you? Mr. Pilkey cried with ferocious concern.

Miss Hendrickson poised a finger on her chrysanthemum and winked a roguish eye:

—I'm telling no tales out of school. . . .

And she sat down amid buzzing and headwagging from the faculty. For she was nitroglycerine while teaching or standing up for her own chaste dignity. Mr. Pilkey called for order, and casting a significant glance at the Comptroller said in a solemn voice:

—Well, before we get on to further business, I want to talk briefly on a subject very close to my heart. And it's getting more pressing all the time. I am referring to the cardinal virtue of economy. This Academy, for the first time since the last depression, has a deficit. . . .

There was a concerted gasp from the faculty. The Principal was pleased, for he knew that they all envisioned an immediate salary cut; it was the sharpest sword he could wield over them. And slow tears began to seep down the jowls of Mr. Whitney. But suddenly the oldest member of the faculty raised a hand. Doctor Hunter hadn't spoken in faculty meeting for ten years. Was he going to gloss the theme of economy with pertinent passages from Livy and Tacitus?

—The Head of the Classics Department. . . .

Everybody stared at the goateed old man in bored reverence. Doctor Hunter hoisted himself to his feet in his pew, his joints creaking under the mildewed shoddy of his garments. He leaned against the hymnal rack; his spade beard moved several times before he found his voice, which presently issued forth as from a sybilline cave, rusty and incredibly ancient:

—I am older than anyone else in this room. And I have occupied myself, wisely or foolishly, with the Humanities for more than fifty years. Of course no one pays any attention to Latin and Greek any more. But that's beside the point. I merely wish to raise my tired old voice in protest. . . .

—Pray do, Mr. Pilkey said courteously, wondering what was coming from his oldest faculty member.

Doctor Hunter looked into the moonlit snow outside the chapel windows, gathered himself, and said:

—I cannot bear to sit through any more talks on economy. Has faculty meeting become a training school for young messengers in the banking business? I am sick to death of hearing about the state of our Endowment, of wasted coal and wasted food. Why do we teachers have to be birched like naughty schoolchildren for wastefulness? Haven't we enough on our minds, simply doing a decent job of teaching? Or do we have to be scolded like a serving maid who has stolen butter from the pantry? . . . I have the right to talk this way, for I was teaching when our excellent Principal was still in a pinafore. And I think this harping on finances and economy is an insult to every American teacher. I am an old man relieving my bosom of many years of disgust. Are American schools becoming just like everything else in this country? Are we, after all, only another form of corporation? Do we have to make money and show a profit? Who, then, is clipping coupons from the sweat of *my* brow? Yet we are being constantly adjured to watch out for the capital of our investors. Let us hear the truth. Do American schools think of themselves merely as plants, out to increase their capital and their buildings and their gymnasia and their athletic fields every year? Upward and onward with aggrandizement! Why, then, let's not call ourselves a school, but an icecream factory, doling out chocolate and strawberry to the young. But *not* learning! For if this is the pass to which American schools have come—economies and buildings—then we may as well stop calling ourselves schoolteachers and refer to ourselves as workers on a conveyor belt in a closed shop. For the life and heart will have gone out of American education. . . .

Old Doctor Hunter sat down rheumatically in his pew. Mr. Pilkey blushed for the first time since his mother caught him in the jam closet on his eighth birthday. And the tears now rushed unstemmed down the faded cheeks of the Comptroller. Mr. Grimes and Mr. Holly conducted a whispered conference. The Principal sighed deeply and said:

—I will omit my lecture on economy this evening. But none of you understands the seriousness of the problem. I insist that you check on the number of electric bulbs burning in your houses. And there will have to be fewer hot showers and steam baths by your wives. . . .

For he was afiire with what had been ignited inside him. He hadn't forgotten his contretemps of the afternoon with the Chairman of the Board of Trustees. And he thought of the $12,000 he'd spent remodeling his son's bungalow, and wondered where the money was to come from. Mr. Whitney's tears fell faster; he asked for recognition from the chair. He got it, stood up, and said sobbingly:

—Mrs. Miekewicz and the chef are protesting that the faculty are arrogant to them. . . .

Mr. Pilkey's rage was diverted into another channel:

—*That* I simply will not tolerate! Why is it that the dining hall staff and the janitors and the secretaries are always complaining against the faculties? My school is a democracy, and I insist that you treat all other employees here with consideration! . . .

He calmed himself, for his left side was really fiddling up a rare music now:

—Shall we get on to the prizes for Commencement? . . . These, as you all know, are open to vote by the entire faculty, though there's nothing to prevent our naming committees to inquire more deeply into the merits of various candidates. . . . The first is the loftiest distinction The Academy offers an undergraduate. I refer to the Sophia Abercrombie medal for Valor, Application, and Dignity. This medal traditionally goes to that upperformer who, in the opinion of the faculty and of his fellows, has contributed the most to The Academy. Who will make a motion?

—I nominate the President of the Student Council, Mr. Grimes said.

The motion was seconded, but in his chair by the rostrum the Principal fell into a brown study, crossing and recrossing his legs. He lifted his hands in a benign gesture of despair:

—It seems that my faculty is determined to railroad me tonight. . . . I grant that Ben Gordon is a lovely fellow. But remember that our Gentile parents are in a majority. What in the world will they say in June when a Jewish boy gets our highest award?

Mr. Grimes at once withdrew his nomination. But old Doctor Hunter again asked for the floor. His voice now sounded a hundred years older than when he spoke a few minutes earlier:

—It has always seemed to me that prizes to students are an incredible affront to the whole idea of a school. Why do we offer five-dollar gold pieces to children for a task well done? And how in the name of Bacchus are we qualified to evaluate such nebulous abstracts as Valor, Application, and Dignity—especially in a nineteen-year-old boy? But if such a ridiculous medal *must* be bestowed, I say that Ben Gordon is the most striking example on campus this year of a gentleman, an athlete, and a scholar. I'm delighted that he's a Jew. So was the Saviour of the human race. . . .

—Let us not be hasty! the Principal cried. I hereby appoint a committee to look into this matter. Mr. Grimes will be chairman. . . .

The faculty was buzzing again. Mr. Pilkey rapped for attention on the arm of his chair:

—Next is the Isabella Wilson Pratt prize of fifty dollars to the first scholar of the graduating class. Here there can be no question of electioneering, for it all depends on the numerical average of the grades of the upperformers. Will the Dean of the Faculty speak?

The old Hoosier answered, consulting a memo:

—The highest student among the upperformers had a scholastic average at midyears of 93.6 percent. And his name is Ralph Du Bouchet. . . .

287

—No question but what Ralph gets the fifty dollars, the Principal said summarily.

There was a round of applause, and the faculty began to smile again. Mr. Pilkey rose and trundled toward the rostrum, tucking his thumbs in his vest pockets:

—And now a prize very dear to my heart, and I hope, to all the faculty. The Eleanor Pilkey Cup. This trophy is designed by the incomparable art of my wife, and paid for by her out of her own pocket. It goes by vote of the faculty to that upperformer who has most distinguished himself on the football field. You all remember this award? A bronze athlete atop a loving cup of silver, and waving a football. Nominations please. . . .

From the rear pew there spoke up two hulking men (tonight without their everpresent cigars and turtleneck sweaters) who were the professional coaches at The Academy:

Demaree Walter Montgomery. . . .

Mr. Pilkey nodded with pleasure; he felt like taking off on an anecdote of what had happened when he himself coached First Football. Miss Hendrickson was bemused. She called across to Mr. Grimes:

—Is that the boy they call Mung?

—Shhh, my dear! Yes! Mr. Grimes whispered.

—And the Horace Greeley Press Prize? Mr. Pilkey said. That goes automatically, I believe, to the editor-in-chief of our school paper *The Academe*. . . .

—Howard West Lathrop, Mr. Grimes said instantly.

—Is he the boy they call The Body? cried Miss Hendrickson, clutching her chrysanthemum.

—Shhh, my dear! Yes! . . .

Mr. Pilkey now walked back and forth on the chapel platform, bursting with the confidence he was about to impart to his faculty:

—I have now the honor of informing you of the latest and greatest scholarship endowment of this Academy. I got it in the mail this morning. . . . Mr. Marlow Brown, father of one of our manliest upperformers, has presented us with four thousand dollars, to finance a candidate of our choice through four years of any college. . . . I now throw the nominations open. . . .

—Why not that little stinker his son? an anonymous voice murmured.

Mr. Pilkey heard it. His white eyebrows blinked up and down:

—This is no time for jesting, gentlemen! I doubt very much that the donor intends his own son to benefit by this scholarship. Still if it's the desire of the faculty. . . .

Doctor Sour arose in his pew, pressing his tummy in its flowered tattersol against the hymnal rack, so that it produced a rubbery ululation:

—I'ddd like to nominate Billie Maginisssss. You all know him, that lovely sssstrapping boy who's presssident of the Arts and Craftsssss Club. He's done wonderful work in carpentry here all year, and nobody appreciatesssss him but me. He's built all that fabulous sssscenery in our theater. . . .

—A slight case of prejudice or favoritism? the anonymous voice asked.

—Who said thatttt? Doctor Sour screamed, falling back with a plop into his pew.

—Billie Maginnis is a lovely fellow, the Principal said. But from his scholastic standing he couldn't get into a reputable college if he paid *them*. . . .

—I'd like to nominate either Johnson Tilbury or Edward McWaters, Dell Holly said with his scared and embarrassed snicker.

—Are they the boys known as The Abbot and The Abbess? Miss Hendrickson wanted to know.

—Shhh, my dear! Yes! Mr. Grimes said, bobbing back at her like a hen.

—I'm not sure that I wholly approve of either Tilbury or McWaters, the Principal said frigidly.

Then Old Doctor Hunter was again recognized and stood up:

—May I ask what this scholarship is to be called? Does it have abstract qualifications attached to it?

—It will be known as the Unitex Plastic Scholarship, Mr. Pilkey said grandly.

—God help us! Doctor Sour said over his wheezing breath. There is only one boy in this school poor enough and brilliant enough to warrant what is to be known as the Unitex Plastic Scholarship. And that is Ralph Du Bouchet. . . .

There was another roar of applause from the faculty. Mr.

Pilkey stopped his pacing and clutched the rostrum. His side had flared up again:

—But Ralph Du Bouchet has already been voted a prize of fifty dollars. And I happen to know that Mr. Amos James, our revered organist, intends recommending him for the Fidelio music prize. Which involves another fifty dollars. . . .

Miss Hendrickson jumped up in her pew; her chrysanthemum shivered.

—But Ralph is such a *sweet* boy! And certainly he can do more with a prize of four thousand dollars than he can with fifty! . . .

Mr. Pilkey coughed and flexed his left fist:

—I hate to bring personalities into this. But I happen to know that Mr. Marlow Brown wouldn't care to have his scholarship awarded to his son's roommate. He doesn't think he's a redblooded American boy. . . .

Doctor Hunter had remained standing, looking over the faculty with his bleared scholarly eyes. Now his goatee shook like a prophet. And he cried out in his Gethsemane voice, which had become suddenly young again:

—How long will this sordid commercialism go on in a school that calls itself respectable? Are we going to be honest in the awarding of these prizes or are we going to be liars who call themselves teachers? . . .

Then the buzzing in Mr. Pilkey's left side shot up into a shivering sound of agony. His body seemed to split in two. He tried to steady himself on the rostrum, but he fell out into the floor of the chapel. The faces of the faculty seemed to be pelting him like hysterical sunflowers.

7

On the seventeenth day of March—Saint Patrick's Day on all calendars but Mr. Pilkey's—The Academy closed for the Winter Term. The snow lay in filthy drifts in the quadrangle;

to its degradation was now added a fine cold drizzling rain that fouled everything into a mealy slush. Today the Boys' and Girls' Schools voided their denizens back to the laps of parents. It was the concluding afternoon of two and a half months of incarceration and private despairs.

Mr. Pilkey was unable to see his boys and girls off, or to warn them of the perils of an undisciplined vacation. He lay upstairs in his Cape Cod house after passing out in faculty meeting. To tend her son his old mother had arisen from her electric blanket for the first time this winter. She had even contributed her electric blanket to his welfare. She'd shooed away the Principal's wife, since artists, she said, are no good in sickrooms except to paint touching death scenes.

Guy Hudson, because exoduses fascinated him, who was himself a displaced person, walked in the quadrangle of the Boys' School, watching his students take off. He had yet to get out his grades and letters to parents. He liked seeing boys slough off their formality to him, and shake the dirt and snow of The Academy off their shoes. They were like souls checking out of Purgatory, with a faint and holy sneer for those who must remain behind.

From the entry to Hooker Hall he heard voices:

—Think the Old Bastard will croak?

—Not a chance. The skin of a turkey buzzard. Mister Death would be scared to lay a hand on him. . . .

For every boy knew that the Principal had taken a dizzy spell in faculty meeting. And the hatred of students for those over them knows no bounds of fairness: teachers and Principals were to be hated en masse—that was what the code said. And they were good haters. Guy Hudson lit a cigarette and waited for the voices to emerge. They came out of the dormitory carrying suitcases. They were Buddy Brown and The Body. Two blond young men who in less initiated circles would pass for fine specimens of Clean Young American Manhood. They hadn't yet seen Guy Hudson.

—This vacation, The Body was saying, I'm going to try my nookie all the ways it describes in the book. Seventy positions. . . .

—Ah, drop dead. I've heard rumors you can only get it up on Sundays. . . .

They paused and flushed when they saw their history

teacher loitering under the colonnade. For a second their defence mask of humility went up. Then they remembered they were going home for vacation. The Body put out his free hand to Guy Hudson with a rancid sneer and a sample of the undergraduate humor for which he was famous:

—Well, bye now, Mister Veteran. Have a perfectly SOP vacation!

—Same to you, Mister Civilian.

—Well for m-e-r-c-y-'s sakes! Buddy Brown said in falsetto. Still around, huh? . . . O, by the way, s-i-r, my pop is out gunning for your hide. Just thought I'd let you know. . . .

—He could get me with his pea shooter, Guy Hudson said shrugging.

Then the two upperformers swaggered on, leaning comically against each other for support under their bags. He heard them mention his name as they quit the quadrangle. They knew. Every boy in school knew that Mr. Pilkey had ordered him out of faculty meeting, for there were many leaks of gossip. Doctor Sour might have told his brawny boys with much lip smacking .

There now descended Mr. Grimes in a camel's hair coat, carrying his smart luggage, which he would pile into his Packard and whisk home to Mother Grimes in Baltimore. He would say goodbye to the Pilkeys and be off. Guy Hudson thought that Mr. Grimes was calculating the probabilities of snubbing him. But the colonnade was too narrow for them to look the other way or to pretend not to notice each other. So Mr. Grimes paused, setting down his spruce airplane luggage (as advertised in *The New Yorker* for the chic bachelor). His handclasp was swift and dry, like the brushing of a mole's radar:

—So long for now, Doctor. . . . I hope you'll do some tall thinking this vacation. As you probably know all too well, you're in bad odor Around Here. . . .

—A mouse died in the walls, Guy Hudson said.

—Of course I'm doing everything in my power, mon vieux. But lately you seem to have a decided penchant for faux pas. . . .

—My faux pas are always intentional. . . .

—O? But it *is* possible for a teacher to commit educational suicide. . . . Au revoir, doctor. Bonnes vacances. . . . Think on my words, as Father Shakspere says. . . .

Mr. Grimes picked up his luggage and scurried off. Guy Hudson put his hands in the pockets of his jacket and leaned against a pillar in front of Hooker Hall. He was waiting for another exit. Meanwhile he read the plaque inset in the masonry, stating that this dormitory was a memorial to Hooker Abercrombie (1808-1897), the distinguished nineteenth century painter, and brother to Our Gracious Foundress.

Ralph Du Bouchet, carrying a battered suitcase, came down with a tall sad-looking woman. He paused and flushed.

—Mother, may I present my history instructor, Mr. Hudson?

Mrs. Du Bouchet took his hand. He felt the calm pressure, thinking that she was a true woman, outside the pattern of the Venus. He was somehow reassured. There was majesty in her; he now saw the reason for Ralph.

—Won't you come to us for part of your vacation, Mr. Hudson? Ralph often speaks of you in his letters. Unless I'm very much mistaken, you're the only one for whom he has any feeling on the faculty. . . .

—Mother, Ralph said almost inaudibly.

For an instant the eyes of the redheaded teacher and the slender black-eyed boy met. It was the first and last time they looked directly at each other. More was said in that glance than even that night over the German etching. The gaze was regretful and triumphant all at once. It said: our time was here and is now gone. . . .

—You're very kind, Mrs. Du Bouchet, but I have commitments in New York. I leave tomorrow morning. . . .

—That is our loss, the firm distant voice said. I think that Ralph could profit by living with you for a week or two. It's a pity that the relationship between a fine teacher and his students isn't closer in America. I suppose it just isn't allowed to be. . . . We're so uneasy about the hearts and souls of the young . . . and for all the wrong reasons, I think. . . .

He felt the lift of his old familiar blush. Ralph looked at the bricks on the colonnaded walk with his brilliant wild eye.

—Are you ready, mother?

But some dam of reticence had broken in the woman. She seemed to have been pondering something for a long time.

Guy Hudson guessed that ordinarily she wasn't this loquacious:

—Remember this, Mr. Hudson. You've meant something to Ralph this year. I don't know what it is, but his father and I owe you much. He has a certain toughness that he lacked last fall. I mean surface toughness. Underneath he'll always be the same....

Guy Hudson said goodbye and watched them make their way to a decayed station wagon—the resilient and wonderful boy, who had stirred him as no other male ever had, and the meek somber woman who had mothered Ralph. And he thought how many raging hungers in this life never make the headlines. And how much more is expressed in a gauche moment than by arson or murder.

He climbed the two flights of stairs to his room, feeling in every fiber a drained sweetness such as he'd never known from having sex with anybody. In this moment the shell of The Academy's overorganization and the crust of its nonsense fell away. He saw what the teacher, unfettered, can be: the untouched walker-through-fire, the awakener, the liberator, and the goodbye-sayer to youth. But few looked so deeply into it. He knew also that there was something touchingly unmaterialistic about all that he'd tried to do here: to bring to life the unrevealed, to sympathize with it, but to let it go unblurred by his own breath. Perhaps he wouldn't long be suffered to do this. Hostile forces were already encamped against him. Soon he would be called a seducer when he was only a leader, a destroyer when he'd merely tried to melt the dross of the ore.

He sat down to his desk, slamming a typewriter on his blotter. Ahead of him were three hours of Mr. Pilkey's favorite sort of paper work. It wasn't correcting papers, for that didn't show to the outside world or get mentioned in the catalog. No, he had to forward to fifteen parents the midyear grades of their sons, with what the Principal called a Friendly Letter on each. For one of the glories of The Academy was the Counsellor System.

First he had to copy on printed forms the grades of his fifteen little charges. True, there were seven secretaries in the offices, but Mr. Pilkey disliked overstraining them with clerical work. So the faculty did it. But mere grades didn't suffice in a school that offered such exhaustively clinical teaching. There went home also an Effort Mark. By this Effort Mark Mr. Pilkey reversed the critical processes of the modern world, which say that if you make a mess of something you have made a mess of it. That would be unkind in teaching. The Principal was fond of saying that it didn't matter if a boy got all F's as long as he *tried*. Academy teachers weren't permitted to state that a pupil failed because, in the language of our grandfathers, he was just plain stupid. No, Mr. Pilkey decreed that his teachers write out psychological reports on all students who did poorly in any subject. They must account for all failures, which, after all, were caused by faulty teaching. Consequently the instructors at The Academy were forever snowing one another and their Principal under in little notes of analysis and apology:

—HUNTINGTON, JONATHAN, French 2b. Midyear Grade: D minus. Effort: Excellent. I honestly believe that Johnny is doing his darnedest! The death of his Aunt Martha in February has naturally been preying on his sensitive mind, and Johnny hasn't been able to concentrate too well in my class. Then too he has developed a tendency to untie the shoestrings of his neighbors while I'm teaching. Should he perhaps see a good psychiatrist? I suspect he suffers from a grief complex. I've noticed a tendency to sniffle and twitch. He doesn't know a great deal of French, but it's a rare pleasure to teach him! He has a creative mind. Last week he wrote me a theme on Les Rues de Paris. The grammar was out of this world, but he had such interesting ideas! I think we'll hear from Johnny when he matures. . . .

Guy Hudson moaned. His desk was littered with some fifty such little notes, written by teachers to the interested Faculty Counselor. These were pinned up every rating time on the faculty bulletin board by the ripe Miss Budlong, the youngest secretary. And every teacher who dared write a juicy F in his gradebooks must show account for it with a long case history.

Guy Hudson unhooked his typewriter and perused the Principal's mimeographed Suggestions on Writing Letters to Parents:

* * *

1. Be as gracious and chatty as you know how.

2. A mere listing of attainment grades is unsatisfactory and unacceptable. Write the sort of letter you would wish to receive if *you* were the parent of a boy.

3. Include gossip and personal anecdotes about the boy; this delights the parent.

4. In cases of serious academic failure or disciplinary trouble, tone down any language which might give offence.

So for the next three hours he concocted letters to the mothers and fathers of those lowerformers for whom he was responsible as Faculty Counselor:

THE ACADEMY

17 March 1949

My dear Mr. and Mrs. Barstow:

(I remember the time I met those stuffed shirts. They came up when Malcolm stole the watches of the daughters of Mrs. Dell Holly. It was all settled by psychiatry. And Mrs. Barstow wept at the Principal's desk. I think the old devil felt her pretty knee.)

—I have more welcome tidings for you this month than last. . . .

(That mealy word *tidings*! I'm no angel announcing the birth of Christ to shepherds. But Mr. Pilkey thinks it has a mellow ring; so we all cringingly use it in our letters to parents.)

—The overall scholastic picture . . .

(What does that turgid phrase mean?)

—is about the same. There have been some improvements. Malcolm has brought up his French and Latin. His algebra and ancient history, I regret to say, have gone down. . . .

(Just like a seesaw in a slum.)

—Mr. Grimes reports that Malcolm's application in English class has been most faithful, particularly in the study of myths. . . .

(Especially the Rape of the Sabines and the story of the begetting of the Minotaur.)

—But Doctor Anderson points out that Malcolm

296

makes unnecessary noise in Latin class. However, as we know, boys will be boys. . . .

(They will as long as you go on encouraging them to be little bastards. Malcolm needs only a good beating up.)

—But we need not be too excited about certain deficiencies in the academic record. . . .

(Gobbledygook and jargon!)

—Eventually with my close supervision he will develop adequate study habits. . . .

(I'll not waste ten seconds on the little turd. And what are study habits?)

—Mr. Barstow will beam with pleasure over Malcolm's athletic record, since, if memory serves, he himself was a hockey star at the University of Pennsylvania. . . .

(I got that out of Miss Pringle's files.)

—And Malcolm has been a most aggressive goalie on the Pequot hockey team. . . .

(Broke Lewis Seabury's retroussé nose last week.)

—On the corridor too his citizenship has improved. . . .

(A truly Platonic citizen of the republic. He learned to masturbate this term.)

—Only the other day he said to me: Gosh, Mr. Hudson, how did it feel to be a doughboy? I think this proves that Malcolm has patriotic spirit, don't you? And that is the educational picture for midyears. He will have to raise his grades a little to be promoted to the next class, but much can happen before June. And I close by wishing you and Mrs. Barstow the happiest of Easters.

Cordially yours,
Guy Hudson, Faculty Counselor

After fifteen such letters as these he was ready to vomit on his typewriter. He clipped them to grade reports and other notable documents. So much went into the envelopes containing the monthly grades that the parents must have thought they were getting a wallet wrapped in paper. But it looked worth the $1800 a year they were putting up.

—Teacher? he said to himself, sheathing his typewriter. I'm a male whore with gonorrhea of the dignity. . . .

He took his paper work downstairs and laid it on Mr. Pilkey's desk in The Den. The Principal read every letter to parents. If it wasn't sufficiently fawning, he returned it to the writer with a sharp note to do better. Only rarely did anything ever escape Mr. Pilkey's censorship—once Guy Hudson wrote a mother that her boy needed a cake of Lifebuoy soap. The Principal missed the sentence, and the mother was on the next train for The Academy.

He came upstairs and lighted the lamps in his room. Outside the March evening was drizzling and dark. There was no noise in the Boys' School now. He could hear the slow rain defiling the snow; there was a whirring trickle in the gutters outside his window. He undressed, shaved, and took a shower. Then he dressed messily, as he liked to do, in a pair of dungarees and a checkered lumberjack's shirt of flannel. As a gesture of defiance he took his pornographic picture out of the closet and put it on his mantel beneath the crossed fencing sabers and the captured Kraut helmet. Ralph couldn't surprise him with it now. Then he donned his green combat jacket (without lieutenant's bars) and his corduroy hat, and went out in the cold rain and slush to the cocktail party of Mrs. Launcelot Miller.

All year long Mrs. Miller was so busy entertaining her favorite athletes and whining over their muscles and their amours that she had little time for the faculty, except for visits to the salon of Mrs. Dell Holly, to keep up her culture. But since she possessed a private income, each March a sense of guilt compelled her to do something to pay back any social obligation she might have to the faculty. It would shut up their tongues for the next fifty-two weeks. So on the day that the Winter Term ended, she threw a fabulous cocktail party. It was the only and greatest Saturnalia on campus. Guy Hudson heard it was such a milestone that people used it as a snobbish frame of reference for the school calendar:

—It was the morning Marie had such a head from Mrs. Launcelot Miller's cocktail party. . . .

—The phone rang just as I was dressing for Mrs. Miller's. . . .

The Principal didn't approve of this orgy, but it was explained to him by the Dell Hollys that a party was just what the doctor ordered for the faculty after an exhausting Winter

Term. Only two persons never came to swallow drinks at Mrs. Launcelot Miller's: Mr. Grimes, since there was no further operating to do after the shut of school; and Doctor Sour, since he was only interested in the boyssss.

Guy Hudson walked through the foggy drizzle to the bungalow of the Millers, a little off from the quadrangle. The Millers could never be fired from The Academy because Mrs. Miller's father had put up the money to build this cottage of theirs. It was a dovecote designed by the official Academy architect. Mrs. Pilkey had done the landscape gardening around it, also with a fee from Mrs. Miller's father. It looked like a dollhouse covered with vines, giving to one corner of the campus a rustic prettiness, which pleased parents as they drove in. In the catalog Mr. Pilkey referred to it as the Lean-to. But Marxian-Socialists on the faculty called it privately The Outhouse.

Guy Hudson staggered through the melting snow up the artificial slope to the Millers' bungalow. Round it were flagstone terraces on which in fair weather Mrs. Launcelot Miller, lying in a hammock, drank tea with her special athletes. The entrance was flanked by wrought-iron lanterns (designed by Mrs. Pilkey) that in the dim rainy March night looked like the heads of political criminals. The little house shimmered in moisture. He saw people with glasses in their hands passing to and fro behind the curtains. The front door, adorably divided in Dutch fashion, would open at the top and he heard shrieks and laughter. The faculties were taking their pleasure.

Against the March thaw he was wearing his old combat boots. He walked up the snowy flagstone walk and stamped them on the welcome mat. He pushed at a bell button under a brass plate that announced in chaste lettering the names of Mr. and Mrs. Launcelot Miller. It was the sort of doorplate belonging to people who put HIS and HERS on their guest towels and have amusing murals painted on their bathroom walls.

The ring was answered by Launcelot Miller, professor extraordinary of biology. He put his arm around Guy Hudson's shoulders.

—Come in, come in, fella! Party's incomplete without ya!

It seemed something he'd read in a book on jollity entitled How to Give a Party. Launcelot Miller was an ape of a man, tall, fat, and hairy, with tickles of black hair protruding over the collar of his polo shirt. Under this waggled breasts like a woman's. His heartiness was so deliberate that Guy Hudson felt as though he was being welcomed to the house of a sociable gorilla. He held a martini in his furry fist.

—Leave ya things in my den, fella. Then step this way for somethin warming. . . .

Guy Hudson took off his hat and combat jacket in the den, hung with autographed photos of Mrs. Miller's reigning favorites of the past ten years, preferably in athletic costume that revealed their bodies. There was also a kidney-shaped desk of blond maple, from which she addressed her round-robin circular letters to those alumni she'd loved as boys. The room was chintzy and feminine, the flowers and furniture dust covers strangely contrasting with the athletes' faces, which belonged in a downstairs bar of the Princeton Club.

Launcelot Miller again put his arm about Guy Hudson's shoulders and propelled him into the living room, already filled with drinking people. Most of the faculties of the Boys' and Girls' Schools were here, stowing away free liquor as fast as they decently could. Their fatigue from the Winter Term was taking its toll too, for some were already well oiled and talking shop and irrelevancies like telephone girls chained to their switchboards. Mrs. Launcelot Miller, in slacks and corncob pipe, was circulating with a crystal cocktail shaker. Her aim seemed to be to get these people drunk and out of her house as soon as possible. Then she'd be rid of them for another fifty-two weeks. She bore down on her newest guest, the pipe fulminating in her mouth:

—Guy! This is the first time you've *ever*. . . . I feel so blue since Ben Gordon and his crowd left. . . .

Already she wasn't feeling too much pain, for she thrust her pimply face toward his.

—Am I supposed to kiss the hostess?

She set up an anguished scream:

—Why, that's so *sweet*! Nobody else ever had the courage to say that. You know, if you were ten years younger, you'd be in Ben Gordon's crowd. . . .

So he pecked at her neck, which had corrugated skin, like a charwoman's.

—I'm glad you're dressed sensibly for my brawl, she said. In fact, that's the way First Hockey dresses when they come for tea on Sunday afternoon. I miss Ben so. But Launcelot and I have been invited to visit the Gordons in Chicago this vacation. What a table they set! . . .

And stroking her neck where he'd kissed it, she was off down the room. He retired to the fireplace, where great logs were purply and slowly burning, as they do in colored magazine prints of Houses Beautiful. He was damp from his walk; so he turned his rear to the blaze and drank his martini, which was strong and sour. And he examined the room, already in considerable commotion.

—You're blocking my view, said an especially ladylike voice.

He wheeled and beheld Mrs. Mortimer Wesley, wife of the scoutmasterish Director of Admissions. She was sitting practically on the andirons. In her hand was the one martini she was said to nurse all evening long. The faculty prude, she lived for this one evening all year long. For at this party she got enough daggers to throw until the party would be repeated next March. She disapproved of every one and everything. Holding her one drink, she followed everybody in the room with her little yellow eyes. Nothing that happened by way of indiscretion was forgotten by Mrs. Mortimer Wesley. Even now she pointed out to him a lady and a gentleman conversing, each married to somebody else:

—See that? Did you *ever*! That's a new combination! . . .

She was famous all over school for her stinginess. She was reported to wake her husband each morning at five, have him do the housework, and bring her breakfast in bed.

—And look at Doctor Anderson! Alcohol certainly arouses the beast in men, doesn't it?

Her eyes looked at him as though she was hoping he'd give her some scandalous ammunition by propositioning her. He moved away:

—Why not have another martini, Mrs. Wesley? That must be getting warm in your hand. . . .

—Now really! . . .

By an ebonized grand piano (also loaded with pictures of athletes) Mrs. Mears had the faculty of the Girls' School ranged round her in shepherdess poses. They were all solicitous of their Directress. He guessed that only when the drinks had begun to work would the lady teachers desert their boss, who was wearing a fur-trimmed cap. The ladies were doing their share of guzzling. Mrs. Mears tossed off the olive in her martini and imperiously waved the empty glass at her hostess:

—My! How delicious! And only an hour ago I was so nerrrvous and keyed up after seeing the girls off. . . .

It was Miss Habib Demerjian who spotted Guy Hudson slowly wandering and watching:

—Mister Man! Sashay over here and bend an elbow with us. . . . Yoo-hoo!

—My dear, Mrs. Mears said. Well, I suppose it doesn't matter. School's out. . . .

He winced into his cocktail glass. He was watching a pair of wonderful eyes pass from Miss Demerjian's mustache to his own sloppy attire. It was the gaze of Miss Betty Blanchard, sitting on the piano bench and spying over the rim of her martini, which she drained with slow steady intensity. She was wearing the black velvet gown and gardenia he'd noticed weeks ago. Her face was flushed and excited. He looked harder. She wasn't quite the teacher of Spanish now. She was a beautiful girl meditatively drinking by herself in a roomful of yelling people. Her thoughts seemed to nest on some Himalaya. He walked toward her and took the glass from her hand.

—May I?

She nodded with the first gust of excitement he'd ever observed in her. God, was she an alcoholic? Or was she happy to see him for the first time in their strained meetings? He got her glass refreshed from the roving shaker of Mrs. Launcelot Miller.

—Chivalry! Mrs. Miller said, champing on her pipe stem. And who are *you* being so gallant to?

—A lady.

He garnered a round olive and put it in Betty Blanchard's glass. Somehow he wanted her drink to look festive and special. Had he been a magician-bartender, he would have contrived to frost the martini too, or have it foam amberly in the glass. He returned it to her hand. Her gown had long sleeves, fastened at her wrists, but her shoulders were bare in the firelight; they seemed to have been cut from marble that was warm and poreless. As she took a sip, she threw back her head; her breasts thrust proudly.

—Thank you, Mr. Hudson.

302

He felt queerly happy. But he bowed and walked away, for he believed he was going to blush. As he left, Mrs. Mears squealed to her mistresses:

—Look at Betty! She's positively gay! Not a trace of nerrrrvousness now....

—Je suis désolée, Miss Demerjian muttered.

—Et moi aussi, said Miss Carpenter, the tinny mistress of music.

There was a rattle of applause from the drinking faculties. Led in by Mr. and Mrs. Launcelot Miller, the three Pilkeys arrived at the cocktail party: the Principal, a little pale and leaning on a cane; Mrs. Pilkey in an outrageous evening gown with sequins; and the Principal's aged mother, looking as though she'd made her electric blanket into a dinner dress.

—He made it! a young teacher cried, anxious to convince his boss that he was a true bully boy, Yale fence style.

The Principal bowed to his inferiors, making much of his invalid's cane:

—Yes, I'm much better, thank you all! There's life in the old dog yet!

There was further applause, and those who hadn't called at the Cape Cod house during the Principal's prostration hastened to pay their respects now. But a depression settled on the party with the arrival of the Pilkeys. There was less sprightly conversation, and an increase in covert drinking. A noggin of the rum he loved was thrust into the Principal's hand; a seat was found for him by the fire, displacing Mrs. Mortimer Wesley, who had to go elsewhere to spy on what she hoped would turn into a Bacchanale. Launcelot Miller (though he couldn't be fired) personally wrapped a bear rug about the bandy legs of Mr. Pilkey.

—Just like Dickens, the Principal cried. Thank you, thank you! Later tonight I may read aloud....

The faculties shouted their enthusiasm, each one making a mental reservation to make a drunken getaway before this happened. Mrs. Pilkey consented to take a glass of sherry. And old Mrs. Pilkey, remembering she'd reached the age of ninety-three without having tasted a martini, cried that she'd sample one then and there.

Guy Hudson tried noiselessly to pass by the Pilkeys. He had now the beginnings of a pleasant buzz on. And the fuss of all these alien people blurred his agreeable consciousness like balloons against the sunlight. He knew it wasn't etiquette to quit a room so soon after the arrival of the Royal Family. But there were too many in the drawing room; even the flowers sickened under the exuding warmth of the Principal convalescent. Mrs. Pilkey was simpering over her sherry and the oldest lady was holding her novel martini to the light. He was almost out of the living room when the Principal called out gaily:

—There's our young anarchist and hothead! Cooling his brains in spiritus juniperii. . . .

Everybody laughed. Guy Hudson flushed. He went out of the living room, into the corridor, and entered the dining room. Here people were sitting around the Miller dinner table, drinking fraternally, or leaning against the buffets and windowseats merely drinking. They were talking shop as frenetically as they did in termtime. He wondered if teachers ever got unwound. For months now he'd noticed the trademark of their conversation, some occupational virus that they must have picked up in their classrooms. They never talked casually; they lectured one another. The voices of teachers are edgy; they don't *say* something, they insist on it. He found their society as poisonously aggressive as a convention of salesmen.

Then he saw where the attention of the dining room was focused. Herman Pilkey had come to the party in his uniform of a Marine Lieutenant. Through his shoulder loops a fourragère was threaded; on his breast assorted ribbons for valor in defence of the American theater of operations; for Herman had never been farther overseas than boot camp at Parris Island. He had hold of his pregnant wife Nydia, swiveling her on his knee, and pretending that her plump torso was the barrel of a machine gun. He feigned to feed a belt of bullets into Nydia's left breast and out her right.

—Ack! Ack! Ack! There's enfiladed fire on Hill 207. . . .

Mrs. Dell Holly looked in tired fashion over her martini at Guy Hudson:

—The dear boy is storming Atlanta all over again. . . .

—Ack! Ack! Ack! Herman Pilkey cried, turning his wife in another direction.

Nydia was wearing a violet gown; and when her gunner swung her around her meaty rear faced Guy Hudson. Her mouth was woolly against her husband's lap:

304

—Hon-ey! Cahful! Remembuh the condishun of yoah lil fruitcake. . . .

—Ack! Ack! Ack! Herman Pilkey cried, sighting along Nydia's buttocks. Bet you never saw anything like this overseas, Hudson. . . .

—No, I didn't. . . .

Guy Hudson sat down next to Lisa Holly, who smelt of jasmine in her white frock. She looked like a model frozen under Klieg lights to best advantage. She was feeding martinis into her face with cool speed. He saw that she loved her tea, that it gave her a certain cushion in being the grande dame. She nodded her elegant coiffure in Herman's direction:

—Does this spectacle disgust you?

For a moment he thought she might be vibrating with compassion for him, but he decided she was angling for gossip for her salon:

—What do *you* think?

For Herman Pilkey playing at soldiering had thrust him back more than four years ago to the heartbreak of the Forest of the Ardennes. He saw again the hands of dead American soldiers, meaningless spread gloves in the bloody snow. And in that winter of sorrow that fat steak who happened to be the Principal's son was stateside, strutting around as a gyrene officer and playing with Nydia Pilkey in Atlanta. The travesty was almost more than he could bear. And now, for the edification of the ladies and gentlemen in this room, Herman pretended his wife was a pillbox surrounded by barbed wire, and he was storming her single-handed. Lisa Holly didn't miss the clenching and flexing of Guy Hudson's fists:

—Relax, my child. Life is more of a game than you're prepared to admit. . . .

—That I will never believe, he said passionately.

He was sorry at once, for he had no intention of laying himself open to knowledge by such as Mrs. Dell Holly.

—Ack! Ack! Ack! I'm an 80 millimeter mortar. How'm I doing, Hudson?

He didn't answer. Only his scarred mouth twitched with remembrance, as a joint does at cold. Mrs. Launcelot Miller came by with her cocktail shaker and refreshed his martini.

Her corncob pipe was near his cheek as she bent toward him:

—Guy! Enter into the spirit of things! You're not having fun!

—Sorry.

—Pffft! Pffft! Pffft! Now I'm the fuse of a landmine. . . .

Invaded by a loathing such as would cause him to trample on a centipede, Guy Hudson had a desire to smash his glass to the floor. Then he would take Herman by the collar of his Marine tunic, tear off the fourragère, and make the redfaced slob eat it inch by inch. It would be like feeding a rope of punk into a hamburger machine. But Lisa Holly was watching him all the while, her eyes satirically cocked. He was almost grateful when she took off in her Bryn Mawr voice on her three daughters:

—I've just finished the most fascinating book on psychoses in children from three to seven. Did you read *The New Yorker* review of it last week? But I'll give you to understand that I *bought* the book. Ten dollars for two thick volumes attractively boxed. . . . A Mother has a duty to see that her girls grow up free of traumas. . . . I find now that Julia, my eldest, is an egregious example of voyeurism. Isn't that shattering? She just stands and looks at me with those green eyes till I'm ready to scream. . . .

—I can't imagine what she sees, he said absently.

—I really don't know myself. Unless it could be me. . . . And Helena, according to this fabulous book, is the Aphrodite type. We've had to remove all the mirrors from her bedroom because Dell and I have caught the little vixen plying her trade. . . .

—Pardon? he said, hypnotized.

—Yes! Helena danced naked in front of her own image!

—Isn't that what most women do?

—Mr. Hudson, for pity's sake! . . . You're not even looking at me. . . . And let me tell you what I learned about Lydia, my youngest. She has the oddest compensations. The book says that little girls are unfortunate who are the daughters of women who . . . aren't . . . exactly . . . bad looking. . . . So now Lydia, because of some suppressed jealousy toward me, her poor mother, has taken to disfiguring her pretty little face with the colors of her paintbox. She comes in with horrible splotches of indigo and yellow all over her cheeks and says she's Lena the Hyena. . . . Heavens! the trials of parents! . . .

He saw that Lisa Holly was getting drunk. He watched her sway in her white frock, struggling to preserve the queenly tilt of her chin that lent atmosphere to the salons of Mr. Grimes. Suddenly she closed one eye and looked at him. She held her martini as though it was a scepter. And suddenly he saw her as an old woman, still reading *Vogue* and *Harper's Bazaar* and scheming for fine gowns, and memorizing book reviews. Her conversation was simply a feat of memory. But now under the alcohol it had stopped. She seemed to have fallen into a cistern and was peering out at him, ludicrously drunk and bewildered.

—Mister Hudson! Why are you staring at me like that?

—Admiration and paralysis, he answered listlessly.

Herman Pilkey had a new imitation to wow the dining room:

—Plop, plop, plop! I'm an atomic bomb. Just watch me mushroom!

Then to screams from his wife that he would hurt himself, the Principal's son prepared to stand on his head in the middle of the dining room floor. His belly jiggled as his palms groped for balance; the bluegreen trousers of his uniform slid up his fat red hairless shins; his tunic and bars dropped away from his torso. He seemed like a joint of beef hooked up in a deep-freezer. To applause Herman maintained himself upside down for a full minute, while an obliging lady counted off the seconds on her wristwatch. Dell Holly could be heard droning to a confrère in a corner:

—There's nothing dubious about the value of the Iowa Reading Test. . . .

Mrs. Dell Holly sighed to Guy Hudson; it was the first trace of coquetry he'd ever seen in her posturing:

—Do you want to take me outside for a breath of fresh air?

—No. I came here to drink. . . .

He arose. He had an urge to return to the living room. But he feared that Mr. Pilkey would be lecturing the faculty from the hearth. But all the same he wondered if Miss Betty Blanchard was yearning for another drink.

At another corner of the dining room the seven secretaries were placidly pouring martinis into their throats. They were dressed to the sky, since they hadn't associated in a party way with the faculties since last September. The youngest, Miss Budlong, was drinking avidly and gracefully, like Joan Crawford playing a well-coiffed dipsomaniac. She was only nineteen, and since she was the juiciest of the office ladies she expected some of that attention given her by the Boys' School. But here there were only teachers getting drunk. She looked at Guy Hudson and struck a winsome attitude, wrinkling her nose. It was the sort of thing that would have pleased him in pretty women, ten years ago at Amherst. But not now. He was way beyond ingenues. . . .

Miss Budlong called out to him in an accent lacquered onto her when she was a student under Mrs. Mears:

—Don't be standoffish!

—I have that reputation.

—Tell us about your war experiences!

He shrugged and pointed to Herman Pilkey, who had now arisen from standing on his head and was publicly fondling his wife:

—I want you people all to take a good look at this po lil white trash wife of mine. . . .

—Humman! Nydia murmured, nestling against his four-ragère. Hon-ey!

—Yessir, Herman said, tossing off a martini with his free hand. She does what most of you duckies don't. I mean she produces. She's a one-woman meat market. One last year. And now if you'll all look at her tummy c-a-r-e-f-u-l-l-y with your opera glasses. . . .

Nydia Pilkey dutifully assumed the stance of a model and pirouetted in the center of the dining room. As she turned, shimmying a little, in the soft lights from the iron sconces, everyone was made aware of Her Condition. Guy Hudson, nauseated, looked away. Once he'd assisted at the delivery of a German girl, with child, by an SS man. But that was less obscene that this. And the foetus of Herman Pilkey's second child, under the blighting vulgarity of the father, became a piece of carrion in his mother's womb. Guy Hudson choked on his martini.

—Look at that belly, Herman said, like a lecturer in obstetrics. I bet Nydia's got two in her. What shall we call it? The name lottery is hereby thrown open. . . .

—Sophonisba, Lisa Holly said thickly.

But Miss Pringle tottered to her feet and clicked down her

308

sherry glass on an end table. Her eyes were moist behind her glasses; she shook a finger and quavered:

—Well, really! Herman Pilkey, you'll never be the man your father is. I've known you since you were a little shaver. And I must say I've always detected a . . . vulgar streak in you. Do you realize there are maiden ladies in this room? Do you? . . .

—Ah, go back to your shorthand, Herman said, encircling the blossoming waist of his bride.

Then Miss Pringle turned up her toes. Her last epileptic fit had been in February. She gave several abortive little moans, clicked her teeth, and rolled her eyes behind their spectacles. And almost immediately, with the daintiness of not knocking over her sherry glass, she was down on the rug under the dining room table. Her high buttoned boots stuck out, and a few saw her frilly panties.

Miss O'Mara, head nurse of The Academy's infirmary, lurched to the rescue:

—O, the dear saints in heaven above! Trust the likes of *her* to ruin my day when I'm plannin to lay in a little spot for my poor liver. . . .

The twitching Miss Pringle was carried out by Dell Holly and a teacher of French. They were followed by stout Miss O'Mara, who hastily swallowed another martini to fortify herself against her disappointment. Miss Pringle was littered out the back door. The last thing they heard was the champing of her jaws.

—Herman, Mrs. Dell Holly said. You're a swine. . . .

The Principal's son began to blubber like a little boy caught at the brandy bottle.

—Gee! How was I to know the old doll would throw one of her fits? . . .

There was a brief silence in memory of Miss Pringle, but the party picked up again after a few moments of shock. Guy Hudson thought it was because that people drinking expect the worst anyhow, and are delighted in their cups by catastrophes, such as epileptic fits and seductions. In the corridor Launcelot Miller could be heard phoning the school doctor, begging him to keep Miss Pringle's epilepsy out of the morning papers.

Guy Hudson watched the other secretaries settle down to their drinking. They seemed delighted at the elimination of the Principal's private secretary. Miss Budlong said she felt woozy; so he opened a window. And Miss Robenia Hoskins, charmed at the violent trend things were taking, described a cash shortage in the books at the Bursar's Office. It took ten minutes to tell in Miss Hoskins's nonstop sentences, and she acted out running her carmined fingernail down yellow ledger sheets:

—And just as you might expect we found it in the debit column! she yelled.

The secretaries were making visible inroads into the liquor, for at twenty-seven fifty a week they could rarely afford to let down their back hair. Miss Robenia Hoskins next took up most of the faculty, running through them in her unpunctuated stream of consciousness:

—And while I'm on the subject I might just as well frankly confess that the much touted Mr. Philbrick Grimes is almost as big a gossip as yours truly. . . .

—Glass houses, my dear! Glass houses! Lisa Holly said dreamily.

She was now leaning on a windowsill, her forehead in her hand. Guy Hudson had never seen her when she wasn't bolt upright, like a dowager sitting for her daguerreotype. She was a pretty study in slow melting, like old cheese.

Just at this moment the Comptroller and his wife trundled into the dining room. Mr. Whitney was late because he'd been balancing his books for the Winter Term, and possibly weeping over the shortage described by Miss Robenia Hoskins. And to make a gaudy showing as Second Lady of the Faculty, Mrs. Whitney had spent all afternoon on her paint job. Her fat form was squeezed into a gown of flame-colored velvet, so that she looked like a whale on fire. She had an egret in her gray hair.

—Yoo-hoo to all! Better late than never, I always say, ha-ha. . . .

And while the Comptroller sipped a martini and mused mousily on his shortage, his wife kissed nearly everyone in the room, keeping up her function as faculty mother. Now she stood before Guy Hudson. From her breath he gathered that she'd been nipping from a bottle on her toilette table as she got herself up. Her huge corseted figure shut off the light from its source; she gave him a rollicking kiss. He felt as though his face had been pushed into a grapefruit stewed in rum:

—Yoo-hoo to you, Mr. Hudson! Know *what*! I've had a temptation to do this all year long. But I *do* suspect your political affiliations! . . .

He turned his cheek so that she needn't be embarrassed by the slit along the left side of his mouth. Mr. Whitney looked wearily at the enthusiastic embrace. Mrs. Dell Holly on the windowseat put up her lovely pale claw of a hand to stifle a hiccough. Then the Comptroller's wife rolled over to her great confidante Miss Robenia Hoskins, who vied with her in literary tastes and the intricacies of the card table:

—O, Robenia, you haven't read *Wild Thyme*? Literary Guild. . . . There's this octoroon, you see. Her name is Sophie. The whole thing takes place in the bayous of Louisiana. She's pursued by a hairy halfbreed who's a perfect *bounder*. And do you know what the scoundrel does to her after a thousand pages? Takes a whip to her, Robenia, my dear, and *rapes* her! . . . O, dear, I *do* hope they'll put the card tables out later. . . .

Guy Hudson had had enough of drinking and watching in the dining room. He was beginning to feel that the whole thing was a shimmering mirage. He loved to be mobile when he was drinking, to hate people out of a mist of omniscience and bitterness. And he wondered how the Boys' and Girls' Schools would feel if they could now see their models and mentors in various phases of alcoholic amnesia. He was against all fake delicacy in teachers. But this was shrill and ugly. These people were drinking to forget their trade, as a sand rat drinks to obliterate his. The life had dried up in them, and their very attempts at humor took a horrible vengeance on their desiccation. Their students would have been as disgusted with them as Guy Hudson was. They were trying to be party boys and girls tonight. It was a witches' sabbath in an old people's home. Their false poses and their phony morality now assured that they couldn't even enjoy themselves. . . .

—Come back soon, Red, Miss Budlong called.

He shuddered at her name for him, but he turned in the doorway with the empty glass and looked at the smoky dining room. Everyone but Lisa Holly was jabbering. Mrs. Whitney's egret kept poking into the eye of Miss Robenia

Hoskins. He himself had drunk five martinis now—enough to make him lubricated. But in his head, because of these people, there was only a fume of resentment.

In the corridor to the living room he met Mrs. Launcelot Miller, who, to give the festivity a shot in the arm, had donned an amusing paper hat, such as is supposed to lift the spirits of people at New Year parties. It was at a mad angle on her stringy hair. She poured him another martini; some ashes from her corncob pipe fell into his glass.

—Loosen up, she said.

—For what?

She took his arm and leaned on it. With the other she flourished her cocktail shaker and said plaintively:

—I wish the boys were here. They're *such* fun. . . .

—You're right there.

—You know, I wish Launcelot had a mouth like yours. Then maybe I could have babies. . . .

But you do have babies . . . other people's. . . .

She took a swipe at her paper party hat:

—Don't think I don't know what people say about me. But those other old hens haven't got what I have. Not on your tintype. Every woman here would love to have Ben Gordon visit her. . . . Did you ever see his shoulders? . . .

But he was in no mood to have her nymphomania flower under his eyes. At the entrance to the living room they came upon Mrs. Mortimer Wesley, still holding her one and only cocktail and peering around the corner like a witch checking on the efficacy of her voodoo. Her yellow eyes candled with her note-taking:

—O, how scandalous! . . . please don't go in there. . . .

—Why, this is my house!

—O, my dear, I'm afraid I'm going to have to go home. . . .

—Have another drink, Mrs. Miller said, brushing her aside.

—What I've *seen*! Mrs. Wesley said, passing a hand over her eyes. The morals! . . .

From the living room came the innocent tinkling of a piano and a clapping of hands, as at a barn dance. Mrs. Launcelot Miller renewed her confidences to Guy Hudson:

—Takes only a little alcohol, doesn't it? And the boys are so much nicer and tell you *every*thing for a cup of tea. . . .

Considerable decay had set in since he last saw the living

room. Many people slumped to the rugs, where they drank and watched or experimented with one another. Miss Habib Demerjian was exchanging mincemeat kisses with Doctor Anderson of the Classics Department. These he was returning in a grave Horatian fashion and lecturing her on the proprieties:

—Libera me, Domine, de ore leonis. . . .

—N'éloignez-vous pas, mon amour! cried Miss Demerjian, helping herself to another suety kiss.

She licked her mustache after each salute, as though she was a cook sampling a bisque. When she saw Guy Hudson, tall above her in the French doors, she beckoned him to sit on the rug beside her:

—Who's counting? Let's make it a *trio*! . . .

—Thanks. I kiss Doctor Anderson only when there are no ladies around.

—He appears well grounded in Petronius, the classics scholar said fussily.

At the piano, playing Country Gardens as a duet, were Mr. Amos James, his glasses on cockeyed, and Miss Carpenter, who contrived to slip her elbow under his in their Cockney tinkling. During this mechanical and rattling little song Mr. Pilkey had cast off his rug to arise from the fireplace and dance a jig with his wife. Some of the faculties joined in the up-and-down hopping of the Principal. Mr. Pilkey was ruddy with rum.

—Zowie, McTavish! the Principal roared. Get me my kilts and my plaidies!

The dance was an improvisation borrowed from the schottische and the polka. It was the only spontaneous and good thing Guy Hudson had seen all evening. He wandered to the couch where Miss Blanchard sat next to Mrs. Mears, who was screaming that the party was making her nerrrrvous and she *loved* it. He too was nervous about what he was going to say:

—If I bring you another drink, will you let me sit next to you?

Her eyes were lucent from watching the dancers; her lips were apart from her quickened breathing; a vein welled in her satiny throat from the drinks and the music. She turned to him. He'd never seen her face so alive.

—No, I don't think so.

He shivered and, about to turn away, said roughly:

—I'll be goddamned. . . .

—I mean, she said quickly, will you dance with me? I haven't danced in ages . . . except with the girls. . . .

—Makes them nerrrvous too! Mrs. Mears pointed out.

To calm a spasm in his limbs he put a knee against the sofa. He hesitated:

—I don't dance . . . ordinarily . . . but let's try. . . .

Betty Blanchard surrendered her long cool fingers to his. He pulled her to her feet, for she was wedged against the flank of the Directress of the Girls' School. Then they walked out on the rug. The Pilkeys were taking up more space than anyone else with their fervent hopping. Guy Hudson and Betty Blanchard joined in the communal dance to the tune of Country Gardens, which was getting brisker all the time. He didn't quite know what step to do, but after a few essays they hit upon an appropriate movement—strutting back and forth, clapping hands, then leaping into the air to a Cossack war cry of Hoi! He watched her shyly. She wasn't looking at him or at anyone, she was just giving herself up to the abandon of free movement; they were merely part of a pattern of excited people. He felt in that same giddy humor as when his basketball team at Amherst had challenged and played Smith College girls. Being taller than she, he towered over her and all but hit his red head on the low ceiling during their leaps. And the smacking of their palms together when they clapped hands excited him, and he wanted to laugh and shout foolish things in her little hidden ear. But they were seldom close together, for the dancing of these drunken people was more rhythmic than personal. Nearly everyone in the room was bouncing and shrieking and clapping to Country Gardens. They weren't ingrown teachers any longer; they were peasants working out some old Daphnephoric rite. Once Betty Blanchard tripped on her spike heels; he caught her waist and lifted her high into the air. Her loose black hair flew behind her like a Fury's.

—Really, sir, she said with a touch of her old prissiness when he'd set her down.

—Really, madam, he answered, feeling both sad and foolish.

He noticed that as she became heated with her exertion there arose from her tossing slender body, in its black velvet,

314

a cool wave of perfume. And his one contact with the sheath of her virginity caused him to run his tongue over the smashed side of his mouth; it was like licking a jagged pretzel. Several times too he had an impetus to kiss her experimentally on the cheek. No one except Mrs. Mortimer Wesley would have noticed, for couples were dropping out of the dance and onto sofas or the floor, to neck or to go on drinking. Several wives were kissing the wrong men, working off in their drunkenness the subdued and clandestine passions they might vent only once a year.

He looked at Betty Blanchard, skipping opposite him. Some fire had been lighted through her violent exercise. She'd thawed to him considerably; yet if he overstepped himself he knew there'd be that chill white hand and that studied voice to tick him back to his place.

—Lissen, he said, trying not to sound smoochy, everyone else in this room is lovin it up. Would you have any hard feelings if I. . . .

—Leave us not, she said.

And she underscored the coy vulgarism with a frost he'd known many times before.

Suddenly the music of Country Gardens stopped, for Miss Carpenter of the Girls' School had thrown a tepid kiss in the direction of Mr. Amos James of the Boys' School; he was wrestling with her on the piano bench for his intact male spinsterhood. The dancing stopped, and watchers applauded the valor of Miss Carpenter. Guy Hudson took Betty Blanchard's hand in that affectionate courtesy, leisurely and reflective, with which one conducts from the floor a girl he's enjoyed dancing with. But she took hers away, as though to leave him no doubt that the nonsense was over. The portcullis was closing again.

—Thank you. I can still walk, Mr. Hudson. I've had only four martinis. . . .

—You've had five. Same number as I've had. . . .

Those Oriental eyes slitted at him before she smoothed her skirt and sat down beside Mrs. Mears:

—Really? Have you been spying on me?

—On no one else, he said, twisting his mouth to its ugliest.

Mrs. Mears waggled a drunkenly chaperoning finger at him.

—You've made her nerrrrvous again! S-h-a-m-e!

He had an impulse to burrow under the rug like an armadillo. He lit Miss Blanchard's cigarette, but already she was withdrawing from him into her catatonic stare. So he picked up his empty glass and walked away to the French windows, stepping over affectionate couples on the floor. He'd never felt such a whimpering chagrin. The impulse came upon him, as when he was in sexual heat, to shout out all sorts of four-letter words in the mewing overheated room. He was pretty drunk too—a blurring intoxication in which any mad thing would be welcome. He'd danced with Blanchard and put his hands about her waist! For at least ten minutes she'd been gracious and relaxed to him. He sat down alone on one half of a loveseat to reflect on these deliciously tantalizing implications. Launcelot Miller refilled his martini. Guy Hudson shook his head like a befuddled dog; he was fighting to keep detached, for something was bound to happen to him tonight. He knew it as his ruined mouth knew the twinges of cold weather. So he watched the people in this living room. Everyone was involved with everybody else, for no particular motive except that they were getting spifflicated together. And, as is the rule in parties, they got tangled up with people they wouldn't have spoken to, sober.

The mistress of gymnastics, Miss O'Leary, too muscular to be necked by anyone, stood, pulled up her evening gown, proceeded to demonstrate feats of strength. She pushed several of the lighter male teachers so hard that they hurtled against the windows like medicine balls. She bulged her biceps, which looked odd in an evening gown. And to get a little attention she bellowed in her parallel bars basso:

—I challenge any lil ole man in this room to a bout of Injun wrestlin!

There was a ghastly silence from the drinkers, and a drunken gasp of disapproval from Lisa Holly, who'd been swaying over a martini and babbling to the air about her three daughters. There was also some grunting from Doctor Anderson, for Miss Demerjian was trying to lie on top of him. She was doing her damnedest to open his shirt and plant her mustache on his collarbone.

—I will take you on, Amazon! cried a virile old voice.

And Mr. Pilkey charged out onto the rug from his chair by the fireplace. His wife set up a little wail:

—Dearie, remember what the doctor said!

—There's no fool like an old fool, said Old Mrs. Pilkey.

The eyes of Mrs. Mortimer Wesley were almost out of their sockets. She'd never be able to recall all the tidbits of *this* party! She held her half-finished first cocktail and observed all the riders on this fantastic carousel. Everybody was flying around and reaching for rings! . . .

Like a wrestler at the bell Miss O'Leary lowered her skirts and put herself on guard. The Principal, tearing off his evening tie, hulked toward her:

—En garde, mademoiselle!

Just at this moment Mrs. Launcelot Miller, drunk, but not so much so as to forget her duties as hostess, tottered into the room. Her pipe was still in her mouth; in both hands she carried an enormous silver salver, a gift of the family of Ben Gordon. This tray was loaded with serried ranks of shrimp, lettuce, mayonnaise, and whole wheat toasted crackers. She took a look at the imminent carnage between Miss O'Leary and Mr. Pilkey:

—Everyone's off their rocker! she screamed. O, ha-ha, what a scrumptious party I'm giving! . . .

Mr. Pilkey, who loved hors d'oeuvres, was distracted from moving in on Miss O'Leary. He wheeled, his boiled shirt open, his bang of white hair in his bloodshot eyes:

—Does anyone remember how I used to coach the first football team?

And the Principal retracted his right leg and brought it forward again in a high-flying punting kick. The toe of his patent leather pump connected with the salver. The whole tray shot up out of her hands, knocking her corncob pipe from her mouth. There was an echoing bong like a Chinese tam-tam. Shrimp and crackers and mayonnaise flew heavenward in a perfect typhoon of flying groceries. Then the hors d'oeuvres began to descend in a thick hail of pink and green. To plopping and prickling, gobs of saffron mayonnaise landed where they would. Fillets of shrimp settled in the hair of many a lady who had visited her hairdresser that afternoon. A cracker belted Miss Demerjian on her mustache.

—My house! my lovely little house! wailed Mrs. Launcelot Miller.

She was overruled, for the drunken faculties were united in laughing together for the first time in the history of The

Academy. Mr. Pilkey stood in the middle of the ruin and bowed to his employees:

—Who does that doctor think he is anyhow? Telling *me* to spend a month in bed! ...

Mrs. Miller retrieved her pipe from the mess of shrimp and mayonnaise and burst into tears. Her husband looked the other way. And Guy Hudson had the same sensation he'd known in Berlin, seeing human beings and swine rooting for sustenance in the same rubble pile. He decided in judicial drunkenness that The Academy was a pigsty, where learning was the muck in which these feral creatures rolled, oinking of their scholarship and their superiority. Wild boars and sows of all ages and creeds. ...

Only Miss Blanchard gave a long agonized sigh. Then the Principal's attention was turned to her, and he waded toward her through the garbage. He looked like a hairy iceman intent on spoliation:

—I don't want to fight a woman! I want to pluck the sweet mimosa of love! ...

—Dearie! Mrs. Pilkey cried, arising.

Old Mrs. Pilkey clicked her false teeth:

—Just like his father and his grandfather before him! They're all Adams with a few shots in their bellies. ...

Mr. Pilkey advanced on Miss Betty Blanchard, his pumps sloshing with the mess from the hors d'oeuvre tray. He made her a courtly and intoxicated bow:

—My pretty duck, may I have the next one? And the next and the next and the next? ...

The eyes behind the old man's glasses were cunning now, with a more brutal cunning than he even used on his teachers. Miss Blanchard got to her feet. In her long velvet gown, half drunk, she had a melting imperiousness about her. She set down her cocktail glass:

—Don't touch me! You ought to see yourself! You're like a door-to-door swill collector. ...

—That's telling him! Old Mrs. Pilkey cackled.

—Young woman! cried the Principal's wife, rising too. Discharge her at once, dearie!

—I'll discharge her! the Principal cried, licking his lips. I'll discharge a duty on her! Come here, minxie-minxie! ...

And he caught the girl's hand in his own great white one and swept her greedily to his breast.

318

—That's my pop! Herman Pilkey said from somewhere.

The Principal groped mistily for Miss Blanchard's mouth. She set up one shattering scream that caused Guy Hudson to jump up and walk forward, his fists tight. Herman Pilkey barred his way, staggering in the Marine uniform.

—O, the army's gettin tough, hey?

—Almost as tough as the gyrenes. . . .

And he slapped the Principal's son across the mouth with a dull crack. He felt Herman's buck teeth against his palm. Then the fat figure staggered to a couch, where he lay down in Nydia Pilkey's lap, blubbering.

—Hon-ey! Did a big bad man's get tough with oo? . . .

Betty Blanchard got free of Mr. Pilkey. She kicked her long skirts out of the way and raced for the door of the living room. She was moaning to herself.

—My house! mourned Mrs. Launcelot Miller, picking up a piece of shrimp here and there.

Catcalling, everyone watched Betty Blanchard fight her way over sprawled bodies into the study, snatch up her cara-cul coat, and dash out into the raw drizzle of the March evening.

—What a poor sport, Miss Demerjian said loftily.

—Think so? Guy Hudson said.

—No place for nerrrvousness at this party!

The Principal was bumbling about now, lifting up the chins of ladies and searching them passionately:

—Where is she? Where's my little lotus flower?

—Sit down and contemplate your navel, Guy Hudson said. Good night to all of you. . . .

Then he too ran for the study and put on his combat jacket and green hat and raced out into the evening. He told himself that he was chasing for her, not after her. The damp air hit his chest, bringing out the final madness of the drinks he'd had. A hoop of panting enclosed his ribs. And a voice inside him said as he ran: What are you doing? Posing as a protector of a lady's virtue? Ha-ha. He caught sight of her through the light rain and fog. She was clambering up a snowbank and sobbing. Her fur coat was open, her hair a delta of ink on the night. On the downside of a melting drift she slipped and fell. He caught up with her, bent down, and pulled her to her feet. Her eyes were closed, as children pretend not to see an unpleasant sight. She was soaking wet;

there were brilliants of snow and rain on her long black lashes.

—My dear, he said. Can it be that you aren't as self-contained as you pretended? . . .

He chafed her wrists and wiped the snow from her face and hair. Her gardenia was powdered with the filthy white of old snow. And oddest of all, her slow tears stirred instead of irritating him.

—Let me alone.

It was because her crying was like ripping. Other women blubbered.

—Walk along with me, he said. Call me your Saint George.

He was delighted with himself for being so pompous. They staggered together through the slush and melting snow-drifts of a March night. It was like being lost on a polar ice field. Sometimes she reeled against him, swiftly retracting her body when it touched his. He sneered with his damaged lips. What was the difference between this and helping a drunken French whore home from a bistro?

—I'm pretty tight, she said. And crazy too, I think. Can you get me a taxi?

—So far as I know, there isn't one within fifteen miles.

—Go back to that horrible party, please. I'll get over to the Girls' School somehow. . . .

She began to laugh and hiccough. They stumbled out of the snow and muck onto the quadrangle of the Boys' School.

—I'm not leaving you, he said. And stop entertaining that pleasurable sense of panic. . . .

—What really causes me panic, she said, hiccoughing again, is that I'm not afraid of you. I always thought I would be. . . .

—Why, how interesting, he said dully.

Her glove was dangling in the crook of his arm. He felt idiotically thrilled. For he was feeling protective and compassionate toward her. Only with his friend the French boy Marcel Bonne had he ever known this yearning in the pit of his stomach. Instinctively, as when he walked with Marcel, he took her hand and idly, calmly, stroked her gloved fingers.

—Don't, she said almost inaudibly.

—Well, not if you don't wish it. I wouldn't do anything you don't want. It's strange, but I have a horror of hurting you.

She paused in the snow and looked at him. Her brilliant eyes didn't quite focus. He saw that she was fighting for a balance between laughter and tears. Something was sweeping them into confidence, an armed truce:

—Stranger still, I almost believe you. . . .

Then, as though she'd reconsidered, she gave him her arm and they went on. Both their faces were crystaled with the light rain. He led her to the door of that dormitory where he lived; a single light burnt in the entry to which he'd expected to return drunken and solitary.

—No, she said, pausing again. Goodnight. Everything's going too fast for me. . . .

—You can't go away soaking wet like this. . . . Come up and dry off. . . .

She tightened the collar of her caracul coat and took a stance he'd seen many times before. She murmured waveringly:

—What do you take me for?

—A damned fool. I know what's in your mind.

Then he swept up her figure into his arms; she was most unlike a dead weight, for she was almost as light as a bubble. He kicked open the entry door with those stout combat boots he'd buckled on against the March weather and carried her into the corridor. Through this passageway six hours ago had passed little lowerformers on their way home to vacation. They'd never have imagined that now their mentor was carrying the limp figure of a girl. It was something out of Gothic romance.

—Please put me down, Mister Hudson. . . .

—It's you who are being corny.

Nevertheless he let her pumps touch the stone floor, and in her drenched evening gown she climbed the stairs in front of him. The rain and snow glinted on her fur coat like dew on the pelt of shy deer. She was holding up her skirt and walking quite steadily now.

—I'm mad, she said in a low voice.

—Probably. But I don't see that it makes much difference. Madness or pneumonia. Pay your money and take your choice. . . .

At the third landing she hesitated again; he saw the desire for flight pounding around her temples. He kicked open a door for the second time:

321

—We teachers boast that we're reasonable people. Do I have to pick you up again?

She appeared deciding on whether to cry:

—You'll never remind me of tonight?

—Never without your permission. . . .

She entered his one chamber. He lit some lamps. He noticed how a certain prurience in her mind, which he believed to be a reflex in all women, made her edge away from his narrow bed, covered with a taut slip of cobalt blue and ridiculous flowers. Then he helped her off with her coat. Even as her arms were sliding out of the sleeves, Betty Blanchard stiffened like a scarecrow. Guy Hudson followed the track of her eyes; she'd caught sight of the obscene etching on his mantelpiece under the crossed sabers. And he regretted somehow that he'd put it there when he left for the cocktail party.

—My art, he said lamely.

—The harm is done now, she said lowering her eyes and sitting in his favorite chair in her bedraggled velvet finery.

—Goddam it, *what* harm?

He left her and busied himself with tindering and lighting the dry logs stacked in the fireplace behind the screen. Presently under his ministrations a tongue of smoke licked out, blew into a blaze, and cast a golden halo round the electric lights. The fire softened even the lines of the pornographic etching. She continued to stare at this picture as though she was mesmerized in her chair. She looked like a beautiful withdrawn paranoiac in a medical journal. From where he crouched supervising his fire he looked over his shoulder and spoke harshly to her:

—Well, when you're through with Madame Tussaud, take off your clothes and get into the shower down the hall. . . .

She darted up at once, like a queen summoned to her execution.

—For God's sake stop acting Edwardian! . . . I'll get out of the room. You'll find a towel, slippers, soap, and bathrobe in my closet there. . . .

And he went gruffly downstairs to the second landing Common Room for lowerformers and lit a cigarette. In this room, where little boys were served hot chocolate and read football stories on Saturday evenings by order of Mr. Pilkey, hung Academy pennants and plaques of rich and famous

322

alumni. He sat in a chair and listened hard. He heard Betty Blanchard upstairs go into the boys' showers. He heard the water swish on. It was possibly the first time in the history of The Academy that a lovely girl had taken a bath there. He sat smoking viciously and clutching his knees. Often before he'd waited impatiently in a bedroom and listened to a woman douching herself. But for the first time this woman was one he really wanted. His desire for her was cold and rational, though he was capable of enormous passion. It was a need of body and soul this time. For Guy Hudson was in love with this tense girl. And he could have her only if she wanted him to. He sat and smoked and thought. It had never been like this before. Instead of wanting to taste her for a night, he knew, almost with amused horror, that he wanted to give her everything of himself and everything he owned. He wanted to put his queer bitter heart in the palm of his hand and say: Here, Blanchard, take it for keeps. He was ill with a tight unmessy core of desire. It was a sensation altogether new.

He mashed out his cigarette and ran noisily up the stairs to his room, which betrayed her recent presence by its honey-eyed dampness. Her clothes, as he expected, were lying on his bed in a prissy semblance of orderliness. He stretched a cord from his bed to the firescreen and hung all her garments on it, sneering to himself at the housewifely motherliness of his action. Then he noticed that she'd turned his German etching to the wall. He turned it around again, and found that it shocked him for the first time. And he guessed that this was because he was having his first intimations of the difference between love and raw sex. He got out his cheap pot and electric plate and began to make coffee. As the brew began to bubble, there was a knock on his door. If it was any of the drunken faculty, he meant to thrash them with his sabers.

—No ceremony! he called out.

Betty Blanchard came shyly in. She was a riotous combination of Diana and a circus queen in his bathrobe and slippers. Her hair was enclosed in a turban she'd wound of his bath towel. And her face, now that the makeup had been washed off was a figurine of pure marble. She was even lovelier unbedizened. She clutched the twill robe loosely

323

about her, so that none of the tight marvel of her body was apparent.

—Your bathrobe smells of you, she said.

She didn't look at him, but sat down primly in his chair.

—How's that?

—O . . . like grass and tobacco and soap . . . what my mother called the Man-Smell. She hated it.

—That's too bad for your mother.

He poured steaming black coffee into two cups, the only ones he owned, bought at a five-and-ten. She picked up hers; he was entranced the way her nostrils flickered over the vapor. Never before had he been delighted by details of a woman's actions; only a cardinal point in their bodies had been his focus and his aim. Then she noticed her drying garments and began to laugh. It wasn't anything like her clucking schoolmistress laughs. There was something of wildness in it.

—That sounds good. Things are looking up. . . .

—I was thinking what a good wife you'd make some man. . . .

—I was much in demand in the army, he said with stage modesty.

As she blushed at this, a wave of pink rosied her pale fine features.

—I've always felt that you think of sex most of the time. . . .

—Don't you . . . sometimes? he said gently.

The necessity for her to answer was obviated by tilting her head to swallow her coffee. She did it with such maddening grace that, had she been anyone else, he'd have rushed upon her then and there. Instead he simply closed his fists and said:

—I'm not what you American women, with your false delicacy, would call a *good* man. But I try to be honest with myself and others.

—Some of that is true, I guess. . . .

He sat on a scatter rug by his coffee cup, drawing up his legs in their loose dungarees. He stared at the fire, for he knew she was regarding the back of his head in the flickering intensity with which a mouse assesses an unaware cat.

—I wish you'd trust me, he said. If nothing else, we could

324

be friends, good friends. You need someone badly, you know. . . .

There it was. He said unembarrassedly to her things he'd shrunk from with all others. Ideas came to him from deep inside, words often used softly in betrayal and seduction. But with her they were wrenched out of him, and they had a tense reality and truth all their own. . . .

—Yes, I do, she said.

There was a silence, and she stirred in his deep chair:

—When do you think my things will be dry?

—Soon. . . .

Then it came tumbling out and he didn't give a damn how she took it:

—Look . . . lie down on my bed for a while and rest. . . . You might even take a nap. . . .

—Mister Hudson. . . .

—For God's sake, Miss Blanchard! You look so much like a boy now that I'm tempted to beat you up. . . . Didn't I give you my word?

—You didn't say Honor Bright. . . .

—I say it now.

He believed himself. She lay down, small and shivering a little, on his cot. He covered her with an army blanket. Her eyes flickered toward the ceiling, piteous little points of light from the blazing fire. He shook with a desire to tear open his bathrobe and nip her shoulders, crying crazy things.

—Don't look at me that way, a small voice said from his cot.

—No, he said nastily, I shan't even stay in the room with you. Call me Galahad. Recite Tennyson. You've made me just as filthy minded as you bourgeois women. . . .

He tried not to slam the door and went again downstairs to the Common Room. He lay down on a divan, crossed his combat boots, and smoked a cigarette in the dark, with the swish of rain outside. For he was fighting an impulse to go back to his room, lie down beside her, and force her to his will. But that would be a sort of murder of something newly come to birth within him. He had no thought of saying Well, So Long, to her tomorrow. He now wished to solve with her help something rich that had appeared in his barren life. It was a problem not to be solved by the bottle or by a one-night stand. He groaned at the physical tension between his loins:

—I'm almost thirty. I'm in love. It has made me into a little girl solicitous of her doll. I'm retreating from reality. God, God, God! . . .

And finally he fell into a tossing sleep on the couch, which was too cramping for his length. In this slumber he revisited his mother's womb for the last time, to sink there his longing and his bitterness. It was the end of a long-enduring and somewhat vindictive boyhood.

He awoke. His watch said three o'clock. The moon on the melting snow had passed into her phase before dawn. Outside there was a continual dripping and a movement, as of spring. He was amazed he wasn't in his own cot. He jumped up, stiff and matted from snoring in his clothes. Then he clapped his temple and remembered. Surely she'd be gone by now, stolen away, and he having made himself the bleating fool in her eyes. Two at a time he ran up the stairs to his room. He opened his door. In the moonlight he saw that Betty was still asleep. His grand bonfire was only embers now, but the moonlight made a diagonal strip on the head of his poor cot. His bathrobe had fallen open from her; one hand was under her escaping hair, blackly alive on his pillow. With her relaxed and childlike breathing her breasts rose and fell. He felt like a tending gardener of sweet flesh. He watched her asleep for a long time, savoring the tense rising miracle of his desire. Then he took her hand. She started up as though she'd been pretending to sleep.

—My Betty. . . .

He knelt down on the floor, his red hair against her bathrobe. He was running his tongue over the deformity of his lips. She lay rigid, but she didn't move away. For what seemed ages he knelt there, feeling their spirits fighting each other. In their slight contact there was some mingling, but much warfare of their bloods. Then he laid a hand on her bare shoulder and opened the bathrobe all the way down. She began to cry very softly.

—It's necessary, he said in her ear. Necessary for both of us, my dearest girl. . . .

He waited another age, in which he could feel his own pulse pounding in the fingers that grazed her cool shoulder.

326

Then he laid his face under her breasts in the moving valley of her belly. And she spoke through her calm hopeless weeping:

—I'm afraid. . . .

—But only for a little while, he said softly. And isn't that better than being afraid all your life? And you'd never know quite what you were afraid of. . . .

—But I'm a woman, she said, sounding miles away, for he heard her voice through the sheathing of her ribs.

—You are. But not *quite* a woman. . . . O Betty. . . .

—Why do we have to go through with this? Why couldn't there be another way? I wish I'd never been born. . . .

The sweetness in which he whispered to her was at variance with a madness that was creeping up on him:

—That's because you haven't begun to live yet. And the stars and fate and I and everything else good in this world say you should begin. . . . Now, Betty. . . . now. . . .

She gave an intense soft cry, like a bird bereft of her young. And he became demented after long hours of repression and conscience. He was over the precipice of mortal flesh. He became an executioner, an avenging icepick against virgin ice. Crying aloud murderous and ravaging things, he reduced her beneath his hands and his lunging body to what she essentially was, to what she had come into the world to be. He drew her on like a glove. He took out on her whimpering shell all the little meannesses with which she had piqued him. This first time, he knew, he couldn't be tender or solicitous. At another time he'd have loathed himself and called himself a butcher. But now the need of penetrating her was too strong; he was rampant and boiling, and the ferocity of this first time annihilated whatever gentleness and wooing would come later. She screamed aloud in her agony:

—Won't you even kiss me, you devil? Kiss me, for the love of God! . . . No, no, not *there*! Dear God! Kiss me on the mouth!

He shouted her down in fierceness and hate:

—No, not this time, you whore! Later, Betty, later! But not now! . . .

And in the moment when everything was sucked out of his bowels, he gave one bellowing shout and crashed forward on his elbows:

—This is *me*! *Me*, you whore! . . . O, Jesus! . . .

She gave a final scream, which broke off into a long low sobbing. He knelt up and looked at her in the moonlight. She was broken, slaughtered, as she lay on the white sheet that was smeared with her blood. And he too began to cry, the hard rending sobs of a grown man:

—Betty . . . Betty. . . .

At last she spoke, far away from him:

—I . . . have never felt such pain. And it's you who caused it. . . .

—Don't ever forget that, he blubbered. It was my way of killing you. And now, Betty, you'll live. . . .

He lay a little distant from her, his hand on her shoulder, listening to the weeping of both of them. Hers had a new and burgeoning note—no longer the fretfulness of a violated girl.

At last he fell asleep and slept till the sun stood outside his window. She was regarding him with unblinking eyes.

—I watched you sleep, she said. And I found out who is really victorious. It was *I*. . . .

And she laughed a low laugh he'd never heard from her before.

—I wonder, she said, if it would be all right for you to kiss me now? . . .

He put his arms around her neck and pushed his face past her shoulder, as though he was contemplating something on the pillow. Then he put his spoiled mouth on hers. It was their first kiss, and it came after he'd despoiled her. But it was all right now.

—Guy, she said in his ear, I'm going to say something that would have horrified me yesterday. . . .

—What, my darling?

—I . . . want you to take me again. The sickness and the pain are all gone now. . . . Forever, I guess. . . .

And turning to her, as tender as before he'd been devilish, he taught her what love is like. She was indeed reborn. She joined him in all delights, surpassing him in invention and sensuality. Finally he was exhausted and lay weak and laughing beside her. For her mouth had said wild words he'd never expected to hear from her, and their excitement and climaxes were dual now.

—O you men, you men! Betty Blanchard said in magnificent scorn, stroking his red curly hair, and the cleft in his chin.

—That's the answer, darling, he whispered, and you've learned it all too fast. . . .

Then he fell asleep again. She arose in his dressing gown. An access of domesticity was upon her. She made coffee and toast, ransacking his larder and making little disapproving sounds over the messy manner in which he lived. Then she sat down and in the morning sunlight looked at him sprawled alone on the cot. She laughed at the crimson splashes on the sheet. His red hair was tangled from her fingers; his long muscular legs spread like a caliper. He was a cruel and sensitive little boy. And now she pitied him in an odd detachment. She knew that henceforth he'd be always at her mercy, unless she hurt or debased what he'd given to her. She sensed it was meant for herself alone. In one night nonsense and pretense had been burned out of her. In their place was a new surety such as even *he* would never attain to without her help. She kissed her hands to the sleeper and went to waken him for his breakfast.

—The snow's melting at last, she said.

She guessed it must be so too over by Miss Sophia's grave.

IV

The Book
of
Spring

1

By the first days of April waddings of snow melted away from the grave of Miss Sophia. A mealy slush befouled the ground, later to be dried by a cold winking sun. Once again children passed through the churchyard on their way to school; once again a tiny sexton bobbed out of the door of the meetinghouse with his broom, like a cuckoo excommunicated from a clock. In these first days of spring, mornings were leakily sunny, afternoons rainy with a warm tearful shower. About these new days of April there was something intimately sad, as though the New Year entertained regrets and doubts about his birth.

In swampy flats by the slow river cows once again stepped out to pasture. The air was sweetly fetid with their dung, and mellow with the music of their mooings. Sometimes they climbed to the barbed wire along the river edge of the graveyard and gazed with their melancholy eyes at the headstone where Miss Sophia lay. Flossie and Brownie and Melissa, munching on the wet new grass, stared at the graveyard and meditated appropriately. Soon their udders would yield milk to the tables of The Academy's dining hall. It could carry the first poignant taste of spring.

From farms that surrounded The Academy came a lowing of kine and of bulls testing their new bullhood against the spring. When the Boys' School entered its last session, students on fragrant afternoons would pilgrimage to convenient barns and comment on the prowess of Old Nickie, as, ring in nose, he inseminated chosen heifers. And the crowing of cocks that had been blanketed all winter long by the snow now trumpeted forth every morning, for barnyards are as susceptible to spring as children, or the poor in spirit. From below the damp earth came sounds of icy freshets thawing out, a bleating of new calves, a scampering through the grass.

Earth was opening her eyes and her arms once more after a hibernation of six months.

At the close of the Winter Term (and after the disasters of the cocktail party of Mrs. Launcelot Miller) Mrs. Mears and her daughter Midgie entrained for Miami. The Directress of the Girls' School had mild fun in Florida pretending she was the widow of a brigadier general (killed in the Pacific, my dear!). She was so busy talking to other ladies in the fabulous hotel that she didn't notice how often Midgie was slipping out nights. In Miami the pageboy-bobbed President of the Student Council met a young actor who claimed to be a protégé of Ethel Barrymore. Midgie and her actor danced and got drunk nightly by lagoons, and soon they were engaged. The young man was somewhat effeminate and sibilant, but Midgie was delighted to be wooed by Someone in the Theater. Mrs. Mears gave a tea for her daughter's fiancé at the Roney-Plaza, for that was the way engagements were signalized in *her* girlhood. When she got a good look at Adrian, she upset the cream pitcher and said she was nerrrvous. So Midgie was whisked north on the next train—unwed. Perfumed letters from Adrian would arrive at the Girls' School for some time to come. Mrs. Mears steamed them open before they fell into her daughter's hand. Adrian begged for money. Henceforth—if her mother had anything to say about it—Midgie would confine her sirening to approved candidates at the Boys' School.

The Pilkeys too passed a sad spring vacation. At Mrs. Launcelot Miller's, after the departure of Miss Betty Blanchard in a huff, the Principal got drunk with fine old rum he doted on. Next morning he awoke to a hangover, and that afternoon he had a stroke. His whole left side was paralyzed, but the school doctor saw no reason why with rest he shouldn't recover full use of his faculties. He lay all vacation upstairs in his Cape Cod house, tended by old Mrs. Pilkey, by his wife, by the Negress Florinda, and by two trained nurses from The Academy's infirmary. Miss O'Mara told Miss Houlihan that as a patient the Principal was a bigger baby than any of his boys. On Mr. Pilkey's counterpane were thousands of letters of regret and get-well-quick cards from parents, alumni, and the Governors of six states.

Mr. Philbrick Grimes had himself a shuttlecock vacation, as he later described it in the spring salons of Mrs. Dell Holly. He'd planned to pass the two weeks chez Mother

Grimes in Baltimore. With the Principal's stroke Mr. Grimes had to fly every other day from Baltimore to The Academy, to see if there was anything he could do for those poor Pilkeys. He finished by spending most of his spring vacation on the quadrangle, holding the trembling hand of the Principal's wife and transcribing for the Alumni Bulletin stately memoirs of the Principal. Even Miss Pringle (who came nicely out of her epileptic fit at the Millers') wasn't allowed in her boss's bedroom, out of consideration for her modesty. So Mr. Grimes did most of the secretarial work of the Academy. Thereby he learned a few things he hadn't known before.

—I'll see that you lose nothing by giving up your vacation, my boy, Mr. Pilkey promised from his bed.

There was a grave impediment now in the old Principal's speech; all day long he tentatively flexed his left hand, which was as flabby as a doll's.

Upon the striking-down of their Principal, the trustees (without the presence of Judge Hopkins V) held a special emergency meeting. They named as acting co-Principals (for the duration of Mr. Pilkey's illness) the Messrs. Dell Holly and Philbrick Grimes. They voted that Herman Pilkey was still too young administratively to step into the shoes of his bedridden father. Lisa Holly's delight was unalloyed. She politely but fervently hoped that Mr. Pilkey would croak by summertime. Then there would be a contest between her husband and Mr. Grimes for the Principalship of the Academy. And Philbrick, poor dear, was unmarried. But two desks were installed in The Den where Mr. Pilkey had reigned undisputed. There sat Mr. Grimes and Mr. Holly, politely glaring at each other and fighting in nasty delicacy over just how the school was to be run and over questions of protocol and curriculum.

Nydia Pilkey was perturbed over the freezing-out of her lover-man, who, as the Principal's son, was logical successor to his chair. Her Georgian accent turned rancid, and she gave birth to her second son prematurely on the second of April without so much as a hon-ey for the obstetrician. Herman went on a bat the night his second boy (christened Hooker) was born, and he didn't show up at The Academy till four days after the spring term was underway.

During this vacation too Doctor Sour, who was trying to wangle into the State Department through his intimacy with European languages, ended up only in the dossiers of the

FBI. He got drunk in Washington while he was there for interview and picked up two sailors, who were not so compliant as his boys at The Academy. Next morning his plump unconscious form was found in the slush of Constitution Avenue, near G Building. Some of his ribs were broken, and his nose smashed. His false teeth were missing. Mr. Grimes eventually heard of these disgraceful circumstances, said several tsk's, and decided that Doctor Sour would have to *go*. The Hollys agreed over their sherry.

And Mr. Guy Hudson of the history department spent his vacation in New York, as he'd planned—but not alone. He was never drunk now, as becomes a despairing war veteran in a country rearming. He was serious and solicitous, as befits a man in love, but always with his sense of humor. For with him at all times was a handsome black-haired girl in a caracul coat. Her name was Betty Blanchard, but during their stay at Tudor City she and her lover registered as Mr. and Mrs. Charles Francis Ames. From a hard precision in their manner, from a removal from the acquisitive life, sharp desk clerks at the hotel guessed that the Ameses were a pair of schoolteachers on their honeymoon. The two spent much time in their little suite, where the handsome girl prepared spicy dishes. Every evening the redheaded young man with the distorted mouth took her to the theater. Then the bell captain and elevator boy would see them return about midnight, glowing with pleasure, carrying a bottle of something to drink in their room. They were oblivious of the whole city. It was the gayest and deepest ten days that Guy Hudson and Betty Blanchard had ever known in either of their lives. Every night till late in the morning these Ameses lay in each other's arms, never using both twin beds. They loved, amused, and consoled each other—which is about all that two lovers can do. And the girl whose alias was Mrs. Ames would sometimes look at herself in the mirror while Mr. Ames was in the shower:

—Blanchard, at twenty-five, you've suddenly burst into bloom....

Or sometimes he who was registered as her husband would say:

—Betty, let's go to the theater tonight. We've got all of thirty dollars left.

—Shall I be with you, Guy? she would ask.

And he'd laugh and scrape his scarred mouth across her

petally neck. He taught her all the ways of love he'd learned in Europe. And she responded fiercely. His tongue and mouth on her body had drawn her to him far more closely than most men know how to hold their mistresses.

Again, students of the Boys' and Girls' Schools spent their free two weeks in fashions no less varied than their teachers. Some few holed themselves up with books or parents. Others sampled the last skiing of the winter. But most experimented with life wildly or cautiously, as they had done at Christmastime. All this while their mentor and apostle lay at home in bed, never guessing what his released boys and girls might be up to. Indeed for once Mr. Pilkey didn't much care what happened to his boys and girls. His own health was of paramount concern to him. He made the infirmary nurses bring him medical books, from which he studied and doped out his own case. He told Miss O'Mara he'd have made an A-1 surgeon if he hadn't taken up schoolkeeping.

In Chicago Buddy Brown and a chum got drunk on the evening of the twenty-eighth of March. They borrowed Mr. Brown's Cadillac and somehow managed to kill a slum child crossing a black windy avenue. But Mr. Marlow Brown, by contributing eight thousand dollars to Police charities from the capital of the Unitex Plastic Corporation, managed to keep his son out of jail on a manslaughter charge. A smart corporation lawyer proved that the dead child came from an unscrupulous family who made their living throwing themselves under the automobiles of the rich and suing for damages. So Buddy was able to return for his final term at The Academy—a little paler, a little shaken, but firmer in the knowledge that his pop could move the world. Cynthia Brown got wind of the accident and engaged herself a more expensive analyst.

Howard West Lothrop (The Body) and Demaree Walter Montgomery (Mung) flew to Alabama for the warm dry spring. There they tampered enthusiatically with Negresses and gin. On the streets of Birmingham The Body was moved to beat up a Negro who didn't know his place. But Mung, gentle even when he was drunk, managed to spirit his blond friend away to the home of his father, the aggressive cottonbroker.

The Abbot and The Abbess stayed with The Abbot's aunt in her suite at Hampshire House. When the aunt was out having seances with her Park Avenue friends, there was a continual little cortege of callers entertained by the two boys: ballet dancers, Y instructors, Marines. Through the corridor of the ninth floor of Hampshire House roared the strains of a Capehart phonograph which solaced The Abbot's aunt during her headaches. It played Ravel and William Walton. Finally even bellboys, waiters, and elevator operators came to the enlarged New York salon of The Abbot and The Abbess. Famous actors and chorus boys strutted their stuff. That spring there was little labor trouble at Hampshire House, for there was always a sound of jumping and gurgling and tittering on the ninth floor. The aunt, Mrs. Van Vleck, found out one night what was going on, and retired to an expensive sanatorium.

Or in Detroit a Negro boy went to visit his friend the high-yaller cabaret dancer Rita Christmas. She had as warm a welcome for him as ever. But near the end of his vacation Tad discovered that she'd made a little contribution to his physical wellbeing, which necessitated his taking shots for twenty-four hours at a free clinic. He pretended to be a penniless chauffeur. It was a difficult pose, what with his imperious bearing and suave accent. And his father was the best doctor in town; his mother owned a dress shop patronized by blazing Negresses. This vacation was the last time in his life that the boy ever wept. He never told even his friend Ralph of his little encounter with disease in Detroit.

And near Cape Hatteras Ralph found himself a job in a little stonecutting place owned by first generation Italians from Cremona. All day long his brown hands chipped at little fauns intended as the rock garden statuary or memorials of sentimental rich people. He chiseled at the wings of little angels, at the veil of Saint Thérèse of Lisieux letting fall a shower of roses on her Carmelite convent, at Neapolitan San Gennaro holding the vial of his liquefying blood. Mother Du Bouchet was well pleased that her mysterious and beautiful boy was picking up a little extra money. And Father Du Bouchet told other unsuccessful painters over his vin ordinaire that Ralph had matured without going bourgeois or businesslike. Two days before he returned to The Academy Ralph played the Lalo *Symphonie Espagnole* with an orchestra of amateurs in a nearby city proud of its cultural renascence. The critics said that at eighteen he was already a great artist. His fiddle under his arm, Ralph bowed gravely

338

to his audience; he was wearing a borrowed white tie and tails. The evening of his triumph a party was given for him by a dowager patroness of the sinfonietta. He spent the night at her villa. As he slept, there came to his bedside her daughter Babs. She wore the feather cut of a bright young woman. She was a senior at Bennington, interested, she said, in the incidence of silicosis as an occupational disease. She undressed and crept into his bed, murmuring that his aloofness had destroyed all her inhibitions. She took him into her arms, and her manner in heat was different from the embraces of Mrs. Miekewicz at The Academy. That night under the admonitions of her excited hands and quotations from Eliot and Rimbaud, Ralph passed forever out of his boyhood. She shattered the ties that bound him to his mother, to the ambivalence of his feeling for Guy Hudson. Ralph didn't particularly enjoy his baptism, for he was indifferent to Babs and her modern medievalism. But he went through with it. She said he was Marvelous Bed. Next morning at breakfast, over cherried grapefruit and pancakes with crisp bacon, his hostess looked suspiciously at him. For her daughter kept insisting that Ralph was much more than just a fine violinist—much, much more. . . .

Ben Gordon, and his roommate Bill Hunnicutt, who was forever giggling and being athletic, had themselves a real man's vacation. Father Isidore Gordon brought them a jalopy, and they drove on a sightseeing trip through the South. They stopped with becoming reverence to inspect Monticello and Mount Vernon and Black Mountain and Charleston and Asheville and Atlanta. It was a canoeing trip on wheels. They had plenty of money, and they were perhaps the only two who took Mr. Pilkey's advice in his termend letters that students should have clean restful fun. Along their route waitresses and policemen all agreed that the two were perfectly swell American boys. By the side of the road where there was a sandlot Bill Hunnicutt had to have the car stopped so he could get into a pickup game of baseball. He visited a southern training camp, his clear eyes pools of glee. Ben did most of the driving in his usual warm silence. . . .

The Academy opened for the Spring Term on the fifth of April at five o'clock in the afternoon. Mr. Pilkey still lay in his bedroom of the Cape Cod house, clenching and unclenching his useless left hand. It was the first opening of term in twenty-five years that he hadn't attended. When a bell in an Academy tower struck five, the old gentleman began to cry into his pillow. His wife heard him, for she sat near his bed painting on china which would be offered to all alumni at $10 the plate as the Pilkey Memorial Table Service:

—My dear, my dear! They can get along without you just this *once!* . . .

—No man is indispensable! cried Old Mrs. Pilkey brutally.

The wife rallied before the mummified mother:

—How can you say that, you dreadful old woman! You haven't had a human sentiment since your seventieth birthday. . . .

—Which is just your age now, dearie! the crone railed triumphantly.

Mr. Pilkey turned away from his two warring ladies and continued to dampen his pillow, his shoulders shaking. He felt like Moses dying—but there was no Lord to show him a Promised Land.

In their delightful new functions as Acting Co-Principals Mr. Philbrick Grimes and Mr. Dell Holly decided to do away with the rite of handshaking by The Den. It was so old-school-tie-ish. Since they'd once been minions here, they knew how students and faculties hated to shake hands with the Principal on the opening of a new term.

—We will give a tea, Mr. Grimes said. In my suite. Won't that be much cosier?

—But your apartment is up *two* flights of stairs, Philbrick, Lisa Holly said sweetly.

She won. Welcome Home was held in the apartment of the Hollys. Mrs. Dell Holly forgot her sleepwalking glide and flew around making preparations. It was a foretaste of what her life would be like as wife of the next Principal if she played her cards right. So she worked all afternoon on a monster tea (to be financed by the Comptroller). All returning students of both schools would be treated to a warm cup and a friendly handshake. But Mr. Grimes still had an ear to the ground and reminded her tartly:

—You know perfectly well, my dear, how The Head would frown on coffee and sherry for the faculties. . . .

Lisa Holly and Mr. Grimes weren't so close as they used

to be. She smiled at him in a superior way and smoothed her rose tea gown:

—Darling, don't be a schmoe! We'll serve coffee and sherry to the faculties of the Boys' and Girls' Schools. It will put them on our side right at the outset. . . . And as for the Head knowing or caring, he's lying in his house half-paralyzed and with one foot in the cemetery. Never forget that, darling. . . .

Mr. Grimes was horrified, but he fell in with the Hollys' plan. He knew how ill the Principal was. But he also knew that he would never be Head of this school unmarried. Therefore the Hollys were one up on him, and he was in considerable controlled agitation. All vacation long he'd schemed on how to effect a mariage de convenance. . . .

Thus in the Common Room of Sophia Hall there was re-enacted the old ceremony of opening school—but with a difference. Returning students now had to shake hands with *two* people. Mr. Grimes knew a thing or two about acting; he had little difficulty in upstaging the Hollys in the reception line.

—Our Mister Grimes, said Lisa Holly secretly to her husband, has all the earmarks of a gangster. Intellectually, I mean. . . .

And when Miss Blanchard arrived at the tea, Mr. Grimes went out of his way to woo her. He was astonished. The girl on whom he'd now set his heart had miraculously altered during vacation. He was frightened by her radiance. She had (as the poets say) roses in her cheeks. He took her hand fussily:

—Hello, my dear. Of course you've heard I'm acting Principal now? You'd better be nice to me or else. . . .

He affected a satire on a nickelodeon villain. But for once he felt it wasn't coming off.

—I know all that, Mr. Grimes.

—May I call you up some evening? Who knows? Perhaps we might go to the city for thick steaks and Old Fashioneds. I have a pitiful little Packard, you know. . . .

—Don't, please, Mr. Grimes. I don't think I care to go out with you. . . .

He turned parakeet yellow. He hadn't tasted such chagrin in fifteen years. What had happened to this girl? Didn't she want to be the wife of the next Principal? He felt so liverish and on edge that he felt justified in being a *mite* high-handed with Guy Hudson:

—Doctor, take a tip from an old friend. Did you look around this vacation for a new job? You should, you know.

Guy Hudson looked down on him as though he really wasn't there:

—What did the woodpecker say to the telephone pole? . . .

Mr. Grimes nearly fainted at such arrogance. And Hudson also looked wonderfully well and content. Didn't even mind losing his job! Mr. Grimes wondered if there was any way to dismiss a teacher under contract, even before the end of the scholastic year. He'd talk with Mr. Pilkey. . . .

Finally five hundred students went away after tasting a dish of tea with their new twin Principals. But the faculties lingered on, drinking coffee and sherry, and savoring the wild license of this departure from the old Pilkey Puritanism.

—Best party yet! cried Mrs. Launcelot Miller.

She lit her corncob pipe, for she was thinking that, now the Hollys and Mr. Grimes were in absolute ascendancy here, she'd have to do more entertaining, or else sink out of sight.

But they were caught with their pants down. When they were washing up five hundred teacups, and the Hollys and Mr. Grimes were congratulating one another on their new triumvirate (each with mental reservations), Mrs. Pilkey came limping into the kitchen on her varicose veins. She looked like an old sorceress. She pointed over her shoulder in the general direction of the Cape Cod house, and she trembled with an old woman's rage:

—I . . . don't think he'd like what you three have been doing . . . at all. Of course I shan't tell him, for he's too sick. It might kill him. . . . But . . . I think you three are attempting a Palace Revolution.

—Sit down and have a cup of tea, Lisa Holly said quickly.

—No, thank you. . . . I just wanted to say that it takes a long time to find out who one's *real* friends are. . . .

Then the Principal's wife limped away—back to her Cape Cod house, to her painting on chinaware, to her sick titan, and to old Mrs. Pilkey. Mr. Grimes and the Hollys stopped their dishwashing and looked at one another, surprised to find that they were all furiously blushing, like children caught in a flagrant enormity of cookie-stealing.

342

2

The May afternoon swam in a heterogeneous perfume. From his dormer window Guy Hudson could see hundreds of boys lying on the quadrangle, taking sunbaths in the slanting warm light. They lay on their bellies on Academy-issue blankets, wearing shorts and sunglasses. Sometimes a book was propped beneath their elbows, but oftener they called out insults to one another, or wrestled, or played with their yoyos and their water pistols, which were the fad this spring. Sometimes an almost naked foursome sat on one blanket and engaged in what looked from a distance like an innocent hand of Old Maid or whist. The catalog said that gambling was forbidden at The Academy, but Guy Hudson's ear could detect the chink of dice being rolled on these blankets.

And now that the boys exposed their bodies to the spring sunlight, Mrs. Launcelot Miller often went abroad for a constitutional on the quadrangle, wearing slacks and a bandanna, and puffing on her corncob pipe. He watched how she made it a point to sally up to groups of her favorite boys, to admire their muscles. Once he caught her rubbing her recommended brand of suntan oil into the umber shoulders of Ben Gordon. The boys talked politely to her. When she moved out of earshot, Guy Hudson saw that they laughed at her in adolescent mockery.

At five o'clock knots of athletes returning from their sport on the fields ran among the sunbathers. Among them Guy Hudson noticed Tad McKinley sweating and glistening like an avocado in his baseball uniform. This spring Tad had come into his own as pitcher for The Academy nine. Or passing also among the sunbathers was Ralph, slender in his red-fringed track shorts, with The Academy letter on his jersey. But mostly the quadrangle was a sea of reclining bodies soaking up sun, a series of bronzing limbs at many listless angles. Sometimes they were joined by greasy ambiguous little Poles who washed dishes in the dining hall. These would try to share the boys' blankets. Then the bathing gods would freeze up into a Greenland snobbishness: the sons of millionaires would draw snottily away from twenty-one-dollar-a-week pantrymen who tried to share the sunlight with them. Guy Hudson watched all this from his window and smiled to think that the creator of student democracy lay in his bed at the Cape Cod house. Mr. Pilkey desired his faculty to be buddies with the janitors and secretaries. But it was a little too much of a good thing when cleanlimbed boys fraternized with the hired help.

By hook or by crook Guy Hudson got his papers corrected in the afternoon, even though he had to coach the Pequot baseball team. He was finishing them up now, every so often looking out at the pavilion of sunworshippers below him. Then he got dressed slowly. This spring the sloppiness of his clothes had been corrected for an obvious reason. He put on a seersucker jacket and a snapbrimmed hat of Leghorn straw.

He went downstairs and walked out of the quadrangle toward the Girls' School. He swung along the road, a blade of fresh grass in his teeth, whistling Addio al Passato, for Betty had introduced him to *Traviata* on their March honeymoon in New York. Along the edge of the road the first daisies and wild flowers were pushing up their heads. He bent and snapped off the prettiest for a bouquet he brought every evening to the Girls' School. The sun was falling down; the air was sweet and dry. From barns along the valley his nostrils picked up a wavering incense of milking, of straw, of the excreta of farm animals, which on hot afternoons stank up the breeze like a miasma. But today there was little motion in the air; it carried a whiff of new seed and flowers.

As he walked through Miss Sophia's village, he noticed a remembered figure moving ahead of him and gazing into the window of a hardware store. Ralph. He overtook the boy, who gazed at him with pleasant languor:

—I saw you taking the 110 high hurdles this afternoon. . . .

—Was I good? Do I have style? . . . I like to run. I imagine I'm escaping from something. . . .

—From what, for example?

344

Ralph didn't answer. Guy Hudson watched him thoughtfully: Ralph too had changed. He wasn't any longer the indeterminate and delicate boy who'd come to The Academy last fall. The shyness had evaporated, and most of the questioning. Then the boy spoke again, articulating what both were thinking:

—You know, it was sort of wonderful, those days when you and I were friends. . . .

—Can't we continue to be? Guy Hudson asked, chewing on his blade of grass.

—Not the way we used to be. . . . How silly I was about you! I guess I had what my mother would call a crush. But you were silly about me too. . . . I suppose the comedy in being a schoolboy is that the gizmo doesn't see how ludicrous he is to older people. . . .

—Why, you're still a kid, Guy Hudson said stuffily.

—No, I don't think so.

And he gave his teacher one of his sidelong glances from his black lashes. It was roguish and learned. Guy Hudson had seen that expression in dogs preparing to mount, in all arrived males who've broken through the tabus of their childhood. And he understood:

—O, I see. You've finally discovered girls? . . .

Ralph nodded with a hint of his old eager diffidence.

—Good. That's the way it should be. . . .

They came to a greasy sandwich joint. Inside lounged girls from the village high school—a hundred teen-agers listening to a gilded juke box, dancing tentatively, and swilling Cokes. In a circle by themselves (but prowling the girls) a dozen Academy boys were playing the slot machine. Through the window Guy Hudson saw blond Buddy Brown, with his arm around the waist of Ginny Snelgrove, the town pump.

—May I buy you a cheeseburger? Ralph said, pausing at the screen door.

—For old times' sake, you mean? No, thanks. . . .

The dark boy smiled and went into the screaming eatery. Guy Hudson crossed the lazy river, passed Miss Sophia's churchyard, and came to the white buildings of the Girls' School. In the warm dusk of May, Daygirls were hopping into their buses and singing popular songs. Safe in their numbers, they called out yoo-hoos and taunts to him, for they well knew who he was. A fat little girl in bobbysocks bumped into him, and drew back with a coy scream.

—Is Miss Blanchard around? he said gently.

—Well, *you* should ask *me*!

He had no intention of getting tangled up with Mrs. Mears or the other mistresses. He stood by a flowering Japanese cherry tree and looked up at a lighted window on the third floor. Then he tossed a handful of gravel against it. whistling softly his phrase from *Traviata*. Then he retired to the main road to wait, lighting a cigarette. Presently Betty joined him. Out of sight of the seventeenth-century house he pulled her into his arms and kissed her. She fastened his flowers to the lapel of her light spring coat, which rustled against his cheek. Since he knew her so well now, he was a little hurt that she didn't fully respond. She seemed to be communing with herself—a practice he remembered in the cold days before their love.

—Did the mistress of Spanish have one helluva day?

—No, she said, looking at her feet as they walked. No more hellish than usual.

—There's something on your mind. I won't have you reverting to the nun you were once. . . .

She let him hold her hand, but he knew that it was restive in his clasp. They walked back to the village and entered a Lithuanian tavern on an avenue off the main thoroughfare, which by edict of the town fathers was called Sophia Street. No one from The Academy ever came to this restaurant but them. It was out of bounds to all students, and inelegant and beery to the faculty. Only tobacco workers and post-office clerks and butchers from the First National Store came here at sundown to drink beer and lament that soon they must go home to supper and their aproned spreading wives. Or young high school athletes (denied admission to The Academy because of their I Q's) came here to get drunk and fight over the scores made by the baseball team of the American Legion's Twilight League. These wore grimy uniforms paid for by the leading garage in the village, and carried advertising on their backs.

He helped Betty with her light coat. They sat down and ordered steaks and beer. It was the only restaurant in the state with anything like 1939 prices. Then, as was his wont, he tried to take her hand across the table:

—Did anyone ever tell you how beautiful you are?

She withdrew it:

—Guy, this is no operetta. I've got news for you. . . .

Then a letter carrier, pickled on the strong ale of the place, tottered up to their table:

—Gentry, by God! Why don't you people stay where ya belong? Dontcha know this is the wrong side of the tracks?

—We like it here, Guy Hudson said.

—He likes it here! Well, ain't that ducky? . . . Say, best news that ever hit this town is the sickness of Old Pilkey. Every church in town is offerin up prayers for his quick decease. . . .

Guy Hudson was silent. He had no desire to fan the animosity between the town and the school.

—You're all Commies over there, the letter carrier said.

—Then don't bother to associate with dirt like us.

—Jesus, come off ya high horse, perfessah! Who you kiddin?

Then the gray wrinkled government employee turned his bleared attention to Betty Blanchard:

—Saaaay, this is *nice*! . . . and are *you* blind! Why, the little lady's got that same touch-me-not look about the eyes my missus got when she was expectin her first. But she got over it by number two. . . . Jesus! Free love! Communism! . . .

And the letter carrier tottered back to his cronies to talk baseball and the next war. Guy Hudson noticed how his girl had stiffened in her place. He reached forward again to take her hand, but was once more rebuffed. But her eyes were shining in a way different from those times he'd loved her with all the drive of his body and soul.

—Betty! Did you hear what that character said?

—Yes. And did *you*, you stupid, stupid man?

—Betty! For God's sake! Is it true? What delusions I suffer from! And I always thought I was rather clairvoyant. . . .

She said with a lovely weariness that he never completely fathomed:

—Guy, you're like every other teacher in the world . . . in possession of a few facts, which give you a sense of omniscience . . .

—Put me out of my misery. Is it *true*?

—Yes. I've missed two periods. This afternoon I went to a doctor. You'll be a father around Christmastime . . . And don't tell me to have an abortion, because I refuse. . . .

He took a powerful swig of his beer and sat gaping at her.

Then he began to tremble. He who'd always imagined himself aware of all implications now found a new set of them battering at his consciousness.

—Who said anything about an abortion?

—I know you well and love you better than you'll ever know. But . . . well, Guy, I thought that in this instance you might act like a lot of other men I've heard about. . . .

—I . . . I . . . wouldn't. . . .

They ate their steaks and drank their beer with a new sort of silence between them. He fought to make himself master of the facts of a reality he'd often read about. His girl was going to have a child. Swallowing hard the morsels of the rare meat, he saw the true nature of Betty's victory over him. She'd withdrawn from him, as she'd been before he'd first made love to her. But this time the withdrawal was in the interest of their child, which even now was ripening in her fair body. In a sense she'd lost all interest in himself. He'd served his purpose. Now all her deceptive strength was turned inward. She seemed to be listening to herself, to messages from her blood. Suddenly he felt very much alone. Christ, how strong these women were! Like a little boy he made another grab for her hand; this time she let her wrist lie in his palm:

—Betty. You're angry with me. You hate my guts. . . .

—Guy, you've been to too many movies. I'm not angry and I don't hate you. . . . As a matter of fact I'm the happiest girl in America. . . . Even at school they notice how happy I am, and I guess they suspect something. Mrs. Mears said yesterday that I'm not the nerrrvous young woman I was. And as for my teaching . . . why, now it has warmth. I feel like a mother to those girls, instead of a meat cleaver.

—I'll marry you.

He felt like a Boy Scout. She shook her black head:

—Think it over. I'm pulling none of the nonsense that you got me in trouble. It's not trouble and I wanted it. I wanted you to have me. And you don't *have* to marry me. All that interests me is some provision for your child. . . .

—Of course, Betty, he muttered, putting his forehead in his hand.

—And I might point out to you that we love each other. There's no question of my being some poor little telephone girl whom you slept with in a mad moment. . . . I'm of your own intellectual class—whatever that means. I was bred to the idea that someday I must marry and be a good wife. And because I love you, I know I could be that to you. . . . But whatever happens, I mean to have this child. I mean to bear it with devotion.

—It was . . . just . . . the shock.

—Once, a few months ago, I thought you were the toughest-skinned man I'd ever seen. Now I see that you're almost as confused as those little boys you teach. . . . What do you think happens when you make love to a girl? The first night you took me, I was aware of all the implications. It seemed to me a privilege to conceive a child by you. I'd have protested had you taken . . . the usual precautions. . . .

—I always had before. . . .

He drank another beer in silence, paid the check, and arose, helping her into her coat. His flowers were brighter on her lapel than he himself felt; the daisies mocked him. Now he felt different toward her. For they were at war—not the delicious torture of a war between lovers, but the internecine strife of a man and woman over their child. He knew that the formalities of marriage were easy; he and she were already truly married—had been since that rainy night in March. Not once had he ever thought of her as his mistress, to be kept in an apartment to give him the luxury of pleasure. From the beginning he'd loved her as his woman, not as his whore. . . .

She buttoned her coat and said in her low voice:

—Guy, whatever you decide, don't think of me as the proverbial millstone. If you wish to marry me, our marriage will be as happy as any such enforced social arrangement can ever be. And if you don't . . . I'll have that child. And that's what every woman is finally interested in. All other things pass, Guy, even passion. . . .

Meditatively he put his light straw hat on the back of his red hair:

—But subconsciously you're already treating me as your seducer.

—Don't be silly. I'm merely being frank with you. You men are so fond of believing that women are all subterfuge that it knocks you off your feet when you hear the whole truth from one. We're ultimately more honest than you. . . .

Musing, but with none of his usual acrimony, he took her arm and walked her back to the Girls' School. Inside the seventeenth-century house Mrs. Mears could be heard telling her daughter Midgie that charge accounts made her nerrrrvous. By the Japanese cherry Guy Hudson took his girl into his arms and kissed her. It was a contemplative kiss, contemplative as she herself had become. And he observed that, though she was pleased with the new tenderness of his salute, she no longer yielded to his lips and tongue as she did on those frequent times when he'd been her lover.

—Take plenty of time to think things over, Guy. . . .

—I have, my darling. We'll be married next month when school closes. . . .

She smiled a little sadly:

—You love the magniloquent gesture. . . .

But she didn't fall into his arms with the rapture of a white slave released from bondage.

—Thanks, Guy. But keep thinking. . . . When I first knew you, you were a boy, a bitter and ingrown one. Now you show promise, as Principals say. . . . And I was worse. I was a henny schoolteacher gnawing at her own vitals. You delivered me from that. . . . But during the months till Christmas don't be surprised if I'm not interested in you the way I was. . . . But I do love you. You're the only man in the world I love. Probably because I trust you. . . .

He watched her go up the path to Mrs. Mears's house in the May moonlight. She ran in little steps, but with queer dignity. He heard her shut the door after she'd waved to him. Then he lit a cigarette and walked back toward the Boys' School. He scowled, but he threw back his shoulders and began to whistle Sempre Libera.

Ordinarily he'd have gone back to the Lithuanian tavern to drink beer, pull apart the puzzle of his mind, and put the pieces back together again. But at nine o'clock that evening he had an appointment with Mr. Pilkey in the Cape Cod house. He knew that the ailing Principal couldn't fire him till June, when his contract with the Trustees expired. Guy Hudson spat out his gum and knocked on the famous door, designed by Mrs. Pilkey from Joseph C. Lincoln stories. From the quadrangle came the lamenting and violence of lowerformers being put to bed.

The Negress answered his knock. She was at least as old as old Mrs. Pilkey, but some embalming process had preserved her, in the way that everything at The Academy

350

lingered on in mummy, to the very extinction of dust and orneriness.

—Dey been talkin bout yo all day, Florinda said, taking his straw hat of Leghorn.

—Don't they talk about everybody?

—Some dey does, some dey doan't. . . .

The mammoth old maid waddled ahead in her carpet slippers; he followed her up the stairs of the dimly lighted house. Everywhere there were portraits of the Principal and his wife, done by students of the Art Class and those alumni who had turned to canvas and oils. All the rooms were set-pieces, designed by Mrs. Pilkey after rooms in the House of the Seven Gables. There passed him on the stairs old Mrs. Pilkey, thorny with her ninety-three years, and sniffing to herself.

—Firebrand, she said, as he stood aside to let her pass.

—Yes, mam.

And on a landing he met Mrs. Pilkey, wrapped in a kimono, her white coronet braids up for bed. She approached him in her half-scared, half-crusty fashion:

—I hold you personally responsible for a great deal that has happened here this year. . . .

—The yeast was working before I was born, Mrs. Pilkey.

From the door of the Principal's bedroom Philbrick Grimes and Dell Holly were emerging.

—Doctor! Mr. Grimes said. Summoned to the Presence at last?

But Dell Holly said nothing, skirting Guy Hudson as though he was host to bubonic plague.

In a huge bed surrounded by Dickens and the Bible and choice works of English history the Principal lay in state. He wore an oldfashioned nightshirt. He looked remarkably hale. In another month the old man would probably be out of bed, again asserting his supremacy after the interregnum. Mr. Pilkey surprised his subversive teacher by beaming on him, much as he beamed on prospective parents or on the donors of a million dollars to the school's endowment:

—Come in! Come in! Shut the door! Sit down! . . . No, not there! Close to my bed. . . .

There was something oddly pitiful the way the old hypocrite now stumbled over his words—he who in chapel had been so eloquent in the use of stately English. Mr. Pilkey kept clenching his atrophied left hand. But otherwise it seemed almost as genial as Guy Hudson's interview for his job, when the Principal had said that The Academy needed fresh teaching blood from war veterans. Guy Hudson sat down hesitantly but courteously in a cretonned chair.

—I didn't think you'd have anything more to say to me, sir. . . .

The Principal made a gallant attempt to lean up on his elbow:

—On the contrary I have a great deal. . . . Now you know, as any fool knows, that the United States is in a bad way. I don't know where *you* get your information from. Young men tend to read radical journals. I get mine from the New York *Times* and from influential business men and politicians who send their boys and girls to my school. . . . But it behooves us Americans to be watchful. Even since the recent war we have allowed our national defence to slacken woefully. That war in which you and millions of other young patriots fought seems to have been in vain. I believe we are heading for another. . . .

Guy Hudson leaned forward in the first enthusiasm he'd ever felt for the old man:

—I believe we are too, sir. We should concentrate on straightening out the messes in our country, in proving to the world that we can make democracy work at home. But I believe we're preparing for a third world war unless millions of Americans wise up to the menace of the cartels and to the reactionary tactics of the Republican party. . . .

—Dear me! That isn't precisely what I meant. I think it necessary for us Americans to build up our citizen army once more. Preparedness is the best insurance against attack. Since 1945 we've allowed our armed forces to weaken in numbers. We must be prepared against foreign red infiltration.

—Guy Hudson stood up excitedly:

—I disagree with you, sir! Building up a tremendous military machine is the surest way to get ourselves involved in war, for it starts a worldwide armament race. And we should learn from history that those who have trained armies are going to use them. . . . Whom do we think we're kidding? We're yelling all the time about the danger of attack. But who's in any position to do the attacking, except us, the

352

strongest nation in the world, the only one uncrippled by what you choose to refer to as the late war?

—You don't talk like a loyal American.

Guy Hudson took out his handkerchief and dabbed his scarred lip with it:

—I love my country more than those who do the shouting and write the propaganda. I only know that another war will be the end of everything for most of the people in the world, except possibly those who engender it. America herself couldn't escape the cataclysm. I've been through one war. I know what it's like. . . .

—You're a radical alarmist, Mr. Pilkey said blandly. Please listen to me. . . . Now my newest policy for this school (even though I am at present indisposed) has to do with universal military training, which I am certain will soon be passed by Congress for all the youth of America. Do them good too! Discipline them out of their soft decadent ways. . . . I propose that my Academy beat out more lethargic schools. Military drill will be instituted here. Better now than next year. . . .

Guy Hudson raised his voice by the old man's bed:

—I think it's an outrageous, dreadful, and opportunistic idea! You're hopping on the political bandwagon. It's all of a piece with this sinister infiltration of the military into all phases of American life. It horrifies me! What do you want, another Nazi Germany? You're pulling down the colors, Mr. Pilkey. People like you surrender education to the steely fingers of the military. Why not close your books for good? Then you yourself can accept the brevet of a colonel and call your school a Military Academy. . . .

Breathing hard, the Principal lay back on his bed and put out his unparalyzed right arm:

—I'm too old to become a colonel . . . and I see that you're just as wrongheaded as ever. . . . You know perfectly well that you've already caused enough trouble in my school for me to fire you three times over. But your contract runs till June. . . . Now I called you here tonight to offer you a last chance to redeem yourself. . . . A chance to return to my good graces. If you do as I ask, I may even renew your contract next year with a raise in salary. . . .

Guy Hudson's red hair bristled and glinted in the subdued lights of the sickroom. His mangled mouth was twitching:

—I'm quite sure I don't want to return to your school at any price. . . . And may I ask where you got this fiendish idea of military education for your whole school?

—From men of vision . . . like Mr. Marlow Brown. . . .

—Jesus Christ! There'll be another war because the Marlow Browns of the world stand to profit by it. . . .

—I beg your pardon! This year you've insulted everything I hold dear. If I were younger, I'd thrash you, young fellow. . . .

There was a trace of the old panther in the sick man's stammering voice. Guy Hudson bent toward him, coiled and tense, as on the night he'd strangled a German parachutist:

—May I know the price of what you call my *redemption*?

—Now you're talking turkey, the Principal said, sinking back into his pillow. You were a lieutenant of infantry. Have you retained your commission?

—I'm still in the ORC, damn it. . . .

—Don't damn it, man! Bless it! You have a chance to make your country strong again. . . .

—Spit out your proposition. . . .

—I propose that you give courses in close and extended order drill and classes in the use of infantry weapons three times a week to all students of the Boys' School. . . . And I would like to recommend that you wear your army uniform. The boys will respect it more. . . .

—And if I refuse?

—You will leave here forever next month. And I will refuse to recommend you for any teaching position. That means you can never get a job in a decent school. . . . And don't think you can hamstring my program. If you refuse, I shall hire a friend of my son's, who is a captain in the Marine Reserve to give the military courses. . . .

Guy Hudson's voice roared up to the old scream of battle, that Mr. Pilkey and his fat son had never known:

—Good God! How can you be so cynically shameless? You call yourself an educator. And the farce is that Who's Who and nine tenths of the world take you at your own evaluation of yourself. That's because you're so goddam smug and they so goddam stupid. . . . Let me tell you one thing. American education has sold itself down the river. Once to the parents. And now to the brass hats. The militarization of this country is a tragedy that every intelligent person should fight

354

to his last breath. . . . In this school and hundreds like it you might have brought civilization and learning to the boys and girls of a free peaceful America. But instead you want to train them for murder. Because you and men like you haven't the guts to stand on their own feet, you're going to make democratic education a tool of the state. Yes, blow with every political wind, instead of insisting on the true greatness of a school! Turn out little fascists for the military machine! And what will be the net difference between American schools and the kindergartens of totalitarian states? Answer me, you old ruffian! . . .

Mr. Pilkey turned purple and gasping, and sank back among his pillows:

—You're a dangerous fool. You're a Communist! All right. Get out of my house. And next month pack your bags and get out of my school . . .

—With the greatest of pleasure.

And in what he didn't realize was a gesture from his own army life, he did a right-about-face and marched out of the room. In the corridor outside, the Principal's wife, who'd been eavesdropping at the keyhole, laid her trembling hand on his arm:

—I agree with you. But I don't want you to kill him on me. . . . He's an old man. . . . He's done much good. . . .

—All to be undone by what he's contemplating now. . . .

And hating himself for his rudeness, for the seraphic cruelty of the idealist, he stamped downstairs. There old Mrs. Pilkey was waiting for him, her shriveled hands crossed almost like a madonna's on her ninety-three-year-old bosom.

—You're right, said her fierce old voice. You should talk to the women of America. I heard you raising the roof up there. When you're mad you sound like Dan'l Webster. I heard him when I was a tiny girl. . . .

—The women of America have the vote, he said melo-dramatically. Let them rise against inhumanity. . . .

He left the Cape Cod house. He thought: there is so little time left, so little time for human love or learning or decency. It was all being swept away by hypocrites, conjurers, and demagogues. And his own voice was piping against a hurricane.

Mr. Grimes and Mr. Holly, upon leaving Mr. Pilkey closeted with Guy Hudson, descended the stairs looking at each other like two assassins primed for a coup.

—Now is the time, Dell Holly said in his plaintive pious voice.

—Yes. While he's up there, we can do it safely. . . .

They ran in a cabalistic zigzag from the Cape Cod house to the moonlit quadrangle. There they picked up their Mata Hari—Lisa Holly vibrant in a moire gown.

—Now! Darlings, are you sure what we plan to do is *all right*?

—Certainly, they hissed. The school is blowing up, and we're certain that Hudson has planted the nitroglycerin. . . .

Each taking an arm, they whisked her toward the dormitory for lowerformers. She was in an ecstasy. Not only did she see herself as the next First Lady, but here she was on an intoxicating May night engaged in something like a prank out of Alfred Hitchcock. The trio ran up two flights of stairs, to the corridor where lowerformers were already asleep.

—How can we be sure he's not back already? Lisa murmured.

—He'll be tied up an hour, Mr. Grimes said. You know how the Head is when he gets talking. . . .

Lisa Holly's skirts whistling as she ran, they entered Guy Hudson's room. Mr. Grimes switched on a light without even feeling for it.

—Philbrick knows everything! she said.

—I lived here twelve years ago, he said humbly. One whole year with these screaming brats. . . .

She looked about her at the simple room—the narrow cot, the crossed sabers, the little radio, the littered history books.

—The man lives like a peasant, she said, turning up her famous little nose.

Then running her white finger over the ledge of the mantelpiece:

—And he's not a very good housewife. . . .

The Messrs. Grimes and Holly, with the deftness of graduate felons, went through the drawers of Guy Hudson's desk. Then Mr. Grimes with a snicker caught up a silverframed photograph by the blotter.

—His dear old mother? Lisa Holly said, reaching for it.

—No, her husband said. Only Miss Betty Blanchard. . . .

The second most beautiful woman on the faculty let out a gasp of delighted surprise:

—So! I *thought* something was going on. . . .

—Quiet, Lisa, You'll wake the kids. . . .

The slim woman sank into Guy Hudson's favorite chair:

—Well! something for Mrs. Mortimer Wesley's book! Something even *she* didn't dream of, for all her anteater's tongue. . . .

Mr. Philbrick Grimes pounced, holding up a sheaf of periodicals from the bookrack. They were *The Nation, The New Republic, The New Masses,* and *PM.*

—Will you *look* at what he reads?

—He's in the pay of Moscow, Dell Holly said in his graveyard voice.

—Mon ami, he *must* go. And before June. He's probably made this campus a headquarters for A-Day. . . .

Then Lisa Holly thought she'd have a look at the closets.

—What a messy man, she sighed.

She loved to go into other ladies' houses and check on their maintenance and dusting. Rummaging among skis and laundrybags, she came upon a framed picture, which she extracted and held up to the lamp and the moonlight. It was the German pornographic etching. She dropped the print to the floor with a little shriek, but not before she'd examined it thoroughly.

—Lisa, Dell Holly said piously. Such things are not for the eyes of the mother of my girls. . . .

Then the door opened and the rightful inhabitant of this room stood on the threshold. His hair, under the hat he was removing, was a soft ruby in the moonlight. His scarred mouth worked in amusement and rage:

—So, my friends, invasion of privacy too?

3

Ben Gordon stood watching squadrons of bees deploy on the June air, which was like warm milk vaporizing. He smelled a hint of intermingled flowers; the heat pressed pleasantly on his dark brow. He was standing with arms folded against his plaid jacket, leaning half out of sight against one of the many columns that bounded the quadrangle. For on soft green grass, where normally students were forbidden to saunter by double edict of the Messrs. Pilkey and Whitney, the Boys' School was having an afternoon of military drill. All but Ben.

—Riiiiight flank, haaarch! . . . Left flank, haaarch! . . .

It was the voices of Herman Pilkey and his friend Marine Captain Wolcott conducting the drill. Ben watched with stoic amusement. The columns flashed this way and that in wanton zigzags. Life at The Academy had become increasingly regimented: the quadrangle was now a field where mock soldiers played at war. Every male student was out for drill. Except himself. A week ago as President of the Student Council he'd refused to have any part in the new program of military training. For this defection in patriotism to his country and loyalty to his school he'd been cashiered from his presidency and stripped of all his honors. The student vote on his resignation had been 211 to 188. But from his sickbed Mr. Pilkey had insisted that Ben resign his presidency or be expelled. Ben had done so. Then Mr. Pilkey had said that democracy and student government were all very well—when they worked. But if they didn't work then it was the duty of elders to *see* that they worked. Thus Ben had been disgraced in the eyes of the faculty and of most of the students. In this first week of his degradation the dark muscular boy had wept often in his room. The first scars were healing now. He was just another upperformer at this Academy, waiting to graduate.

But he'd never forget that interview in the sickroom of the Principal. Mr. Pilkey had called him a subversive Jewish intellectual, had with his own unparalyzed right hand removed the badge of The Academy's Student Council. And Buddy Brown had been elected President in Ben's place. Whatever illusion the young Jew had nurtured about his glory was gone forever. He desired now only to get to Yale, where he could hide his face in the anonymity of a thousand freshmen.

Other nineteen-year-olds would have sneered. But not Ben. He accepted his fate with a shrug he'd learned from his father, the Chicago magnate, and from his mother, the vibrant Jewess who was such a clubwoman for philanthropies.

Their hearts too had broken at his removal from the Council. They said he'd been right to stick up for what he believed. It was such a puny stand of idealism he'd taken, but its consequences in the eyes of a boy were huge. Refusal to drill, carrying the wooden guns carved by the Woodworking Class. Refusal to wear the oversized chevrons of a master sergeant, stitched up by Mrs. Launcelot Miller. Refusal to believe that America had so far broken down that she was already girding herself for another war. Yes, a Jewish intellectual and a world federalist! But it had cost Ben every honor at the Academy. Some of his old chums had turned against him. Even his roommate Bill Hunnicutt spoke only when he had to.

The warm June air teased Ben's wide hairy nostrils almost like a whiff of musk. He changed the crossing of his thighs and attended to the drilling. He alone had refused to countenance this farce. And one faculty member—Mr. Hudson. They were both fools who'd flown into the face of public opinion. A nineteen-year-old boy and a wounded ex-lieutenant of infantry....

He watched the Boys' School marching in closed battalion formation—a rectangular column that all but brushed both sides of the long dimension of the campus. At its head marched Herman Pilkey and Captain Wolcott, two Arabian stallions in full-dress Marine uniforms. They turned their heads sideways or backward to shout out their idiotically stylized commands. Their voices sounded like bison with grippe:

—To the rear ... haaarch! Dress it up! ...

Six paces behind them and also strutting his stuff was Buddy Brown, undergraduate sergeant major. Ben observed that his successor to the presidency had invented a stride all his own, reminiscent of the goosestep. Since new honors had inundated him, the blond boy spoke to no one in school except his noncoms. And he'd revived an ancient custom of violence to recalcitrant or unorthodox lowerformers. At night, when he was crying into his pillow, Ben heard the screams of little boys being paddled on their naked buns for real or imagined slights to Buddy Brown's regime. Mr. Grimes presided at these spankings, keeping note on his clipboard of the number of lashes. Even the sick Principal approved of the beatings, for he said that now The Academy was under quasi-martial law.

Ben watched the drill even more closely. As sergeant major Buddy had exempted himself from carrying the crude lathe rifles turned out by the Woodworking Class. No, his father had bought him a genuine Springfield '03 army rifle, and Mr. Pilkey had given Buddy permission to keep his newest toy in his room, provided he owned no live ammunition. Buddy was expansively proud of this real rifle. Nightly he oiled and cleaned it, and lowerformers who toadied to him were sometimes permitted to fondle it. He was also custodian of the Browning .50 caliber watercooled machine gun which was used in the new weapons classes. And he'd designed his own uniform. He'd bought an Eisenhower Jacket from an army surplus store in the city, and dyed it red. On its sleeves were oversized chevrons, stitched up by Mrs. Launcelot Miller; these were creamcolored, so that his rank could be descried acres away. His trousers were officers' pinks, dyed cream. Lastly he wore combat boots which he kept at a high burnish. Thus Buddy conducting drill looked like a sinister version of the Chocolate Soldier. He was permitted to wear his uniform at all times, even to classes. When they met in the corridors, he sneered at Ben Gordon. But he didn't quite dare elbow him out of the way. . . .

Out on the quadrangle Buddy began to play to the gallery of faculty. He wheeled and began to prance backward in order to check on the dressing of his marching battalion. His blond head tossed backward.

—Those two fags in the front rank step lively!

Ben winced and shut his eyes. The two addressed were The Abbot and The Abbess, who weren't marching in step with anyone else. Their toy guns were listing at a crazy cant off their shoulders because their elbows weren't locked to their sides. They minced along in pastel slacks of powder blue. Beside them huffed The Bishop, sweating profusely.

—Shut your hole, Mary! The Abbot and the Abbess squealed back at their sergeant major.

Several of the faculty standing about expressed shame that The Abbot, The Abbess, and The Bishop were so unmilitary. Buddy Brown's face turned purple:

—No talking in ranks! I'll get you three queers after lights tonight! . . .

Ben Gordon opened his eyes again. He watched a sergeant on the left flank of the leading column, Howard West Lothrop, also known as The Body. He and Buddy now ran undergraduate life, for The Body controlled the press, the school's paper known as *The Academe*. Each week now it came out with editorials on the soldierly approach to school life, and a fresh list of military rules, infringement of which meant a paddling by Buddy's Elite Guard. So effective was the writing of the new minister of propaganda that the Acting Co-Principals, with the sanction of Messrs. Pilkey and Whitney, had fired most of the dining hall staff. And all students who weren't noncoms did a stint of KP. . . .

Or that other sergeant lethargically chewing on a blade of grass and marching on the right flank of the first file was a boy Ben had once been fond of—Demaree Walter Montgomery, also known as Mung. He and the Alabaman had been happy together on football trips, for Mung knew the secret of laughter and relaxation. But Mung had let him down, hadn't had the guts to stand up against military training:

—Whah, boah, everabodah loves woh. . . .

Ben turned his eyes to a slender dark corporal on Mung's left, carrying his fake rifle tenderly, as though it was a violin. Ralph Du Bouchet, made wretched by military training. Ben pitied Ralph most of all, for as a scholarship boy he hadn't dared protest the new regime. Had he done so, Mr. Pilkey and Mr. Grimes and Mr. Holly would have shipped him home on the next train. So Ralph now drilled excellently in silence.

After watching this spectacle for half an hour Ben began to feel like laughing and vomiting and crying all at once. He was in disgrace, and three hundred and ninety-nine boys were making fools of themselves. But he merely drew farther into himself and folded his arms more tightly against his big chest in his loose well-cut jacket. A scream of pleasure went up from the other colonnade where faculty ladies were knitting and watching the drill. The loudest was the corncobbed mouth of Mrs. Launcelot Miller, who found her boys even more bewitching as soldiers than as athletes.

The whole battalion was executing a tour de force—the Left Turn, in which one flank moves out in a great sweeping arch, the other marking time as pivot. The movement of this wheel of boys so tickled Mrs. Miller that her pipe fell from her mouth. Ben looked at her and shrugged. She no longer entertained him since his fall from favor. Suddenly in the rich heat of a June afternoon he felt sick. It was the nausea and the loathing that come when people of inflexible principle feel themselves betrayed and dragged through swill.

—If you feel like puking, I'll get you a waste basket, a familiar voice said.

Ben turned quickly. Mr. Hudson was standing on the other side of the column from him. Ben blushed and swallowed the parbreak that was rising in his throat. The redheaded history teacher was wearing baseball pants and a polo shirt open at the front, revealing the coarse rug of hair on his chest. Ben felt suddenly soothed and not so much alone. He'd always liked this man, who wasn't someone he had to *cope* or *deal* with. And now the functional garb, the intense face with the scarred lip reminded him of something removed from the twentieth century. Was it John the Baptist? . . .

—O, hi, sir.

Guy Hudson stared mock-critically at the drill:

—You know, at Fort Benning in 1941 I could never figure out what saluting and parading had to do with modern warfare. I said to myself, Shit for the Birds. . . .

Ben smiled. It was the first four-letter word he'd ever listened to on the lips of a teacher. And Mr. Hudson's use of it, sparing and scathing, cut to the core of what Ben was feeling. It excited him. It made a bond between them, the tie of two men who'd got a whiff of the modern world. Weren't they two in the same doghouse? Ben's mouth formed lovingly around the word, which some delicacy in him had never permitted him to use before, even with The Boys in bull sessions:

—Shit for the Birds? he repeated tentatively.

Guy Hudson smiled:

—Good, Ben. You sound like a baby learning to talk. Some day, when you're older, your pronunciation will improve. . . .

The Boys' School was now standing at Parade Rest. Herman Pilkey and Captain Wolcott ordered their sergeant major to dismiss the battalion. Buddy Brown came to attention and threw a stylish highball salute at his two commanders, which delighted them and evoked applause from the faculty ladies for its military precision. Herman Pilkey, nipples joggling and sweating, trotted off to his wife Nydia, who held her second son in her plump arms. Buddy called the school to attention and:

—In-spec-shun . . . harms!

There was no rattle of bolts, for the sergeant major had the only real weapon on campus—and that was in his closet. But almost four hundred wooden rifles were brought to port, the imaginary chambers were looked into for imaginary bullets. Then the dummy guns were brought to Order Arms with thuds that scored holes in the new grass of the quadrangle. The Abbot, The Abbess, and The Bishop dropped their pieces, which as any soldier knows, is a serious matter. Guy Hudson murmured in Ben's ear.

—When I was a kid, my father was hurt that I didn't take more of a shine to the lead soldiers I got for Christmas. I suppose I was looking forward to real-life obscenities such as this . . . boys playing sodger. . . .

—We're in a minority, sir.

—We always are, Ben. But we won't be shut up. And it takes more than those lathes they're shouldering to knock us off. . . .

Ben smiled one of his sweet almost-forgotten Chassidic smiles. Suddenly his dismissal from the Council and his degradation before the school didn't seem quite such a strangling pill. He knew at nineteen what he'd always guessed from his father and his mother—that one terrible thing came after another, but you got used to anything. The aloes and myrrh of his race and religion began to be palpable to his tongue.

Before he dismissed the school, Buddy harangued them in the style of a conscientious sergeant major:

—Let me remind you, men, to watch your conduct at the dance tonight. The Academy's Spring Proms have always been known for good manners and hospitality. Let every girl who is our guest this weekend go away raving about how we conducted ourselves like officers and gentlemen. We'll soon be both, you know. And think of the free advertising of good will for the school! . . . Remember that commissioned officers in the next war will be largely drawn from schools like ours. . . Heelers, runners, and dance committee

report at once to Mrs. Whitney and to Mr. Grimes. . . .
Battalion dismissed!

Ben Gordon walked quickly along the colonnade, trying
to keep concealed from the released soldiers, who were running in all directions off the parade ground. They had to
dress and shine themselves up to meet their dates for the
Spring Prom. He walked withdrawn and negated. A few
boys who still loved him spoke, but most were thinking of
the girls they'd meet in the next half hour. A few now
snubbed him. Buddy Brown and The Body were running to
the entry of their dormitory:

—I dished out the old globaloney, hey? Buddy was saying.

And on a terrace by the schoolhouse Mr. Grimes and his
clipboard were entertaining two gentlemen of the press from
the city. He encouraged the attendance of reporters at military drill. Good free publicity.

—Damn good show you fellas put on here, one of the reporters was saying.

—Well, we *try*. Perhaps your readers will be interested to
hear that this Academy is one school that realizes her responsibility to the nation. You may say that Around Here we believe that the education of gentlemen of leisure and esthetes
is a thing of the past. Our ailing Principal (whom God grant
many years of health and usefulness yet) concurs with these
opinions. I am only his mouthpiece. . . .

—Good deal, good deal, the newspapermen said, scrib-
bling on their little pads. We'll want a rotogravure spread on
all this for the Sunday supplement. . . .

The reporters walked to their convertible by the gym, and
Mr. Grimes consulted his clipboard for his next appointment. In his wispy tense face there was an expression of a
mission well consummated. Then he realized that the ex-
President of the Student Council was regarding him. He
stepped back a few paces and adopted his conciliatory tone,
as when his classes were naughty:

—Ben, mon vieux, I think perhaps you've learned a valu-
able lesson in the last week, more important than you'll ever
get from books. . . . It's better to make such blunders as you
have made in the privacy of a school, rather than out in the
world. . . . All's not lost yet. . . .

And having doled out some of his own brand of compassion, he prepared to take flight, for among other duties

he'd taken upon his shoulders the running of the Spring Prom, though he pretended to take the advice of the under- graduate Dance Committee. Ben stood his ground; Mr. Grimes bridled:

—Ben! What a way to look at me! I'm your friend! It may interest you to know that I was one of the few people Around Here who protested your being put off the Council. . . . You have your points, you know. . . . Ben, I'm busy! . . . Don't look at me that way. . . .

—I was just thinking, sir.

And he walked to his room and dressed to meet Judith Strauss, whom he'd invited six weeks ago to be his Prom Girl. Now all his world was changed. He wished that he was cleaning streets somewhere, many miles away. Bill Hunnicutt sat on the other cot shining his shoes, whistling so he wouldn't have to make conversation. All over the dormitory kids were showering and yelling of exploits they planned at the dance tonight. According to them, the boots would be put to Helen, to Marietta, to Skippy, to Martha, and to Connie. But Ben could think only of how the boots had been put to himself. . . .

In splashes of June sunlight the village railroad station was the converging spot of three groups—one of boys and two of girls. These knots of hosts and guests were even now coming together, like the elbows of a long dismembered triangle.

First there were several hundred boys, in a huddle of bets and trepidation, waiting to meet their dates for the Prom. This contingent was headed by Buddy Brown in uniform. He'd also compelled the attendance of The Academy's band, even now tootling out brassily:

—I don't want her, you can have her; she's too fat for me! . . .

There were also a half dozen crack cheerleaders to make the arrival of the girls at least as portentous as a football victory or a Roman triumph.

Second, making their way to the railroad platform from the Girls' School were fifty select misses chaperoned by Betty Blanchard and Habib Demerjian. Only the cream of the Girls' School were bidden to the Spring Prom.

Third, coming on the train which would presently heave

into view, were out-of-town girls who were the homegrown steadies of particular boys. The true Bloods of the undergraduate body turned up their noses at the proximity of the Girls' School and preferred to have their gash come from New York, Baltimore, Atlanta, and Chicago. It was costly, but it was worth it. This train was now five miles down the track. Girls were already looking expectantly out of the windows of their Pullmans and coaches, jabbering to one another on the beauties of the scenery and the social delights they hoped to taste this weekend. This train carried its quota of beautiful heiresses too stupid even for finishing school. But they all had in common the fact that someone in the Boys' School thought enough of them to invite them from many miles away.

The delegation from the Girls' School, duly instructed in etiquette and reminded of their virginity by Mrs. Mears, arrived on the train platform and were sorted out to their respective hosts. The Misses Blanchard and Demerjian carried a roster, from which appropriate girls were matched with the names of Academy boys. Each girl, carrying her suitcase, would be handed over to the boy who had requested the favor of her presence. There would be screams from girls meeting their blind dates for the first time, shouts of reunion as members of the Boys' School met up with young women they hadn't seen for a week or so. Most marked, however, was a certain shyness of the boys to break away from their consolidated phalanx, or the girls from theirs. Safety in numbers. Later the rapport would be more thorough, but the ice must be broken. The Boys' School and the Girls' School were regarding each other with regret and some animosity and trepidation.

Miss Demerjian began to read from her roster:

—Mister Buddy Brown and Miss Midgie Mears. Step forward, please. . . .

The Presidents of the Student Councils of both schools stepped out of their formations. The Girls' School set up a scream of delight:

—Oooooh! Why didn't they *all* wear uniforms?

The blond heads of the boy and girl touched as they kissed defiantly (by rubbing noses) before the assembled schools. Midgie was wearing a flat straw hat and a dirndl.

—Hi, pig, Buddy said in her ear.

—Hi, wolf, Midgie said.

Then Buddy led Midgie, taking her arm in cocky masculinity, off the station platform to a jalopy he'd wangled from somewhere; it was to be their bridal coach. Miss Demerjian looked at Miss Blanchard with some apprehension after the affectionate greeting:

—Well, really! I'm glad our Directress had a headache this afternoon. She wouldn't approve at *all* of public osculation. . . .

Miss Blanchard smiled absently. She was looking for her own date in the crowd. Miss Demerjian wiggled her mustache and raised the roster:

—Mister Ben Gordon and Miss Judith Strauss. . . .

The ex-President of the Student Council of the Boys' School, looking like no waiting bridegroom, stepped out of the ranks to greet the daughter to a delicatessen king.

—Aren't you two going to shake hands? Miss Demerjian cried.

—Hullo, Judith, Ben said, casting his eyes to the boards.

For some reason most of the Boys' School looked away from this meeting. Judith Strauss took her host's hand and spoke softly:

—Listen, I'm a good sport. Naturally after what's happened, I didn't want to come, and you probably didn't want to have me. Just remember that I accepted your invitation long before. . . . You haven't even tried to understand. You might at least have released me from the engagement. I can scarcely hold up my head. . . .

—Please, Judith, Ben said.

He took her suitcase and hurried her off the platform.

—What's eating those two? Miss Demerjian cried.

—Shhhh. He was kicked off the Council last week, Betty Blanchard said.

—Ooooooh, baby. Then he's *nobody* any more? . . .

Eventually all the dates from the Girls' School were turned over to their respective hosts from the Boys' School. Then Miss Demerjian turned herself over to Doctor Anderson, whom she'd badgered for an invitation for the past month. And Betty Blanchard surrendered her company to Mr. Grimes. Last night she'd had her first real quarrel with Guy Hudson. He'd refused to invite her to the Prom. He said she *knew* he didn't dance. And she said she was going any-

how because she loved dancing. Consequently permitting
Mr. Grimes to squire her about for the weekend was to be
a sort of snub and revenge on her lover. . . .

—There's room in my hack for four, mes amis, Mr. Grimes
said. But we must drive slowly along the road behind the
boys and girls to see that they don't get into mischief in the
hedgerows. . . .

Betty sniffed and didn't allow him to carry her suitcase.
So she and Miss Demerjian and Doctor Anderson, who was
quoting Ovid, got into Mr. Grimes's Packard, which mod-
ishly had its top down to the visits of bees and the flower
smells of June. Here they must wait till the out-of-town
girls got in.

The train came round the bend, to a shout of waiting
boys who hadn't yet been paired off. Out of its windows
waved a host of overdressed or frightened or brazen or bored
girls. The band played more enthusiastically, and the cheerleaders went into their yell:

—Girls! . . . ra ra! With a siss boom ah! . . .

Miss Demerjian imprisoned the arm of Doctor Anderson:

—O, I know how they feel! I remember my first formal at
Niantic Classical High! . . .

—You're not happy this afternoon, Mr. Grimes said to
Miss Blanchard.

—Give me time, sir.

She didn't tell him that she'd taken to being sick in the
mornings. And she was much aware of new life within her
body, a life that had nothing to do with Mr. Grimes. She
shot a swift horrified glance at the little man whom she'd
selected to be her knight for the weekend. Already her regret
at her treatment of Guy seared her. And she was spiting
him simply because he didn't care to dance. . . .

The out-of-town girls were clambering off the train en-
cumbered with enough luggage to last a pilgrimage. They
were paired up with the remaining boys by the Mesdames
Dell Holly and Launcelot Miller, who read from rosters
typed up by the epileptic Miss Pringle:

—Howard West Lothrop and Miss Bonnie Ann
Schultz. . . .

—Demaree Walter Montgomery and Miss Fuchsia
Brown. . . .

—Ralph Victor Du Bouchet and Miss Harriet Spencer. . . .

Then the voice of Lisa Holly trailed into a gurgle, for she discovered that she was presenting Tad McKinley to a lush colored girl who was stepping off the train with the enthusiasm of a Moabitess.

—Good heavens, Mr. Grimes said at the wheel of his Packard.

After straggling over in pairs, holding hands, from the railroad station, the boys and their girls somehow got together in the corridor of the schoolhouse, by that alcove known as The Den, normally the office of Mr. Pilkey. But this June the Principal wasn't here to greet the dancers, to be the Fezziwig of the festivities. He lay upstairs in the Cape Cod house. And at one of the two desks of the Acting Co-Principals sat the Comptroller's wife, an orchid at her shoulder and a bestselling historical novel under her jeweled hand. For Spring Prom was the one time of year when Mrs. Whitney all but exploded with the dynamite latent in her duties as Second Lady. Since Mrs. Pilkey couldn't be bothered with details, Mrs. Whitney was solely in charge of everything requiring the sure hostess touch of a married woman. God help anyone who disputed her position! Single-handed she hired the orchestra and compounded the punch and ordered the chicken patty shells and assigned girls to rooms in dormitories or in faculty houses. She was socially responsible for the success of Prom weekend, and she went about her chores as temperamental as Dolly Madison. Her husband's budget be blowed! This was her party and the boys were paying for it! . . .

When the boys and girls were all assembled, she closed her novel on a fruity scene, arose from the desk, and signaled for silence in the buzzing and twittering. Behind her the darkening canvas of Miss Sophia looked down on the revelers: this was perhaps different from the croquet and garden parties Our Gracious Foundress had romped at as a girl, more than a hundred years ago.

—Welcome all! cried Mrs. Whitney dulcetly. We'll all cooperate to make this a banner occasion, *won't* we, girls! . . .

Then she had her special reception committee of lower-formers distribute room assignments to the girls, each of whom received a mimeographed copy of her celebrated Tips for a Happy Weekend:

1) Smoking is not permitted at this school. Remember that a true lady never tries to be smart—i.e. seducing her escort into flaunting rules. When in Rome. . . !

2) Leaving the dance floor except at intermission is expressly prohibited, and renders your date liable to expulsion from school.

3) No alcoholic beverages are to be consumed before, during, or after Prom Weekend.

4) This is, after all, a school. Schools run on schedules. Kindly do not embarrass your escort by being late to any function. This includes meals.

After her official greeting, caressing the orchid bestowed on her by the Dance Committee and holding her breath to keep her afternoon frock from splitting, Mrs. Whitney went off to her house and her tiny husband. There she would finish her bestseller, nag at Mr. Whitney, and worry about chaperones.

Accommodations for the girls in dormitories and faculty houses were complicated and ironclad. For the past month Mrs. Whitney had assigned and reassigned, having frequent tantrums like a landlord. Woe to any brash upperformer who wished to change his girl's room, or have her move in with a chum! Sophia Hall had been emptied of all boys, who were sent off somewhere for the weekend on a camping trip, whether they wanted to be evicted or not. Once a year, in June, the stately ivied dormitory found its boy-smelling, boy-marked rooms and corridors echoing to young girls showering, getting dressed, fussing over their hair, giggling, and comparing dates. Seventy girls were squeezed into the double bunks, where for the rest of the year restless boys studied their Cicero and groaned under the police state of Mr. Grimes. Tonight not even he might enter Sophia Hall.

All other girls were put up in faculty houses, with special injunctions from Mrs. Whitney that hostesses be kind—even to sewing up a torn evening gown or providing aspirin for a little headache. Mrs. Launcelot Miller, for instance, bedded down the girls of the ten Biggest Wheels on Campus in her bungalow. Ben Gordon's girl Judith Strauss wasn't staying at the Millers' this June.

Mrs. Dell Holly was also a principal hostess. This year she was harboring (she protested she could house no more

370

than three) Miss Midgie Mears and Miss Betty Blanchard and Miss Habib Demerjian. Even now she stood at the screen door of her apartment with her skinny husband lurking in the background. All afternoon Lisa Holly had been practicing gestures of pre-bellum graciousness:

—Why, Betty! . . . and Habib! . . . and Midgie! O, what a gleesome threesome! . . .

Privately she'd told her husband that Miss Demerjian was the sort who left rings in the bathtub and brown stains on the toilet seat. But now she was all affability. The Misses Blanchard and Demerjian inherited the guestroom, done up by Lisa Holly from whimsical suggestions in *House Beautiful*. And Midgie Mears was assigned the nursery of Lisa Holly's three small daughters, this weekend evicted from their cribs to sleep squalidly on the couch in their father's study. Midgie made a face at her two mistresses before disappearing into her chamber:

—Well! Just like old times! I can't ever get away from you two. All we've done is to move across the river. All we need now is my Mom. . . .

—You'll be late for dinner, Betty Blanchard said.

She and the mustached mistress of French entered their fragrant bedroom. Miss Demerjian flung out her arms and inhaled the lilac scents from the pastures outside; she cocked a pastoral ear to the clicking of mechanized lawnmowers:

—Baby, I've always wanted to live with you. . . .

—I hope you can put up with me for the weekend, Habib, Betty Blanchard said wearily.

—Put up with you? Miss Demerjian said, gathering enthusiasm. Why, baby, we're going to be so *close*! And after the dance we'll hash the whole thing over and confide in each other till the wee hours! Won't that be *nice*? Just like two Jane Austen sisters tittering in their garret. . . .

She began to whistle After The Ball Is Over and to unpack Syrian finery from her suitcase.

—My God, Miss Blanchard said to herself.

She sat at a dressing table and put her face in her hands. She thought that she was a pregnant girl coming to a dance she cared nothing about, simply to tease her lover. And with Mr. Grimes. It was the most adolescent thing she'd ever done in her life. She was as bad as those little girls who, to mortify

371

their mothers, threaten to go out in the garden and eat snails. . . .

—Baby, aren't you well? Miss Demerjian called out from a forest of hangers in the closet.

—Quite well, Habib, she answered, lighting a cigarette.

—Frankly, baby, you could have knocked me down with a feather when you came to the dance with Grimesie. I'm no fool. I know who's *really* on your mind. . . .

—You can be first in the bathroom.

Miss Demerjian, in bra and panties, retreated, but when she closed the door she was still rattling on:

—Of course Doctor Anderson is no wolf-cub. But when he's not thinking of Latin, he sometimes thinks of me. As the feminine gender, genitive case. . . .

Now that she was alone for a few minutes, Betty regarded herself in the mirror of the dressing table. Once she put a hand below her breasts and pressed very gently and exploringly.

Then the telephone bell rang out. It was the sort of instrument one would expect to find in the guestroom of Lisa Holly; it was in canary plastic and its cord was braided like an alligator's tail. She picked it up to hear the quick officious voice she was expecting:

—Philbrick speaking, my dear. I'm dressing for dinner. Just thought I'd see how my Promgirl is making out. . . . Comfy and snug?

He'd called her once like that before, last September. . . .

—Mrs. Holly is most thoughtful, Mr. Grimes . . . Philbrick. . . .

—Dandy. See you in an hour then at the main entrance to the salle à manger. . . .

She replaced the phone thoughtfully and icily. No sooner was it in its cradle than it shivered her by ringing again. She picked it up angrily. But the voice that came out now was a low rough one, that many times had been closer to her ear than at phone's length:

—Betty. . . .

—Guy, she said, lowering her voice so that Miss Demerjian shouldn't hear even over the rattle of the showerbath.

—I just wanted to give you the pleasure of knowing that if you think you're crucifying me, you are. . . . Do you know what I'm planning to do tonight?

372

—Guy, I really don't care. I asked you to take me to this dance and you refused. For all I care, you can get drunk. . . .

—Don't worry, darling, I will. . . .

—And I might add that you're behaving like a brat. . . .

—And you like a bitch. . . .

Betty hung up. She brooded over the dressing table, filling up as though she was going to cry. As moments of their love were painful in the savagery of great physical delight, so there was something perversely delicious in their hurting each other out of bed. They were both the sort to savor every twinge of the screws. He was quite capable of coming to the Prom drunk and making a spectacle of himself. . . . For a moment she meditated on walking out of her commitment to Mr. Grimes. She'd run to Guy's room. They would get tight together in the city, eat steaks, and tomorrow leave this place forever. But then she dabbed at her eyes, shook her tight black hair, and undressed. As she slid out of her last stitch and was standing naked in the breath of June that floated through the open windows, she looked with fascinated tenderness at her white belly. It was already an obviously distended hemisphere. She cupped her hands about it and gave a mad little cry, known only to her lover.

There was a knock at the door, and Lisa Holly entered immediately, carrying two heavy bath towels:

—O, excuse me. I thought I heard you two still talking. . . .

She set the towels on a chair and left the room at once. But not so fast that Betty didn't intercept one divining glance from those gray eyes to her own hands clutching her body. Lisa Holly had seen everything—how the body of an unmarried girl was beginning to swell and bloom. Betty pulled on her dressing gown and burst into laughter. Now it was out!

Miss Demerjian emerged dripping from the bathroom:

—Baby, how you're laughing!

At truth, Habib. . . .

After phoning his girl, so raging was his envy and resentment, Guy Hudson sat in his favorite chair and scowled. His jealousy was all the wilder because it was directed at a phantom. God knew he wasn't afraid of Mr. Grimes's having Betty to a dance. That eunuch! No, it was just what she was doing to him, reminding him of their cleavage now that she carried his child. But he was piqued that his wife in all but

373

name would even care to go dancing with an emasculated Machiavelli. That hurt oddly. He saw no point in dancing, which he'd always considered a recent compromise and social perversion—artificiality coupled with a mild libidinousness. But *she* enjoyed it! She could take her deep sweet pleasure in bed with him and still enjoy whirling on a floor and muttering nothings to silly music. Well, she could have it. None of which allayed his fury in any way.

He lit a cigarette, crossing and uncrossing his legs restlessly. All over the quadrangle was the sound of slopping showers, of the last rites of sweetness and purity—even to that depressing Americanism of boys dabbing deodorants under their armpits that they might stink sweetly during their gyrations tonight. It wasn't what Guy Hudson thought of as a party, but he was never one for titillation without climax. Even at Amherst he'd been amused at the idea of grappling with a girl on a dance floor, hoping that at the end of the evening, through purring and suave insistence, something passionate might come of it. To his taste, dancing of the ballroom sort was something velvety and catlike. A man might hop into bed, but why have a dry run standing upright and gently shoving to brass and clarinets? It made one into a mumbling tiger lily, swaying listlessly on a stem. It was this impatience with preludes and irrelevant details that had made him unfit for drawing rooms. He was meant to live on locusts and honey, with an occasional roll in the hay to sweeten his discipline. Was he perhaps only a Puritan with social conscience? He was furious with himself as well as with his girl. She was a bitch, and he a fakir who lolled on nails. . . .

—He'd all but decided to get into his evening clothes and go to the dance like a country bumpkin, Abe Lincoln gangling in the Vienna of Franz Joseph. Then he snapped up his head. Ralph stood in the door of his room, washed, half dressed, and almost Spartan in his gaiety.

—I was wondering if you know how to tie a bow.

The boy faced toward the window; Guy Hudson approached his shoulders from the back and put his arms about Ralph's neck. As he took the loose black ends and knotted them from behind, he felt like an Indian pederast. He ended the neat bow with a flourish and freed his erstwhile victim.

—Thanks, Ralph said. You know, you should be coming

to the dance yourself. It would do you good. . . .

At six thirty the dietitian was still running from table to table in the dining hall. She hurled curses at her husband the chef; she shouted out examples of his growing incompetence in her bed to the student KP. For she was setting out flowers on every table, a Spring Prom extravagance of adornment that Mr. Whitney must countenance every June. There were cosmos and gladioli and fern and pompoms and zinnias. At important tables on the parquet floor (no one was to sit at the High Table tonight) bouquets stood in proper vases. But the supply of these was limited; and when it ran out Mrs. Pilkey, pursued by her demon of symmetry, called into use every available receptacle. At the table where the Hollys would play host to ten boys and girls, flowers had been jammed into a silver loving cup, a trophy awarded to the baseball team of 1937. On an out-of-the-way table at the fringe of the dining hall, flowers bent shamefacedly out of an old hat rack that Mrs. Pilkey had ordered disguised with crepe paper.

When with the ringing bells the first couples ticklishly entered the dining hall, Mrs. Miekewicz had planted her last urn with an oath and retired to the pantry where she blazed away in Polish at such folderol as would dare throw her whole ménage into an uproar. She regarded the dining hall as the personal concession of herself and her husband the chef. Though she was theoretically in the pay of little Mr. Whitney, she regularly flattened him with threats that she was quitting. She regarded him as a meddler who'd somehow got mixed up in her restaurant business. She was proud of her casseroles of macaroni, served daily to the Boys' School throughout the year, but she was wild with rage when Mrs. Whitney ordered her to serve chicken patty, green peas, and French fries on Prom Weekend. She hoped the girls would choke on it. . . .

Though the supper bell continued to whir at six thirty, couples were dilatory in getting to the dining hall, for the girls took their own good time about dressing. It wasn't often that a lady played to an audience of four hundred gasping boys. The only people on time at the dining hall tonight were boys who couldn't afford, or hadn't been permitted, to invite a girl to the Spring Prom. They took their places at a ring of tables in the fringes of the vaulted room. They were neatly dressed, but not formally, and they stood at their places watching girls enter with their lucky or unlucky escorts. They made comments on the wardrobe of each young lady, on her legs, on her general personality. These critiques were rarely flattering, for males mewed up for months together are always in danger of turning against the opposite sex. It was a brave girl who entered that dining room tonight, she knew that four hundred pairs of eyes were stripping away the diaphanous veil of her party frock.

Faculty members in evening dress entered and took their places at opposite ends of tables on the main floor. Tonight they would be hosts and hostesses, receiving their brevet of hospitality direct from the sickroom of Mr. Pilkey.

Mrs. Dell Holly and her husband came in, she with a vast and weary handsomeness, having just communicated her spicy nugget of intelligence to headquarters in the Cape Cod house. Now perhaps she was thinking of herself at Wellesley fifteen years ago, before she graduated to being just another matron in a reception line. From Dell Holly she'd demanded (and received) the orchid she wore on the shoulder of her mauve gown, which floated a small bustle like a bicycle rack over her trim buttocks.

Mrs. Launcelot Miller, for once without her corncob pipe, wore a black sequined gown at her table, where naturally sat the leading athletes of The Academy with their dates. Buddy Brown was there with Midgie Mears in salmon-colored satin, her pageboy bob apparently lacquered to her head. She solaced herself also with Mung and The Body and their dates. Tonight during dinner she regaled their young mistresses (and embarrassed them) by stories of her boys on the athletic field. She displayed familiarity with the skeletons and muscular development of Buddy Brown and The Body and Mung—till at last their girls began to eye one another oddly. Opposite Mrs. Miller, serving their chicken patty and scarcely speaking a word, sat Mr. Launcelot Miller, looking like an uncomfortable teddy bear got up for an important occasion. His stiff shirt buckled over his breasts, and occasionally a wiry black hair would pop out of his stiff collar, causing the little girl on his right to imagine that his chest must be a pelt of steel wool. His fat hairy hands also passed around the celery and olives under the vigilant eye and corrective voice of his wife. These little minxes were named Janet and Betsy and Ducky—but she didn't really care in the slightest for the tepid little creatures who had stolen her lovers away from her for the weekend.

The eyes of celibate Academy boys who weren't going to the dance bulged and moistened at the spectacle of two hundred girls nibbling on chicken in their dining hall. It was almost the only time of year when desirable women came into the quadrangle. Thus boys without dates twitched on their chairs and eased the tension in the trousers of their Sunday suits. They muttered to one another over their chicken patty and peas, stiffened into papier mâché by the revenge of Mrs. Miekewicz:

—Look at that one in yellow. Wouldn't kick *her* out, wouldja?

—Betsy Wagner's got one helluva paira boobs, and look at what she's got em covered with. If it ever falls down. . . .

—Ah, Liz stood me up yesterday. Otherwise I'd be sittin over there too in my soup and fish. . . .

—I tell ya I can't stand it. Gonna gimme a handjob before the evenin gets much older. . . .

But the two hundred girls, pretending prettily to be unconscious of the stares and the murmurings of lust, scarcely touched their chicken and peas, which would drive Mrs. Miekewicz to further distraction. American girls delight in conveying to their hosts the impression that they are dainty in their appetites, that they don't eat enough to keep a bird alive. Later tonight they'd assuage their ravening hunger from faculty iceboxes, and their hostesses would understand, having once been schoolgirls themselves. All the time they kept up a nervous conversation with everyone at table within shrieking distance. Except for a few mice whose first party this was. These wished themselves home with their moms.

The dresses of these two hundred girls were a compromise between what their mothers thought they ought to wear to a dance, and their own taste, which was to arouse their partners to a discreet frenzy under a warm Technicolor moon at dance intermission. Pretty girls of fourteen and fifteen were wearing their first evening gowns. They hinted that the girl inside them was a blossom, a slip of a thing just out of babyhood: please handle her delicately.

But there were ladies of eighteen and nineteen and twenty,

dressed to the ripeness and promise of their years. Many wore gowns that debouched their charms to a maddening degree; their young men found their gazes wandering between a bewildering bosom and plate of chicken patty. Such upperformers passed their gala supper in an epidemic of bemused desire: they wanted to chew the chickenflesh on their plates, and they wanted to put a tooth into the girlflesh beside them. These young men were in a bad way indeed. Such was Ralph next to his girl at dinner. Miss Harriet Spencer no longer wore the uniform of Emma Willard School. She had a gown that had transformed her into a little green watermelon, gushing with sweet pulp and juices.

There were of course a few girls who, in spite of the cold eyes of the faculty ladies, had dared appear in a boys' school decked out like arrived courtesans. Chronologically they might not yet have reached twenty, but they were arrayed like glittering New York women of thirty-five weary of everything but psychiatry. Here the four hundred boys noticed mantillas and snoods, gilt or jeweled combs in the hair, wimples under chins, expanses of Renaissance headgear, beauty patches on rouged cheeks, slashed skirts with inset satin in complementary colors, earrings and fantastic necklaces.

Tad McKinley sat uneasily beside his date, whom he'd imported from a Cotton Club in Detroit. He knew that everyone in the room was peering at him, and especially at her, whose name was Mirabel Jackson. She wore an evening gown of cloth of gold, her lacquered hair was studded with tea roses. About her saffron neck hung a gold chain, the end of which had originally been attached to a live white mouse. He'd persuaded her to detach the mouse before she entered the Dining Hall, and it was now having its supper in a cage in the Biology Lab. This young Negress was the only girl present who attacked her chicken patty with unfeigned relish. She had several helpings, humming in contentment to herself. Every so often she called out to the faculty lady in charge of the table that this was a fabulous school and everyone and everything at it were fabulous. Between courses she told an anecdote about Nellie Lutcher that made the other girls at table turn into red Indians. But Tad, though he planned later in the evening to taste the sultriness of Mirabel Jackson, felt a wave of blood strumming under his smooth black cheeks. It was shame, not lust; and he told himself that these whites were getting to him after all. He was taking on their damnable genteelisms.

—Shut your mouth, Mirabel, he said to his date as the strawberry parfaits were borne from the pantry.

—I'm being fabulous, the glittering Negress replied, raising her voice out of sheer orneriness to its nightclub level.

Doctor Anderson couldn't keep his eyes off Mirabel Jackson; her coffee breasts rolling almost open in her bodice reminded him of the apples of the Hesperides in a golden basket. Miss Demerjian often shot her escort a glance of withering scorn. Tonight her mustache was hidden under three layers of white liquid rouge. Often she lashed out at Doctor Anderson in purest French. Mirabel Jackson heard her, understood, and decided that Miss Demerjian was also fabulous. Indeed she told her so in French, and Miss Demerjian raised the flag of a blush.

At another table, with boys and girls between them, sat Miss Betty Blanchard and Mr. Philbrick Grimes. It was almost as though they were man and wife, and these boys and girls their children. She now knew the fate Mr. Grimes was plotting for her, and the horror of it made her swallow her parfait and drink her coffee in silence. She wore a white brocade gown, with a single yellow rose in her black hair, which she'd combed out till it fell and coiled above her pallid shoulders. Mr. Grimes, while he was telling the table stories, occasionally scanned her face with petulant possessiveness. Dear God, he'd decided to make her *Mrs.* Philbrick Grimes! If he had his way, she'd one day be the wife of the Principal of this Academy! Was that her child stirring within her in protest against another father? Nor was she unaware that all the way across the dining hall a redheaded man, in charge of a table of lowerformers too young to attend the dance, was watching her like a lynx over a dark waterhole. Even at this distance she could make out the red scar along his mouth. That mouth had known every cranny of her body, had helped transform her into the vessel of life that she now was. As Mr. Grimes told of his last meeting with Katharine Cornell, Miss Blanchard fell to wondering if her child would be marked with his father's twisted mouth, with those fierce eyes which watched her every move with feral hatred. . . .

The dinner ended when Doctor Smedley arose to chant

379

Grace After Meals. He also conveyed to the visiting girls the best wishes of the ailing Principal. Mr. Pilkey regretted that he was unable to be present at the twenty-fifth recurrence of the Spring Prom. Mr. Pilkey hoped that his boys and their dates would conduct themselves like ladies and gentlemen, for dances at The Academy had never been savage or modern. They were planned for innocent merriment of good young people. Mr. Pilkey's message by proxy went on to speak of the unsullied purity of American womanhood and the gallantry of American manhood. Then Doctor Smedley lifted up his old voice and thanked God for dances, for youth, for chicken patty, green peas, and strawberry parfaits. The diners rose from table; rarely was there such a portentous rustling of skirts in the dining hall of the Boys' School.

The Spring Prom was held in the gym of The Academy. But a bare room for athletics had been transformed by the inspiration of Mrs. Whitney and by the work of Ben Gordon and the Decorating Committee. When the first dancers strayed in by couples out of the dark mosquito-humming June night, they found themselves in a gymnasium all but transfigured. The bleachers were still there in the gallery; there still remained the basketball hoops and the black painted lines on the waxed hardwood floor. But all else had become that fairyland of limbo and somnambulism in which Americans prefer to do their dancing and night-clubbing. Under normal light the change wrought in the gym would have been intolerable to any but a seahorse. But in the flecked light of a revolving crystal ball (begged or borrowed from a nearby outdoor dance hall) it had become a place of retreat many fathoms under the sea. From her reading in historical novels Mrs. Whitney had decided on a submarine motif for this year, and Ben Gordon and his sweating committee had faithfully carried out her nightmare of the Palace of Neptune. Dried seaweed seemed to thatch the walls in deposits of mottled green; it was really only shredded green tissue paper. From the glass skylight far above the floor of the gym, rowboats were suspended over the heads of the dancers—in these scarecrows got up in sailor suits seemed to be rowing through the air. Hanging also about ten feet above the floor were octopi, sharks, crabs, and five or six mermaids. These last were achieved by silvery naked figures of dress models (from an uncle of Ben Gordon's in Chicago) with scaly tails attached, and dulse and seafruit clinging to their indecent bosoms. And green gelatins from the Academy theater (courtesy of Mr. Grimes) masking baby spots filled the air with a heavy luminousness of emerald. The faces of the dancers took on in this light the codfish color of passionate seasickness.

In keeping with Mr. Pilkey's new Austerity and Economy Program the music was provided by no name band, no wriggling girl vocalist at three thousand dollars for the evening. No, the twenty dollars apiece for the Prom tickets had gone to Mr. Pilkey's favorite charities, or to pay for the gym decorations, or for Mr. Whitney's extra expenditures on the chicken patty. The music came from a coaxial pair of loudspeakers fastened to the basketball goals. And it came off phonograph records belonging to Buddy Brown. The turntable was in charge of the plump lowerformer who cleaned Buddy's room; all evening long he watched it and diligently changed records.

The boys were embarrassed to be dancing to canned music, and their girls murmured to each other that when it came to throwing a party The Academy was a pretty cheap place.

—O, my! Ain't she purty? . . .
—Golden earrings. . . .
—Just because . . . my cheeks are pearly. . . .
—Your red wagon. . . .

For two hours couples glued themselves together, the boys' lips buried in their girls' hair, swaying silently in voluptuousness broken only by overamplified music, needle scratch, perfume and sweat wafting from bodies writhing in communion or escape.

Sets of gym double doors were open against the descending oppression of a hot June night. Here stood tables with punchbowls floating with Mrs. Whitney's Special Mountain Dew—a dismal syrup of limejuice and carbonated water. Here heated couples refreshed themselves and tried to murmur party things over the brassy scream of the recorded music. They looked longingly at the playing fields outside, smouldering under a tangerine-colored moon. But egress from the stuffy dance floor was denied them till eleven o'clock, when they were free to woo for twenty minutes. And lest any girl or boy attempt to sally forth to the pleasures of the fields and the witchery of the night, faculty ladies stood as chaperones by every exit. Within hailing distance of these dragons loitered muscular corporals and sergeants of The Academy's military training corps, in full drill uniform, twirling nightsticks, camouflaged in green crepe paper. Not that revelers were to be bludgeoned. But if any tried to leave the gym before intermission time, the Acting Co-Principals were advised of the break immediately.

Though he was dancing elegantly and decorously in the embrace of Miss Blanchard, Mr. Grimes knew everything that went on on the dance floor. He whispered delicacies into the inattentive ear of his partner, his little eyes whisking everywhere in the ghoulish green half light. The only thing he missed was a redheaded man hunched in the gallery bleachers, who all evening followed every move made by a girl in a white gown.

—Whirl, ballerina, whirl. . . .
—If ah can't sell it, keep sittin on it. . . .
—Falling in love with love. . . .
—Do you call *that* little thing an affair? . . .

Finally came intermission, the only excuse for the dance, the real reason why two hundred boys had each spent twenty dollars to have here for a weekend girls in whom they had no interest save the possibility of release. The dancers went for the lime punch, wiped their brows, and sallied forth into the darkness, walking hand in hand with specious relaxation and comradeship. Couples seemed to be sucked into womb of night upon leaving the gym. Where did they disappear to? Not even Mr. Grimes could tell. They had only twenty minutes. . . .

A few wandered hand in hand along the paths by the hydrangea bushes, but these were boys and girls who were timorous, coldblooded, or dedicated to an old Protestant code of reverence, self-deception, and Plato.

Many went in to the sofas of the darkened library, especially to its remote book stacks which one night a year shivered with hot whispering and entreaty, and sounds of mouths doing other duty than card cataloguing. Others hurried down to the cinder track to make love stretched out on the bleachers.

Betty Blanchard, feeling her fevered forehead, said to her escort:

—Let's go up to your room and have a cool drink. . . .

—My dear! heavens, no! Mr. Grimes said. We'll just have to stroll here by the gym and see that nothing goes wrong. We can't very well come back to the second half of the dance with our breaths reeking of liquor, can we now?

—I forgot our responsibilities as teachers, she said in a feigned simper.

—Don't ever forget them, ma chère. . . .

Buddy Brown had lost no time during the first half of the Prom. He'd been whisking Midgie Mears into a dusk corner under the belly of one of the hanging mermaids. Under his purple cummerbund he carried a little silver flask of bourbon; and with the connivance of his noncoms the handsome blond boy and the frowsy blond daughter of the Directress took heartening nips for themselves. By intermission time their bloods were ablaze. He took her to the librarian's office. There on a settee he loved her up in a heavy way. When they clung together in gasping madness, and he attempted to lift her dress, Midgie refused him the normal prerogative, but whispered an alternative in his ear. She opened her bodice and Buddy took his satisfaction there. Out in the moonlight, a few minutes later, she began to cry when she discovered that her pageboy bob was as wild as a haymow. And when she saw the stain on the bodice of her dress, she began to vomit.

In twenty minutes Mung and The Body, in the cellar of Hooker Hall, performed an amorous feat unique in the annals of The Academy. They'd tested their teamwork in Birmingham last vacation. For the first seven minutes Mung made Miss Fuchsia Brown and The Body enjoyed the favors of Miss Bonnie Ann Schultz. Then with much giggling and neo-courtesy they changed partners and went through the same motions with each other's date. They returned staggering to the gym just as Mr. Grimes was proclaiming the end of intermission.

Ralph Du Bouchet and Miss Harriet Spencer walked in a little grove neighboring the gym. For five minutes they said nothing; then he grabbed her.

—I'll scream, her voice said under his mouth.

—Please, he muttered.

—Nooooo. What would mother say? What would I tell them at Emma Willard?

Ralph sank down on the soft grass:

—You little goon, he said.

Ben Gordon and Judith Strauss sat silent on opposite ends

of a bench on the terrace in front of Hooker Hall, she tapping the heel of her dancing pump:

—This is one hell of a weekend, she said decisively.

—Judith, can't I even hold your hand? We used to be such good friends. . . .

—*Used* to be, you dope!

Then she got up and walked away.

And on the grass by the cinder track, in company with many other boys and girls experimenting in minor and major liberties, Tad McKinley and his guest requited themselves for the sneers of the whites at dinner. She gave herself as freely as she did to her honkytonk audiences in Detroit. With her there was none of the coyness, none of the unfulfilled teasing and *No, no, please*'s! of white girls who in crisis suddenly remember that they were reputed to be heiresses and respectable young ladies of old Protestant families. Indeed Mirabel and Tad lost themselves so completely in each other that they returned to the gym thirty minutes after the end of intermission. They were still glistening and panting from their poontang. The Messrs. Grimes and Holly were summoned to meet them at the door by an adolescent storm trooper and an outraged lady of the faculty. On the spot Tad was expelled from The Academy one week from his graduation. And Lisa Holly, attracted by the uproar, told the beautiful young Negress to put herself and her bags on the next train. They really didn't want *her* sort defiling a chaste institution.

The second half of the Spring Prom ground on till the specified hour of one o'clock. Its true purpose had already been reached at the twenty-minute intermission; the rest was anticlimax. The eyes of chaperones and MP's at the gym doors grew heavier and more prudish. And children of from fourteen to twenty, still clinging to each other on the musky dance floor and staggering together under the fitful phosphorescence of the revolving crystal ball, began wearily to remember that they were still children, though dressed up like sophisticated ladies and gentlemen at a party. It was already long past their bedtime. Still they swayed and tripped together in the exhaustion of marathon dancers. They'd had enough by midnight. In vain did Buddy Brown command the little lowerformer to stack hotter platters on the turntable. The dancing got more and more dispirited, except for an occasional flare-up of jitterbugging. Miss Midgie Mears had got rid of her liquor and her supper, and somehow she'd washed the smear from the bodice of her gown; she and her partner were kicking away with the best of them, their blond hair streaming. A circle was cleared for them; the spectators sleepily applauded their vitality.

Only one person in the gallery was untired, watching and still resentful. Guy Hudson was the last one left on the basketball bleachers, chewing gum and observing the stale comedy beneath him. The mermaids and rowboats were hanging on a level with his eyes. He felt like a pearl diver watching his loot swimming below him. But still his girl swayed in the arms of the faculty's number one operator.

Precisely at one o'clock, when the phonograph was blaring Goodnight, Sweetheart, and there wasn't anything for the boys and girls to do but go back to the dormitories and drink lemonade and champ on cookies, a wheelchair was pushed out onto the gym floor. Behind it shoving were old Mrs. Pilkey, and fat Miss O'Mara. In it upright and martial sat the Principal, natty in the evening clothes he'd been married in. His wife in one of her incomparable evening gowns marched loyally by his side. There was a sprinkling of applause, but also a scattering of boos and hisses that sent the old man's white eyebrows crinkling up and down. Waving his cane, he summoned Miss Blanchard to audience by his wheelchair. She came slowly, but with the first hauteur she'd ever presented to him. Mr. Grimes melted away somewhere.

—Well. Have you decided to dance with me again, as in March? she said in her low voice.

She was smiling, tired, but unafraid. The Principal strove to keep his prophetic voice down to an outraged whisper:

—No, young woman. I shall never want to dance with you again. Only *pure* women interest me. Get off this dance floor. From what I've heard, you're not fit to be in company with my lovely boys and girls, nor my nice respectable faculty. . . .

The last waltz of the evening was concluded as Miss Blanchard slipped out of the gym. Guy Hudson was waiting for her on the walk outside and gave her his arm. The air was cooling. They laughed together and laid their cheeks side by side, kissing:

—You ought to be ashamed of yourself, you scarlet woman. I trust you had a perfectly rotten time?

—I did, Guy. Till now, that is. . . .

The envelope of June darkness enclosed them. Inside the

gym the phonograph ground back and forth on the eccentric groove on the inside of the record. The little lowerformer was too sleepy to pick the needle off the turntable. Some of the waltzers still swayed out of a reflex of sheer fatigue. Mr. Grimes buzzed round the Pilkeys in horror and apology. For Mr. Pilkey was flailing about him with his cane.

By Pilkeyan dispensation participants in a Spring Prom were allowed to sleep late on the following morning. Till nine o'clock. Since last evening they'd paid homage to Terpsichore and to Aphrodite, today they were exempted from worshipping the Christian God in The Academy chapel. But for those boys who hadn't put up twenty dollars to attend the Spring Prom, Doctor Smedley held a special revival meeting in which he wrestled for their souls. He talked on the unbusinesslike vices of drinking, dancing, and cardplaying.

At nine o'clock groggy dancers and their dates were routed out to breakfast in the dining hall. Mrs. Miekewicz had lain awake all night cursing at the extra trouble, and now she served them cold fried eggs, bacon rancid with its own grease, and gummy coffee. Did anyone complain to the Comptroller? That little gentleman would weep and protest that in these times he couldn't afford to hire a new chef and dietitian. Besides, the Miekewiczes had served The Academy for twenty years.

But the gayest tradition of the morning after Spring Prom was that students of the Boys' School might bring their girls to classes. Mr. Pilkey himself invented this graceful relaxation of discipline twenty-five years ago. It proved to the girl (who might later be mothers of prospective students) that work at his Academy was as effortless as a vaudeville show. The older teachers got, the more kittenish they became on that one morning of the year when girls invaded their classes in bright morning frocks. Only Doctor Sour refused to have a girl in his classroom. Mathematics teachers showed how to bisect and trisect a divided skirt. Even Doctor Hunter rose to the occasion of feminine inspiration. Courtly in his goatee, he read aloud and translated for young American ladies the love poems of Catullus which tell of Lesbia and her sparrow. And the girls giggled amiably and voted Doctor Hunter a Perfect Old Dear.

Guy Hudson planned to hold class in European History 2a

as usual. He slammed churlishly into Room 18. He sat on his desk with his legs tucked up under him, toying with a piece of chalk. He was determined that this morning he wouldn't alter his teaching in the slightest, nor put on a coy act for the girl guests. For this was the last class he would ever teach at The Academy this June or any June.

His class began entering, but with a difference. This morning there was no loitering, no whistling, no defiance. There was a certain jubilee in the air. Couples came prettily and politely to his desk, and he had to stand up. He was introduced to Midgie Mears, to Judith Strauss, to Harriet Spencer. He was as gracious as the scar at the corner of his mouth would permit. Only Tad and his Negress were missing, for everyone knew with hideous silence that they were on a train heading somewhere. The Academy would see them no more. . . .

The girls sat with their escorts in the front rows, holding hands and giggling solemnly, for Guy Hudson's appearance wasn't such as to augur a period of strained comedy, like whatever classes they'd just come from. It was the first mixed class he'd ever taught. Buddy and Midgie were sitting close together, playing footie-footie with their loafers. Midgie wore a peanut-colored sweater, over which dangled her badge as President of the Student Council of the Girls' School. Buddy glittered with his insignia too. Together the blond boy and the blond girl seemed incestuous twins, hatched from the same brash ovum. Gud Hudson forced his eyes off Midgie's redoubtable breasts. He got up and all but slammed the glass door to his classroom:

—My dear children, I haven't the slightest intention of putting on a circus for you this morning, no matter what other teachers at this institution are doing. . . .

Midgie, aware of her privilege and prerogative, put up her hand as spokesman of the group:

—Let's just have *fun*! Don't be a stuffed shirt all your life!

The boys and girls said *aw* and applauded. Guy Hudson turned his most twisted sneer on Midgie:

—In many respects I *am* a stuffed shirt. All teachers are, because they pretend at least to stand for something. And I propose to go on teaching this morning. . . . On second thought, I wonder if I can teach *you* so very much. . . .

There was ribald laughter from the regular component

387

of the class; some of the girls demurely hid their faces.
Midgie flushed; Buddy's blue eyes sparked, as though to
say that his SS would take care of Hudson after class, all
right all right.

—I intend to talk to you about America. . . .

Guy Hudson sat down at his desk, leaning forward, his
hands folded in a repose he never felt. Comfortable smiles
lapped the cheeks of the boys and girls. Ah, this was the pap
they'd been fed during and since the late war. They could
relax and hold hands while this redheaded fool beat his
gums about dying for one's country and the glories of free
enterprise and the inevitability of an atomic war with Russia. They wouldn't have to think once during the next hour,
and they could nod appreciatively at the old bromides. It was
going to be a perfect after-Prom class at that! . . .

—Do you love America, Mr. Hudson? Midgie asked innocently, batting her false blond lashes and smoothing her
storied breasts.

—Very much, Miss Mears. And now may I do the talking?
This isn't a vaudeville routine. You're not my straight
woman, feeding me the gags. . . .

There was a knock on the door of Room 18. He thought
it might be the revived Principal rolling up in a wheelchair
to tell him to get out of the school, or at least Miss Pringle
with a pungent note. But no. Outside in the corridor stood
Mr. Grimes and Miss Blanchard, waving and smiling, as one
does to a convict on visiting day. Guy Hudson got up and
opened the door, for even at The Academy a teacher teaching was a sacrosanct as a criminal who has found haven in
a sanctuary.

—Doctor, Mr. Grimes said airily, good morning. It seems
she wants to sit in on your class. Of course I didn't approve,
but she insists. . . .

With delicate distaste Mr. Grimes handed his erring Prom
girl into the classroom and withdrew, snickering piously.
Nor was Betty the same girl from whose side Guy Hudson
had arisen this morning at seven in the village's ratty hotel.
She had on a gray suit with pearls; the round beauty of
her maturity made every other girl there seem a little shrill.
There was considerable stir at her entrance, which drowned
out her saying in her lover's ear:

—They say you can't love a lumberjack till you've seen

388

him ride the logs, and you certainly can't be married to a teacher till you've watched him teach. . . .

She sat down in a chair near the door, seeming abashed at the commotion she'd caused. Guy Hudson returned to his desk, scratched his red curls, and tossed a stick of chalk in his palm.

—Where was I? he said a little thickly.

—Somewhere in America, Midgie prompted.

—O yes. . . . Look, you and I and millions of others are living in the most wonderful country, the most horrible country the world has yet seen. Most of us know very little about its tradition, in spite of the shouting about American history that goes on in most schools. And all the saluting of the flag. . . . Most of us, sadly enough, really aren't interested in our country. As a matter of fact, you may write this down as a first and dominant quality of Americans. When nothing gets in their way, they're possessed of a kind of amiable madness. We've so much freedom that, in the process of acquiring and maintaining it, we've seen fit to throw over every tradition, every link with the past. In many ways this American chaos is a good thing. But we do go sliding cheerily through the fourth dimension. Perhaps God laughs at us for our arrogance. For we've given up every check except political opportunism and a zeal for what is blasphemously called the Almighty Dollar. Yes, my friends, whatever is right for the moment is okay with us Americans. This is the philosophical side of that trait known as Yankee ingenuity. . . .

Thirty or so pairs of eyes were wide open now. Judith Strauss let out a stabbing sigh, thinking perhaps of her father, the delicatessen mogul. But Guy Hudson continued slowly, expanding his chest and keeping his voice low and monitory :

—You and I can never understand ourselves or our country till we realize that we aren't whole personalities. We're all split by virtue of the dual nature of America. Two traditions run side by side here, and few are aware of the dichotomy. Unity has disappeared in America. It will never be achieved, and perhaps that's the way we want it. . . . Nevertheless, when one overthrows the orthodoxies, one yearns for them and strives to invent new ones. You see, we're the heirs of a Jeffersonian agrarian democracy, which liberals

389

have recently begun to shout about. But they're mistaken to invoke it now. It was wonderful in 1800. It was the most luminous ideal of modern times, and the last Christian one. We got it from the French Revolution—Liberty, Fraternity, and Equality. What more could a man ask *in theory*? O, my friends, the Founding Fathers had a breadth of vision that few in America of 1949 dare look into too closely. It might blind them. There are many groups today in America who shrink from the implications of the revolutionary ideas of those great men whose names are paid lip service to, at least on their birthdays. Our only and our greatest boast should be that we're *still* a free people. . . .

There was uneasy applause. He raised his freckled hand:

—And still a revolutionary one. . . .

The applause died. Judith Strauss raised her hand and said in her madonna voice:

—Do you mean revolutionary in the Marxian sense, Mr. Hudson?

—No. But you're using Marxian in its strictly derogatory sense. For the record let's make it clear that you boys and girls in this room associate Marx and Revolution. The Founding Fathers had never heard of Marx, had they? . . . Marxism, as *I* understand it in its fullest implications, would be a dreadful catastrophe in America. For it devolves logically into smaller and more vicious dictatorships than we have here locally. The Marxist ideal is vicious because it infiltrates into our sense of pity, our awareness of an unfair distribution of the world's goods. Thus Marxism makes a fool of the idealists. As it works today, it hasn't settled the problem of distribution any more than *our* system has. But so far our system at least makes pretences to the old Jeffersonian freedoms. Capitalism, at least when it's unpanicky, has always been tolerant of revolutionary criticism *from within its own body*. . . . And that's what I mean by the revolutionary sense in intelligent Americans. We don't seek to overthrow our own government, but to keep it as a living and constantly evolving organism. We try vigilantly to square and harmonize the old agrarian tolerance with a system of finance and distribution which, allowed to run wild, would eventually swallow up our freedoms and ourselves. This sort of revolution is true democracy. It isn't mentioned in the pages of Karl Marx. I think that a false dilemma is set up when we Americans are offered a choice between dictatorship by the machine (and those who own it), and dictatorship by the state, which might at first pretend to be paternal and purely socialistic. In our time, my friends, we must show up this false dilemma, or be silenced forever. . . . Which brings me to the second element in our split personalities as Americans. I just said that in one hundred and fifty years we've passed from the original agrarian republic into a complex industrial nation which is striving to remain a democracy. Few politicians are willing to point out that we no longer live under a system analogous to that with which we started. The DAR babbles of our great progenitors, but it refuses to face the truth that their great-great-grandchildren live under a different sort of economic society. . . . Yes, we might as well face the fact that few Americans (except possibly some artists, Christians, and village idiots) are governed by any ideal except to get rich as fast as possible. And here our freedoms operate to our disadvantage. The artificial concept of equality really perpetuates what was going on long before it was dreamed up—survival of the fittest and dog-eat-dog. For that's Life, as the cliché says. . . . Who of you in this room this morning has any real sense of pity? And who desires to understand anything that isn't approved of by the comfortable bourgeoisie from which you come? I'm sorry to use Marxian phrases, but sometimes they're applicable. . . . Let's face the fact dominant in the head of every boy in this class. He's at this school to be educated, educated in the sense that possibly he may go out and amass more of a pile than the so-called uneducated or less fortunate. . . . And some of the pretty little deals I've observed even at this school assure me that Americans justify anything from which money can be turned. I suppose all nationalities do. . . . But let's consider for a moment the ultimate consequences of a civilization in which everything but the motive of profit is suspect. . . . Bright rapacious entrepreneurs get control of the American radio and the American movies and the American reading public. All these channels are good in themselves, since communications make the world smaller. But suppose these vast audiences are fed nothing but dinosaurian vulgarities, half-truths, and sheer poison? Then we have nothing but deadly pills, peddled under the banner of freedom to millions of good men and women who are caught in a mesh devised by a few. . . . These suave entrepreneurs assure us that the American public gets what it wants. But does it? Are Americans really so tasteless, so violent, and so stupid? Can they live on a diet of singing commercials, of well-dressed dipsomaniacs, of seductions geared to lonely clubwomen? I refuse to believe it. . . .

—You talk like a Communist, Buddy Brown said sulkily and suddenly.

—I am *not* a Communist! And the fact that you've called me one proves my point about the second half of the American split personality. It can be spotted by Puritanism, or by attempted standardization of all thinking. It's a method of suppressing the things which are wrong with America. These must be faced squarely, for we all feel guilt about them. . . .

There was a little applause and much booing.

Quiet! This class isn't a democracy; it's a dictatorship. By *me*. . . . I'm only a teacher, and perhaps soon I'll be gagged from teaching because I'm all out against the evil monster that lurks in the American subconscious. This dragon is Hydra-headed. It manifests itself in petty moral censorship, or in a glorification of useless work and useless manufacture, in all tasteless and horrid things which industrialism and commercialism uncontrolled can do to the human spirit. But all this evil is protected under the name of the American Way of Life. . . . Some people would have it that if I point out evils in our democracy I'm being unAmerican. Am I? There can be wonderful good in the best aspects of this American Way of Life. But we can't afford to lump both good and evil under the name of democracy. Then one of the noblest words in history would be degraded to just another catchword, covering and justifying holy wars, exploitation, suppression, vulgarity, and hypocrisy. And democracy will end as a dictatorship, like anything else. . . . As a teacher, my hope rests in more and finer education for more people. I say that nothing serious can happen to the world if everyone's eyes are opened. . . .

The bell in the corridor truncated his class and anything more he had to say. Boys and their dates rushed out the door. Lulled in the pleasures of their weekend, most hadn't attended to what he'd tried to say. Why should they care? They had plenty to eat. And this afternoon they were going

392

to a track meet and a tea dance. They'd been listening to a man almost thirty, who could only be described as embittered. It was a neat word, embittered. Didn't it explain completely the Guy Hudsons of this world? . . .

He dusted the chalk from his hands and strolled to the door of his classroom, the last time he would ever enter or leave one at this Academy. He understood at last how the teacher may find himself in conflict with society, because, like the artist, his integrity forces him to slice across its strata.

Betty was waiting for him at the door. She at least hadn't rushed away with the rest. She took his arm gently:

—Guy. I think I like you. You're a fanatic. Your eyes never shone that way in my arms. . . .

—And I like *you*.

He knew that for all the talking men did, for all their shaping and groping after abstracts and laws (where none were), their women knew something deeper. And these poles met and married when men and women truly loved.

4

The fifteenth of June came in with blast-furnace weather and a sense of utter ripeness. Over Miss Sophia's grave in the churchyard burdocks and mallows bent like crutches of old people leaning together for a picnic time in the sun. Eighty-two years now she had lain in the cemetery; all memory of her was blotted out, save as an impetus, a shining Christian anonymity of accomplishment, to be invoked whenever the going got rough. But on her headstone in full summer an influence seemed to be smiling, as though here lay a female Anacreon.

And on the macadam road by the churchyard, by the Girls' School, there passed a stream of automobiles elegant and inelegant, repeating a procession they'd participated in nine months ago. Nine months. The gestation time of a human foetus, and in American education the seedtime of the student. Mr. Pilkey said so in his catalog.

The Boys' and Girls' Schools held their Commencement jointly on the quadrangle. This ceremony (which edified parents and proved to them that their $1800 was well spent) was like estranged brothers and sisters getting together for the reading of a legacy.

In the preparations Mr. Pilkey was everywhere in his wheelchair, provided with a battery motor so that he could scoot from chapel to quadrangle, inspecting the alignment of the folding chairs on the grass under a rented circus awning, peppermint striped. Mr. Twarkins and his crew of janitors were setting up the chairs. In the chapel Mr. Amos Jones practiced the War March of the Priests.

Mr. Pilkey's electrified wheelchair veered like a little boat through the rising mists of the June morning. He greeted hundreds of arriving guests, lingering over them in exact proportion to their national reputation or income. Running behind him was Mr. Grimes, carrying a clipboard of memoranda and a thermos bottle of iced lemonade, lest the convalescent Principal work himself into another stroke on this most crucial of days. The mechanical wheelchair pried into everything like an enchanted rickshaw: Mr. Grimes had all he could do to keep up with it; the Principal was as happy with his new mode of conveyance as a child with a toy automobile.

—Did you know it reverses too?

And he veered backward, all but knocking down the faithful Mr. Grimes, the clipboard, and the thermos bottle.

To these graduation ceremonies also came five hundred or so alumni of the Boys' and Girls' Schools. Tonight they would throw a drunken brawl, at which they would be dunned for contributions to their school's endowment. The eldest of them was no more than forty-five. When they were at school, they hadn't been the most brilliant of The Academy's boys and girls. For clever alumni have no reason to be interested in school reunions. No, the ones who kept returning year after year to their Alma Mater were dreary ones whom no one had been aware of, half-baked politicians, athletes whose single glory in four years had been that day they cut the tape on The Academy's track team. They'd never been so happy since, and they came back to remind themselves of it. On Graduation Day men and women escaped from their present lives and stole back to look hungrily upon an institution they'd perhaps hated while they were here. But now they told their children that the greatest single influence on their lives had been Those Good Old Days. Thus once a year the barren womb of Miss Sophia was peopled with hundreds of men and women. Perhaps this Coming Back Home was what she'd really wanted in the last days of her life. She, who'd never known human love, was cherished by thousands of American men and women, for whose education she'd provided. And each June they returned to her with a sigh for their boyhoods and girlhoods, lingering for a day in her shadow. This perhaps was the essence of her triumph. Few mortal lovers are as faithful as men and women coming back to a school which has meant something in their lives—they don't know what, precisely. Was it that in their four years here these men and women got their first and last intimations of the scope and power of love? . . .

Anyway, graduates came back in hordes. Alumni of '26 and '27 walked with their wives and daughters, nostalgically pointing out the gym and the chapel, or observing platitudinously that such and such a building or dormitory hadn't been built in *their* time. Even to the eyes of teachers there was something inordinately touching about these old alumni and these parents on the last day of the school year. It almost atoned for the humiliations of nine months. It touched even Guy Hudson, who would be dismissed this afternoon. For he saw a final vindication of teaching—that many men and women had nothing left to love or cling to except a school which at least, of all worldly things, pretended to idealism and disinterestedness. To his wry eye there was something vaguely sad about Commencement. Only on such days do Americans indulge in leavetaking and retrospection; only then are they foggily aware of the grandeur and potentiality of schools.

The one hundred and fifty upperformers graduating today wore The Academy's blazer—a jacket of maroon and black stripes, the colors in the coat of arms of the Abercrombie family—and white flannel trousers. Even Mr. Pilkey in his wheelchair wore just such a loud blazer. He looked like

Zeus gone collegiate. Mrs. Pilkey, who'd had one of her Bumps this morning, wore a garden party frock in The Academy's colors. And the Principal's mother had on something in maroon and jet. She was ninety-four yesterday, and she hunched along refusing to speak to any lady under sixty.

Parents kept arriving, got up in gay clothes, for the graduation of a son or daughter is a solemn festivity for American mothers and fathers, who are pushed into the background with the birth of their heirs. Soon the colonnades clicked with the strolling of hundreds of smiling men and women, vaguely proud and yearning.

Mr. and Mrs. Marlow Brown strutted like cock and hen. Wasn't their boy President of the Student Council? Mr. Brown bragged to other fathers of the sumptuous prosperity of his plastics business, and of the smash his son was going to make next year at Princeton. And Cynthia Brown, pomaded and mascaraed, flipped her long cigarette holder and recommended to troubled mothers her latest analyst, a Viennese who'd studied under Jung. She felt *so* at peace on his couch. . . .

Mother Du Bouchet had bought herself a new gown for Ralph's graduation—a dignified and handsome silk—her first in two years. She had on a flowered toque and a little veil, and she'd contrived to look less tired and worried than usual. She told Father Du Bouchet that it could happen only once or twice, this tribute to Ralph. And they walked under the colonnades, their arms about their only son, who other mothers said was the prettiest boy in the graduating class.

A Negro doctor and his wife turned up and left the grounds in ashen chagrin. They were the mother and father of Tad McKinley, recently expelled. He hadn't notified them, and they'd come on from Detroit. When the McKinleys heard what had befallen their son, the little Negress put her head on the shoulder of her husband and sobbed without a sound. Mr. Grimes was detailed to drive them in his Packard to the railroad station, and he did it in horrified silence.

There was a sad twosome of parents who tacitly avoided Mr. Pilkey. The father was a stout merchant from Chicago, the mother an intelligent Jewess, somewhat loudly dressed. Their son was being permitted to graduate, but he'd lost all his honors. Thus the Gordons scarcely held up their heads, or spoke to anybody else except the Du Bouchets, who had

396

quick sympathies. They stood in shady corners of the ivied dormitories and didn't look at a soul. Even their boy couldn't bear to be with them. Often the Jewess dabbed at her eyes with a lace handkerchief; her husband put an arm around her shaking shoulders.

The quadrangle now swarmed with loitering parents and all the male and female teachers of both schools. Upperformers about to graduate were drawn up in processional line, their striped blazers moving like a stroboscope. From loudspeakers hung everywhere there blared forth the music of Dr. Amos James, for the organ was piped outdoors through the public address system. He began the fanfare to the March from Mendelssohn's *Athalie*. The graduating class marked time and stood at attention for marching. Buddy Brown shouted a military order. Guests moved forward to take seats in the chapel.

Mr. Grimes was chief usher. He had under him a corps of cute lowerformers in full military regalia. Unfortunately only five hundred guests could be seated in the chapel—the graduating class, the faculties, and the more distinguished guests. Mr. Grimes had worked a week on who was to sit where. Upperformers about to be transfigured would sit in the front pews after they'd marched in. Behind them the two Mrs. Pilkeys, Mrs. Mears, and the faculties of the Boys' and Girls' Schools. Then the Marlow Browns, and so on down the ranking parents.

The chapel was alive with gladioli, their golden bells pealing in all windows. Mrs. Pilkey had been hounding faculty ladies in flower arrangements since eight this morning. On the platform, under the enormous copy of Miss Sophia's portrait (done by Mrs. Pilkey) and beside an American flag, sat Mr. Pilkey in his wheelchair, Doctor Smedley, and a guest speaker with words of warning for the graduating class. He was a scientist, a brigadier general who'd assisted in the development of the atomic bomb.

But more than a thousand guests couldn't be seated inside. It was to accommodate these nobodies that fifteen hundred folding chairs had been installed in the quadrangle. Here sat most of the parents, poor alumni and alumnae, and an assortment of villagers who'd wandered over for the party. Everything that went on in the chapel was piped to them through the loudspeakers. Among these hangers-on were the

397

mother and father of Ben Gordon, sitting far back under the circus awning.

The graduating classes of the Boys' and Girls' Schools entered the chapel. The girls in their pastel dresses were led by Midgie Mears. She almost didn't graduate; yesterday she'd failed two Spanish makeups. But since it was unseemly that the daughter of the Directress shouldn't receive her diploma, Mrs. Mears had put the pressure on Miss Blanchard, who'd refused to raise the grade to 60. Finally Mrs. Mears prevailed by pointing out that Miss Blanchard would be the first unmarried mother on the faculty. . . .

When all candidates were seated in their pews, Mr. Pilkey bent the microphone down to himself as though he was wringing the neck of a stork. He wouldn't be permitted to stand up for another month. His voice rang through the chapel, to a metallic echo of it from loudspeakers in the tented pavilion of the guadrangle:

—Give ear, ye children, to my law, devout attention lend:
  My tongue, by inspiration taught. . . .

And graduating boys and girls answered him in an antiphon of mixed voices, for this was the Commencement Litany and Responsive Reading. He'd used it every June for twenty-five years; it was the last time he would lead these children in choral prayer. It had been rehearsed for a week. It came off so perfectly, in such devotional cadence that many mothers bowed their heads, and Cynthia Brown was heard to sniffle into her handkerchief.

Then they all rose, except Mr. Pilkey. In the Dutch Prayer of Thanksgiving two thousand sang, but the Principal's baritone dominated them all, for his mouth was close to the microphone:

—We gather together to ask the Lord's blessing;
  He chastens and hastens His will to make known. . . .

It had an organ prelude and interludes over a sustained pedalpoint on D, beloved by the organist, since by it he could keep a congregation in suspense. Beginning softly, graduates and congregation sang three stanzas in gathering crescendo to:
—Lord, make us freeeeee!

398

This too had been rehearsed by both schools, but its seeming spontaneity at the climax so overpowered Buddy Brown's mother that she collapsed in her pew and sobbed all through the ensuing Collect by Doctor Smedley. The chapel microphone picked up her emotion and transmitted it to the undistinguished audience outside in the quadrangle, who couldn't decide the reason for the grief during the old chaplain's interminable prayer.

Then from his wheelchair Mr. Pilkey made a few remarks. He told of the success of The Academy's new military program, of how his boys were developing new virility and reliance under it. He paid tribute to the new President of the Student Council, a gallant sergeant major in the field. But he didn't mention the ex-President. He spoke of The Academy's need for an increased Endowment if it was to continue to make its contribution to American democracy against the rising costs of living; he hoped that parents and alumni (included the new graduating class) would contribute generously, for schools like this one couldn't afford to go out of existence.

Guy Hudson sat almost out of sight in the Choir Loft, a handkerchief stuffed in his mouth. He was staring at the blownup replica of Miss Sophia behind the rostrum. He could have sworn that the left eye of Our Gracious Foundress was giving him a shrewd old woman's wink. But then he and Betty had had several shots of bourbon to steady their nerves for The Service. . . .

Then the Principal awarded diplomas. As their names were called, each boy and girl stepped forward for the rolled parchment tied with a two-color ribbon of The Academy's hues. Boys whose initials ran A to K received theirs from the hand of Mr. Grimes; Dell Holly took care of the L to Z's. The girl graduates (A to K) got theirs from Mrs. Mears; L to Z from Lisa Holly, luminous in strawberry satin. And Mrs. Mears had her last say to fifty members of her school who were making their fledgling flight from her lap:

—Girls! We've laughed together and we've cried together! But it's been worthwhile, hasn't it? . . . Yes, it *has*! . . . And remember next year in college, and after that, when you're wives and mothers that a graduate of Miss Sophia's Girls' School is the ideal American woman. She is resourceful.

Never under any circumstance does she allow herself to become nerrrrvous. . . .

Mr. Pilkey, who like a true monarch knew the secret of being kingly while seated, awarded medals, prizes, and scholarships. These went as the faculty had voted them in March —with two exceptions. The Sophia Abercrombie Gold Medal for Valor, Application, and Dignity went to Buddy Brown, not to Ben Gordon. And Ralph Victor Du Bouchet got a $4,000 scholarship to Juilliard, subscribed by Mr. Marlow Brown and the Unitex Plastic Corporation. Lastly Mr. Pilkey announced that a vital and mature sparkplug of his faculty was about to receive a signal honor: the Shakespeare Memorial Instructorship in Literature. It carried an honorarium of $5,000 a year, and was awarded by unanimous vote of faculty, Principal, and trustees to Mr. Philbrick Grimes, a loved and distinguished teacher. Mr. Grimes came shyly forward and received a scroll suitable for framing. His brigade of ushers acted as claque.

Finally the visiting brigadier general spoke long and earnestly to the graduating class. He told them with military modesty of his small part in the development of the atom bomb. He doubted, however, that His Baby would make humanity junk its concept of national sovereignty, of individual rapacity, of inherited hatreds and prejudices. He told them that humanity was probably living on borrowed time. But he predicted that in the few years left to the human race great scientists and humanitarians of the future would continue to be graduated from such schools as this one. And he wished the graduates joy, success, and prosperity in their chosen careers; he would follow them with benign interest.

After a somewhat damp singing of America the Beautiful, the newly laureated, their parents, the faculties and older alumni and alumnae adjourned to the circus-awninged quadrangle. For there during the Commencement Exercise Mrs. Miekewicz and her Polish husband the chef and lower-formers impressed into KP duty had set up tables laden with salads moulded into designs of the American flag and The Academy's seal. Also potato chips and pickles and iced tea and coffee and icecream under fresh raspberries. It was the last expense of the school year for Mr. Whitney, who watched almost two thousand distinguished and undistinguished guests make away with all these victuals. Half an hour later nothing was left but the tablecloths.

There was no respite to the ceremonies. A concert was given to the folding chairs, into which replete people lowered themselves and looked tolerantly at the arts, sleepy in the warmth after their buffet luncheon. The afternoon sun had cooked the top of the awning, and many a mother fanned herself with her mimeographed program and imagined herself listening to music in a steam room.

The Academy orchestra of fifteen squeakers, blowers, and beaters under the baton of Mr. Amos James worked their way through *Finlandia*, the Boccherini *Minuet*, and the Overture to *Tannhauser*, leisurely savoring their tortured dissonances. Even in the open air under the canvas pavilion the chaos and the din were such that the players seemed to be learning their various instruments.

Then the Girls' Glee Club warbled By the Waters of Minnetonka and Heigh-Ho, Come to the Fair! and The Foolish Lover Squanders, and such girlish glees under the direction of Miss Carpenter, mistress of music. Mrs. Mears nodded her flowered hat in time. Their fluty girlish soprani and altos sounded tepid in the open air. Mothers fanned themselves like metronomes; alumni were reduced to taking snifters out of bottles under their folding chairs. For this was the way American ladies were expected to sing, in a genteel tradition of innocuous ballads by the family piano; it must not be suggested that music was a passionate and dangerous pastime.

Ralph played a Bach unaccompanied violin sonata in E major. After two minutes of it the alumni decided that something troublingly decadent had crept into the school since *their* day, when suspicious artistic impulses were confined to mandolin clubs and manly barbershop harmony. And Mrs. Marlow Brown peered angrily at her husband—four thousand good dollar bills for *that*? She looked a little happier when Mr. Amos James came out and sat down to the ebonized Steinway for Ralph's second number. But alas, this was the Fauré Sonata. There was polite applause, and Ralph left the platform under the stigma of being a terribly cultivated young American. Was he perhaps a little queer?

Then the Boys' Glee Club sang a brief recital. Their program was a compromise between the thwarted taste of Mr. James and the concept of what is healthy music for young Americans to sing. There was Palestrina's *Adoramus Te*, which was voted to introduce an unpleasantly ascetic note into the graduation. And flies buzzed in the heliotrope during pianissimo delicacies of Antonio Lotti's *Crucifixus* and Carissimi's *Plorate, Filii Israel*. The mothers were getting quite depressed with this morbid music and the heat, and Mrs. Mears, who liked the operetta *Robin Hood*, was getting nerrrvous. Mr. Amos James hovered between beatific ecstasy and despair that he couldn't *draw* his chorus out, even after nine months of perfectionist rehearsals. They sang their music perfectly, but they felt nothing of it. Their voices, the voices of American young men, were happier in scat singing and football cheering.

Interest revived in the last pieces of the Boys' Group which were sung by express order of Mr. Pilkey, and conducted with gingerly embarrassment by Mr. James. These were the Winter Song, with its fake conviviality and zum-zum's; and humming dialect songs about darkies and pickaninnies and mammies and cornpone which infuriated Guy Hudson; and the Yale bathos of the Whiffenpoof Song (in which the Alumni joined with whiskey enthusiasm); and The Academy's football song: Pigskin, Play!

But Mr. James got a last revenge on the sweltering audience and a vindication of his own humiliation and musical taste. For the last number of this Commencement Concert he brought together the choirs of the Boys' and Girls' Schools, the dreadful orchestra, and the Steinway, played fourhanded by The Abbott and The Abbess. These choral and instrumental masses all but lifted the rented awning off the quadrangle. They performed the florid chorus *Wie Will Ich Mich Freuen*, from a Bach cantata. For Mr. James was determined that the last memory of graduating boys and girls should be the name of his treasured Johann Sebastian Bach. The Abbott and The Abbess, giggling over their music at The Bishop, sometimes lost their places in the polyphony, but the total effect was of a rococo pinwheel spinning out all the colors of the spectrum. A few stunned alumni were heard to remark that it was a damn shame to train American kids to sing the language of Adolf Hitler.

Commencement Day was over. The alumni would have a fund-raising party given for them tonight. Parents and guests began to drift away after shaking hands with the Pilkeys and thanking them for all they'd done in maturing their children.

Summer vacation was beginning. Many boys and girls of the graduating class would never revisit this quadrangle—whether through inclination or fate.

Buddy Brown and Ralph Du Bouchet said goodbye forever without shaking hands.

Ben Gordon put his things into his father's Cadillac. Most of the way back to Chicago he looked out of the window with wet eyes.

Midgie Mears was swept into the white seventeenth-century house by her mother, to begin a summer of tutoring to insure that she might last at least one year at Bennington.

And a contingent of safely graduated upperformers who weren't going home till this evening or tomorrow made up a foraying expedition to the village under Buddy Brown. Even The Abbott, The Abbess, and The Bishop were in this gang, which had much steam bottled up in it. They ran to the Lithuanian tavern on Sophia Street, no longer Out of Bounds to them. There they proceeded to throw down beers. By six o'clock they were sloppily or violently drunk. The Bishop tickled the back of his prelatical throat and threw up all over the graduation blazers of The Abbott and The Abbess. The Body attempted to beat up Mung. The group was united only in scattering raw hamburg and salted peanuts on the citizenry of Miss Sophia's village. They kicked in the stained glass and the oscillating beads of the juke box. And having picked up Ginny Snelgrove and several doxies from the local high school, they returned to The Academy loaded with beer inside and empty bottles outside. They stood outside the Principal's Cape Cod house and serenaded him with:

—Roll me over
In the clover....

When their Principal didn't appear, they gave him a noisy and flatulent razzberry. Mr. Grimes might be seen peering from behind a lace curtain on the second floor. He didn't venture out. But when the mob began smashing their bottles against the white clapboards of his house, the front door opened and Mr. Pilkey's mechanized wheelchair dashed out with him in it. He rode right into the yelling rioters, using his cane to rich advantage. And they quailed before him though they'd boasted they were no longer afraid of the old foghorn. Drunken revelers, shouting from their cudgeling, scattered in the direction of the westering sun. Mr. Pilkey used his voice too:

—Get away from my school! . . . Go to your homes! . . . Three hours ago you woudn't have *dared*! I'll call the police! . . .

His cane caught fleeing Buddy Brown and Ginny Snelgrove, running with their arms about each other's waists, across the flat of their backs. And the recent leader in student government shouted, mostly for his girl's benefit.

—Why, you old bastard!

—And you're a young one! Mr. Pilkey bawled, belting him again.

When all had melted before his wrath, the rubber-tired vehicle picked its way back among the shards of the bottles. The door was opened for him by the invisible hand of Mr. Grimes. Inside his old mother and Mrs. Pilkey and Florinda the Negress received him as a conquering hero.

—Shut the door, Old Mrs. Pilkey said. Those hoodlums! We belong to a vanishing generation. . . .

—*Vanishing*! cried the old gentleman, mopping his brow with the bright striped sleeve of his blazer. Not while there's right and wrong in this world! . . .

And the Cape Cod door slammed shut.

Guy Hudson and Betty Blanchard were walking slowly toward the Girls' School. He was loaded with bags. She turned in the road and took a long look at the Boys' School, its towers and ivy gilt and tender in the sunset.

—How lovely it is from a distance, she said softly. One would never suspect. . . .

—One never does, he answered, sweating. It's when you move in close to things that they begin to hurt. . . .

Coming insouciantly toward them was a Packard convertible coupe, stirring up a wake of June dust and ground beetles.

—Here comes the Shakespeare Chair, Betty said.

Mr. Grimes applied his brakes and skidded to rest beside them. He leaned out with his famous shy snigger:

—Remember your John Milton? . . . Adam and Eve making their solitary way out of the Garden of Eden . . . a touching spectacle. . . .

—Shall we call *you* the angel with the flaming sword? Betty Blanchard said, turning away.

A huge bitterness surged up in her. She wondered if Guy would squash this little scorpion. But her lover took on the expression of a pained frontiersman. He quietly set down his bags, offered a cigarette to Mr. Grimes, which was daintily declined, then lit one himself and mopped his freckled brow.

—Do you call *this* place Eden?

—Yes, doctor, Mr. Grimes said with a shrug. It's *my* Eden. . . And I'm rather sorry to see you two being expelled from it. . . . If you'd played your cards right, you'd still be looking at the Tree of Knowledge. . . .

—I'm surprised to hear you mix a metaphor, Guy Hudson said smiling.

Mr. Grimes winced. Betty took up the quarrel:

—Do you imply, then, that the difference between heaven and hell, between angels and devils, is simply the rules of a poker game?

Mr. Grimes shrugged gallantly, but he didn't answer. Then he resumed:

—I feel like offering to drive you kids wherever you're going. But I just haven't time. I'm in a hurry.

—You always are, Guy Hudson said. You always will be. But never in such a hurry that you can't gloat over unpleasant little incidents. . . .

—Can't we part friends? Mr. Grimes said.

He put out his hairy slim paw, but Guy Hudson didn't take it. And to cover up his rancor Mr. Grimes talked swiftly on:

—I'm going to Lisa Holly's for a spot of sherry. Don't you two wish you could still play in our backyard? It's fun, you know. . . . Adieu, mes amis. . . . It's been fun knowing you two . . . in ways. . . .

And the Packard jerked off, leaving Guy Hudson and his girl in a puff of dust. She pretended to retch toward the retreating car.

—Don't.

—Why?

—Because there's no point in it, my darling. Save your bile for the big people. . . .

—I'm sorry. It's just that I think we've been given one helluva creaming. . . .

—We can take it, he said.

He picked up his suitcases, and they walked slowly through the village, down the glen, and toward the white church. By some impulse they sought out the headstone of Miss Sophia, yellow and mossy in the sunset. He put his arm about Betty's shoulder:

—You know what? I have a fiendish desire to love you up here and now. The old girl would rise from the dead, with us writhing on top of her. . . .

—See if I care.

But some last flaring of the pettishness he used to know compelled her to kick the tombstone with her shoe, which was soft and high laced like a ballet slipper.

—Don't do that, Betty.

—And why not?

And now in ire she bent down, took the headstone into both her hands and shook it like a raging child. She called into the grass and the weeds and the mallows:

—Miss Sophia, can you hear me? Listen! . . . Speak to us and tell us that you've been cheated like us! Say that your heart is broken too! . . .

He lifted her up to his chest:

—Her heart *isn't* broken. . . . Neither is ours. . . . She had faith. She saw what she had to do and did it. . . .

Betty began to cry:

—What do you mean? What are we going to do?

—Go right on teaching, I guess. It doesn't matter how or where. We were born to be teachers. You love it and I love it, I *know*. The work transcends the irritation and the heartbreak. We know that now too, don't we?

She looked at him in a new way, and her tears changed to laughter. It was the laughter of Miss Sophia, of mothers, of watchers over the world:

—Yes . . . I suppose we do have to go on teaching, don't we? . . . Because it's one of the few *real* things. . . .

Come then, he said.

22 JULY 1947—27 FEBRUARY 1948